BEYOND INNOCENCE

Barrie Turner

An M-Y Books Production

M-Y Books
187 Ware Road
Hertford
SG13 7EQ

m-ybooks.co.uk

Chapter 1

As he approached the quarry entrance, he braked lightly in order to slow the car down and then, once inside, he allowed the vehicle to crawl noiselessly between the huts in order to ensure that the car was no longer visible to possible prying eyes. He opened the door and stepped silently into the blackness of the night. For a few moments, he stood quite still taking whatever time he needed to allow his eyes to adjust to the all-encompassing darkness before walking as quietly as possible to the rear of the car. As he walked he became aware that he was becoming sexually aroused by the knowledge that, even though this was his first victim, it was almost certain that this would not be his last.

Without another glance he raised the boot lid and lifted the lifeless body out of the car then, with a quick grunt, he hoisted the corpse onto his shoulder and walked to the edge of the lake.

Before setting out on his macabre journey he had already wrapped the body in black polythene sheeting which he had tied and bound securely; and now he proceeded to attach a quantity of large stones to the parcel in order to ensure that, when he consigned her body to the deep, it would fall rapidly to the bottom some sixty feet below where it would be entombed within the thick layer of mud which covered the floor of the lake. Now he was satisfied that all was ready and he began to smile to himself as he pushed the parcel into the water. He smiled because he knew that he had found the perfect spot and that her body would never be found. Still smiling as the parcel slipped slowly beneath the surface, he had no way of knowing that a trailing rope had snagged itself on an underwater tree root a mere twelve feet below. Totally unaware of the consequences of this fateful happening and the effect the discovery would have upon him, he quickly turned and retraced his steps to the car. He was now more than satisfied with his gruesome night's work and felt secure in the knowledge that girls and sex no longer mattered. Furthermore, never again would he experience the shame and humiliation of a woman rejecting his advances or, even worse, berating him over his premature ejaculation. As he started the car, it began to rain quite heavily and this only served to increase his feeling of wellbeing for he knew that by the time he got back home all trace of his visit to the quarry would be well and truly washed away. Yes he smiled – he felt he was home and dry!

Chapter 2

Detective Inspector Taylor drove into the station yard at Merseyside Police headquarters and he parked his car in his allotted space. As he walked across the yard to the entrance, he was pleased to see the bulky figure of Detective Sergeant West disappearing through the door ahead of him. 'Good old Westy,' he mused, 'always reliable, always there on time.' These days they weren't just coppers, they were also firm friends after having spent more than ten years solving crime together. From the look of things now, they could well be on the trail again.

Some three days earlier following a quarrel with her boyfriend, a young woman from Bromborough had been reported missing. Today, he and Jim West were going over the water from Liverpool to interview the young lady's parents and her boyfriend. Afterwards they would compare notes before deciding upon their next course of action. He was in the building now and he steadily climbed the stairs to the first floor where there were a number of offices including his own and that of Sergeant West. As he walked through the main office he caught sight of his colleague and motioned to him to come to straight to his office.

Detective Inspector Taylor seated himself behind his large mahogany desk, and he began to speak as soon as Jim West came through the open office door.

"Listen Jim I just wanted to have a quick word before we set off. I wondered whether or not you have any thoughts on this missing Bromborough woman. You know the Wilson girl?"

"Do you think it could be one for us or do you think she has just run away somewhere and disappeared for a while?"

Jim West hardly waited for his chief to finish speaking before he replied, "I know it's early days yet, but I've already got a gut feeling about this one. My guess is that the girl's already dead and that it is one for us. I don't know why I feel like this, but I do. Maybe it's just instinct but there it is."

"What makes you so sure?" asked the Inspector, knowing full well that his colleague hadn't quite finished.

"Well, Peter, it's nothing you can put your finger on, and there's certainly nothing definite yet, but the bloody boyfriend has been down at the local nick trying to get them to widen the scope of their missing person's enquiry. He's also been sticking his nose in telling the desk sergeant he thinks she's been done in. Apparently, the boys themselves think he is almost daring them to go and find her. My experience of this type of behaviour in previous cases, and indeed many others in other patches, is that it nearly always follows that the missing person has been killed, and the boyfriend, the husband, stepfather, or other close relative is the one responsible. Despite this, I'll keep an open mind until we've got something definite to go on."

"What about the girl's parents? Do you know anything about them?"

"Not a lot," said Jim. "When I spoke to the boys at Bromborough they just said they were an average, decent, hard-working couple, who are now genuinely concerned that their only daughter has not been seen for a couple of days. What makes it worse as far as they are concerned is the fact that she didn't take any clothes with her."

The Inspector remained silent for a moment or two before speaking then he said, "Well I don't think we have much choice. As always, this is the part of the job that we hate doing – interviewing the parents of missing offspring, but I am afraid we don't have much in the way of alternatives. Come on then Jim let's grab a quick cup of tea then we'll drive over there to see what we can sniff out. Afterwards we'll call in Bromborough nick then, before we leave, we'll go and have a word with the boyfriend to see what he has to say for himself."

The drive through the city centre and the Liverpool tunnel was quite uneventful, and it took barely an hour in Inspector Taylor's unmarked police car to get to the Wilson residence. They were soon seated in the comfortable lounge of the Wilsons' unpretentious semi-detached home.

The Inspector was going to begin, and, in situations such as these, he was always hesitant, and decidedly edgy. The trouble was he always felt for the parents and it was as if he could actually feel what they were going through. In fact, it was almost as though he could read their minds. Naturally, the last thing he wanted to do was to heighten their fears, or increase their own anxieties, and he certainly didn't wish to alarm or distress the Wilsons any more than was absolutely necessary during the course of their initial enquiries. Within a short space of time, he was able to establish that the missing girl had not taken any clothing other than the clothes she was wearing on the night she disappeared. Although she would have had money in her purse, her parents were able to verify that she hadn't taken any of her credit cards, or her cheque book. Noting this, but keeping his thoughts to himself, Jim West was already beginning to think that things were looking ominous. The parents also confirmed they knew she had been going out with Harry Thompson for at least six months, and they had met him on a number of occasions. Whenever they met him he always appeared to be well mannered, and quietly spoken. Furthermore, in addition to being punctual, he was always tidily dressed, even when wearing casual clothes. They mentioned that whenever Diane spoke about him, which seemed quite often especially of late, it was obvious that she thought a lot about him. They also confirmed that she had been talking recently about going to live with him, and perhaps one day getting married. This was something they were more than pleased about, especially as he worked in a local bank, and there had been talk of him being promoted. Finally, they confirmed that Harry appeared to be very upset about the disappearance of Diane, and, it was not until Harry telephoned them on the Saturday morning that any of them, Harry included, realised that she had gone missing.

Sergeant West asked whether or not Harry had told them about the quarrel the previous evening, and they both nodded nervously in agreement. The Wilsons confirmed that Harry had been with them in the house whilst they made contact with every person they could think of in an effort to trace her. At the end of the day after they had learned nothing new, they decided to report her disappearance to the police at the local station in Bromborough. The following day, Harry had stopped by on his way to work, and during that day he had telephoned repeatedly in order to ascertain whether or nor Diane had returned home. During the course of his last call, he told them that he was going to finish work early, and that he had arranged to take some time off work. He also stated that he would call round later after he had visited the station again. Sergeant West intervened at this point to remind his superior that this was the visit by Thompson that he had spoken about earlier before they left Liverpool.

By now, both men could see that they had learned as much as they were going to do at this visit. As they turned to leave, Inspector Taylor faced both parents and said, "As you know it's still very early yet, and, hopefully, when she has got this silly quarrel business sorted out in her mind, she will return home full of apologies for all the fuss and upset she's caused you both, and I am sure you'll be extremely relieved and delighted. Because she's not a minor, she is quite able to run off like this however much out of character to you this might seem, and, because of this, we can hardly treat this as a full-blown murder enquiry at this stage. We will, however, initiate a missing person's enquiry, and carry out local searches. Should our initial enquiries fail, we'll reconsider both our position and our strategy, and proceed accordingly. Having said this, I now have to ask you both whether or not you think Harry Thompson is telling you the truth. In other words have you ever considered the possibility that Harry Thompson may actually have caused your daughters disappearance?"

The effect of this question literally stunned Mr. and Mrs. Wilson as it was totally unexpected and Mrs Wilson put her arms around her husband and began to cry. Both officers were well aware of the discomfort and distress the Wilsons were experiencing, and it was all too painfully obvious that neither of these devoted parents had even contemplated such a terrible thought.

Seeing the degree of discomfort, Sergeant West responded first urging both parents to calm down and offering profuse apologies before saying, "Sincerely, we do understand how difficult it is for you both, but it is equally important that you also understand our position. If your daughter has come to any harm at all, we have to consider, and take account of, every possibility no matter how hard, or far- fetched it may seem to you. Still visibly distressed, and very badly shaken, the Wilsons said that they couldn't bring themselves to think that Harry could possibly be involved.

Tight-lipped and silent both officers left the house, and returned to their waiting car. Neither man spoke until they were safely around the corner and out of sight.

"Thank Christ that's over," said Sergeant West.

"I agree", replied Inspector Taylor, "That's why I always detest this part of the frigging job. Everybody knows, as well as us, that we have to ask the bloody awkward questions and, when we do, just look at what happens. They look at us aghast, as if we're vermin or sick in the bloody mind. At times, I think they just don't realise we have a job to do, and, we have to ask awkward and embarrassing questions. "You know Jim," he sighed, "at times like these I begin to wonder if I might be getting too old for this bloody job because it certainly never gets any easier." He started the engine once again and they drove in silence to Bromborough police station.

Some lively banter with their brother officers revived their spirits a little, then it was time to make the short journey to the home of Harry Thompson which lay just over a mile away in the picturesque village of Eastham.

Within minutes, Sergeant West had the car outside the neat little terraced house situated on the main road just beyond the golf club. The house was overlooked by trees on the opposite side of the road, which formed part of the country park and nature reserve. From the back of the house there were views across the river Mersey to Liverpool in the distance beyond, but neither man had time for sightseeing today as they strode purposefully to the front door. In response to their knock, the door was opened by Sally Thompson, the adoptive mother of Harry Thompson.

"Mrs. Thompson?" Enquired Sergeant West with his warrant card in his hand clearly visible. Quickly noting the nod of acknowledgement, he added, "Sorry to disturb you, Ma'am, but we are police officers investigating the disappearance of Miss Diane Wilson, and we would like to ask your son Harry a few questions in connection with this."

Rather nervously, Mrs. Thompson ushered both men inside. Before closing the door, she took a hesitant look up and down the road in order to determine whether or not any of the neighbours were about, or watching. She followed both men into the house and into the small front room, where she urged both officers to sit down and make themselves comfortable whilst she put the kettle on and made the tea. Whilst waiting for the kettle to boil, she volunteered the information that, although Harry was out at present, she was certain he would be back within the next ten or fifteen minutes. She poured the tea, and returned to the room with a tray and some biscuits, then, somewhat apprehensively, she sat down to await the officers' first question.

After what seemed an eternity and unable to bear the silence any longer, she asked both of the officers if she could be of any help.

Jim West was the first to respond and he replied, "Well we doubt very much if you can, because the purpose of our visit is to speak to your son to see if he can help us with our enquiries. So we need to speak to him first."

Although she was almost afraid to speak by now, she still felt it essential to point out the officer's mistake as she countered, "No officer, he's not my son; he's adopted." With time passing agonisingly slowly she was becoming increasingly worried, and her mind began to blur with the events and happenings of recent days and weeks.

The impact of her statement wasn't lost on either of the two men as they both made a mental note that all might not be what it seemed to be here in the quaint little backwater village of Eastham. A fully trained and observant officer would have noticed immediately the glance, which said it all, as it passed between them, quite unnoticed by Mrs. Thompson.

At this moment however, their thoughts were interrupted by the sound of a key being inserted in the lock on the front door. Within a few moments, both men were looking at Harry Thompson.

Stating the nature of their business, Sally Thompson

introduced the men to her adopted son.

"Mr. Thompson," began Sergeant West, "Can you confirm to myself and Detective Inspector Taylor your movements on the evening of September 11th 1988, and can you also state and confirm the last time you saw Diane Wilson alive?"

Harry didn't need any time to think about his answers to the questions because he knew full well what the truth was. Furthermore he reasoned, if that is what they wanted to know, he was more than prepared to tell them everything he knew because, as far as he was concerned he had nothing to hide. In this frame of mind, he told the officers everything he knew, including the sex session, and ending with the quarrel, which culminated in Diane's refusal to allow him to see her safely home.

It was the Inspector who terminated the interview. Then, presumably in an effort to catch him unawares, he fired his final shot. "Harry Thompson did you kill or cause any harm to come to Diane Wilson on, or after, the evening of September the eleventh?"

Harry heard his adopted mother's involuntary gasp of breath as the impact of the question hit her hard and he saw her mouth begin to open, and her jaw begin to sag momentarily. He also observed the anguished look of fear in her eyes. Looking at all three people in the room, he answered as firmly as he could, "No I did not and that is the truth."

Neither officer had anything further to say apart from keeping everybody fully informed about any future developments and that, for the moment, Diane's disappearance was being treated as a missing person's enquiry. Following on from this, there would be local searches, and appeals to the general public through the local press, for help and information.

As they walked back to the car, Inspector Taylor asked the Sergeant to drive, together with a request to pull in at the pub just down the road, stating that he could murder a pint, and that no doubt his colleague was in the same frame of mind.

Jim West readily assented as he brought the car to a standstill in the pub car park. After locking the vehicle, he followed his boss into the almost empty bar. Comfortably seated, with glasses in hand, they began to compare notes.

"Well, Jim, give me your thoughts on today's proceedings."

Sergeant West took a copious draught of the amber liquid, put down his glass, and replied, "He's done it. He's done her in. Obviously, he's hidden the body somewhere and now he's challenging us to find it. As things stand and without a body, we can hardly charge him and my guess is, at this moment in time, he's feeling very pleased with himself because he thinks he is very smart and that he's put one over on us. In fact, I wouldn't mind betting he is already thinking to himself that he's got away with murder."

"Jim, I have to say that I agree with you," the Inspector replied, and, despite the fact that he seemed to be so concerned, I felt that he was far too composed and very sure of himself. I'll tell you something else as well, did you see that terrible worried look on his mother's face when I asked him point-blank if he had done it. Although she can't bring herself to admit it, let alone think it, deep down she's wondering whether or not he's killed his girlfriend. Also, and before I forget, what about Mrs Thompson's reaction when she pulled you up about him being adopted? It looks like she has her own suspicions about it as well. So Jim, where do we go from here? My suggestion is, and it's only a suggestion at this stage, we just wait a couple of weeks for developments then, irrespective of what transpires, we put him on TV together with the girl's parents."

Jim West responded quickly by agreeing with the Inspector adding, "Yes, and like most killers, he won't be able to get there quickly enough. He'll see this as his big chance to shine on TV in front of millions of people." By now they were on their way back to Bromborough police station where they planned to brief a number of people on the results of their enquiries to date and the next moves to be made in connection with the case. Above all else, they wanted all personnel to be fully aware that, even without a body, and with nothing solid to go on in their eyes, Harry Thompson was still their number one suspect. Before leaving, they also arranged for more local searches to be carried out with the added proviso that the operation would be scaled up very rapidly whenever the time came to take matters further.

Chapter 3

For the first few days after the killing he could barely contain himself as he scanned all sources of news in an effort to see what progress, if any, was being made by the police. Two weeks had passed since the disappearance of Diane Wilson, and, as far as the general public were concerned, it had now become old news. Without a body, he reasoned, there could be no worthwhile developments, and this led to a gradual decline in the feeling of euphoria he had experienced at the time. He kept telling himself that the police, as well as the public at large, didn't have a clue, and the reason was simply due to the fact that he had been far too clever. Once he faced up to this, he knew that, next time, he would have to give them something to go on, and if that meant a body, then, he would give them one. He also knew that he couldn't go back to Chorley Wood, nor could he raise the body of his first victim, Diane Wilson. That was too dangerous, and far too difficult. This meant he would simply have to find somebody else, and this would be a far greater test of his skill and intelligence. Pitting his wits against the combined talents of the police, and all their resources, he knew he would have to adopt a different plan and, also a varied approach. He'd learned a number of lessons from the first killing. This time, the planning would have to be meticulous, the attack and the killing, would have to be both swift, and sure. He was well aware that he would have to choose his victim with great care, and although it would still be a person selected at random, this time he would determine the time and the place. He would make certain that the girl was on her own and, above all else, he would have to ensure that she did not have the opportunity to scream or shout for help. In addition, he didn't wish to travel any great distance with the body, or even move it too far from the actual killing zone. Finally, when leaving the scene, he would have to ensure he left no traces behind, and whilst he did not wish the body to be discovered too easily, he would have to make sure that it was not too well hidden.

He decided that his first priority lay in the location of the disposal point. Then he would find the most practical route there. He made up his mind that it would be far more practical, and easier, to conduct this search during the hours of daylight. He told himself that he must act normally without drawing undue attention to himself, or arousing any suspicion. With a new sense of purpose, the adrenalin began to flow through his body and he was making himself become visible once again. He began by walking along the nature trails and pathways through the woods at Eastham Nature and Country Park. He was trying to find a path, or a place, on the extremities of the woods and the golf course. Every day, scores of people walked the same pathways, and he found it very easy to stray and wander away from the recognized pathways and routes. Surprisingly enough, it didn't take long to find a spot. It was partly fenced off, just beyond a boundary path. Beyond the fence there was a small, tree-lined incline where the ground beyond fell away to a ditch. The spot was absolutely perfect. If you didn't know the ditch was there you would walk straight past it, and yet, on the other side of the fence, there were four full sized football pitches together with all the changing room facilities provided by the local council. Each of the football pitches were used twice on Saturdays and Sundays which meant there would be over three hundred and fifty footballers plus reserves and other minions as well as spectators and dog walkers passing by. Throw in the odd golfer or two and it was difficult to imagine the body lying undiscovered for too long. Later, and after further investigation, he found the place was even better than he had first thought when he discovered he could drive his car quite close to the fence without taking any silly risks or chances.

Now the location had been established, all he required was the killing zone, and the next victim. He began by taking the train along a local branch line which ran between Liverpool and Chester. From his starting point at Hooton station to his exit location at Bebington this involved a total journey time of nine to ten minutes which covered the seven stations along the route... He always made sure he had a valid season ticket in order that he could get on and off the train at any station of his choice along the route. As a result of these journeys, he discovered that, periodically, the station at Spital was left unmanned at night. He knew if he could be on the station at a time when it was unmanned, he could simply lie in wait. His chosen victim would then be made to walk some twenty or thirty yards along the railway path towards Port Sunlight station where he would be almost opposite the spot where he had lain in wait for his first victim. Once again it was perfect. There were no houses for at least a quarter of a mile and, with no lights, it was absolutely pitch black at night, plus, it was no more than three minutes maximum to get the victim loaded into the car for a further four-minute journey in order to dispose of the body. Now, the adrenalin really began to pump through his body and he could see himself, waiting on the railway platform steps, hidden from the platforms, just waiting, waiting for someone alone. Perfect. He permitted himself a smile, whilst considering that he had thought of everything including his course of action if more than one person alighted from the train. Obviously, if the sole person alighting from the train was a man, he would simply abort the mission and try again later when the next train came along ten or fifteen minutes afterwards. Alternatively, he reasoned, he could always check out the station earlier and then ride the train back and forth between the stations, waiting for the ideal opportunity; a woman, on her own in an empty carriage. Then, as the train approached Spital station, he would make his move. As the train slowed down on its approach, he would simply show the woman the knife and walk her off the train. More risk, no doubt about it, but well worth it, considering the excitement, the thrill of the chase, followed by the discovery of the body, and the hunt by the police for the killer. Yes, he was ready for it now. There was no need for a dummy run. 'Just do it and let's do it tonight,' he told himself.

Angela Clarkson was a prostitute. Working her pitch on Rodney Street, Liverpool, you could usually spot her, and her colleagues who worked the same patch a mile away. However, whenever she visited one of her regular clients on the Wirral, she looked totally different. On these occasions, she always looked a much changed person. This was something that she had to do because the person she visited in his hotel left nothing to chance, due to the fact that he had far too much to lose. On these assignations all the clothes that she wore had been carefully chosen by her mentor and, whenever they met, he always asked her to wear a particular outfit from the many clothes that he had bought for her. Business completed, she walked from the hotel to the station in order to wait for the next train to Liverpool. Angela was feeling a little sad this evening because she was going away to live in London and this meant that she would not be seeing her regular client again. She had to go to London as she needed to earn more money to feed an ever-increasing drug habit and, at one time, she had even considered asking her mentor for help, but she just couldn't bring herself to ask him. Sighing to herself that's what life was all about, she looked at the watch her client had given to her as a parting gift and she wondered, would she would ever see Timothy Harris again. At this time of night the station was usually deserted, and tonight, apart from one other person on the platform, was no exception. Angela could hear the train approaching and she began to walk towards the edge of the platform.

As the train drew slowly along the platform she could see that it was almost empty. She deliberately chose to enter the last carriage, which was next to the carriage occupied by the guard who doubled up as a ticket and fare collector. Almost unnoticed, the other person on the platform also moved towards the same carriage, only he chose to board at the opposite end of the compartment to Angela. The guard was halfway down the train carrying out his other duties, and, other than a most cursory glance in their direction, he paid them hardly any attention whatsoever.

With the guard engaged elsewhere, he entered the compartment, and although he didn't show it, he was already considerably aroused, and becoming increasingly excited. He could see her at the other end of the carriage facing the same way as the train. This meant she had her back to him and this was so important to his plan. He moved just over halfway down the compartment and sat down. In next to no time the train was leaving Bromborough Rake station, and it was next stop Spital. With excitement mounting within him, it was almost time for him to make his move. No point in rushing things, he told himself. He had to wait until he felt the brakes slowing the train down, then it would be all systems go. He felt his body becoming tense, his rate of breathing increased, and his heart began to pound faster and faster, louder and louder, so loud in fact it was a wonder she couldn't hear it. He stood up, and he made his way silently towards the door. Each step brought him closer to her, and to death. He felt the train braking, then he was abreast of her. Making it appear he had lost his balance as he stumbled against her, he had the knife at her throat in an instant. God, it felt so good to see her stiffen and freeze, that he almost ejaculated on the spot. Then, observing the fear on her face, and the look of abject terror in her eyes as she saw, then felt the knife at her throat Angela became aware that he was talking to her.

"Whatever you do don't scream and you won't get hurt. Just get off the train with me at the next stop and do exactly as you are told." The train stopped and they both alighted. The guard was standing quite some distance away by the first carriage, and as he stepped back on board and signalled to the driver to start the train again he didn't seem to notice anything untoward. As they stepped from the train, Angela noticed with considerable apprehension, that the platform was empty. She saw the train for Chester pulling away from the opposite platform and, as she mounted the footbridge steps, she knew full well that the station was totally deserted. Making their descent over the other side, she saw the rear lights of the Liverpool train swiftly disappearing in the distance.

Realising that her life was now in jeopardy, Angela decided that she had better take a chance with her own destiny. Rightly or wrongly she reasoned, if she gave him whatever he wanted she might have a chance of staying alive. All she had to do was to stay calm and keep him under control. She shuddered at the thought of him losing it especially with that knife, whilst telling herself this was one of the hazards of the trade. As they came to the edge of the platform, she tried to turn to him saying, "Look here friend, I'm on the game you know so, if it is a jump you're after, it's no big deal. I can promise you that I'll give you a bloody good time and say no more about it. He didn't speak to her in reply. Instead, he pushed her down the path at the side of the track where the inky blackness of the night swallowed them up. In the woods beyond a night owl hooted and Angela Clarkson began to hope and pray that she would get out of this alive. They reached the disused bridge, which they skirted and he guided her down a path to the right of it. It was here that he told her to stop. They were only thirty yards from the Old Chester Road, and almost opposite the place where he had lain in wait for his first victim. "Take your clothes off and turn around," he ordered. Nervously, she began to comply. He saw her clothes falling to the ground, until she was naked, facing away from him. Her body stiffened as she sensed him getting closer to her and, when he placed one of his hands on her buttocks she flinched involuntarily. Whether or not it was because she touched him, she never knew but without any warning, her tights were around her neck and she was desperately fighting for breath and her life. Unable to breath, she sank slowly to her knees then she felt his knee in her back, forcing her head into the ground. Her face sank into the soft black soil causing her to vomit and retch violently as she took her last breath on earth. Angela died a horrible death and she didn't die easily. In his highly emotional state, he found himself ejaculating. As he relaxed his grip he began to smile. All the tension was leaving his body and he started to regain control of himself. Just as he had done with his first victim, he began to fondle her breasts before telling himself that he had to stick to his plan. He adjusted his own dress and pulled the dead woman's blouse over her head covering her breasts and the top half of her body. Leaving the macabre scene, he returned to his car, which he had parked nearby. Upon his return, he parked the vehicle as close to the opening as possible. Resuming his task, he moved the lifeless body to within a couple of feet of the car, then, he lifted the inert frame, and placed the body in the passenger seat. He reasoned that if by chance anyone saw them, they would automatically assume she was drunk or asleep. Again, leaving nothing to chance, he positioned the seat belt around her. Gathering up all her belongings which he placed in the boot, he seated himself behind the wheel, and, before moving off he satisfied himself that all was well. He turned to the body beside him saying, "alright love, let me take you home." As the car moved forward her head rolled onto his shoulder. He thought this highly amusing, and he began to smile. It was a smile of sweet satisfaction at a job well done, well almost. In no time at all they were at the extreme edge of the car park.

During the short journey he hadn't seen a soul and now, in the pitch black of the night, he had the place to himself and the lifeless body. He switched off the lights and waited a few minutes whilst his eyes grew accustomed to the dark. Then it was time to go. Time to finish off his grim night's work. He manoeuvred her legs out of the car, and placed her cold hands upon his shoulders then, with a swift lift, and an imperceptible grunt, she was on his shoulder and he made his way to the ditch. Her body was getting colder and it actually felt heavier but it hardly mattered as he reached the designated spot. He let her body slide into the ditch, and in a final macabre gesture, he lifted her blouse to expose her breasts. Even in death he was not prepared to afford her any dignity at all. After collecting all of her clothes, he returned with them to the ditch where he threw them beside the stiffening corpse. He rifled through her handbag, pocketing all the money and two plastic sachets that he assumed would contain drugs. "Great," he murmured as he stood up to go. "Absolutely great, sort this one out you clever bloody coppers."

He walked casually away from the scene with the night's events to be reviewed, and enjoyed constantly just like a living picture, only this one was firmly implanted in his mind.

Chapter 4

Harry Thompson was out walking with his dog, Lady. Lady was a tri-colour border collie and she had been a family pet since she was eight weeks old. She was now ten years of age and, as often as he could, Harry walked her three times each day in and around Eastham woods and Nature Park. This was something which they both enjoyed, especially Lady, and more so if he could find a stick to throw for her. On this walk they soon found a suitable stick and he threw it for her to chase just off the nature trail. Lady chased after it, her sleek coat flowing like silk along her body. After picking up the stick she walked a few yards before sitting down with it between her front paws. Lady sat patiently; eagerly awaiting the next throw, her eyes shone with excitement, and as Harry bent down to retrieve it he noticed the watch lying half hidden in the long grass. He could see immediately this was quite an expensive item and, as he put it in his pocket, he resolved to hand it in at his local police station in Bromborough. He felt sure the owner would have missed it and reported the loss. 'Who knows?' he mused, 'there might even be a reward?' After he'd taken Lady home, he went down to the police station to report his find and it was duly entered in the lost property book. He was quite a regular visitor owing to the disappearance of Diane, and, by now, his was a familiar face to most of the officers on the desk. With a minimum of fuss, the formalities were completed, and he returned home satisfied that he had done the correct thing. Despite his public-spirited action, he was still unhappy because there was still no news about Diane and it was now almost three weeks since she had disappeared. That same evening there was an announcement on the evening news stating that the body of a young woman had been discovered in the woods at Eastham. The body had been discovered by a local man named Eddie Simpson who had been taking his dog for a walk in the woods. No further details were given in this first bulletin and he prayed that it was not the body of Diane that had been found.

Events proved it was not the body of Diane Wilson but the body of a Liverpool prostitute named Angela Clarkson. Later, there was a further announcement saying that the woman had been strangled with a pair of her own tights and it appeared that she was the victim of a sexual assault. He shuddered as the announcement continued with an appeal for help from the police, asking local people from the surrounding parishes of Eastham, Hooton, and Childer Thornton, to donate voluntary samples of DNA for checking against samples taken from the body of the dead woman. The public were assured that, once checked, all the samples donated would be destroyed. He picked up the telephone immediately and rang the number given, in order to enquire about the voluntary sample testing. His call was put through to a person on the desk who assured him that it would be quite in order to attend any time the following day.

There was a knock on the door just as he was replacing the receiver and his adoptive mother, Sally, went to answer it. When she returned to the room her face was ashen as she solemnly announced "Harry it's the police again. You know the two who were here recently…." She didn't finish the sentence Sergeant West did it for her. In a very firm and in his authoritative voice he said,

"Harry Thompson, we are police officers investigating the death of a woman found recently. My name is Detective Sergeant West and this is Detective Inspector Taylor and we want you to accompany us to Bromborough police station in order to assist us in our investigation into the death of Angela Clarkson."

Sally couldn't not understand, let alone believe, what was happening, "Are you arresting him?" she asked the Inspector who replied "No, Mrs. Thompson, not at the moment. As my sergeant just said, we are asking him to come down to the station to assist us with our enquiries. Dependent upon what happens, we will probably ask him to make a statement. With that he was ushered into the car and driven hurriedly to Bromborough police station. Once inside, he asked why this couldn't wait until morning as he would have been visiting the station anyway to give a voluntary sample as requested on the TV appeal. In answer he was ushered into the drab interview room where the only furniture was a desk and three chairs.

Then the questions began.

"On or about October 2nd Angela Clarkson was murdered and her body was thrown in a ditch. We want to know when you last saw this woman and were you in the habit of seeing this woman on a regular basis for paid sex?"

Harry Thompson's replies were quite specific. He said quite emphatically that he didn't know any woman of that name and that he had never seen her in his life. He vehemently denied that he had ever had sex with her at any time whatsoever. The questions continued.

"Where is Diane Wilson? What have you done to her? Where have you hidden the body? Did you strangle her with her own tights?"

Adopting the good guy pose, when Sergeant West left the room, Detective Inspector Taylor said quietly, "Why don't you get it all off your chest and tell us all you know. You'll feel so much better and we can help you. Let's face it, we all know you didn't intend to kill either of these women and, if the truth be known, they had it coming. This happens all the time with women they do, or say, something absolutely stupid and they're too thick to realise the consequences of what they've said or done. So, come on now, be a lad, tell us all about it, help us, and we'll do all that we can to help you..."

The reality of the situation began to dawn on him, especially now Diane's name had been mentioned. It was all becoming painfully obvious they were putting him in the frame for two murders. This was becoming a deadly serious business indeed.

Sergeant West had now returned and the Inspector left him to it.

"Look son," he said in a very aggressive and, almost threatening manner. "We know you did this one. We can arrest you right now for this job. At this very moment we're just wrapping up our own local enquiries then, it'll all be over. Rest assured, eventually we'll find the body of Diane Wilson and you'll have to go through all this again. Doing it like this, the hard way, you're not doing yourself any favours and, you're only making it worse for yourself. When the time comes you won't be able to say 'oh yes I did it. It was me, but I didn't know what I was doing at the time.' Also, remember this, when we take a DNA sample and compare it with yours, you won't have a leg to stand on. So, do yourself a favour and, whilst you are at it, think of the relief your girlfriend's parents will feel when they know what happened to their daughter. At least put them out of their misery."

Harry looked straight at the detective and said firmly, "I've told you everything I know. I repeat I have never seen the dead woman in my life. I did not know her and I cannot help you any further in connection with the disappearance of Diane Wilson. Furthermore, I am not going to answer any more of your damned stupid questions without a solicitor being present."

His request was noted, and he was given access to a telephone. He contacted the office of Michael Mulrooney, and from the answer-phone message, he obtained the number of a duty solicitor. Michael Mulrooney had a formidable reputation and, if you needed the best, they didn't come any better. Although he knew that Michael Mulrooney would not be coming himself, he felt comforted by the fact that it was somebody from his office, and that when the time came, Michael Mulrooney would take charge. One hour later he was relating his story to Brian Donnelly, the duty solicitor. He also included the fact that he had telephoned earlier to offer his own sample in an effort to help the police with their enquiries...

Both of the detectives were back in the room as his solicitor took them to task. He told them in no uncertain manner that they didn't have a shred of evidence upon which they could detain Harry and that they now had two choices. They could either charge him with something or they could release him. He also pointed out that Harry had already volunteered to donate a DNA sample in order to assist the police in their enquiries and, when it had been tested, the police would find it would bear no resemblance to that obtained from the unfortunate young woman. Before allowing the police to take a sample from Harry, Brian Donnelly insisted the police accepted the fact that this sample was being freely given, on a purely voluntary basis and on the strict understanding that Harry's sample would be treated in the same manner as all of the others... Although the watch had been mentioned by the police during this interview, it had not been established as belonging to Angela Clarkson. Brian Donnelly reluctantly conceded that, if such a link was ever established, it would be in order for Harry to take the officers to the spot where he had found it.

At last Harry was standing on the police station steps and he was free to go. Before leaving, his solicitor confirmed he would arrange for an appointment with Michael Mulroony as he felt sure the police would not be content to let matters rest.

All the volunteered samples, including Harry's, proved negative but, they were not destroyed as promised. Instead, Detective Inspector Taylor ordered them to be put on hold at the laboratory. His reasoning was that he could hardly authorize the destruction of all the samples, except the one from Harry Thompson because, if Thompson was ever charged and the defence got hold of that information, they would have a field day. No, it was far better to hold on to them all and say nothing to Thompson's legal team.

Chapter 5

The next day, Detective Inspector Taylor was discussing the case with his colleague, Detective Sergeant Jim West. Both men agreed they were getting close. "Look Jim," said the inspector, "the crux to both cases is the Wilson girl. If we can find her body then we're in with more than a good chance. Thompson has admitted to having sex with the girl and with any luck when we find her, we may get a good DNA profile result that will be enough to convict him. We now know that we have no DNA in the Clarkson case so we have to discover if the watch belonged to her and if possible, who gave it to her assuming that she didn't buy it herself. At this stage I can't see that we'll trace her last client and, even if we did, that doesn't necessarily prove he paid her for sex and then killed her. My guess is that, if we can trace the watch to Clarkson, then we can have a go at arresting Thompson and making it stick. Once that happens, who knows, he might decide to cough on the Wilson case which would give us all a break so let's just see what we've got so far."

1. Thompson argued with his girlfriend who then disappears
2. Thompson lives four to five-hundred yards from the spot where Clarkson's body is found.
3. Thompson admits he walks his dog daily by the very same spot.
4. Thompson admits he used to take his girlfriend in the woods in very close proximity to that self same spot.
5. Thompson finds a watch some twenty yards or less from the ditch where Clarkson's body is lying.

6. Thompson hands in this very expensive watch at his local nick.
7. Enquiries have revealed that Thompson drinks in the Roundhead pub on occasions and he is known to be quite a loner.
8. Thompson keeps visiting Bromborough nick and asking about the Wilson girl.

"Quite honestly, Jim," he continued, "although it's all supposition and circumstantial, I think it's almost too much."

"I agree, Peter," said Sergeant West, "and I really do believe we have the right man in the frame. I also think we should get Thompson and the Wilson girl's parents on TV to do a national appeal for her to come home or at least get in touch. Then, because we are only talking about the watch at the moment, why don't we see if we can get the BBC to squeeze it in on the next Crime Watch programme to see whether or not anybody can identify it as belonging to Clarkson. Regarding DNA on Clarkson or, in this case, the lack of Thompson's, maybe Thompson knew she was on the game and he couldn't, or wouldn't, have sex with her. Perhaps he let her give him a hand or a blow job, after which, he kills her. So for us the answer is simple. We don't talk about DNA. In other words we don't introduce it and we just go for the circumstantial evidence. Again look at it like this, this guy Thompson's an out-and-out nutter, a frigging psychopath, who's been trying to make fools of us. He takes the Mickey out of us by pretending to be so concerned about his girlfriend's disappearance and all the time he's laughing bags at us because, without a body, there is no charge. Now we're supposed to be chasing him but, all of a sudden, he realises that we aren't and why? I'll tell you why boss, because we haven't got a bloody body. So he decides – balls to this, I'm not getting any kicks out of this so I had better give them one and then they'll have something to get their teeth into. Result, two weeks later he kills again. Dumps the poor girl's nearly naked body in a ditch, lifts up the top of her blouse, to show off her tits and then, after this in another show of bravado, he brings in a watch to us that he claims to have found about twenty or thirty yards away from the body. Really, Peter, I can honestly imagine him, in fact, I can almost see him now walking all over the scene, gawping at the body every day and in all probability, he's playing with himself each time he passes by.

Whilst listening to his colleague, the inspector pulled out a brown manila envelope from his brief case and immediately his colleague had finished he passed it to him saying," just have a look at that report from Professor Love. It's a murder suspect profile report I think you will find it quite interesting. Jim West opened the envelope and began to read;

From the details given it is my opinion that the person who committed this crime is a local man or, if not, he is certainly very familiar with the area. I say this after noting your remarks concerning the location of the deceased woman. If this is his first victim, then I would not be at all surprised if he kills again. I say this because of the fact that it has all the hallmarks of a killing of hate or lust and, in both instances, his desire has to be satisfied hence his choice of victim a prostitute or a stranger to him. I expect this person to be a loner, a person who does not make friends very easily or finds it difficult to enter into relationships with persons of either sex. Similarly, he will have had a difficult childhood although, to those persons closest to him, this might not be so apparent e.g.; difficulties perhaps with a step-parent of either sex or, quite possibly, a drunken parent. I think you will find that he is probably in regular employment and that he works in an office environment rather than holding a manual occupation.

Finally just to recap, if this is not his first killing then he will have killed by strangulation using tights before and, whether this is his first murder or not, he will kill again. His positioning of the corpse in an open place with no attempt to hide it leads me to this belief. During your investigation you should search thoroughly for trophies collected from his victims but, because he is playing some form of game with you, this could well be something very simple such as a clipping of pubic hair or something equally innocuous to the human eye. In any event it is possible that his killing is sparked by something in his past life such as his mother doing something that his father took exception to and, as a result, the mother, or the pair of them, end up with a beating. Maybe the mother wore the wrong colour dress one day and this type of behaviour was the result.

Should this be the case, I expect our murderer to carry on playing his game until you succeed in apprehending him because, to him, this is a game and he wants you to catch him. When you do apprehend him you will find that he will make subtle movements to tell himself that he is in control of the interview. This may take the form of him wrapping his arms around his body in order to comfort himself. Alternatively, he may place his hands behind his head and look at the ceiling. Whilst doing this, or indeed something similar, he will be more than aware of exactly what is going on even to the extent of following your examination and answering your questions. Therefore it is essential that, if anything such as this occurs, then you should bring the meeting to a close even if it is just for a minute or two as this will break his thoughts and his attempt at controlling matters. It is essential that you remember that your murderer will at some time want to confess but this will only be at a time and place of his own choosing.

Yours faithfully,

(Signed) Professor B. G. Love.

Jim West put down the report after reading it and looked across the desk at his boss before saying, "Well Peter it looks very much to me that Professor Love has got it spot on and that his report confirms that Harry Thompson is our number one prime suspect."

Peter Taylor agreed with his man adding, "That's exactly what I thought but we still have to nail the bastard first so, in the meantime, we will have to stick very closely indeed to Mr. Harry Thompson."

The following week Harry Thompson, together with Diane's parents appeared in an emotional T V appeal for her to return home or to at least get in touch. Opinion on Harry Thompson's performance was at best divided, as most people on the police team thought that he had killed the girl. Mrs. Wilson broke down completely long before the end and, somehow, the whole thing seemed quite unreal.

Sadly no new leads came from the appeal and it came to the evening of the Crime Watch Programme.

The clip began with the announcer, Glenda Johnson, holding up a watch and saying to the audience viewing at home, "Does this watch look familiar? Did you buy it for someone special? Or, was it was purchased for a special occasion? Did you lose it recently and, if so, where and when did you last wear it? Could it have been on a visit to Eastham Country Park on the Wirral?" At this point a photograph of Angela Clarkson appeared on the screen together with the voice of the announcer saying, "This is a picture of Angela Clarkson. Her near naked body was found in a ditch in Eastham Country Park a few days ago. Did you see her in the vicinity with anybody? And, if you did see her, was she wearing a watch like this? As usual, all enquiries will be treated in strictest confidence and you can contact the police by telephoning any of the following numbers."

At the end of the evening when the update was featured, the police admitted that apart from a railway guard who reported that he thought he had seen a similar person to

Angela Clarkson board his train at Bromborough Rake Station some time after ten thirty one evening, there had been a poor response to the appeal. Inspector Taylor made arrangements to interview the guard and, although the guard was quite sure that it was Angela Clarkson, he couldn't offer any further information. Later, the murder team thought that they might get a breakthrough when they contacted the English agents of the watchmaker who quickly established that fifty two of the same watches had been sold nationwide. In all instances, except six, completed guarantee cards had been received and, as each card gave details of the purchasers, they were all quickly traced and eliminated from the investigation. The six outstanding had been exported abroad and these persons were traced through the VAT refund scheme.

Chapter 6

Timothy and Paula Harris were relaxing at home. These days, they didn't spend too many nights together because Timothy Harris MP was a government minister as well as a powerful figure in the city. As a consequence, he was often away from his home in Cheshire either on government business or looking after his own interests as he was on the board of a number of companies. Tonight he had been quite content to pour himself a large brandy and catch up with reading 'The Times.' In the spacious lounge, with a log fire blazing away, he felt at peace with himself. In a far corner of the room the TV set flickered away and the Crime Watch programme was about halfway through. Sleep was beginning to fill his eyes and 'The Times' newspaper was about to slip slowly from his fingers. His wife watched with some amusement whilst thinking to herself, 'he'll be asleep any second now.'

At that moment the screen was filled with the picture of Angela Clarkson. Timothy was awake instantly as he recognized the face on the screen. There was absolutely no doubt about it at all. It was definitely Angela Clarkson. Then the watch was featured again. "Jesus Christ", he muttered under his breath as he reached for and began to spill his brandy. "Angela Clarkson killed when? Oh my god," he muttered again "that was the time I was in Bromborough and Birkenhead." Although he was in an acute state of panic and sweating profusely, he knew he had one saving grace as he had spent the latter part of the evening watching the football highlights on the TV in the residents' lounge in the company of the assistant manager so he wouldn't be in desperate need of an alibi. 'Good lord,' his train of thought continued, 'if any of this got out it would be the end. It would probably mean a messy divorce and he would be made to resign from the government. After which there would be all the usual snide gossip in the Tory press, together with the consequent disgrace that would ultimately follow.'

Meanwhile, Paula Harris was no longer looking at her husband with amusement. She had just witnessed him transported back into the real world with such rapidity that she could only conclude he had been given one of the biggest frights of his life and she began to wonder what on earth could it have been. She had just seen him jolted upright in his seat, watched the colour drain from his face and, as far as she could see, this was all because the face of a murdered prostitute had appeared on the television screen.

"Are you all right Timothy?" she enquired. He mumbled "Yes, yes," in reply, "I'm alright I was almost asleep when I suddenly remembered that I have to see Norman Collins at the Golf Club about ten o clock. I'd better get down there now and see what it is he wants although I have a sneaking suspicion that it will be something to do with some share deal he wants me to pull off. I'll get down there now and see just what it is he wants. Although I don't think I'll be delayed, I won't be long so there's no need to wait up for me," And, as an afterthought as he disappeared from view, he added, "You probably won't have time to make a brew before I'm back."

She watched him scurry out of the room. Then, she heard his car start up and the sound of the engine slowly fading away as it turned out of the drive.

"Liar," she shouted, when it really was too late to matter, but still wondering all the time what on earth he needed to lie through his back teeth for. Somehow, she vowed, she would have to find out and, if it was as bad as she suspected, then he would have to bloody well watch out. She went over the events of the past few moments in her mind and the more she thought about it, the more convinced she became that this was something to do with the murdered girl featured on the television. She walked quickly to the bedroom, and took out her diary from the bedside cabinet. She searched rapidly through the pages until she found what she was looking for. It all checked out. Timothy was in Birkenhead at that time. "The filthy bastard," she shouted at the empty room. "I'll shagging prostitute him. I'll stitch him up so good this time he won't be able to lie his way out of this." She made her first telephone call to Directory Enquiries; from there she obtained the telephone number of the television station. A further call gave her the number of the Crime Watch hotline but then, as an afterthought and before ringing the number given, she telephoned Quentin Russell, a reporter on the political scene. After she had identified herself to Quentin by the use of her code name "Rose", Paula suggested to him that he should carry out some sensitive enquiries into the Angela Clarkson murder case, hinting that an errant government minister might be able to provide the police with some help in their investigation into the murder. Finally she called Sheila Collins. She was relieved when Sheila answered the phone and Paula soon ascertained from her that Norman was not in the golf club. At that very moment he was, in fact, working in his study. Upon hearing this Paula smiled to herself as she realised that it would be no use Timothy returning home, telling her about his and Norman's, plans for making a bit more money on the side. She also knew that, even if he did, she wouldn't confront him and expose his lies just now. There would be no point in that, not at the moment anyway for, with any luck, there would be much better opportunities later. Well satisfied with her few minutes' work, she sat down to contemplate what she should do next. One thing was very clear in her mind, Timothy wasn't just history, he was as good as dead, especially, if her worst suspicions were confirmed.

Paula Harris had more than enough reasons to be annoyed and upset by this latest turn of events. Throughout all of her married life, she had been subjected to beatings and assaults from her husband Timothy. She readily acknowledged that in some way she was not entirely blameless. After all, she reasoned, if she hadn't told him she was pregnant all those years ago maybe it wouldn't have mattered so much. At the time, although Timothy had accepted the child as his own, over the years he had continued to voice and show, his displeasure to her and to their son Anthony. As a result, throughout their married life she had never been able to share the guilt-laden secret which troubled her tormented mind so deeply. Every time she came anywhere near to pouring out her heart to her husband, she became so traumatised with fear that she simply couldn't go through with it. Then, there were the beatings, which both she and Anthony had been made to suffer whenever Timothy flew into one of his uncontrollable rages. Each time this occurred, she vowed to herself, "next time, I will get out. I will tell him," but she never did, because, she always assumed that the consequences would be far greater than she could possibly imagine. As a result, for all of these years, Paula Harris had to hope and pray that her other son, the one she had secretly given up at birth for adoption, was alive and well and that one day she would be able to withstand that final confrontation with her husband and achieve her secret goal of tracing him. Every night she prayed that God and his adoptive parents would look after him. Although she always reproached herself for what she had done, she took some comfort from the fact that even if Timothy had been told at the beginning, things might not have been any better. Then, there was Anthony himself. Where on earth was he at present? All she knew after another blazing row with Timothy all those months ago, Anthony had stormed off vowing that if he had to stay in the house any longer with his father, he would probably end up killing him. On this occasion she had had to take Timothy's side, as the incident had been sparked by Anthony's arrest for possession of a small amount of cannabis which, ultimately, Timothy had been able to get covered up thanks to his 'connections.'

At the time Anthony had denied the drug was his and he had always maintained that it had been planted on him and, although she was prepared to accept this could well be true, she also knew that she had voiced her suspicions in the past to her husband and after all it had to be said that there was no smoke without fire. She recalled the many times she had methodically searched Anthony's room looking for some evidence of drug taking but she had never been successful. Apart from her own forebodings, her own mother's instinct confirming that he was involved in the drug scene centred on the fact that she was well aware that some of Anthony's best friends, including Simon Collins, were heavily involved themselves. In fact, Simon Collins was in a rehab centre at this very moment. However, none of this stopped her from worrying about the whereabouts of her wayward offspring and all she could do was thank God he was financially independent and thus able to support himself.

Despite all these problems, the number one item on Paula's greatly troubled mind was the continued infidelity practised by her husband. All these years he might have thought he was extremely clever and, that he had always got away with it but she knew better. Most of Timothy's affairs had been one- or two-night-stands and she knew nearly all of the women involved. As a result, she was able to warn them off or, in some subtle way, ensure that their own husbands suspected what their wives were up too. Usually this worked but this latest episode though was something far worse. If he was associating with prostitutes and paying for sex, this was something that she could not cope with and, one way or another, she would have to find out. Once she had the required proof there would be no going back. First of all she would announce to all who would listen that she was leaving him and then she would institute divorce proceedings against him. Then, and only then, she would try to find her first born son. 'Who knows, she thought, 'with Anthony united with a brother he never knew existed, maybe there was a possibility that after twenty-six years, she might be able to play happy families again always assuming, of course, that Marcus, her adopted son, still wanted to meet and greet her.

Timothy Harris, although still very worried, was mightily relieved to get out of the house. He congratulated himself on how quickly he had deceived his wife and, if all went well with his plan, he might escape unscathed but that would all depend on his big brother-in-law. He reached out in order to check again that his mobile phone was beside him as he drove in silence to the golf club. He parked away from the main body of cars already there and picked up the phone and began to dial. He was sweating as he waited for the connection to be made at the other end as he tried desperately hard to think of the words to say. When the receiver was raised at the other end, his train of thought was interrupted momentarily but, recovering quickly he said, "Hello Robert, look I'm terribly sorry to trouble you but I have to tell you that I could be in quite a spot of bother and I'm wondering whether or not you can help me. You see it's about this girl, the one, you know the one er on the Crime Watch programme. Yes. Yes Clarkson that's the one." Now he was fumbling, and struggling to find the words and he could hardly bring himself to say it but he finally blurted it out. "The watch, the watch. It was me. I was with her in Bromborough and after we had dinner and a couple of drinks she left. She said she was going to catch the train back to Liverpool and she told me that she was going to work in London afterwards. After she left, I went back to my hotel you know the one – the Roundhead, and then I stayed in the bar for a while watching the football highlights. If you want to check this out, ask for Mr. Rogerson, the Deputy Manager, because he was with me until I went to my room just after midnight."

There was a pause at the other end of the line then he heard Robert's voice saying, "all right Timothy leave it with me, I'll have it checked out and, as long as it's as you've said, then I'll try to keep your name out of it you silly bloody pillock. Give me a ring at the office tomorrow morning and I'll let you know how I got on." With that, Robert Tyson, Chief Constable of Merseyside replaced the receiver muttering to himself, "bloody pillock why he can't keep his dick in his frigging pants I'll never bloody know." Before retiring, he left a message at HQ for Detective Inspector Taylor to see him first thing in the morning.

Timothy sat in his car for a moment. He knew that he'd been very fortunate and that he wasn't out of the woods yet. There was no point in him going home yet he had to go in the club, if only to ascertain whether or not Norman Collins was there. If he was, all well and good; they could have a quick drink together and his alibi for tonight was established. However, if Norman wasn't in the bar all he needed to do was to grab a quick drink and once again his presence at the club would be confirmed. Timothy knew he had to cover his tracks very carefully now. In fact, probably more than ever before. He was well aware that his wife always suspected he was being unfaithful but, up until now, he was sure he had always been able to show that her fears were groundless. Well, almost, he smiled whilst thinking to himself that that was one of the benefits of having good friends. Friends, which one could always rely upon. After locking the car he walked briskly into the club and straight to the bar. He saw at a glance that Norman wasn't in and he also knew there would be very little chance of him coming in now. He ordered his drink and asked Alec the barman if Norman had been in that day. In reply Alec told him that Norman had left at eight o'clock after having a couple of drinks. There was no point in Timothy prolonging the conversation with another part of his alibi in place; it was time to get off home in order to ensure that his ever-loving wife didn't get too suspicious because, if this all went wrong, he knew he would be destroyed and, he really did stand to lose everything at this time.

When he arrived home he was quite surprised to find that his wife had gone to bed. Once again, he complimented himself on the art of his deception then he came up with his master plan. Tomorrow, he would buy another watch identical to the one that he had given Angela. He'd pay cash for it, and use his original visa bill for the purchase of the first watch, as proof of purchase should his wife suspect anything. He'd keep the watch hidden until their wedding anniversary at the end of the year and, with any luck, he would be in the clear. It had been a close shave, a little bit too close for comfort but he assured himself, that's what life was all about.

Little did he know it but it was all beginning to come apart at the seams. It would still take quite some considerable time and, when it did finally happen, the effects upon everybody would be catastrophic.

The following morning the Chief Constable went over the things he was going to say whilst he waited for Detective Inspector Taylor to arrive. There was a faint knock on the door and, in answer; he shouted "Come in." Peter Taylor entered the room.

The Chief Constable put down his pen as the Inspector entered. "Sorry to trouble you Peter I know you've a lot on at the moment, but, this is important so I felt that I should tell you myself. This concerns the Angela Clarkson case. I had a tip off last night. I can't disclose my source but I can assure you the watch definitely belonged to her. My information comes from an absolutely impeccable source in fact; he might well have been her last client."

Peter Taylor could not believe what he was hearing and replied, "Well let me check him out."

But he was quickly rebuffed by the Chief Constable who said, "No. No leave it there, Peter, you have the watch positively identified, leave this man out of it now; there's nothing to be gained by destroying him or, his reputation."

"With respect sir," said Inspector Taylor, "in all my years on the force I have never ever had to contend with anybody interfering with the way I conduct or handle a case. If you're going to interfere like this, I will insist that you tell me now that you are taking me off the case and you're going to handle it yourself or, replace me. In addition, I will expect to receive notification of this from you in writing together with some form of explanation giving your reasons for taking me off the case. Upon receipt, I can assure you sir; I will then take up the matter with my Police Federation."

Even though the Chief Constable expected a war of words over this issue, he was totally unprepared for an onslaught of such magnitude. In a clumsy attempt to diffuse the situation he said quietly, "For Christ's sake Peter, sit down for a moment and listen because you're not thinking straight about this matter. Just give me a minute and, I'm sure we can sort something out. First of all, I want you to ensure that this man does not, under any circumstances whatsoever figure in this enquiry. As

I have already told you, my source is without question but, if his name does come out he will be utterly ruined and, as far as I can see, there's no need for that, is there?"

Peter looked defiantly at his boss and, although he was all tensed up inside and positively fuming, he could see the validity of the point put to him by his superior as he replied, "Sir, if we are talking openly man-to-man and this is my case, I really think you should let me be the judge of that. We have a DNA Profile taken from the dead woman and, if it matches his, he could still be in the frame."

This argument raged for over half an hour. In the end, a compromise was reached. Inspector Taylor agreed that the name of the person would not be revealed provided that the matter was handled by himself alone and without any outside interference whatsoever. In return for a DNA sample and a check on the man's alibi then, provided that he was completely satisfied, Detective Inspector Taylor agreed he would keep the name of Timothy Harris out of the case. Needless to say the DNA test did prove to be a positive match but, with a waterproof alibi checking out, Timothy Harris's name was removed from the case. To make matters certain the file was sealed and then placed in a locked drawer in the Chief Constable's office where it would remain until all the papers were filed at the end of the case. Then it would be marked up 'Not to be shown to The Defence' and filed in the Crown Prosecution Central Records Office. As Detective Inspector Taylor closed the door behind him, the Chief Constable breathed a sigh of relief as he realised how close matters had got to being totally out of hand.

Meanwhile, Peter Taylor made his way back to his own office where Jim West was waiting for him. "Hello Jim," he said, "sorry to keep you waiting but I've been to see the Chief. It seems that we have a positive ID on that watch, in fact, there's no doubt about it. It did belong to the Clarkson woman. Sorry, I can't tell you any more as the source is classified."

Jim West's eyes lit up at the news, "Let's go and pull Thompson in then," he said.

"Not so fast Jim, I'm afraid it's not quite that simple." At this point he paused for a moment because he knew that he had to choose his words very carefully now. He was going to propose to his colleague that somehow they needed to find one or two pieces of evidence and, he could hardly come straight out and ask Detective Sergeant West to manufacture that evidence. It had to be a lot more subtle and tactful than that. With DS West almost straining at the leash, Inspector Taylor continued to keep him in suspense even though he now knew exactly what he was going to say. Then he added, "What we really need to find here Jim is one or two of Angela Clarkson's mates on the game who can vouch with absolute certainty that the watch belonged to Angela and that they had seen her wearing it. I reckon if we can tie that up we can go ahead and pull him in."

Inspector Taylor needn't have worried. Jim West knew straight away what was needed and he assured his Chief that he would get on to it immediately in order to ensure that it was taken care of.

However, Jim West did not take care of it and neither did his boss, as later that day events took a dramatic turn when Diane Wilson's body surfaced at Chorley Wood near Preston.

Chapter 7

Two divers from the Preston and District Sub Aqua Club found the body. They had entered the murky waters, and they had only got down twenty feet or so when one of them spotted the trailing rope and this led them to the parcel on the shelf. At first, they thought it might be drugs and that they had stumbled upon a huge haul. This prompted them to leave things as they were until the police arrived.

Word spread quickly throughout the country and it wasn't very long before detectives from Merseyside CID were making their way to the scene. With all sirens operating at full pitch, the convoy of cars sped up the motorway at speeds well in excess of the normal speed limit whilst another car was dispatched to collect Mr. and Mrs. Wilson who would be asked to identify the body.

Accompanied by a trained police counsellor, the Wilsons made the painful journey to the mortuary at Preston where the body had been taken. Brenda, Diane's mother, couldn't face the ordeal and it was left to her husband to identify her.

As John Wilson began to walk slowly to the doors at the entrance, his movement became distinctly laboured and, to those watching him, it was obvious that he must be absolutely dreading this terrifying ordeal. Brenda, his wife, watched with growing apprehension too as the officer accompanying him began to open the dark green doors in order to let him pass and it was at this moment, as she prepared herself for the inevitable, that she knew that all her fervent prayers were now in vain. As she felt her body tighten involuntarily, she somehow steeled herself for the inevitable sounds which she knew would be forthcoming as the sheet was drawn away from her daughter's face and the shock and horror registered with her beloved husband. Despite this, and still hoping against hope, even she could not have prepared herself for what was to follow. As John Wilson disappeared through the dark green doors and, although Brenda Wilson was silently weeping uncontrollably, she was totally unprepared for the sound that followed. When it began it was almost inaudible as though it was emanating from below bowel depth and moving with agonising slowness through his body until, when it finally emerged, the howl of anguish chilled all within earshot as the finality of the all-embracing tide of death washed over all of those present.

Distressed beyond belief, Brenda found it impossible now to express her own grief and release her inner torment, especially in the presence of strangers as she sank into the comforting arms of her husband. She endeavoured instead to attempt to share his burden whilst knowing only too well that together their suffering would now be never-ending. Before their tragic and tearful journey home began, they were both sedated and they listened in solemn silence as Inspector Taylor told them he wouldn't rest until he, and his team, had their daughter's killer safely locked up behind bars.

Although still in a state of shock, John Wilson leaned forward in his seat and directing his anger directly to the Inspector said, "Well, I don't think you'll have very far to look, will you Inspector? Let's face it, if I get my hands on Harry Thompson before you do, there won't be any need for a bleeding trial. With that, John Wilson wound up the window and the car drove slowly out of the parking area to journey back to the Wirral at a much more sedate pace. Neither of the bereaved parents spoke much during their lonely ride back home. There wasn't any need. They both knew the pain the other was feeling and they also knew that their world no longer existed. Furthermore, as far as they were both concerned, Harry Thompson was the biggest evil, lying bastard, on this earth.

Inspector Taylor and Jim West made their way to their car. Before moving off, he checked with his own superiors that the total news blackout he had requested was being observed and that the men that he had asked for were on hand waiting in readiness to make an early arrest as soon as they got back. It wasn't as if Detective Inspector Taylor was presuming Harry Thompson to be guilty. It was more of a case of keeping him secure and unharmed until the cause of Diane Wilson's death had been established and the DNA samples analysed and compared. Once all this had been accomplished, he felt sure that Harry Thompson would end up inside for a very long period of time.

Leaving the mortuary behind, Jim West was skilfully driving the car at speeds within the limits and now they were approaching Ellesmere Port. His boss was on the radio making sure that the men were ready. Receiving confirmation that all was to his satisfaction, Peter Taylor told his Sergeant to go straight to the home of Harry Thompson. In order to make Thompson's arrest official, one of the other officers in attendance had secured the necessary warrant and Inspector Taylor didn't anticipate any trouble or any members of the press to be in attendance.

The cars drew up outside the front door of the neat little house in Eastham village and silently disgorged their human cargo of officers and men. Both men strode purposefully to the door at the front. No time for niceties now thought Jim West as he lifted up the knocker and launched a thunderous assault on the door. Inspector Taylor thought about asking him not to overdo it, but that hardly mattered for the door was beginning to open.

As the door swung open, both men could see the frame of Harry Thompson in the doorway. They saw the smile on his face diminish as he saw the group of men assembled. Thrusting forward his ID card, Detective Inspector Taylor began. "Harry Marcus Thompson My name is Detective Inspector, Taylor, Merseyside Police. I have a Warrant for your arrest in connection with the death and disappearance, of Diane Wilson. You do not have to say anything at this stage but I must warn you that anything you do say may be used in evidence against you. I must now ask you to accompany my officers, and myself, to Bromborough police station where we will continue our enquiries."

With that Harry Thompson was led away to face another ordeal. When they arrived at the police station he was taken in by the rear entrance and, as a precaution, a blanket covered his head. He was then led upstairs to the interview room. Harry knew the predicament he was facing so he didn't waste any time in requesting the presence of a solicitor. As instructed by Brian Donnelly, the solicitor who had come to assist him the last time, he made a specific request for Michael Mulrooney to attend. He also made his position crystal clear to the officers from the very beginning that he would not answer any questions until Michael Mulrooney, or his appointed representative, arrived irrespective of how long it took.

It was late when Michael Mulrooney arrived and he was allowed immediate access to his client, Harry Thompson. Straight away he told Harry that he should only answer questions when he nodded and, whenever he didn't nod, Harry was to remain silent and let him do the talking.

All too soon the officers were back in the room and the interview began in earnest. Inspector Taylor switched on the tape recorder and began as follows.

"We have arrested Harry Marcus Thompson on suspicion

of causing the deaths of Diane Wilson and Angela Clarkson. This interview is being conducted by myself, Detective Inspector Peter Taylor, and Detective Sergeant West from the Merseyside Police Force. Also present are Harry Marcus Thompson and his solicitor, Michael Mulrooney. At this point the Inspector stopped for a moment and looked at his watch, then he continued, "The time is now seven fifty six pm, and, I would like to commence this interview with your affirmation that your name is Harry Marcus Thompson and that you are currently residing at 43 Eastham Village Road, Eastham, South Wirral."

Noting the nod from his solicitor, Harry confirmed that the officer's statement was correct.

"Can you confirm to us the last time you saw Miss Wilson and can you give us an accurate account of your subsequent movements covering the following twenty-four hours?"

This time there was no nod, and, Michael Mulrooney answered, "Mr. Thompson has already given you a full statement concerning this matter, and he has instructed me to say that he has no reason to add to it at this stage."

And so it went on. As each question was put to him his solicitor was there with the answer. The Inspector concluded matters by telling them that the interview would be adjourned until 9 am the following morning when there would be an application for a remand in custody whilst enquiries continued.

Michael Mulrooney nodded his assent to this adding that the police had only 36 hours in which to conduct their enquiries, after which time, they would either have to release Harry, or charge him with murder. He also added that Harry was completely innocent of any charge and any custodial remand application would be vigorously resisted.

The following day the remand hearing was held in the Magistrate's Court and, Harry Thompson was formerly charged with the murders of Diane Wilson and Angela Clarkson. Following a two minute hearing he was remanded in custody to Walton Gaol for 28 days pending further police enquiries. Despite protests by his solicitor and, a not guilty plea, bail was refused and he was led to the cells below to await transport to the prison remand centre.

Later that day, the two officers were discussing the case again over a pint of beer in a little country pub. They had received confirmation that Thompson's DNA had proved a match but only to that obtained from Diane Wilson but they knew this was only to be expected in view of the fact that Thompson had freely admitted to having sex with Miss Wilson just before her disappearance. They also knew that this was the crux of the case against Thompson simply because as far as they had been able to ascertain, he was the last person to see her alive.

The Clarkson case was very different though and much more circumstantial. Both men went over the details again together with a plan of procedure.

The body had been found just a quarter of a mile from the Thompson home and that was too much of a coincidence as they considered it was far too close for comfort when considered along with the other aspects of the case.

Thompson must have known the spot because he readily admitted to walking his dog in the vicinity of the golf course and the surrounding area.

At an earlier interview, Thompson had also admitted walking with his girlfriend around the same area on a regular basis.

Thompson had handed in a watch at Bromborough Police Station that he claimed to have found. When the actual spot was pointed out it was found to be less than sixty feet from where the body of Angela Clarkson lay. Although they did not have specific confirmation that this watch belonged to Clarkson, they were quite sure that, given time, events would prove that this was indeed the case.

Thompson was known to drink in the local pubs and hotels in the area and, although he had been identified as being in the Roundhead Hotel on the night in question, nobody could confirm having seen him there with the Clarkson woman.

The railway guard had come forward following the crime watch programme and volunteered the information that a well dressed young lady, who bore a strong resemblance to Clarkson, had boarded his train at the Bromborough Rake station late one evening around the time of her death. Subsequent examination of the CCTV footage revealed the presence of a man on the platform and, although the image caught on screen resembled Thompson, they were unable to obtain definite proof or, confirmation of this.

"What do you think about it now then?" Jim asked his chief.

Jim West didn't take long to think about his reply.

"Well Peter, I see it like this we have no DNA in this case so all we can do is build up the circumstantial case against him. First of all we treat the DNA in Clarkson as though it doesn't exist. After all, if we don't introduce it the defence cannot comment upon it. Then we devote all our efforts into tying the watch in with Clarkson. If we can show that Clarkson wore that watch, I think we are home and dry simply because it's all too coincidental."

Inspector Taylor agreed adding, it was just a pity that they couldn't get access to her last client but, given a decent break, they would get there in the end.

Chapter 8

Jim West had left his boss in his office and he was driving alone to Walton Gaol where he was going to interview Royston Chambers, an old lag whom he had put away many times before. He had telephoned the prison before he set out in order that Chambers could be informed of his impending visit and dwell upon the implications of it. Over the years Chambers had operated as a paid informer to the police and he was one of Jim West's own snouts. This time however Chambers was in big trouble as it looked like he was going to go down for a long time on the aggravated assault and burglary charges he was facing. In the circumstances, Jim West reasoned, it might just be the right time to call in a few markers and, Roy Chambers fitted the bill nicely.

Meanwhile, many miles away, a train was pulling slowly into Paddington Station. Today, Quentin Russell was not in his usual hurry to make his way to the Commons' tea bar. Today he wanted to take his time in order that he could plan his strategy with the MP he was going to meet. Last night, he had received a tip- off, from one of his most impeccable sources that a member of the house might be implicated in the death of Angela Clarkson, a Liverpool prostitute, found murdered on the Wirral.

Quentin Russell was seen by many of his colleagues as a political assassin but he always played the game fairly and squarely. He never pursued or persecuted anybody unfairly or without just cause or reason. He didn't have to because his sources of information were always spot on. Some people said quite openly that he must have a mole within cabinet circles but he never gave anything away and preferred instead to leave his other political reporter colleagues floundering in his wake. It was academic to him anyway because he would never disclose his primary source even if he'd wanted to, due to the fact that he had never met her. He only knew her by the name she had chosen – Rose. In this instance, it was late last night when the call came on his mobile requesting him to contact one of his MP colleagues in order to ask him to put down a question in the House. In return for this, Quentin Russell knew that the Member would put down his question at Prime Minister's question time. The question would be asked and, as a result, Quentin would have secured a political scoop for his paper. Furthermore, his political nose told him that this might well be a case that could run a long, long way. Who knows? He mused, it might even outrun the Profumo affair or, even the Stonehouse scandal.

Now he was entering the tea-rooms and, he could see his appointed companion already seated. He quickly joined him and told him what he knew. Arrangements were put in place so that he would be advised the night before the question was to be asked, then the following morning his paper would publish an unsubstantiated claim that a Member of the House might have something to hide in connection with an ongoing murder enquiry. He quickly left his colleague in order to circulate swiftly around the room, having a quick word here, a quick word there, hearing all the latest gossip and, generally trying to see if there was anything further to be gained. It was very obvious from his roaming that, as usual, he was out on his own on this one but, as far as he was concerned, that was only to be expected as he already knew that his contact, Rose, was the best in the business.

Although Rose and her information might be excellent, little did Quentin Russell know that in this instance, she would prove to be far too good for herself, himself and the paper's editor! By the time this story concluded, there would be a lot of people cast by the wayside, unable to continue in their chosen field of employment. At the end of the day, Timothy Harris MP would have a lot to answer for.

In Lancashire, Jim West was getting out of his car in the reserved parking area for special visitors to Walton Gaol. He patted his pocket to make sure he still had the watch in his possession which would form a crucial part of his investigations later in the day. Then he strode purposely forward to greet Alexander Fulton the Assistant Governor, who was waiting outside to greet him. He ushered Jim inside and escorted him to his office. Alec knew the purpose of Jim West's visit and he made arrangements for Roy Chambers to be brought to the office where he intended to leave the two men alone in order that the detective sergeant could endeavour to elicit the information he required safe from prying eyes and wagging tongues and ears. There was a slight knock on the door and in answer Jim West swiftly called out, "come in." Roy Chambers immediately entered the room. A quick glance around the room told the hardened criminal he was alone with Jim West, Alec Fulton having left by an interconnecting door. Jim West motioned to Roy to sit down then he began.

"Look Roy you don't need me to spell it out for you this time but, I've got to tell you that I've already had a word on your behalf and my boss Peter Taylor is not prepared to give you a frigging inch. In fact, he's quite adamant that when you get sent down this time, and you will get sent down, you will be looking at seven years at least. I've spent a lot of time arguing with him about how useful you've been in the past but he just will not listen to me. In some respects, I have to agree with him because you didn't have to go on this last pissing job yourself. As you damn well know, you stupid bastard, you could have told us about it beforehand and then we could have picked you up the day before on something or other rather than simply lifting you and the others as we did at the scene. The difficulty I'm facing now, and this is how my chief sees it, you want to pick and choose which bleeding jobs you tell us about and, as far as he is concerned that just isn't good enough. In a nutshell what he's saying to both of us is, Roy Chambers, failed mobster, failed master criminal, has outlived his period of bleedin' usefulness, and now that his sell-by date has expired, the pillock's expendable. Jim West locked his fingers together and leaned forward across the wide desk in order to get a lot closer to his man. Looking the criminal straight in the eye he said, "I hope I am getting through to you, Roy. You do understand the seriousness of your position don't you? I really have done my very best to help you but it's really out of my hands now."

Jim West leaned back in his comfortable chair in order to study his man intently. He could see clearly that his words were impacting dramatically on Roy Chambers and he could sense that, as far as Roy Chambers was concerned, this was just about the worst news he could ever have received. He knew that seven years was a long time and the sheer prospect of serving seven filled him with a deep sense of foreboding. In these circumstances he would be locked up for at least three years before being considered for parole. That prospect didn't go down well with him at all. The most worrying aspect of all this was what might happen to him inside whilst he was doing those three years. After all, there were plenty of people already inside who had long suspected Roy Chambers of duplicity with the police and it wouldn't take them long to exact a very painful revenge.

"Oh God," he mumbled, as he realised that this was more than serious. In fact, this could well be the absolute end.

Grey-faced and tight-lipped, he faced his accuser. He struggled for words as he stuttered and stammered, "What can I do, Mr. West? Is there something specific you want to know, some information perhaps about the St. Helen's supermarket payroll heist? Just tell me, and I'll let you know."

Jim West leaned across the desk, and, locking his fingers together once again, he said as calmly as he could, "Roy, for Christ's sake man. You haven't been paying any bloody attention at all to what I have been saying have you, you stupid pillock? At this very moment, the last thing my boss wants to hear about is the St. Helen's supermarket heist. I've taken time out myself to come here to tell you that you're no longer on my bleeding payroll list and I can't help you any longer. This is an unofficial visit by me as I'm only supposed to be here to interview this Thompson fellow; you know the guy we think murdered that prostitute Angela Clarkson and his girl friend. You know the one we fished out of the lake at Chorley Wood. My boss thinks that any time now he'll be ready to confess because he's never been inside a pissing cesspit like this before and this place soon becomes very overbearing indeed doesn't it, Roy? By the way have you met him yet?

Roy Chambers shook his head before answering. "No. I've seen him about but I haven't spoken to him. People are saying he's probably off his bleeding trolley so me, and most of the other lads, tend to keep well away from him. Even in this place you have to be so careful."

"That's a load of bollocks," said Jim, his face breaking into a wide grin." There's nothing wrong with him. What's more I can assure you. If he was going to use that as a plea it would be down on the sheet now and I can tell you here and now that it bloody well isn't. Off his bloody trolley that's a load of bollocks and that's official." Now he was reaching for his coat, making out that he was preparing to leave. He kept his eyes on Chambers all the time waiting for the right moment to offer Chambers the bait then he knew he would accomplish the main purpose of his visit which was a confession from Thompson to Chambers which would go such a long way to ensure Thompson's conviction. He moved slowly towards the door reaching unhurriedly for the handle. He could almost feel Roy Chamber's eyes staring at his back, boring like laser beams through his body, almost pleading with him. "Please don't go Jim. Please don't leave me here, I'll do almost anything, just tell me what you want."

Judging and timing it to perfection, Jim West didn't go.

He never intended to in the first place and now making it appear like an afterthought, he turned around and said quietly, "Listen Roy, there is something you can do, get us both off the hook so to speak. "Why don't you get to know Thompson? We know he's ready to cough so why not make friends with him and get him in a very talkative frame of mind? You see it's like this. My boss is going to be more than pleased if Thompson confesses and, if I can tell him that Royston Chambers played a starring role in it, maybe, just maybe, I can stop him from leaning so hard on you. Obviously Roy, you must realise this is strictly unofficial and, I can't promise you anything. You do understand that don't you? Jim West saw the colour flooding back into the face of Roy Chambers and he knew that he had his man well and truly hooked. He also knew that when Chambers left the room, he would find that some excuse had already been made to place him in the next room to Harry Thompson. After that it would be easy, dead easy."

It would be impossible to describe the relief felt by Roy Chambers when he heard those last words from DS West. Apparently, all Westy wanted him to do was to make friends with Harry Thompson and if Thompson let go any useful information regarding either of the girls, simply let old Westy know. Well that would be a cinch. In return for this, there was still a chance that good old Westy would put more than a good word in for him; in which case, he might not be staring seven years in the face any longer..,

Roy Chambers couldn't agree quickly enough. He was so anxious and relieved to be off the hook he hardly heard Jim West saying, "I'll pop along in a couple of days to talk to you about the supermarket job."

Jim West's face bore a satisfied smile all the way back to Merseyside Police HQ. As he drove, his mind went back over the meeting with Chambers and, each time the picture crossed his mind, he whispered to himself, "easy innit?" He parked his car in his reserved place and, after taking a quick look round, he set off walking towards Rodney Street. For the benefit of the uninitiated, Rodney Street is one of the places where the ladies of the night choose to walk and ply their trade. Quite often nowadays they can be found plying their trade during the day and this was why he was going there now. He told himself there wasn't any time like the present and that this was as good a time as any to locate Bridget Riley and Theresa O'Rourke, two long-time associates of the late Angela Clarkson. Unfortunately, neither girl was anywhere to be seen on the streets so he walked around the corner and made his way into The Rugby Arms or, the Hookers as it was known locally especially in view of its close proximity to Rodney Street. His was a well-known face in this part of the town, and most of the regulars greeted him. Nearly all of them knew he was a copper and there were a number of people present who had had their collars felt by this big burly and uncompromising policeman. However today it was different. There were only two things on Westy's mind and they were both sat in the corner drinking their double gins and tonics. He caught the eye of Alf the barman, who knew without being asked that he would be drinking a pint of bitter.

He also motioned that he wanted two double gin and tonics for the two ladies in the corner. He didn't give either of them a chance to see him coming. The first they knew about it was when the drinks appeared on the table followed by himself with his pint in hand.

He began talking before he actually sat down.

"Nice to see you, girls. I thought I might find you both in here so I decided I'd just call in for a chat, unofficial business like, you know. Both girls visibly relaxed at this and thanked Jim for their drinks as he continued, "Dreadful news about Angela wasn't it – absolutely appalling and, what's more, no need for it you know." Both girls nodded in agreement and Bridget added, "She never deserved that, and the sooner the trade is licensed and properly supervised, the better it will be for everybody. As the drinks went down, the girls relaxed even more. By now they both realised that today Westy, or Jim, as they often called him, didn't mean to run either of them in and he certainly wasn't here to make small talk about their dear departed friend Angela. They were both streetwise and very smart. They knew Jim West wanted their help and assistance in some way otherwise the Black Maria would have carted them both off half an hour ago. Meanwhile, all Jim wanted was for the general noise in the bar to quieten down a little then they would find out the true nature of his visit and it would certainly involve Angela. A couple of gins later the bulk of the afternoon trade had gone. They were alone in the corner when Bridget decided it was time to act, "tell us what's on your bloody mind Jim. Let's face it, you haven't come down here to spend all the bloody afternoon drinking with a couple of old pro's so, let us be knowing what this visit is all about and what the hell it's got to do with us. This is costing us money you know. Don't forget whilst we're in here, talking to you, we're not getting frigging paid, and yet here we are paying our bloody corner into the bargain."

A smile flickered across his face before he spoke. This was typical Bridget. She didn't mess about or mince words, whatever she had to say she said it, and, if you didn't like it, then tough. "Now the crowd's gone, I can tell you. It is about Angela and we need your help. We have a man in Walton and we're almost certain we have the right man but, we do need a little extra help and I'm wondering if either of you had ever seen Angela wearing this." With that, he drew the watch from his pocket and passed it beneath the table. He continued, "If you want to have a good look at it, take it into the toilets and have a good think about it. You see it's very important that we find out. As the girls withdrew, he ordered another pint for himself and waited. He didn't have to wait too long and, as they approached, he could tell immediately from the look on their faces that his luck was out on this one. The watch was returned unnoticed under the table. Both said sadly that they couldn't recall seeing Angela wearing a watch like it, especially such an expensive watch as that. They both saw the obvious look of disappointment on Jim's face and said they were very sorry they couldn't be of more use to him. Although disappointed, Jim thanked them for their time and said he would see them around. Both girls quickly departed to ply their trade leaving Jim to finish his pint in the almost deserted bar before making his way back to HQ.

Once in his office, he made arrangements for both ladies to be arrested and charged with possession of a controlled substance that evening and that he was to be informed the moment that they were in custody. With that little matter taken care of, he made his way to the canteen in order to get himself something to eat whilst he waited for things to develop thinking to himself all the time, that there's always more than one way to skin a cat. Suitably refreshed, after having eaten the braised steak and onions on offer in the canteen, Jim West began to make his way back to his office. On his way he stopped by the office of his boss, Detective Inspector Peter Taylor, in order to acquaint him of the developments during the day, but today, his mentor had already left for home so he returned to the comparative safety of his own sanctum knowing full well he wouldn't have to wait too long before something happened. He just had time to phone his wife to say he would be late when the word came through that there were two ladies downstairs asking repeatedly to be allowed to see him and that they would only speak to Detective Sergeant West himself. Without any undue haste, he made his way downstairs. Once again he found himself saying 'easy, easy innit?' and, in a way it was, although it was also true to say that Jim West was well aware that both girls dabbled with drugs especially crack cocaine. In fact, it was also true that Bridget did a bit of dealing on the side. He made his way to the desk where the duty constable told him that both ladies were being held in interview rooms 1 and 2. He decided he would tackle Bridget first and he entered interview room no. 2 with an air of complete surprise and innocence. He asked Bridget to explain the trouble she was in and how he could be expected to help. She responded by saying the drug had been planted on her during the search by the constable and that she should be released immediately without charge. At first he listened with some degree of sympathy then he tore into her saying that next door, Theresa was already confessing to supplying the drug and that it would be far better for her if she calmed down and cooperated otherwise, she, as well as Theresa, would end up inside for at least six months.

He went on to say that if she could recall the first time she saw Angela Clarkson wearing that expensive watch he would endeavour to ensure she wouldn't face the prospect of a prison term and that he would do his utmost to get the charges dropped. Gradually the penny dropped and Bridget agreed to cooperate. He took her through the procedure to be followed and arranged to meet her the next day at a place of her own choosing where all the bits and pieces would be ironed out including dates and times. Before leaving, he told her to say nothing when she was released to Theresa and he was now going to interview her after which, they would both be allowed to leave without charge. He made his way to interview room no. 1 where the wrath of Theresa soon descended upon him. Bravely, and compassionately, he told her that he was going to smooth things out for the two of them and that she had better calm down before he reconsidered his decision. As he prepared to leave, he told her in no uncertain manner that, as far as he was concerned, this was to be treated as an interest free loan and that, one day, he would probably call in his marker. In the meantime, both she and Bridget were free to go and the least said about the matter the better. Both girls departed very quietly and went straight back on the game. Jim West went home quite pleased with his day's work and well satisfied that very shortly his man would be well and truly stitched up.

The following day around noon as arranged, Jim West was seated at a table in the far corner of the bar. From here, he could readily observe all the people who entered The Pierhead pub and restaurant. He'd arrived early in order to secure this table and, although it was situated out of the way, it offered a little bit more privacy. Later, as the place filled up with visitors, and lunch-time diners, it became very busy and sometimes it was impossible to obtain a seat. After a quarter of an hour it was apparent that the place was going to be as busy as usual but to Jim West, that meant in a crowded bar such as this, there was less chance of being seen and recognised. Then he saw her coming in alone. When he saw her, he muttered softly to himself, "thank god she hasn't come in her working clothes".

Somehow, he always thought the girls working Rodney Street or any other street for that matter, always stood out like sore thumbs with their somewhat way out or over the top sense of fashion. Once Bridget had taken her seat, he made his way through the crowd to the bar where he ordered two very large gin and tonics with ice and lemon. Returning to his seat, he almost had to battle his way through the crowd but eventually he made it with the drinks intact.

After another quick greeting Jim mixed their drinks and got straight down to the business that had brought them here. "Now Bridget this is what I want you to do for me. As you know we are holding a man in connection with the death of your good friend Angela Clarkson. She was a good friend now wasn't she?" Bridget nodded in reply leaving the detective free to continue,

"We've charged this man with killing your friend and we also know that he stole her watch after he had killed her. Obviously, we are unable to find out whether or not Angela had arranged to meet this man or whether she had been with somebody else first but we do know that we will have a better chance of proving him guilty if somebody would come forward to say that they saw Angela wearing this watch." He carefully pulled it out of the handkerchief where it lay concealed in his pocket in order that she could look at it again. "Take a good look," he urged quietly, whilst holding it just out of the view of the public beneath the table. "Now, you know as well as I do that the fellow who gave this to your mate Angela isn't going to come along to us and say, hang on a minute, that watch you showed on the box the other week, I gave it to Angela Clarkson because, in all probability, the man is married with a couple of kids and he's got to think of them, hasn't he? Again, Bridget nodded in reply and took another long pull at her drink. As she put down her glass, he continued, "So we need someone like you to come along to the nick and make a simple statement that you saw her, Angela, wearing that same watch some time before this fellow Thompson strangled her with her own tights. Now, Bridget, listen to me I swear to you that's all there is to it."

He could see her mulling it over in her mind, and, in order not to appear too anxious, he got up, saying as he did, "so have a good think about it whilst I go and get them in again. Same again for you?" Another nod of the head signalled affirmative and he began to fight his way to the bar thinking, 'Christ, she doesn't say a great deal. I wonder if she is this quiet with all of her punters?' He'd caught the eye of the barman and the drinks were now on the bar counter. Picking up the glasses, he made his way back to the table, whispering softly to himself, 'easy, easy innit?' Once seated he began again, "Bridget, you do understand don't you that if this fellow gets off or we let him go, he'll probably kill again so, in a way, we aren't just doing your friend Angie a favour but the public as well?" Instead of nodding Bridget spoke this time, "are you really sure that it is Angie's watch and, how do I know that this is all you want? I mean I won't have to give evidence will I?"

This time Jim took a long drink before replying, "Bridget, we're absolutely certain that the watch was given to Angela by her last client and that this person has been completely exonerated from our enquiries. As regards giving evidence, I can't guarantee it but I'll certainly do my very best he lied." He saw the effect this was beginning to have on her and quickly added, "Hang on a minute we'll only use it if we have to," he lied again, "after all, we think it's very likely that he'll confess before the actual trial and then you'll hardly be needed." As an afterthought, he added, "don't forget you're not doing this for me but for Angela… plus, at the same time, you must also remember that you owe me one for last night."

Seeing the predicament she was in, Bridget finally agreed to make the statement Jim West so desperately needed before adding, "Bollocks Westy, if I do this, by my reckoning we're even now and if this Thompson fellow confesses, then you keep me out of it. Agreed?"

Once again Jim West tried hard not to smile as he lied glibly, "That's a deal. All you need to do is call in the nick later tonight. Just ask for Detective Inspector Peter Taylor and let him handle things. At this stage you'd better not mention that you've spoken to me about this at all."

After another affirmative nod from Bridget, the Sergeant began to make his way out of the rapidly emptying bar whispering "easy easy innit." In his mind, he had already formulated his next move. Give her a couple of days, a week at the most and pull her in again then, like a knight in shining armour, he would come running to the rescue of a damsel in distress. No wonder this was easy. "Easy innit?" he whispered again under his breath.

Later that afternoon, Bridget Riley walked into Merseyside Police HQ in order to keep her appointment with Detective Inspector Peter Taylor to whom she then made her sworn statement, that before Angela Clarkson's death she had seen Angela wearing the watch shown on the Crime watch TV Programme. She told the Inspector that she hadn't volunteered this information earlier as she hadn't seen the TV Programme when it was shown. As a result she failed to appreciate the relevance or the importance of her information. She also confirmed that she had seen the watch when Detective Inspector Taylor allowed her to identify it whilst she was giving her statement in the police station. During this interview she was able to positively state that it was the watch in question. Detective Inspector Peter Taylor couldn't believe his luck as he took down this statement. He knew full well that somewhere along the line, Jim West must have had a hand in it but he wasn't going to raise any awkward questions with his colleague at this or any other time. As far as he was concerned, this was just one of the breaks they so desperately needed in their efforts to bring criminals to justice.

Chapter 9

Three days had passed since Quentin Russell had spoken to his associate in the Commons tea bar and, when his mobile rang. He knew it would be the call he was expecting. He wasn't disappointed. He was assured that the question would be asked in the House the next day and, by the end of the week, rumour and speculation would be rife following a denial by the Prime Minister himself. All Quentin needed to do was to ensure that he kept the pot simmering with a couple of paragraphs in his newspaper column until the time came to pounce.

At her home in Cheshire, Paula Harris was making afternoon tea for some of her friends from the ladies golf section and she too was wondering when something would be mentioned in the "House" about a certain and, as yet unnamed, MP.

Jim West was parking his car at Walton Gaol. He didn't expect any results at all from this visit because this visit was merely to ensure he kept up the pressure on Royston Chambers in order to ensure that he got what he wanted when the time came. He was well aware Chambers would try to string him along by saying Thompson would not admit to anything, but, when Chambers realised that the chips were down, Jim West knew he would say almost anything that he wanted to hear. To Jim West, prisons were like hospitals or, even worse mortuaries, for they had a peculiar smell about them which always seemed to linger as a result of which, he always liked to get straight down to business in order to get away as fast as possible. Today would be no exception.

Once again he was taken inside by Alec Fulton and conducted to the same office. Within minutes Chambers appeared, and, from the look on his face, he was totally surprised to see his old adversary sitting in the assistant governor's chair. The Detective Sergeant wasted no time at all in coming to the purpose of his visit. "How are you getting along with Thompson, Roy?" Is he talking to you yet, and, if he is, what's he talking about?"

Chambers began to fidget and straightaway, Jim could tell from his nervous demeanour, that Chambers was quite unsure of himself let alone what he was going to say? Jim knew that he was going to say that he had nothing to report, but this did not bother him in the least. After a few moments' silence however, Chambers finally summoned up sufficient courage to speak, "Look, Mr. West, I don't think he's going to say anything at all. I'm the only person he speaks to, and, although we knock about a bit during the day, each time I try to mention the subject he clams up tight or, he just says, "leave it. I'm not bloody guilty, and that's it." After that he goes back to his room sulking. So you see Mr. West, I don't think he's going to say anything."

Jim West tried to look crestfallen and, even a little sad by this turn of events but it was the precise result he anticipated. Replying with as much sympathy in his voice as he could muster Jim said quietly, "Look Roy I know you've tried and I've taken on board what you're saying but, it's early days yet. Just keep chatting to the pillock and, I'm sure that he'll come across before the trial. People like him always do. It's like having toothache; it doesn't go away until you get rid of it." At this point Jim paused, he smiled at his old adversary trying to let him think that he, Chambers, was in control of this interview then he continued, "Anyway Roy, we both know that you've tried don't we and that you're going to keep on trying aren't you? So Roy, I'll pass that on to my boss at the nick. Mind you, I have to tell you that he won't be very happy but, as I said I'll tell him that you'll keep Thompson matey and, you'll stick at it but you must remember Roy without this, I can't get my boss to do a bloody thing for you. You do understand that don't you, Roy?"

Chambers was now only too anxious to terminate this interview. At the outset he was hoping against hope that Thompson's reputed denials would get him off the hook and Jim West would then pull a few strings on his behalf but it was all too apparent that this was not going to be. Very reluctantly he whispered, "Alright Mr West, I understand, and you can rest assured that I'll keep at it." With that, he withdrew hastily from the room.

Jim West smiled broadly now as he watched Chambers exiting from the room, "Easy," he murmured, "Easy innit?"

In the House of Commons after a splendid lunch, followed by a very generous brandy, Timothy Harris settled himself into his seat. He was all set for the PM to launch another scathing and blistering attack, on the Opposition because of their stalling and delaying tactics over the proposed revisions to the National Health Service Bill. After this there would be another PM's Question Time during which he looked forward to the almost ritualistic and savage butchering of the Opposition Shadow PM who looked so much out of his depth on these occasions. Due to his outside business interests he had missed the morning session and he had also ensured that his mobile phone had remained switched off and locked safely away in his ministerial case. Following this, he and his associates had enjoyed an exquisite lunch, and because he'd dallied so long over it, he was completely unaware that his leader and the party whips had been trying to locate and question him before his return to the House and, most importantly, before PM's question time but it was far too late for that now.

The House was silent as the Prime Minister strode up to the front bench. As he saw Timothy Harris, his face bore a look designed to kill, but it passed unnoticed especially by the errant MP and the rest of the house. As the afternoon's business began it was as expected, the usual Government rout of the Opposition and today's pantomime produced a real bellyful of laughs. Timothy, along with most of his colleagues, found himself wondering why on earth the Opposition didn't ditch their leader as he was always so ineffective during these exchanges but then he thought that was their problem not his. Now it was time for questions with the Prime Minister.

The House was repeatedly called to order by the Speaker, Helen Little, but eventually the Members settled down in order to allow business to continue. There followed the usual run and gamut of self congratulatory questions which always showed off the Government at its very best and most efficient. The fact that it wasn't didn't matter in the slightest. This Government still had more than a working majority and it was equally true to say that if the Opposition were in power, things would carry on in just the same manner. Proceedings were looking up now that Denis Panter, one of the Opposition's most effective trouble-makers was on his feet and Timothy began to take a renewed interest. Panter never minced his words. If he had a question to ask it would certainly be of some relevance and, it would probably be acutely embarrassing for the person involved.

Dennis Panter remained on his feet, waiting for the Speaker's acknowledgement to begin, whilst Helen Little, the Speaker, continued to shout 'Order, Order, Mr Dennis Panter, Honourable Member for Knutsford.'

As soon as he received the acknowledgement of the Speaker, he began, "Madam Speaker, Members of the House, is the Prime Minister aware of any involvement by a member of his Government with the murdered prostitute Angela Clarkson and, can he emphatically deny that no member of his

Government is involved and, if there has been any involvement by this Member, will he assure the House that there will be no cover up and that all the details will be given to this House once his enquiries have been concluded? Furthermore, will the Prime Minister ensure that the Minister involved tenders his resignation along with an apology to the House for his conduct in this affair. That was it. Short, and swift and, very precise but, most importantly, straight to the point. As Denis Panter sat down there was absolute pandemonium in the House. Papers were flung in the air, there were cries of 'name him' and 'resign', above which, the Speaker strove manfully to bring some semblance of calm to the proceedings.

During this period of absolute mayhem, the Prime Minister had been on his feet for quite some time waiting for permission from the Speaker to reply and for some sign of order to be restored. As the noise subsided and he received the Speaker's acknowledgement, he answered, "Until I received the question earlier today I can assure the Honourable Member that I, along with all the other Members of the House, had no knowledge of this whatsoever and, I can assure the gentleman that I will carry out a full investigation into this most serious allegation. Obviously, I will advise the House of the full results of that enquiry and I trust that the Honourable Member is satisfied with the answer given."

Dennis Panter jumped to his feet and quickly acknowledged the answer given. There the session ended and, utter chaos reigned once more.

Timothy Harris could not believe what he had just heard. He knew he had to get out of the House fast and, he also realised, he had to seek an urgent meeting with his leader in order to issue a complete denial to the allegation. 'Jesus Christ' he told himself, 'this was terrible news. How on earth had Panter got hold of that scoop? Bob, his brother-in-law had put that safely under wraps for him therefore, what on earth had gone wrong?' The more he thought about it the angrier he became. Inside he was absolutely seething as the implications and the ramifications of that meddling prat Panter and his bloody stupid question rushed around in his brain. With his mind in utter turmoil, he knew one thing. He had to get his act together fast and, whether he liked it or not he knew he would have to see the PM tonight and issue a complete denial in time to catch the news. 'Jesus Christ,' he thought, 'that's another thing, the press; they'll have a bloody field day over this.'

With his mind in such a whirl he realised he might be getting agitated and, worst of all, it might be beginning to show and that would never do. Pulling himself together and, in a determined effort to regain control, he told himself, he had got himself into this mess and, somehow, he'd get himself out of it but first, he would have to go and face the PM.

Before he could go anywhere he felt a heavy hand on his shoulder. It was the Chief Whip, telling him, in no uncertain manner, to get to the Prime Minister's office without delay.

When he reached the office, he was surprised at the amount of body traffic going in and out. Then it dawned on him that all the people involved were MPs from Liverpool, Warrington, The Wirral, and Chester. From this he assumed correctly that his leader was interviewing anyone who might have been in the area at the material time. Seeing and realising this, he began to calm down. He breathed a little easier thinking that this might mean no positive identification details had been made known. This also meant it was unlikely the source had come from Robert or one of his officers in the Merseyside force. In the end, though, this began to bother him because, by ruling out all the obvious choices, it only left somebody at the hotel or the restaurant. There and then Timothy decided, once this interview was over he'd telephone Rogerson, at the hotel in order to ask a few discreet questions of his own. Jesus, there he went again, before he did anything else after seeing the PM he'd better telephone his wife. This was bound to be a feature on the evening news and it had probably been shown on the Question Time show on television that afternoon. Once again he felt the jitters returning but there was no time to think about anything else as he was ushered into the "office."

Initially the PM was brutal. He was taking it out on Timothy because he was the member of the constituency where the crime had taken place. Because the PM knew in advance that the question was coming, he had wanted to see Timothy before question time in order to confer about it, rather than be caught on the hop. Eventually, his anger subsided as Timothy assured him that although he was in his constituency and, in the area at the time, his movements were accounted for. "Furthermore," he added, growing a little in confidence, "if you want to check further ask the Home Secretary's office to check with the Chief Constable Merseyside CID. You see, I was interviewed at the time but this was because I was in the area and I had booked into a local hotel after holding a surgery. Now it is possible that this, er, this er, prostitute visited the hotel maybe she called in for a drink, who knows? I certainly don't because I never met her. The lies were flowing glibly now and his confidence increased as he added, "In fact I've just remembered, I spent the rest of the evening having a couple of drinks with Paul Rogerson, the assistant manager. We watched the football on the television then, when it was over, he locked up whilst I went to bed. After listening intently, the Prime Minister announced that he would check Timothy's story along with all the other possibilities and explanations he had received in order to show he had conducted an inquiry and, that the allegations were groundless. He went on to say that he would be seeking an apology and a complete retraction from the Member concerned who had made the allegation.

No longer sweating and in a much calmer state, Timothy left the office and telephoned home. He was feeling much more comfortable within himself and, as a consequence, he was able to talk to Paula much more freely about the events of the day, including the panic and pandemonium which had been caused in the House. He assured her, despite what she had seen on television, it was nothing more than a storm in a teacup, to be followed by a statement by the Prime Minister demanding a complete retraction by Denis Panter together with a full apology to the House.

As Paula Harris replaced the receiver on the hook she couldn't take it in. She shook her head in utter disbelief as she wondered, how the hell does he do it? How the bloody hell does he get away with it? Every bloody time he wriggles off the hook but I'll nail him yet, I really will, she promised herself.

Elsewhere the newspaper presses were beginning to roll. They would all carry the story but, the early editions were far too late, apart from those controlled by Quentin Russell's employers.

Quentin Russell was seated with his editor looking over the first proof. Once again the editor had had to admit that wherever he got his stories from, there was no question about it, Quentin Russell was without doubt the best. Not just the best but, the best, by a very long way. Yet again, he had left the Opposition miles behind and that's why he was paid such a fabulous sum but he was worth every penny.

On the Wirral, a car driven by Michael Mulrooney was slowly making its way to Walton Gaol. He was not alone because this time, he was accompanied by another man Trevor Bailey QC. He was the man empowered with the job of securing the release from prison of Harry Marcus Thompson and, from what he had heard of the case so far, he did not particularly relish the prospect. To him this job was just another case with a nice fee at the end of it. Secure a not guilty verdict if possible but don't go overboard on it because, the word was already about that Thompson was a psychopath and that he should really be in a secure place. Given half a chance that's where Trevor Bailey intended to place him.

Chapter 10

As Michael Mulrooney and Trevor Bailey entered the gaol, they were shown into a small, dark dank room where the interview was to be conducted. A solitary light bulb hung from the ceiling stained almost brown with the constant nicotine from the everlasting supply of cigarettes and tobacco, which had obviously been consumed there. Paint was peeling from the walls and the only furniture to be seen was a small table with four chairs arranged untidily around it in the middle of the floor. The sound of the door opening heralded the arrival of Harry Thompson and both men stood in readiness for the introductions conducted by the solicitor.

Michael extended his hand to Harry saying, "Nice to see you again Harry, I've brought along Trevor Bailey; he's going to be your defence QC. I've worked with Trevor before on a number of cases and they don't come much better I can assure you. As a matter of fact, I think we have been very fortunate to secure his services so let's get straight down to business." After Harry shaking hands with Trevor Bailey they all sat down and the meeting began.

Trevor Bailey began speaking whilst taking his papers, together with his notes from his brief case. "Mr. Thompson", he began. That was as far as he got, as Harry interrupted him saying, "Please call me Harry."

Pretending not to hear, his QC. began again, " Mr. Thompson."

Harry interrupted him again saying rather angrily this time, "Mr. Bailey, Trevor, I asked you to call me Harry. It might not seem anything to you but I'm cooped up in this stinking cesspit all day long. I appear to be in trouble right up to my bleeding neck and, at this moment in time, it seems to me that I don't have a friend in the world. Please cut out all the crap and try to be a little bit friendlier by saving all the official lawyer bit for the courts."

The QC looked at him for a moment, observing his body movements that he found a little odd considering the circumstances. Unlike many other clients that he had represented, Harry seemed to have this habit of locking his fingers behind his head and rocking backwards on the rear legs of his chair. In addition, he alternated this movement by occasionally wrapping his arms around his body as if he was reassuring himself that all was or, would be well. Finally, dismissing this situation from his mind, he resumed his task, "all right Harry, he said but first of all you listen to me. I don't have to take this brief if I don't want to, so just to make sure that we don't get off on the wrong foot again, I want to know quite a lot about you pretty quickly and, I need to confirm some facts. Your name is Harry Marcus Thompson and you live with your foster-mother at Eastham Cottages, Eastham Rake, South Wirral, Merseyside. I also understand that you are twenty six years of age and that you are a bachelor."

Harry confirmed these facts thus allowing the QC to continue, "You have been charged with the murders of Diane Wilson and, Angela Clarkson. Did you kill either one or both of these women?"

Harry immediately answered, "No," in a very firm and positive voice...

"On the first charge, Miss Wilson, I understand she was your girlfriend and that you had been going out together for some time?" Harry nodded now in assent allowing the questioning to continue.

"Did you have regular sex with this woman and was this

straight sex or did you indulge in any games or fantasies such as role play or, anything kinky?" Again the answer was negative allowing the barrister to continue.

"Whenever you had sex with Miss Wilson was she satisfied or did she want more? Did she ever complain about your performance and did she ever refuse your advances?"

Harry was getting annoyed now and, it was beginning to show as he couldn't see, let alone comprehend, where this line of questioning was going and he responded fiercely, "This is none of your business. We were just a happy, normal courting couple having sex whenever we felt like it. What we did or, how often we did it is no possible concern of yours."

Leaving these issues aside, Trevor Bailey tried a different approach. "All right then Harry consider this. Diane Wilson had a vicious temper, she flew into a terrible rage, perhaps she hit you and, before you knew it you had strangled her with her own tights. Obviously you were out of your mind at the time and you didn't know what you were doing. Afterwards, when you saw what you'd done you knew that somehow you would have to dispose of the body."

Harry was on his feet now. He was really annoyed with this man Bailey after all what did he know and, by what right did he consider that he could assume so much, "Bollocks," he exploded "that's a load of balls, I didn't strangle her. We had sex, we had an argument and she left."

Trevor Bailey let him finish before he began again as though nothing had happened. "Angela Clarkson, why did you kill her?" Although he wanted to follow up immediately with additional questions, Harry, didn't give him the chance.

He was still on his feet and decidedly edgy, "Look and listen to me, this is getting out of hand. I never saw the woman, I never had sex with her and I don't associate with prostitutes."

"How did you know she was a prostitute?" Countered the

lawyer seizing his opportunity to press home another point. "Did she tell you?"

Harry was growing tired with this line of questioning adopted by Trevor Bailey, barrister or not and he was beginning to take a distinct dislike to him as he retorted,

"I never knew the woman, I never saw her and the rest. Well it must have been something I read in the papers."

However Trevor Bailey did understand and his tone became a little more sympathetic, "Mr. Thompson sorry, Harry, I'm here to help you and, I am trying really hard to do just that. What you're going through now is nothing compared to the ordeal you will face in court especially under cross-examination. From my point of view as your barrister, responsible for your defence, I don't have an awful lot to go on. Let me tell you how the case for the prosecution is coming along. First of all, they have the body of your girlfriend from which they have a DNA sample that matches yours. They know you were with her the night she died. They know you both quarrelled and, as far as any other person is concerned, you were the last person to see her alive. Regarding Angela Clarkson, all right there's no DNA but, Harry, this is what the police have. She is found in close proximity to your home. All right that's entirely coincidental but she is also strangled with her own tights, another coincidence. The tights are knotted in the same way indicating the same person who killed Diane Wilson carried out this crime. Another coincidence. Her body is found very close to where you walk with your dog and where you say you used to walk with Diane Wilson. Now I know many visitors walk in and around the vicinity but hardly any of those people would be aware of the ditch hidden beyond the fence but a local lad would and you are a local lad. As if this is not enough, close to the spot where the body was lying and, before the discovery of it, you claim to have found a watch that you hand in at the local police station. Harry, believe me, I really would like to help you but, before I can even begin to try, I have to believe in something about you. To be absolutely precise at this very moment I myself, would have to doubt your innocence. Now, if you were to agree to undergo psychiatric tests to determine your sanity, and, we can show the jury that you were unbalanced or mentally disturbed at the time, then I'm sure I can at least get the charges lessened. Afterwards and once the proceedings are out of the way, we can arrange for you to receive all the help you need and I'm sure you'll find that a much better option to a life in prison."

Harry Thompson had sought the comfort and support of his chair in the face of this onslaught as it had taken him completely by surprise. Now he wanted to stand up and hit him, barrister or not. He felt that, if he could get close enough he would probably kill him. What on earth was he saying, me… Harry Thompson insane? plead insanity? As he rose from the chair he felt his legs begin to buckle and, unable to take the strain, he sank slowly to the floor shouting, "Get out, get out, Michael get this bastard out of here."

Harry had recovered a little when the solicitor returned, and there was an uneasy silence for a moment or two as neither person spoke and with neither man looking the other directly in the eye, Harry knew that he had to speak and that he had to ask the big question now, before the moment was lost. "Michael," he said, "Don't mess about, tell me honestly what's your own frank assessment of my position?" "Harry," he replied, "although I've only known you since this thing started, I can't in all sincerity believe you're guilty but, now that you've asked me, I must be honest and frank with you. At the moment we haven't got a defence and you've probably just lost the best brief I could get you under the present circumstances. All I can do is promise you I'll do my utmost for you on each and every charge they throw at you."

With that, Michael Mulrooney departed leaving Harry alone with his rambling thoughts and deeply troubled mind. His brain desperately searching for one clue or any scrap of information which might provide the key with which he could extricate himself from the unsavoury position in which he found himself. But there was to be no such relief forthcoming and, when he returned to his room on the remand block, he found that he had a new neighbour. Royston Chambers.

Meanwhile urgent enquiries had indeed been made within government circles, and it was confirmed by the Chief Constable of Merseyside that Timothy Harris had been asked some routine questions in connection with initial enquiries about Angela Clarkson. This, and subsequent enquiries, showed he had been able to give a more than satisfactory account of his movements as a result of which, as far as the police were concerned, he would not be of any further assistance to their enquiries. The statement also pointed out that a number of people who had been in the hotel or the vicinity, had come forward in response to an appeal by the police and they too had been eliminated. The following afternoon, the Prime Minister was able to announce to a packed House of government supporters that he was more than satisfied that no member of his government had been involved in any way with Angela Clarkson or with her tragic demise. This announcement was greeted with loud murmurings from the government benches together with a tremendous waving of order papers. The Prime Minister then asked the Honourable Member for Knutsford if he was satisfied with the reply to which, there were cries of "Shame" and "Apologise" from the benches. However, whilst Dennis Panter acknowledged the reply given there wasn't any way he would even consider an apology let alone offer one. He was quite content to wait until his source made contact again, and, he was sure he wouldn't have to wait very long.

As always there's no smoke without fire and this was a story that refused to lie down and die. The curiosity of the press had been aroused and, together with that of the public, it needed to be satisfied. Behind the scenes moles were digging. Digging into every sordid little detail they could get their hands on in an effort to discover the identity of the unnamed member. No. 1 on their rapidly shortening list was Timothy Harris. Later that evening, Paula Harris picked up the telephone and dialled the number of a mobile telephone. It was the number she always rang whenever she wished to contact Quentin Russell. After two short rings she heard his soft voice at the other end of the line saying, "Russell here." In answer to this she said one word, "Rose" and contact was established. She began with an apology because she felt Quentin would be angry or annoyed over recent happenings. Nothing further had resulted from their last contact and she was relieved when he told her it wasn't necessary as both he, and his editor, felt there was still quite a lot of mileage in the story anyway. She assured him she genuinely believed there was some truth behind the question which had been asked in the House and that she would contact him again whenever she found out anything which could be relevant. With the connection broken, Quentin Russell relaxed allowing himself a large smile. He could afford to smile now because he knew he was on a winner and that, eventually, it might prove to be the biggest coup of his journalistic career. It was patently obvious to him now that there was more to follow in this saga otherwise Rose would not have telephoned. She would have let the issue die a natural death and, because she hadn't, that meant she intended to do some digging of her own. It also meant that his other long-held suspicions concerning the identity of his source, Rose, built up over the years from previous calls, were being confirmed. He resolved to put the matter to the test the next time they spoke.

Three days had passed and Michael Mulrooney was on his way to Walton Gaol for another meeting with Harry Thompson. On this occasion, he found he had to concentrate on his driving as he found himself being continually distracted by the thoughts and issues which dominated his mind and, made his journey so essential. As he entered the interview room his face still bore traces of a worried frown that told Harry that all was not well. With the briefest of handshakes, the lawyer came straight to the point. "Listen Harry, I've just spoken to Trevor Bailey." Straight away he could see his that client was becoming visibly annoyed but he made no effort to stop. "It appears the police have got some more evidence in the Clarkson case. They are now saying that one of her associates has come forward and that she is prepared to swear on oath she saw Angela Clarkson wearing the watch you claimed to have found."

"Christ almighty", Harry groaned. It was like a bullet in the brain; he brought his fist crashing down onto the desk in front of him and in sheer desperation, and pounded it over and over as he wondered where or when this nightmare would end.

After a few moments, he realised his solicitor was speaking softly and quietly to him.

"Listen Harry, Trevor Bailey told me to tell you it's still not too late to change your mind about your decision to fire him. In view of this latest information he is urging you to reconsider your position, plead guilty through insanity and he will defend you."

Harry was visibly shaking as he looked up at his lawyer. Through clenched teeth, with as much hatred and venom as he could muster he spat out his reply "Michael, you can tell that bastard to piss off. Tell him I don't need him and, if the worst comes to the worst, I'll defend myself..."

Seven days later, Harry Thompson met his solicitor again. He was in court for another remand hearing and, he was still without the services of a QC. Although he wasn't aware of it himself, within the fraternity of Barristers in Chambers, nobody really wanted his case. Everybody saw it as almost hopeless plus, in their eyes, he had committed a cardinal sin when he sacked one of the few barristers prepared to take it on. Before the Hearing began Michael was waiting for him. He told him he would have a visitor later that day and he would arrange for him to meet Irene Yarwood QC. Irene Yarwood, after gaining her first class honours degree at Chester University had successfully completed her pupillage and she had been offered a junior partnership in chambers with a company called Krief Krief and Isaacs. Over a number of years, she had gained a reputation for taking on cases considered hopeless as well as anything else she could get her hands on. She refused to consider any implications on her career if she lost a case as in her opinion all that mattered was doing her utmost and the very level best for all her clients. Now that she had just taken silk, Michael considered her to be the best brief available and he urged Harry to talk to her in order to see whether or not she would agree to take the case. As the only other alternative was to accept a lawyer appointed by the Bar Council and that there really wasn't any other viable option, Harry readily agreed to this and arrangements were made for a meeting at Walton later that day."

He was already waiting in the interview room when she arrived, accompanied by his solicitor. Harry began to warm to her straight away. She was a small slim woman, no more than 5' 2" with jet black hair. She had big blue eyes, which sparkled and lit up her rounded face whenever she smiled. She was smiling now as they were introduced and shook hands and Harry couldn't help thinking that she looked nothing like a barrister, least of all one who was building up such a fearsome reputation.

As she spoke, Harry was acutely aware she was studying him intently, watching all of his body language and movements especially the way he sat, gently rocking himself on his chair with the front legs off the ground whilst looking at the ceiling. "Now then, Harry, we seem to have got ourselves into a proper mess haven't we? Well, let me say before we begin I can't promise you anything I can't realistically deliver. At this stage, I wouldn't dream of trying to falsely raise your hopes or your spirits, by giving you words of comfort such as I'm going to get you off. Far from it, I'll defend you to the best of my ability and that's it. In other words Harry, what you see now is what you get."

"Over the next few weeks I'm going to have to get to know all about you. I'll ask you questions you've probably been asked many times before and I'm telling you now I'll ask you questions that will upset you and cause you considerable pain and, possibly embarrassment. You have to understand that, when I get you in court I want you to be absolutely word perfect. I certainly won't expect to see or hear you floundering especially under cross examination by the opposition when they ask you awkward or embarrassing questions in an effort to upset or discredit you. I can assure you that with my help when we get to court, you'll be able to stand up to everything they throw at you and you'll answer all their questions calmly and without emotion. Remember this, I don't want you breaking down and, feeling sorry for yourself. After all nobody outside of this room feels sorry for you. Before I go today I want to hear your story and I want to hear everything. You must leave nothing out. If you hit your girlfriend during a quarrel, whether she hit you, I want to know everything. When I put my questions to you I want an answer from you each and every time. Whenever I swear at you which I shall, you will not retaliate or get angry. When I talk to you and ask questions about your sex life and your sexual activities, I'll use all the adjectives and phrases known to man that I can get my hands on. Remember, all the people in the courtroom have heard it all before. They're familiar with all the gutter terminology and the prosecution will not be afraid of using any trick in the book when you're in the witness box whereas, you, Harry Thompson, will be sailing in uncharted waters.

One and a half hours later, after hearing his story from the beginning of his ordeal, during which time she made copious notes, Irene Yarwood, accompanied by his solicitor, left him alone in the remand centre to contemplate and reflect upon life's most recent chain of events.

In the capital city, the pot continued to simmer. The rumours were growing ever more persistent. With each passing day, there were calls for an unnamed Member to make a statement to the House and to offer the House an apology for misleading its Members on the subject of Angela Clarkson. Each time the subject came up, the Prime Minister would be on his feet, referring to his earlier reply given some weeks ago. Then he would go on to say that if the persons behind the rumours couldn't offer any concrete evidence or substantiate the allegations, then they should put up or shut up. Alternatively he assured the House that if the allegations were true then he would ask the person involved to resign. In a concerted attempt to put an end to the matter, the Prime Minister suggested that Dennis Panter, the Member for Knutsford, should invite his journalistic source to persuade his editor to name the Member involved, bearing in mind that if they did, the Honourable Member involved would probably respond with the issue of a writ for libel. Obviously, the Prime Minister had no way of knowing at this stage if that latter part of the statement was true. His reasoning was simply that if the MP was named and shamed by the press then he would either have to sue or he would have to resign. In effect, it would save him the job of sacking him or getting rid of him whenever he carried out his next cabinet reshuffle. Whilst the Prime Minister felt more than comfortable with these exchanges, at least one member of the House felt distinctly uneasy and, each time the subject was mentioned, he cringed inwardly knowing his whole life was balancing on a knife edge. He was also very much aware that, whilst he was safe for the time being, he knew it would only last as long as he had the protection of his leader.

Over the next few weeks, Irene Yarwood had been extraordinarily busy. Besides her normal caseload she had involved and immersed herself in the defence of Harry Thompson. During this time, she and Harry Thompson had discussed all topics of his life with Diane Wilson, including all aspects of their sexual exploits. As a result, he was able to answer all questions in a cool, calm and collected manner. No matter what Miss Yarwood said or how it was put to him he had lost all sign of nerves and embarrassment. At the end of it all, Irene admitted that although she also found it an ordeal she felt confident Harry was at least prepared for anything the prosecution threw his way in an effort to provoke him. Throughout Harry's ordeal, Irene had studied his body language intently. Now, it was time for her to delve a little deeper into the character of her client.

Once again, they were seated in the drab and dreary interview room.

"Harry," she commanded, "you and I, together with rest of your defence team, have to face facts. Don't look away when I ask you this. I want you to look me straight in the eye and tell me honestly did you kill either of these two women?"

Without hesitation, he looked straight at her and answered.

"No, I did not."

She paused for a moment before continuing, "Concerning your association with Diane Wilson you were the last person to see her before her death. You admitted to having had sex with her and then, after a quarrel, she storms off into the night only to fall prey to her killer. She vanishes without trace. After leaving your house nobody but the killer sees her and your DNA fingerprints are all over her. Without finding the killer we only have a slight chance if we have any chance at all. Then there's Angela Clarkson. Agreed, there's only circumstantial evidence to go on but being honest, it's still quite formidable."

Harry knew what was coming next. She was going to ask him to plead insanity and he was determined to get in first. "Don't even think about it Miss Yarwood. If I did it I'd know I'd done it but I didn't do it. Furthermore I'm not insane and I won't allow you to use that as a defence on my behalf."

During this session she had been intrigued by his habits whilst discussing all aspects of his case, especially the way he rocked on his chair or wrapped his arms around his body. Deep down, although she thought that in some way he might simply be re-assuring himself. At the same time, she couldn't stop herself thinking "what if?" as she also recalled her psychology studies under Professor Lambert before she switched to law, when he attributed this, or similar behaviour, to a person attempting or endeavouring to control an interview.

Whilst trying to dismiss these thoughts from her mind, Irene had paused for a moment, and, at first, Harry thought he had won the point until she retorted, "No Harry that's where you're wrong. Schizophrenics usually have no idea they have committed crimes and they can quite easily convince themselves they haven't done anything as they flit between their personalities."

This time Harry looked her straight in the eyes and said

calmly, "Now you tell me do you think I did it? Do you think I'm mad?"

Without a moment's hesitation his counsel replied. "Harry, I'm being paid to defend you not to sit in judgment upon you. My duty to you is to give your case my best shot. After that, it's up to the jury. The only thing I can add is that along with your family I have to believe in you." With that, she scooped up her papers and belongings. Then, with a quick goodbye, she left the room.

Chapter 11

Paula Harris was sitting on the floor. That's where her husband had left her after another blazing row. Carefully, and hesitantly, she put her hand to her cheek, which still stung from the blow she had taken. Still badly shaken, she got to her feet, and made her way to the bathroom. She didn't look at herself in the mirror. There was no need. This had happened so many times before that she knew instinctively there wouldn't be any telltale signs, especially after a few hours. "In the morning," she murmured, "I know what I'll do – take a trip into Chester and have a look around the jewellery shops. Maybe I can spot a watch similar to the one shown on the television and, with an idea of the price, perhaps I can find it on his visa or, access card. With that she was up and running taking the stairs two at a time whilst shouting to herself, "Christ almighty, why didn't I think of this before. If the bastard used his card to pay for it then I should be able to find it and when I do, I'll bloody well prostitute him the little bastard. She was rummaging through the visa statements at speed looking at the prices of the articles bought. Suddenly, one item caught her eye Harrods £350.00, and the date. "Yes, yes," she exclaimed excitedly "that fits." She forced herself to calm down for she knew she had to plan her next moves very carefully. This time, she was going to make doubly sure the slippery bastard did not escape again.

"By God," she vowed, "I'll prostitute the little bleeder in bloody good style this time!"

She poured herself a large vodka and tonic whilst she thought about her next move. She was well aware that she couldn't ring up the store for the account was in his name only and, because of this, she knew she couldn't obtain the information from the bank either but, there was a way. There had to be. As she mixed herself another large vodka and tonic, she reasoned she had no other alternative except to contact Quentin Russell. With his contacts, he must be able to find out but she knew that there was a snag. This time there would be a price to pay. She would have to reveal her identity and that of her husband. It would have to come out; there was no alternative.

She sat alone in the dark. The shadows cast from the flickering log fire danced around the walls making intricate patterns but tonight, she took no real interest because, through her tears, she could hardly see them. She was crying now because she knew she couldn't go through with it. Once again, that cheating, lying bastard of a husband looked like getting away with it and all because she was too afraid to reveal her own identity to Quentin Russell.

Quentin Russell reposed in his comfortable armchair. However he wasn't relaxing at the moment. He had just finished speaking with Robin Millward, a Liverpool based crime reporter, who worked for one of the parent company's papers. Robin had been asked to nose around Bromborough and in particular the Roundhead Hotel in order to ascertain whether or not Timothy Harris could be placed with Angela Clarkson. Robin soon discovered that the politician had been registered at the Roundhead Hotel and that he had shared a couple of drinks with the assistant manager. There the trail seemed to go cold until he met Detective Sergeant West. It was from this gentleman he learned that an unnamed person had been exonerated and cleared from police enquiries connected to the Angela Clarkson murder enquiry. The detective told him that he couldn't add anything further due to the fact that all other details were "classified."

Quentin rang his editor with this information and between them, it was agreed that not a word of this would be published in any of the publishing group's papers until the time was deemed appropriate. For now it was considered to be more than sufficient to let Dennis Panter ask the Prime Minister whether or not Timothy Harris was the Member who had been questioned by Merseyside CID during the investigation into the death of Angela Clarkson, the Liverpool prostitute. Quentin and his editor knew this was just enough to keep the pot simmering until they had enough to break the story.

With that little matter out of the way, he was now contemplating his next move. For some time this evening he'd been thinking about ringing Mrs. Harris at her home. He had the perfect pretence following his last two telephone conversations. When she answered he would simply say, "Rose." He reasoned that he wouldn't need to say anything else. If the phone went dead that would be a confirmation alternatively, if there was a sharp intake of breath at the other end, that would also suffice as a confirmation. In Quentin Russell's mind it was all beginning to fit. Timothy Harris was the Member of Parliament for the area. He was in the area at or about the time the girl was killed. A prominent person had been excluded from the investigation. It had to be somebody close enough to that person to be able to point the finger in the first place and there couldn't be anyone closer to Timothy Harris than his wife. He obtained the telephone number and began to dial.

Paula Harris had stopped crying and she was gradually regaining her composure when the telephone rang. She picked up the receiver and cradling it in her neck, she whispered quietly, "Hello."

There was the briefest moment of silence. Then she heard the word "Rose"...

She was absolutely dumbstruck and she couldn't have spoken if she'd wanted to. Slowly the phone slipped from her grasp as she fainted and lapsed into unconsciousness. When she came to a few moments later, she replaced the receiver and frantically tried to focus her mind. She knew she didn't have much time and that she would have to telephone Quentin Russell if only to find out what he knew and, how he intended to use it.

Snatching the phone from the hook, she dialled Quentin Russell's mobile number. She didn't have to wait. The call was answered with great rapidity, and she heard his voice softly whispering, "Rose is that you Rose? Please don't hang up let me explain."

Without being abrupt or cutting him short she interrupted him in order to explain her findings and suspicions regarding the Harrods' entry on her husband's visa account. Then she confided her fears concerning the effect this information would have on the lives of her and her husband.

Quentin assured her he would treat any information in the strictest confidence and that nothing would be published without her consent. He also promised that once he acquainted his editor of the position, he felt certain he would also comply with her wishes. In actual fact, it went a lot deeper than that. Quentin Russell and his editor were well aware that they couldn't publish anything that might have a bearing on the outcome of the trial due to commence shortly. Paula thanked him for his compassion and, understanding. She gently replaced the receiver and slowly mounted the stairs to sleep a deeply troubled sleep.

Despite his promise, which he fully intended to keep, together with his informant's identity, Quentin Russell could hardly contain himself. With the information just laid before him he knew that if the Harrods' entry on Timothy Harris's visa bill related to a watch given to Angela Clarkson then, obviously, Timothy Harris had lied to the House. On its own that was bad enough but this went a lot deeper for it was also patently obvious that there had been a cover up to protect the identity of Timothy Harris from being revealed. Without a moment's further delay, Quentin rang his editor and put the facts before him, at the same time ensuring he was fully aware of the guarantee given to Paula Harris. That night neither man slept as each of them was totally preoccupied with events about to happen.

In Walton Gaol, there was no thought of sleep for certain people either. Officer Fitzgerald was trying desperately hard not to lose his temper with Royston Chambers. Roy wouldn't agree to leave his request until the next day. He was also adamant that what he had to say could only be divulged in the presence of Detective Inspector Peter Taylor and Detective Sergeant Jim West. Eventually the Inspector was contacted and Chambers was allowed to speak to him. As a result of their conversation, a car, carrying the two officers, was soon speeding on its way to the prison in order to interview Roy Chambers. When they arrived the prisoner, accompanied by a warder, was waiting in the interview room.

Dispensing with all formalities, Inspector Taylor asked the prisoner what all the panic was about to which, Chambers replied, "Harry Thompson that's what it's about. He confessed that he did the Clarkson girl as well as his girl friend. He just came right out with it. Right out of the blue he just came up real close to me and said, "Roy, you had it dead right all along. You know it really was me that did it but what bothers me is, how on earth did you know?" At first I didn't know what to say because I was getting a bit afraid, especially as he's in for topping two of them, but then it got like I had to think of something to say sort of to pacify him. So I just said that it always seemed to me that he had a lot on his mind, as if something was bothering him, and if I left him long enough, he would be only too glad to talk to someone about it."

For the detectives this was news they could hardly believe. There could be no doubt about it now. Thompson's goose was well and truly cooked, but there was a lot more work to be done as they both realised that they needed more than the bare bones of a confession. For a start, they needed to find out where Thompson had met Clarkson and whether or not he was a client of hers. They also needed to know where he had killed the girl and how he got the body to the ditch without being seen. Lastly, there was the watch. Thompson had to say that he hadn't really found it. He had to say he simply pocketed the watch and, realising later he might have to account for it, what better way than to hand it in at the local station and claim it himself in three months' time. Regarding Diane Wilson, all they needed there was confirmation that he had struck a violent blow to her jaw before strangling her. Before they left they made absolutely certain Roy Chambers was going to be word perfect. With start of the trial only three weeks away, arrangements were made for both the officers to return the next day in order to take down the full details of Thompson's confession. Before they left Inspector Taylor told Chambers that although they appreciated what he had done it was vital to get the information requested and if he was successful, it would not go unnoticed by the authorities.

Chapter 12

It didn't take long for the paper to obtain confirmation that the watch had been purchased from Harrods and this information was quickly passed to Mrs Harris. As agreed the previous evening, it was now up to her when the information would be used. All persons concerned appreciated that she needed time to think and reflect upon these matters. However, that wouldn't stop embarrassing questions being asked in the House.

Around mid morning, the two Merseyside police officers were seated around a table with Roy Chambers. Together they were going over all the points featured in the confession Chambers had obtained from Harry Thompson.

All the information had been put on tape and now the details were being taken down on paper. According to Chambers, Harry Thompson had confessed to killing both women. After he and Diane Wilson had sex at his parent's home Chambers alleged that Diane Wilson taunted Thompson about his performance. This led to a violent quarrel, during which Thompson struck his girlfriend a severe blow on the lower jaw. She became hysterical and, in an effort to stop her screaming, he grabbed hold of her tights and wrapped them tightly around her neck meaning to release his grip when she stopped struggling. All of a sudden he realised she'd stopped breathing, and he made frantic efforts to revive her but it was all in vain. Knowing that his foster-mother would soon be home and, in a state of complete panic, he wrapped the body and her clothes in plastic bin liners. Then he drove to the quarry lake at Chorley Wood, near Preston, where he consigned her body to the deep hoping that it would never be discovered.

Chambers then described how Thompson told him he met Angela Clarkson in the Roundhead Hotel and he admitted he was a client of hers. They left the hotel in his car and he drove to the deserted car park on the edge of Eastham Woods. They got out of the car and, at his request, she got undressed. Because he was having some difficulty getting an erection, she became impatient and wanted to leave. This led to an argument during which she started screaming. In an effort to keep her quiet, he wrapped her tights around her neck. Chambers then described how Thompson told him that, in a state of absolute panic, he looked around for somewhere to "dump" the body then he remembered about the ditch just beyond the fence. He said that after he had placed the body in the ditch he went back for the rest of her clothes and belongings. After rifling through her handbag, he threw everything into the ditch except her watch and the money, together with two plastic sachets, which he assumed would contain drugs. Thinking that he might need an alibi later, he returned to the public bar of the hotel where he purchased a glass of bitter. After drinking his beer, he went home to bed.

The document was signed and dated as a true statement freely given by Prisoner Roy Chambers whilst on remand at Walton Gaol, Liverpool. Chambers also confirmed that the statement he had given had not been sought by the police nor had he been offered any inducement or subjected to any coercion to obtain the confession from the prisoner Thompson. The officers duly signed the document. Following this, it was signed by the warder who had remained in the room as a witness to the proceedings.

Roy Chambers was then led away feeling very pleased and smug with himself. He felt that he no longer faced the prospect of a long gaol sentence and with any luck he reflected, he might even be released without charge. It was simply a matter of waiting for another visit from Detective Sergeant West. "Good old Westy", he muttered on his way back to the remand wing.

On their way back to the murder HQ both officers were well pleased with their work so far. The confession altered the run of events dramatically and it would considerably shorten the length of the trial. Furthermore, when it was eventually revealed it was bound to cause a sensation but, as far as both officers were concerned, that was now going to be in the hands of the Barristers. Needless to say arrangements were made, post haste, to get copies of the confession sent to the Chambers of the Barrister leading for the prosecution, Gordon Nuttall-Jones.

The same afternoon, copies of the confession were faxed by the Crown Prosecution Service lawyers to the offices of the defence Kreiff, Kreiff and Isaacs where it made very bad reading for Irene Yarwood. She felt that the rug had been well and truly pulled from beneath her feet. It was one thing to have very little chance of securing an acquittal, but to be faced with this, just before the start of the trial, this had made it a different ball game altogether. Refusing to panic, she decided pretty quickly what she was going to do. She knew she would have to see Harry Thompson first and, if the confession was genuine, she would advise him there was no other alternative except to plead guilty. As she contemplated this scene she found her temper rising fast. Harry Thompson had better watch out because she knew she would be sorely tempted to throttle him herself. If and this was a big if, the confession was false then she might have to consider asking for a delay to the start of the trial whilst some enquiries were made on behalf of Thompson. Whilst her secretary made arrangements for an unscheduled prison visit, as a matter of courtesy, she went to see Sebastian Kreiff the senior partner. First of all to acquaint him with developments and to see whether he could think of anything else or if he could offer any additional professional advice. It was pretty much as she expected from Sebastian. Go and see the prisoner first. Then take it from there. With that brief case in hand, she left the Chambers and headed for Walton.

As soon as she arrived at the prison she was escorted to the same drab and dreary interview room where her client was already waiting together with a warder. There was no time for any preliminaries other than a curt hello. The warder had already left as her brief case hit the desk. She rounded on Harry immediately and, thrusting the papers containing the statements from Roy Chambers into his hands, she said, "What exactly do you mean by this Mr. Thompson? Adding, "of course if this is true I trust you realise that you've no alternative now except to plead guilty to both charges." Inside she was positively seething, but she knew she had to put aside all her personal feelings whilst she waited for him to finish reading. Harry didn't keep her waiting long. In fact, he barely read the first page before he let the pages slip through his fingers and onto the desk where he sat. He was ashen faced and visibly shaken. When he opened his mouth to speak he had the utmost difficulty in getting the words out. "It, It, it's er, er tthththere's nnnot, it's just not true, I I I I've hardly spoken to the man" he stammered. How can I confess to committing two crimes I didn't commit and what does the man expect to gain by making this up?"

Throughout the last few moments, Irene Yarwood hadn't taken her eyes off her client and, she had carefully observed each move and tiny mannerism he had made. From this observation, she rapidly concluded that either he genuinely hadn't murdered the two unfortunate women and that the confession was false or she was confronted by one of the best actors she had ever seen. There was still the possibility that if he was acting out yet another scene; he could still be the raging psychopath that other people maintained he was. That thought, and its possibilities, sent an involuntary shudder down her spine as she replied, "Harry we are not playing games here. This confession alone is quite sufficient for any jury to find you guilty on both counts. Once you have been found guilty you will be sent away for life. In your case, life will probably mean just that. In fact, you'll be lucky to get out of prison this side of twenty years. I received those documents a very short time ago and your trial is due to start in less than three weeks' time which leaves me very little time to do anything. I can ask for a delay to the start of the trial but what will that achieve? At the end of the day, whenever we go to trial, this confession is still going to be there forming a large part of the case for the prosecution and we can't mount any challenge to it until Chambers is in the box answering questions on oath. Not that that will mean a lot to him. In view of that, I'm going to spell it out for you right now in order that you'll be in no doubt whatsoever what your alternatives are!"

First, you can plead guilty as charged and face the prospect of a lifetime in prison.

Second, you can plead guilty and plead insanity, spending the rest of your natural life locked away in a secure mental institution.

Lastly, you can continue to plead not guilty knowing full well that, if we can't secure a not guilty verdict or an acquittal, you're going to go to prison for at least twenty years without any prospect of release. During this period of incarceration, you will probably be subjected to many medical examinations to determine your sanity and, at the end of it all, you could still end up being locked away in a secure unit. So Harry Thompson, I'm asking you to tell me how you wish me to proceed?"

Without a moment's thought or hesitation, he answered,

"Not guilty" as firmly, and as positively, as he could.

"All right then Harry," Miss Yarwood replied, "I'll leave you with a copy of your alleged confession and I want you to study it intently. You must read it over, and over, to see if there's anything in there only you could have known about or anything you can spot where we might be able to catch Roy Chambers unawares. By the way, there is something else for you to consider and that is this. If you didn't give any of this information to Chambers there are certain things in there that he could have only obtained from the police which can only mean that there has been some collusion with one or more of the investigating officers themselves. This will be a very difficult thing to prove, and it can only mean one thing. In a nutshell, Chambers has been offered a deal on his sentence when his case comes up for trial. Obviously I'll give this all my spare time myself but we really do face an uphill struggle now. As I said earlier, I could ask for a postponement but it won't accomplish anything, so we'll just have to live with it and hope for the best. Besides, who knows, by adopting this approach, the prosecution might even have overlooked something. For now the best thing you can do is keep your spirits up and if by any chance you see Chambers, which I doubt very much, do keep well away, and say absolutely nothing about this to him or, anybody else..."

Chapter 13

Timothy Harris could see clearly that the Prime Minister was not amused; in fact he was decidedly edgy. Timothy was glad they were alone in the leader's office safe from prying eyes. Even so, he found himself wishing that his ordeal would soon be over. He knew, or at least he thought he knew, why he had been summoned to the leader's office and he assumed that it would probably be about the murdered prostitute. However, he felt quite sure he would be able to weather any storm which might be blowing his way.

The Prime Minister finished his nervous shuffling of the papers on his desk, then he stood up in order to address Timothy Harris, "Look here Timothy," he said firmly, "let's not mess about. You know, as well as I do, this business has gone on long enough and that I've done my very level best for you but, under the circumstances, I have to tell you it's over now and I must ask you to resign your ministerial position forthwith. I would also like you to resign your seat in order to save any further embarrassment to the Government, the Party and the House." Although he was prepared for questions about his reputed involvement, Timothy was totally unprepared for this dramatic turn of events as he asked himself what on earth could have happened to bring about such a change in his fortunes.

Solemnly, the Prime minister told him that Dennis Panter had put down a question for the following day to say that if the person, subject of constant rumour, did not offer his resignation and apologies to the House concerning his involvement in the Clarkson case then a national daily newspaper would name and shame him the very next day.

Realising at once just how serious his position was, Timothy Harris responded by fighting for his political life and, his career. He knew he had no alternative now and that if he couldn't get his leader to move from his entrenched position then he was as good as dead. "Look Sir," he began, "obviously I'm very grateful for your support over these past weeks but I don't think I should have to take such a drastic step as this. With your permission, sir, when the question is asked, please allow me to make a statement and I will categorically deny any involvement or, cover up. In addition, I will personally invite the Honourable Mr Panter to repeat his remarks in any place outside the Chamber and I'll sue him, together with anyone else involved, for libel. Naturally it goes without saying, if the newspaper goes into print, with the same cowardly and libellous remarks then I will sue them without a moment's thought or hesitation."

"Timothy that's all very well and good," replied the Prime Minister but just suppose you can't substantiate those remarks. Also, think about my own position if you sued and lost. In those circumstances, that would reflect even worse upon myself, and, my leadership of the party. We would then end up with the press demanding my head. No, Timothy I'm afraid it is no use. Enough is enough. This unfortunate saga has dragged on far too long and I am determined to put a stop to it right here and now. I shall expect your resignation on my desk here tomorrow before the House convenes and that will be the end of it. I know it's hard on you Timothy but, I feel I've no other alternative and, if I don't have your resignation as requested then I will be left with no alternative except to sack you in a very public and humiliating fashion. With that he began to collect the papers which lay loosely scattered upon his desk.

However, before he could finish that task and before he

could leave, Timothy began again, "Excuse me sir, please allow me two minutes of your time after which, if you still remain unconvinced, I will do as you ask and submit my resignation. First of all your decision has been made on the assumption that there's no smoke without fire and that I really do have something to conceal about this tragic affair. As it happens nothing could be further from the truth because, not only am I not guilty on all charges, I can actually prove it. You see my involvement appears to revolve around the fact that this murdered prostitute wore a watch, which, if my critics are to be believed, I reputedly gave to her. Now the fact is that only days before the lady was killed I purchased a watch from Harrod's which bears an uncanny resemblance to the watch she wore. In fact it could well be identical. However unfortunately for the press, not only do I have the receipt for the watch I purchased but I still have the watch. You see the item I bought was intended as a gift for my wife on the occasion of our wedding anniversary later this year. Now, if I didn't know the poor woman and, if I didn't see the poor woman and I still have possession of my watch, then the newspaper story is going to look decidedly thin. I don't think I'll have too much trouble in convincing a jury either. I have to say I wholeheartedly agree with you that this state of affairs cannot be allowed to continue but please consider my position. I assisted the police in their enquiries and I was completely exonerated along with various other people. I now find, because of my position, I haven't been able to say anything about this as I was told it might prejudice the actual trial but, if the press feel confident to name and shame me, then I don't see any reason why I shouldn't be allowed to be able to defend myself. That is why I think you should at least give me the opportunity to make that statement in the House tomorrow, plus, I think you should also consider the effect the consequences might have on people such as the Honourable Member for Knutsford who has always given people a rough ride with his questions in the House. Who knows, in the not too distant future, people may be less inclined to use his services after this. With this last statement Timothy Harris knew he had struck a raw nerve as the Prime Minister's papers, together with his brief case, were slowly lowered and replaced upon the desk.

"Is this true Timothy?" He asked incredulously to which Timothy Harris replied, "Of course Sir, there's no point at all in me telling you a pack of lies knowing full well that it's going to rebound in such fashion within the next forty-eight hours or so. If that were the case, I might just as well resign now because there wouldn't be any point in prolonging the issue would there?"

"No Timothy there wouldn't," replied the Prime Minister. "There would be no point whatsoever so, in that case, I'll see you in the House tomorrow and, when the question crops up, I'll ask you to make a statement. Better still, when the question is asked be on your feet ready then, when you make your own request to make your statement, I'll give way to you immediately. Oh, and, by the way, thank you Timothy; like a lot of other people, I've waited ages for such an opportunity to really put down that little shit Panter. It's about time he got his own comeuppance and tomorrow might well be his day. Just one more thing before I go, Tim, I'll have a word on your behalf with my lawyers because if I were you, I would want be sure I only employ the best and you can rest assured they'll look after you."

Both gentlemen said goodnight and left the building.

The following morning Timothy Harris kept a very low profile. He endeavoured to fill in his time between the Commons' tea bar and the library. Despite this, it was all too apparent that something was afoot and almost all of the MPs in the House were well aware that today would be like no ordinary day. Confirmation came swiftly after lunch as the House filled up rapidly in readiness for Prime Minister's question time. As the Speaker appealed for order, the atmosphere became almost electric as she acknowledged to the House a question from the Honourable Member for Knutsford, Mr. Dennis Panter. The Speaker, Helen Little, hardly had time to finish, before the MP already on his feet, began speaking, "Madam Speaker, Members of the House. Is the Prime Minister aware of the shame which is being brought upon this House by continuing to allow a certain Member to keep his position within the government despite that person being the subject of continual adverse gossip concerning his involvement in the case of the murdered Wirral prostitute, Angela Clarkson?" Barely pausing to draw breath, he continued "and is the Prime Minister aware that if the Member concerned does not apologise to this House and offer his resignation today, then a daily national newspaper will be forced to name and shame him?"

All eyes were focused upon the Prime Minister who had risen to his feet but, instead of replying, he motioned to the House that as Timothy Harris was on his feet he would give way at once. Seeing the Wirral MP on his feet momentarily silenced the critics and hounds who were baying for blood. As they anxiously waited for his expected resignation speech, Timothy glanced quickly around the Chamber then he began, "Madam Speaker, Members of the House. First of all let me thank the Prime Minister for giving way to me. I have to say that I'm sorry to disappoint those people who have set out to destroy me, and my political career but I am not going to apologise to this House and I have certainly no intention of offering my resignation either. First and foremost, I wish to advise all the Members of this House that I am completely innocent of all charges and accusations made against me. Furthermore, if any newspaper ventures into print in the manner suggested by the Honourable Member for Knutsford, then, I shall respond immediately with a writ for libel. I would like to add that I have a complete answer to all allegations and, if any apologies are due to this House, it is the Honourable Member for Knutsford who should be offering them. With that he strode purposefully from the Chamber trying to ignore the order papers being waved, and the many well-wishers patting him on the back. He paused briefly in the Commons' tea room before leaving the building and making his way towards the offices of Jerome Wolff and Solomon where arrangements had been made for an initial briefing on the basis that his name would be published the next day. Although he was well accustomed to lying his way out of trouble, Timothy was well aware that there was definitely no going back and now, it was all or nothing. Obviously if all went well, as he fervently hoped, then he had it made, but if it all went wrong, he stood to lose everything. The very thought sent an uneasy shudder down his spine as he arrived at his destination.

Timothy Harris emerged some fifty minutes later feeling very relieved. From his point of view things could not have gone better, and he found himself almost wishing the paper would name and shame him. He took his time walking back to his London flat where he intended to spend the night, and he had no intention of spending it alone.

Quentin Russell sat in the editor's office. He had just replaced the telephone after a brief, but all important, telephone conversation with Paula Harris. Turning to his editor he said, "Well Clive you heard that yourself, Mrs. Harris is quite adamant that he's clutching at straws and he's trying to bluff his way out in the hope that we'll back down. She's quite upset about it all and I can understand that, but she wants us to see it through even though she's not prepared to testify herself and

I can quite understand that as well. Obviously Timothy Harris has no idea his wife started all this off in the first instance and that's how she wants to keep it. When it's all over and he's lost, she'll start divorce proceedings against him so, all in all, she's in for a rough time over the next few weeks. Deep down, I get the distinct impression she knows it will all come out in the end, especially in the divorce, so she's only putting off the inevitable but I think we should respect her wishes."

Clive Alderson listened intently to his star reporter and now it was time for action. This would not be an early night for anybody and the first thing on the agenda was a legal conference involving all the senior editorial staff together with a telephonic link up with their legal team of retainers. This was not the first such conference. Over the past few months there had been many others all revolving around the same issues, namely Timothy Harris's involvement with the murdered prostitute, the purchase of the watch from the jewellery department at Harrods and his involvement with the murder enquiry. The article for publication naming the errant MP, had been sent earlier to their lawyers by fax and, apart from a number of minor points raised by the legal team, the final text had been agreed. It had also been agreed that Paula Harris's reluctance to testify would not weaken their case unduly, and they would proceed without her. Now, as the order to print was confirmed, the team repaired to the nearest hostelry to await the first issue from the presses.

In a mews flat off Baker Street, Timothy Harris was relaxing. One of his research secretaries Julie lay naked on the bed beside him. He reached for the telephone saying as he did so, "I won't be a minute darling but I have got to phone my wife. He saw the pained expression on her face and explained, "I know it really is a pain, darling, but I have to do it. Besides it won't last for much longer now so I'm afraid you'll just have to put up with it. Mechanically, he dialled the number of his home address whilst looking at Julie and thinking, "you silly cow if only you knew once this is over and my divorce is through, you won't see my arse for dust!" He felt Julie's hands begin to massage and explore his body and he felt himself responding, as his wife answered the telephone. "Hello darling," he said, "I'm sorry I couldn't ring earlier. I've been tied up all evening. I suppose you saw the Question Time programme on the television but it didn't show me, or my speech. Yes, I was on my feet today, about this dammed prostitute business but I gave it to them in good style. You see they all thought that once I stood up I was going to apologise and offer my resignation but instead I told them in no uncertain manner, if the press published anything about me, then, I'd sue them for every penny. What on earth are you saying love? No I'm not bluffing, I mean it. I have a complete answer to all the allegations and I can prove it. What's more and this is why I couldn't phone earlier, I've been given access to the PM's Lawyers and taken Counsel's opinion. They reckon if the press go ahead and publish tomorrow then I'm home and dry and they'll be asking a fortune in damages for libel. After that, I had another briefing with the PM. Then, I grabbed a takeaway pizza and came round here. So all in all that's good news isn't it?

Paula Harris was now wide-awake and she couldn't believe what she was hearing. Surely, she wondered, there must be some mistake. How the hell could he wriggle out of this? "Well," she answered, trusting to luck that her voice would not betray her true emotions, "that really is good news, but Timothy, why couldn't you tell me this before? After all it's been just as hard for me over the past months with all these allegations and everything else besides which I really do think that if you can prove it you could have told me earlier. I am your wife you know."

"Yes, yes, I know all that but believe me, I really couldn't say anything earlier just in case it prejudiced the murder trial. Now, if the press go after me, I'm entitled to defend myself and that's just what I intend to do."

Paula's brain was reeling. She couldn't believe what she'd just been told as she gently whispered "goodbye and, good luck." As soon as he was off the line she frantically dialled Quentin Russell's mobile number. . As the phone rang, she looked at the clock. It showed twelve forty five and she prayed that she would be in time. Finally, she heard a voice answering as she shouted hysterically, "Quentin, Quentin, get them to kill the story. The evil, lying, little sod, reckons he's got a complete defence. He's just been on the phone to me bragging about it. What's more, he reckons you don't have a leg to stand on. Quentin believe me," she sobbed, "I know this man he's up to something otherwise he wouldn't adopt this attitude and, deep down, I've got this terrible feeling that he'll come up smelling of roses as he always does."

Quentin Russell did his best to calm and reassure Paula that he would attend to matters straight away. He promised to phone back once he'd discussed the matter with the editor. Another phone call to the editor confirmed it was too late to kill the story and that they would have live with it. Quentin also realised that, if the information Paula Harris had just imparted was true, and the action was subsequently lost, then his career was at an end. God, he thought, what a night this was turning out to be. As promised he returned the call to Paula. He explained to her that it was far too late to stop the story now as many of the copies were already being distributed therefore they would just have to live with it and see what happened when the libel action came to court."

Despite this setback, Paula told Quentin that, as far as she was concerned, her husband was still lying through his back teeth and eventually, the truth would be revealed. Without knowing whether or not it would assist the newspaper's case, she told Quentin that she had reconsidered her decision not to testify and she now would be available if called.

Quentin, already resigned to a sleepless night thanked her and assured her that his editor would really appreciate her magnanimous gesture especially in view of the likely cost to her. With that, and a whispered goodnight, he replaced the receiver and reached for the brandy bottle beside his bed. There would be very little sleep tonight.

Chapter 14

The story broke before the dawn. As soon as the papers hit the streets there were flurries of activity everywhere. From five o clock in the morning Timothy Harris's telephone rang incessantly as paper after paper rang seeking his comments on the article. Turning on the television brought no relief as all channels carried the story. To make matters worse, by seven o clock there was a veritable army of reporters and TV crews camped on his doorstep and he knew he would have to issue a statement of some description when he opened the door and walked onto the street. Unfortunately for him that was only part of his dilemma because Julie, his secretary, was still in the flat and the last thing he wanted right now was some idiot from the press discovering that fact. Eventually, he decided upon a course of action whereby he would leave the flat alone and say a few words to the assembled press whilst he collected his car for his journey to the Commons. Julie would have to remain where she was until it became safe for her to leave then, hopefully safe from prying eyes, she could let herself out by the rear entrance. Before leaving Timothy stressed to her the importance of keeping well away from the windows and making any noise at all. He knew he had taken a huge risk bringing her round last night and, an even bigger one, letting her stay the night. He knew that as soon as he opened the door the eyes of the world would be upon him but once he got away from the scene she would be able to slip away.

He whispered a swift "goodbye my love," and made his way down the stairs. As he opened the door he made as much noise as he could in order to ensure all the assembled media persons were aware that he was coming out. Inwardly he was dreading the moment, but this was a situation which had to be faced and, over the next few weeks, it would probably get very much worse so he just had to put on a brave face and get on with it. As soon as the door opened there was a rush of people towards him. They were all shouting questions and trying to attract his attention. Microphones were pushed into his face and, despite the noise of the mêleé; he could hear somebody saying, "Minister, have you seen the morning papers. Are you going to resign? Would you like to make a statement?" He stopped at the top of the steps. There was no point at this stage trying to get away as he knew that he wouldn't even make it to the ministerial car waiting for him. Experience told him that, if he gave them something, he would be able to get to the sanctuary of his car and be able to get away to the Commons. Making sure once more that the front door was firmly closed, he turned to the assembled crowd of reporters and said, "I haven't seen the papers yet but I know only too well why you are all here today. This morning, I have seen from the television that a leading national daily paper has decided to name and shame me. They have insinuated that somehow I have been involved with a murdered prostitute on the Wirral, and that my reputed involvement has been the subject of a cover up. I can only say that I have spoken to my lawyers, Jerome Woolff and Solomon and I have been advised by them to say nothing further at all until our meeting later today. The only thing I can say at this stage is that I emphatically deny all the allegations made and it will be my intention to defend myself, and my name with the utmost vigour. Now I am sure you all appreciate my position. I still have a job to do and, I must be allowed to get to the House of Commons without further delay. Ignoring the pushing throng of reporters and all the questions which continued to be hurled his way he made his way to the car and made his escape. Although the car was soon swallowed up in the morning traffic, he didn't worry about being followed as he had made it quite clear to the assembled crowd that he was going straight to the Commons where he would have a brief word with the Prime Minister before seeing his appointed legal team.

When he arrived there, he went straight to the Prime Minister's private office where the results of last night's meeting were outlined. Then, with the best wishes of his leader ringing in his ears, it was time for his appointment.

Three hours later, outside his lawyers' offices, and accompanied by Jerome senior, a brief statement was issued by his solicitor to the waiting press stating that, "A writ for libel, asking for substantial damages, together with a full apology, has been served at the offices of International Press and Associated Media Publications. My client wishes us to point out that this law suit will be pursued with utmost vigour and that time is of the essence as it is impossible to calculate the amount of harm or damage to my client's reputation that these baseless, and completely false accusations have caused my client. Neither is it possible to quantify or put into perspective, the financial losses he will inevitably suffer. As a result, we shall be demanding a complete and utter retraction of every word of the article printed. Time alone will show that my client is completely innocent of all the allegations made, and that he is more than happy to await his day in court when all will be revealed. It didn't take long for Jerome Jerome to set the wheels of justice in motion. After a series of meetings with the Crown Prosecution Service, in order to ensure proceedings would not prejudice the fair hearing of the murder trial in Liverpool, it was agreed to allow the libel case to proceed. During these meetings, Jerome outlined the case for the plaintiff, Timothy Harris, including all details of his questioning, and the subsequent statement he had given to Merseyside CID. This duly revealed he had answered questions about his stay at the Roundhead Hotel, including an account of his movements on the night in question, and that he had volunteered a DNA sample. It also showed that he had been seen in the bar from 10 pm in the evening in the company of Mr Rogerson, the assistant manager. This gentleman confirmed they had both left the residents' bar sometime after twelve thirty. The statement confirmed he had only been questioned due to the fact there had been unconfirmed reports that the dead woman had been seen in the hotel on the day in question. Finally, there was a statement from Merseyside CID saying Mr. Harris had been exonerated from police enquiries in connection with the murder and his DNA sample had been destroyed.

Jerome indicated to the Crown Prosecution Service that the interests of justice would be best served if this case could be allowed to proceed first. He pointed out that the whole affair had proved to be particularly worrying and stressful to his client, who would be able to show independent proof that the allegations were false, and malicious. He also added there was absolutely nothing in the evidence he was going to present before the jury which would have any significant bearing upon the murder trial. Finally, he pointed out that, during the ensuing period, the defendants had been given ample opportunity to withdraw from the action, and settle out of court, but they had steadfastly refused to do so.

Naturally the defendants objected to all of the arguments raised, pointing out that it would be far more beneficial to their own case to await the trial and the verdicts in Liverpool.

With neither side prepared to concede, the issue went before a high court judge who ruled it was the fault of the defendants that they now found themselves in the position they were. He pointed out it was the defendants who had made the allegations and, at the time, they didn't consider for a moment whether or not their actions would prejudice the outcome of the murder trial. Stressing that as long as there would be no objection from the Crown Prosecution Service, the judge said he would allow proceedings to commence as soon as a vacant date could be found in the court calendar. With no objections from the Crown Prosecution Service forthcoming, the stage was set for the case to proceed accordingly. Within a week, a vacant date was located in the High Court listings and the go ahead was given for the case to proceed. Media interest in the case was very high with cameras positioned everywhere, and reporters trying to interview everybody as they made their way up the steps and into the building. With such a high profile government figure involved, the court was filled to absolute capacity as the public and the press clamoured to be admitted.

The case was to be heard before His Honour, Sir Campbell Mckenzie, and representing the defendants, The Independent Newspaper Group, were Robert Jackson QC, and, Elizabeth Collins QC.

The trial had hardly got under way when it collapsed in dramatic fashion. Timothy Harris had just given evidence relating to his purchase of the watch together with his receipt, when his attorney produced the watch that Timothy was now claiming to be the watch he had purchased at the time. The judge quickly intervened. Very sternly, Sir Campbell pointed out that supposition alone was not enough. Then to the surprise of everybody he stated that, if the defence were unable to say that this was not the watch Harris had purchased, they must rest their case. Without a defence witness who could positively say that they had observed Harris give the item to Clarkson or somebody who could testify that Clarkson had told them Harris had given her the watch as a present, their case was bound to fail. Stressing the point that there was only a period of twenty-four hours between the purchase of the watch by Harris and the death of the woman, in his opinion that made their case nothing short of hopeless.

Seizing on the fact that the defendants had been provided by the plaintiffs with ample opportunities to apologise and withdraw, which they had steadfastly refused, Sir Campbell then launched a scathing attack on the defence. Referring to the fact that they could have sought to limit their own liabilities by making the plaintiffs an offer or, by paying that same sum into the courts before the start of the proceedings and yet they had done neither. In that case he said they were hoist upon their own petard.

After ruling in favour of a jubilant Timothy Harris, the judge announced that the jury had recommended damages for libel at £2 million pounds plus, all legal costs. Approving this settlement, the judge also ordered the newspaper group to publish a complete retraction of its article in their next editions. The repercussions from the case and the verdict were enormous and quite unexpected.

First of all, the board of directors demanded the resignation of the editor and promptly dismissed Quentin Russell from their service. Two days later it emerged the group were now in serious financial difficulties as a result of the case and they were trying to find a suitable partner for a takeover. Like a pack of wolves, other papers rejoiced at their plight with banner headlines denouncing the Independent for running the story in the first place. It hardly seemed to matter just a few short weeks before the rest of the press had been clinging to the papers shirt-tails in an endeavour to get a lead on the same story. In the rush to pillory the Independent all this was forgotten, not because they had got it wrong but because they had lost and in Fleet Street, that was the biggest sin of all.

In parliament Timothy Harris was accorded celebrity

status. He revelled being in the spotlight and hardly a day passed without him making an appearance on television or radio which allowed him to take full advantage of the turn of events which had swung so dramatically in his favour. Behind the scenes and with utmost secrecy, Timothy Harris issued instructions through his solicitors, Jerome, Jerome, and Woolf, to commence divorce proceedings against his wife. With the money from the damages award, and the spin off in fees for interviews plus his parliamentary salary, the cash was absolutely rolling in. All he wanted was a suitable opportunity for the papers to be served without the appearance of undue haste.

Paula Harris was deeply saddened by this dramatic turn of events, as she couldn't help feeling that she was responsible. Since the collapse of the case, she hadn't been able to contact Quentin Russell and it seemed as if he had disappeared from the face of the earth.

In a tiny cramped holiday flat away from the seafront in Brighton, Quentin Russell knew that it was pointless to apportion blame for, as far as he was concerned, the case was lost and he was just another statistic on the unemployment register. Within minutes of being asked to clear his desk, all of his press associates had made it abundantly clear that he was no longer welcome in their company. His press card had been withdrawn and he could no longer gain admittance to the press club. It was no use anybody saying to Quentin that the future looked bleak simply because there was no future and, he knew it.

Quentin Russell had contacted all the editors he knew and they all expressed the same view. Admittedly some of them were honest and told him straight that, in their eyes, he was unemployable in any newspaper office, whilst others said they would keep in touch but deep down he knew they wouldn't. Alone in Brighton with nothing else to do Quentin Russell did not spend any time reflecting upon what might have been he simply reached out for the brandy bottle and poured himself yet another large drink. It no longer seemed to matter that doctors had told him to leave it alone or else. There was no or else. There wasn't any prospect of employment, and there was no Rose to talk to even if it was only to try to establish where it all went wrong.

The next morning he lay where he had fallen. He was still asleep from the effects of the brandy from the night before. The television was still on but he couldn't hear it. In fact, it would be a couple of hours before he would be fully awake, and, even then, the news wouldn't sink in straight away. When he eventually sobered up he would find that the news itself was even more depressing. Clive Anderson, the former editor of the London Independent Newspaper had been found dead at his London home. It was believed he had taken an overdose of tablets. This announcement was followed by a brief resume of his journalistic career, culminating with his recent fall from grace following the collapse of the libel case. This news would have a profound effect on Quentin when it finally sunk in for he and Clive Anderson had been very close friends indeed. Thus it was a friend he could ill afford to lose at any time of life let alone now.

Meanwhile for Timothy Harris, life was good. Life was to be enjoyed. Life was for living to the full. He never saw the lives of people he'd ruined or destroyed and, even if he had, it wouldn't matter one jot or one iota. All that mattered to Timothy Harris was Timothy Harris, and it was just too bad if somebody got hurt along the way.

Chapter 15

It was a filthy day in Liverpool. During the night, the weather broke and a storm of almost unprecedented ferocity launched itself and lashed the city mercilessly together with the surrounding district. The police van, carrying prisoner 1102 Harry Thompson together with the motor cycle escort swung into the rear entrance of Liverpool Assizes. With accustomed practice and precision, the gates swung open and closed. When the cavalcade came to a halt, Harry Thompson was allowed to alight. In accordance with normal custom and practice a blanket was placed over his head and he was quickly escorted into the dark grey forbidding building where he was taken to the cells below. The rain continued to bucket down in solid sheets, whilst in the distance there came the sound of approaching thunder accompanied by flashes of lightning.

Lord Chief Justice Ewing was already in his chambers even though there were still some two hours to go before the commencement of the trial. He was busy studying his own bundle of documents in order to completely familiarise himself with all aspects of the case, and the evidence to be presented. Most judges carried a reputation before them, and judge Ewing was no exception. He had a deserved reputation for being very strict and stern, as many an errant barrister discovered after falling foul of his temper when they had inadvertently strayed. Nevertheless, he was always considered to be fair and impartial in his summing up and trying of cases

As the hour approached the court filled up rapidly. The court ushers and officials busied themselves with their various tasks, whilst down below Irene Yarwood together with her defence team, were having a last minute consultation with Harry Thompson. All to soon it was time for them to leave in order to take up their appointed places in the court The prosecution team were already assembled, and whilst both teams warmly greeted each other like long lost friends; very soon they would be mortal enemies at each others' throats clutching at every minute detail in order to secure some adversarial advantage for their side. When it was all over, animosity would be cast aside, and they would depart as brothers until the next case arose.

In the court there was a sudden stir of people craning their necks to catch a glimpse of the accused as they heard the doors beneath the dock opening and footsteps coming up the short sharp steps which signalled the arrival in court of Harry Thompson.

Despite the sound of the shrieking wind and thunder, the jury were being sworn in. Great bolts of lightning lit up the courtroom, casting eerie glows amongst the shadows of the once white pillars. The claps of thunder grew ever closer and the great old building literally shook as each peal grew louder and nearer. Outside and overhead, the dark clouds blotted out all semblance of light, whilst the lashing of the incessant rain increased to a percussion sounding crescendo. Then, as the be-gowned Chief Usher entered the Judge's Chambers, a hush descended upon the court. Any moment now the Usher would reappear and, the court would be called to order. Everybody would rise whilst the Judge made his entrance. Then the trial would begin. Meanwhile, the storm continued unabated. Day had almost turned to night as bolts of lightning, which seemed to pass straight through the courtroom, were followed moments later by tremendous claps and peals of thunder. With each flash and explosion, the rain increased in intensity making normal conversation exceedingly difficult. It was against this backdrop and eerie setting, that the Chief Usher intoned, "All

Rise" as Judge Ewing made his entrance. He nodded to the assembled people standing in the courtroom and took his seat. Almost immediately a court official rose to his feet and, in a somewhat melodic voice began his well rehearsed speech.

"In the case of Regina Versus Harry Marcus Thompson, you are charged that on or about the 11th of September 1988 you wilfully murdered Miss Diane Wilson of 21, Carlton Crescent, Bromborough, Wirral. How do you plead in answer to this charge?" Harry Thompson had been through this procedure many times before with his defence team and he turned to face the jury. He replied in a voice as firmly, and as positively as he could, "Not Guilty." Without any hesitation the official began again,

"Harry Marcus Thompson, you are also charged that on or about, 2nd October1988 you did wilfully murder Miss Angela Clarkson of 16, Roby Street, Anfield, Liverpool. How do you plead in answer to this charge?" As instructed, he was still facing the jury as this charge was read. Without showing any trace of nerves or emotion, he replied, "Not Guilty," as he answered the charges. He stole a quick glance at Irene Yarwood who responded with the briefest of nods in his direction to indicate that, so far, she was satisfied with his performance.

The Crown Prosecution case began with an opening address, and Sir Gordon Nuttall-Jones was on his feet in readiness. He got into his stride straight away as he addressed the Judge,

"Your Honour, I am Sir Gordon Nuttall-Jones, and I am leading the case for the prosecution assisted by Bernard Gibson QC, and Dennis Slattery QC. The accused is represented by Miss Irene Yarwood QC, assisted by Douglas Waterman QC and Phillip Froggatt QC. junior.

Your Honour, ladies and gentlemen of the jury, the case for the Crown is quite simple. We will be able to show from the evidence to be presented before you, that the deaths of Diane Wilson and Angela Clarkson were caused by one person only, and that person, Harry Marcus Thompson, is the accused sitting in the dock there. He swung around at this point quite deliberately in order to emphasize the word "there" and the jury duly obliged by following his movement until all eyes were firmly on Harry Thompson. As if to underline the solemnity of the sombre proceedings taking place, the storm showed no sign of relenting. It was as if the elements themselves were trying to exact their revenge for the taking of life as the flashes of lightning continued to light up the courtroom, punctuated by massive claps of thunder which seemed to shake the very foundations of the historic building.

Not to be distracted, Sir Gordon continued, "We will show, to your satisfaction that the accused had sexual intercourse with Diane Wilson shortly before her death, and very shortly afterwards during a violent quarrel in which at least one telling blow was struck, Thompson strangled the poor girl with a pair of her own tights. After wrapping her body and clothing in plastic, which he weighted down with stones as ballast, he dispatched and consigned her body to the cold dark waters of a quarry lake at Chorley Wood, near Preston, some thirty five miles away. There Thompson hoped her body would remain forever some sixty feet down, entombed in the soft deep mud at the bottom. There, but for the intervention of fate, the body would have lain forever. However thanks to the grace of God, a trailing ballast rope snagged on an underwater tree root, and the parcel came to rest on a ledge barely twenty feet below the surface. Later it was discovered by two sub-aqua divers who used the lake as a practice centre for deep sea diving and they notified the authorities of their gruesome discovery. The body was later brought to the surface by a police diving unit and the body was later identified by the father of the dead girl as his only child, and beloved daughter, Diane Wilson."

"A pathologist carried out a post mortem examination and he certified death had been caused by strangulation. This had been carried out with a pair of her own tights that were still tied around her neck. Further tests conducted by the pathologist showed that sexual intercourse had taken place just prior to death, and samples were then taken from the body for the purpose of DNA Testing. During this trial, you will hear the results of those tests and the significant part they will play in this trial. As I have already stated, we will also show that the accused quarrelled with Miss Wilson prior to her death. As far as the police have been able to ascertain, Harry Thompson was the last person to see Miss Wilson alive."

"Harry Thompson is also charged with the murder of Angela Clarkson but, under English Criminal Law, the accused cannot be tried for more than one murder at a time. Where there are two or more charges it is up to the prosecution to choose which case to take first and, in this case, we have decided that the Wilson case will be the case for which he will be tried. However, the law does allow for evidence to be presented before you on the second count and, in this connection, you will hear that evidence. You will also hear that, prior to her death, Angela Clarkson engaged in prostitution, but that is no reason for her to leave this life behind in the manner that she did. As far as the police are concerned, this was a senseless, and motiveless killing, but, as in the first case, this poor unfortunate woman had been strangled with her own tights twisted and knotted, in the same manner as before. Despite the lack of any DNA evidence directly linking Thompson to Angela Clarkson, he is nevertheless the only person who can be considered a suspect in this case. Here the facts will also reveal that Harry Thompson lived barely 500 yards from the spot where the body lay and, before the discovery of the body,

Harry Thompson had reported to his local police station that he had found a very expensive ladies watch lying just off one of the woodland nature trails on the perimeter of the local golf course. The spot where he claimed to have made this find is less than fifty feet from where the corpse was lying. Later, you will hear evidence positively linking that watch to the murdered girl, Angela Clarkson. The Crown will show that Thompson did not find that watch at all. In fact, he stole it whilst emptying the contents of her handbag and, knowing that he had just killed the woman, he could hardly keep the watch in his pocket and say nothing about it in case something turned up later to link him with the crime. But, if he handed it in at his local police station, as indeed he did then, he could claim it as his own in some three months' time."

"During this trial you will hear Thompson's protestations of innocence but I am confident the Crown will show this is nothing more than an elaborate charade to hoodwink you. I am sure that, after hearing the evidence, you won't be taken in." With that Sir Gordon sat down, and it was the turn of Irene Yarwood to open for the defence.

"Your Honour, Ladies and Gentlemen of the jury, first of all there are a number of points and similarities for you to consider before you arrive at any decision. The first thing is that similarities don't make murderers of people so let us examine the facts as stated by my learned colleague for the prosecution a few moments ago."

"Harry Thompson and his girlfriend go to bed together where they have unprotected sex. As a result his sperm, his DNA is deposited inside her. Now that does not make him a killer, after all he has always freely admitted they had sex on the last occasion that they were together. Without attempting to malign or to destroy the dead girl's character, he's also admitted they were intimate together whenever they could or, whenever the opportunity presented itself, and as we all know there's nothing wrong in that. This evening was different because they quarrelled, but that doesn't make him a killer either, because, if every lover's quarrel resulted in death the population of the entire world would be decimated. In this instance, as a result of this quarrel, Miss Wilson storms off determined to go home alone and refusing to allow Thompson to accompany her or to drive her home. Somewhere on her way home Diane Wilson met her killer. She might even have known him. Sex might not have been on his mind or, even if it was, perhaps she screamed and, if she did, then presumably that made her death inevitable at the hands of her assailant. Before cross-examination begins, I want you to concentrate your minds on some facts concerning this case. First of all the police are adamant that Thompson's DNA profile and the evidence of intercourse just prior to death don't just point to Thompson's guilt, they actually confirm it. As a result of this, my learned colleague prosecuting will attempt to prove that Harry Thompson is just a sexual fiend who has developed a lust for killing. If that were really the case, or, if the killing of Diane Wilson had a sexual motive, why on earth should Thompson kill Miss Wilson when he had just impregnated her? In which case, he might as well have walked into his local police station and said to the duty officer *I have just killed my girlfriend.*"

"If, as the police would have you believe, sex was the underlying motive where is the same motive in relation to the Clarkson case? Angela Clarkson was a common prostitute who would drop her knickers, assuming that she wore them, for anybody who had the money. We know that Angela Clarkson had sex with someone before she died because the pathologists report tells us so but in this instance, there isn't any matching DNA sample from those obtained by the police during their enquiries or, with those supplied by Harry Thompson the main suspect at the time. Thompson's only crime lies in the fact that he happened to live within 500 yards from where the body of Angela Clarkson was found and he had the misfortune to find an expensive watch that he handed in to the police. Now I have to remind you that fifty other men lived within a quarter of a mile from this spot and none of them provided a matching sperm sample either. Have any of them been considered killers? Were any of them ever considered potential suspects? The answer to that is 'no' and, they weren't considered simply because they hadn't bedded Diane Wilson or found a watch. Another point to consider is this. If Harry Thompson is guilty as charged, why on earth didn't he dump the body of Angela Clarkson in the quarry as well? What on earth could he hope to gain by leaving her body on his own doorstep?"

"Finally, let me conclude this opening address by saying, it is our contention that Harry Thompson is completely innocent of all charges, that the killer of these two unfortunate women is still at large and, it may well be, that the police should be looking for two killers as it is just as likely there is no established link between the two. During this trial, do not allow the prosecution to fool you concerning the fact that both of these women were killed by the use of their own tights. Remember tights, once removed, present a very handy killing tool and any fool can tie granny knots."

As Irene Yarwood sat down there were slight murmurings from those present in Court and the judge felt obliged to restore order with a loud crack from his gavel.

Looking at the prosecution bench he said quickly, "Mr. Nuttall-Jones I know you're anxious to proceed as quickly as possible but I thought now might be a good time to recess for lunch. Then looking and nodding at both counsel, he said, "Good. Then can we all be back for two o'clock."

As both counsel nodded affirmatively, the Chief Clerk

shouted, "All Rise," and Lord Chief Justice Ewing left the courtroom.

Despite the noise from the storm outside, the courtroom soon became a cacophony of sound with voices everywhere. It seemed as though everybody had something to say about the morning's proceedings so much so the departure from the dock of Harry Thompson passed almost unnoticed as he was escorted down the steps to the rooms below. .

When the court reconvened after lunch, evidence of identification of Diane Wilson was given by her father. All those present were touched in some way if it was only due to the stifled, but persistent sobbing of Mrs. Wilson. Several times the judge intervened to ask if she would like a short recess but she refused all such requests preferring, instead, to get the whole traumatic experience over and done with as quickly as possible. With the voice of Mr. Wilson trembling with emotion, Sir Gordon Nuttall-Jones led him slowly and painfully, through his own traumatic ordeal. Due to the distress caused to Mrs. Wilson during this procedure, Sir Gordon revised his witness strategy by deciding that, in order to spare her any further anguish, she would not be called to give evidence. As a result the case moved on to the testimony of the two divers who had discovered the body.

At this stage Irene Yarwood had not asked any questions because nothing had been presented which could be called into question. Evidence of identification, given by the brother of Angela Clarkson, followed the same procedural pattern bringing the second day's proceedings to a close.

After the lunch recess on the third day, Professor Guy Whittingham was called to the stand to give his expert evidence concerning the DNA results from the samples taken during the course of the police investigation. He was giving his evidence under examination by Sir Gordon Nuttall-Jones. Sir

Gordon was a very imposing figure. He stood at least six feet six inches tall and his very presence seemed to fill the Court. Whenever he spoke his voice seemed to reverberate around the room despite the noise emanating from the continuing storm outside. Continuing his examination of the witness he said, "Now professor, for the benefit of the jury, please clarify that statement once again as I don't want the jury to have the slightest doubt in their minds about the DNA testing. Will you please confirm that you are saying it was the specimen supplied by Thompson, the accused person in the dock. At this point he turned to the jury and ordered them, "Look at him, which provided so many similarities to that sample extracted from the vagina of Diane Wilson and you can put it as high as 98% certain that it came from the same person. In addition, the odds of a similar match being obtained from another person are in excess of 300 million to one."

Not completely satisfied with this, Sir Gordon continued to milk the scene by repeating 98% certain and 300 million to one.

"Yes that's what I said and, that is indeed correct." affirmed the professor.

Sir Gordon was more than pleased with this witness and it showed with the smile that lit up his rounded features. He looked across at Irene Yarwood and said triumphantly in a voice at least an octave lower, "No more questions."

Irene stood up quickly. She certainly didn't wish to appear hesitant especially in front of the jury and in the course of her first murder trial, but even so it still took her almost half a minute before she began her cross examination. "Professor Whittingham, thank you for your comments. Now what else can you tell us about this DNA test? For instance are you saying that, absolutely positively and without any question of doubt whatsoever, this sample could have come from one person and one person only and that the person is Harry Thompson, the accused?"

"No" he replied relishing his glory in the spotlight, "I'm not actually saying that. "What I am saying is, unless Mr. Thompson has an identical twin, the odds of a similar profile being obtained from another person are in excess of 300 million to one."

Sir Gordon couldn't believe his luck when he heard this statement from his witness. He was on his feet in an instant. Banging his fist on the table in front of him he shouted aloud, "But there are no twins here in this case."

Gavel in hand, the judge quickly brought the proceedings back to order once again and, although he rebuked the errant QC for his behaviour, the point had been made and it had been hammered home mercilessly...

Miss Yarwood continued as though nothing untoward had actually occurred, "Now Professor Whittingham, you carried out these tests between the samples obtained from the defendant and the samples obtained from the body of Diane Wilson, did you?"

"That is correct," he replied.

"Did you carry out similar tests with the samples from the deceased and any of the other samples provided?"

"No I did not."

"Well, Professor, that is indeed a surprise to all of us. Perhaps you can explain to this court why no other tests were carried out?"

"That's quite simple. You see I wasn't asked to. I was only provided with the sample referred to and I was asked to compare it as I described earlier."

"What about the sample obtained from the second victim, together with all of those samples obtained from the volunteer donors in response to the police appeal for help?"

Before the Professor could reply, Sir Gordon was on his feet bellowing, "Objection, objection I must strongly object to this line of questioning by my learned colleague. From the very start of this case, the prosecution have made it abundantly clear that we would not be introducing any DNA evidence in connection with this second count of murder. Therefore it isn't relevant and I must ask your lordship not to allow this line of questioning to proceed any further."

Sitting silently in his chair, Judge Ewing banged his gavel repeatedly until order was restored. He ordered both counsel to the bench and addressing Miss Yarwood, he said angrily, "Miss Yarwood what on earth do you think you are playing at? If you do anything like this again I shall hold you in contempt. You know as well as I do, from the documents provided in discovery, that the prosecution are not relying on DNA evidence in the second case, in which case you cannot introduce it."

Unabashed and unafraid Miss Yarwood replied, "Your honour I am trying to establish that there is DNA evidence in the Clarkson case and it is being suppressed by the police and the Crown. Over 200 people gave voluntary samples including my client, none of which proved a match to that obtained from Clarkson. Now, if the sample obtained from Clarkson could be matched with somebody, then it is likely or at least it's possible that this person may well have been the last person to see her alive. In that respect that is where the two cases become almost identical. To my mind, there is a marked similarity in the two cases. On the first charge, the DNA sample relates solely to that provided by my client and he readily admits that he had intercourse with his girlfriend. It is because of this that he has been charged. In the second case we know that somebody had sex with Clarkson and that person was definitely not my client. Therefore, I think it is of paramount importance to my client's case that this point is adequately covered during these proceedings. Please allow me to continue for a little while and, at the same time consider this... If the positions were reversed, then surely it is possible the person who killed Clarkson and left his sample also killed the girlfriend of my client?"

Irene received no sympathy from the judge who told her in no uncertain manner that his patience was now exhausted and she was skating on very thin ice adding, "The point is Miss Yarwood; none of us know the identity of the last person to have sex with the poor woman. Even if we were aware of the identity of that person it seems fair and logical to assume he's not here because the police think he took no part in the murder and he has been eliminated from their enquiries. In those circumstances the Crown are quite justified in not bringing before this court any DNA evidence regarding Clarkson. Now that is my final ruling on the subject so might I suggest that we get back to the business in hand which happens to be your cross examination of Professor Whittingham."

Although she had lost the battle, Irene was not disheartened because she knew she had established there was some additional DNA evidence connected to the case and one day, given that she could introduce it, it could prove decisive. As she took her place she announced, "No further questions," and the Professor was allowed to leave the witness stand.

Nodding to Sir Gordon, Lord Chief Justice Ewing indicated that the next witness was eagerly awaited.

"Call Bridget Riley." This was immediately repeated by the usher and, a few moments later, she entered the court accompanied somewhat symbolically by another crash of thunder. All eyes were upon her as she made her entrance and, despite her obvious attempts to alter her appearance, she still managed to look like a tart. She took her place in the witness box and repeated the oath whilst holding the bible. Sir Gordon disposed of the usual perfunctory questions such as name and address and then, with the onlookers hanging on every word, posed the question they were all waiting to hear "Occupation?"

Sir Gordon	"Did you know the deceased woman Angela Clarkson?"
Bridget	"Yes."
Sir Gordon	"How well and for how long?"
Bridget	"At least five years."
Sir Gordon	"How did you meet her?"
Bridget	"Through the escort agency, sometimes we worked together."
Sir Gordon	"Did you work Rodney Street together?"
Bridget	"Yes we did."
Sir Gordon	"On a regular basis?"
Bridget	"Yes, if there wasn't any other work."

The prosecutor then picked up the watch from the table where the exhibits lay. Turning to Bridget he asked, "Did you ever see Angela Clarkson wearing a watch like this and could this watch have belonged to her?"

He walked slowly over to the witness box holding the watch aloft by the strap in order that the jury could see it as he handed it to Bridget.

Bridget looked at it very briefly and without hesitating replied, "Yes that's Angela's watch. She bought it just before she died."

Sir Gordon	"Have you any idea when she bought the watch?"
Bridget	"I think it was about three weeks before she died but I'm not... absolutely sure.

Sir Gordon then stated that he had no further questions and he asked Bridget to remain in the witness box whilst the defence satisfied themselves about the evidence she had just given.

Even though Irene Yarwood knew beforehand that this evidence would be introduced, she was well aware that it did nothing to improve the chances of her client. Nevertheless, she just had to get on with it and she began her cross-examination.

"Now Miss Riley, you have told this court that you were a long-standing friend of Angela Clarkson's and that you weren't simply street corner acquaintances plying your trade together. Is that really true?"

Bridget was now growing in confidence and to some extent she was relishing her moment in the spotlight as she answered, "Yes I'd known her for quite some time.

Miss Yarwood.	"So when you said that you saw Angela wearing this watch she showed it to you, did she?"
Bridget	"Yes she did."
Miss Yarwood	"Did she take it off in order that you could have a good look at it?"
Bridget	"Yes she did."
Miss Yarwood	"So you had a good look at it and did she tell you how much she had paid for it?"
Bridget	"Yes I had a good look at it but she didn't tell me that. She just said that she'd come into a bit of money and that she had always wanted a decent watch."
Miss Yarwood	"Really Miss Riley, I find that very hard to believe. Are you telling this court that Angela Clarkson your long-standing friend, comes down to Rodney Street wearing a very expensive watch and you didn't want to know where she got it from or how much she paid for it?"
Bridget	"Well I didn't want to ask too many questions in case she thought I was jealous."
Miss Yarwood	"And were you jealous?"

Bridget	"A little bit I suppose."
Miss Yarwood	"I have to remind you now that you are on oath and I am putting it to you that you never saw Angela Clarkson wearing that watch at any time. I am putting it to you like this because I'd like you to tell me how much you think a person might have to pay for a watch of similar quality?"
Bridget	"I suppose she paid about sixty or seventy pounds for it or something like that."
Miss Yarwood	"As much as that, really, and, you're telling this court that Angela Clarkson would go out on the streets touting for business, wearing a brand new watch costing sixty or seventy pounds?"

Before Bridget could answer Irene continued, saying, "Well let me tell you something, young lady. That watch didn't cost sixty or seventy pounds. Actually it cost three hundred and fifty pounds and, I have here a letter of confirmation from the maker's English agents confirming that."

Bridget was no longer in control. She was beginning to feel more than a little uncomfortable especially with the way this cross-examination was going. All she wanted to do now was to get out of the witness box and sink at least a couple of large gins. She stood anxiously in the witness box waiting for the next barrage as the QC continued, "Now Miss Riley, are you seriously telling this court that your friend took off this watch in order that you could have a good look at it, and you could see it was quite an expensive item to put it mildly, and she was quite happy to walk the streets wearing it whilst knowing full well that it had cost three hundred and fifty pounds. I put it to you, Miss Riley, that this testimony of yours is nothing more than a pack of lies because Angela Clarkson never bought that watch and you never saw her wearing it at all, did you?"

Bridget   "That's not true. I did see her wearing that watch three weeks before she died and she did tell me that she'd bought it herself."

Irene then surprised everyone in the court by announcing that she had no further questions but this was just a trick she was playing in an attempt to unsettle or unnerve the witness. Bridget was just about to step down feeling mightily relieved, when the lawyer suddenly turned and said, "I'm sorry Miss Riley but there is something I forgot to ask you. Did you happen to notice the maker's name of the watch?"

Caught unawares and with her guard completely down, Bridget stood there not knowing what to say and whether to answer or not until Lord Chief Justice Ewing intervened saying to her, "You may answer Miss Riley."

The question had caught her completely off guard as she falteringly replied, "Yes, I …I …I'm almost sure it was a Rolex."

Irene knew before she had begun to cross examine this witness that she was lying but she knew that she had no way of proving it unless she could totally discredit her testimony and she reconciled herself to ending her cross examination by correcting her before allowing her to stand down. Just like a conductor leading the orchestra into a finale, she concluded,

"No Miss Riley, you are totally mistaken. It was not a Rolex, it was, in fact a Ramond Viell so I say to you once again, you never saw Angela Clarkson wearing that watch before because the probability is that she only received it on the day she died and, in all probability, it was given to her as a present from a grateful client."

Bridget stood in the box glaring at the counsel for the defence. Then she repeated defiantly, "I am telling you the truth. I did see Angela wearing that watch before she died. I did and that's the truth."

Instead of letting the witness stand down as she had originally indicated, Irene now judged it to be the appropriate time to vary her attack by adopting a different tactic as she enquired almost nonchalantly, "When did you first get fined for soliciting and where did the offence take place?"

For a moment there was no answer. Irene repeated the question.

With utmost reluctance, Bridget replied, "Birmingham 1983."

This was the opening Irene had worked so hard for and she seized the opportunity immediately.

"Miss Riley, Earlier, you told this court that you had known the deceased woman for 5 years but, if you were convicted in Birmingham in 1983, then it's highly unlikely that you knew Angela Clarkson in Liverpool or anywhere else five years ago."

Before she could finish the question, Sir Gordon was on his feet shouting "Objection, Your Honour, I object most strongly to this line of questioning. It's quite clear to all of us that Miss Yarwood is not only badgering the witness but this line of questioning is totally irrelevant and I demand that it should be stricken from the record."

Before giving his decision, Lord Chief Justice Ewing used his gavel to good effect. Then, after looking long and hard at Sir Gordon he fixed his gaze on Irene and invited her to explain the relevance of her question and where her cross-examination might be leading.

After thanking his Lordship, Irene kept her eyes firmly upon him as she answered, "Your Honour, before my learned colleague interrupted proceedings, I was simply trying to show to this court that the testimony of this witness is a complete tissue of lies. If the court will bear with me for one moment I think I will be able to show this provided that I am allowed to continue without any more interruptions."

Noting her remarks, Judge Ewing gave his permission for the defence to continue and Irene repeated the question;

"Miss Riley, earlier you told this court that you had known Angela Clarkson for five years but, if you were convicted in Birmingham in 1983, then it's highly unlikely that you knew Angela Clarkson in Liverpool or anywhere else five years ago because she was arrested in Manchester for drug offences for which she received a custodial sentence. In fact, she was not released until 1984. Furthermore, in 1984 she was again arrested in Manchester and charged with soliciting. Taking all this into account, your testimony amounts to little more than a tissue of lies."

Lord Chief Justice Ewing, looked down from his seat on high above the court. He cleared his throat loudly before pointing at, and rebuking the witness very angrily, "Young lady, I must warn you that the penalties for perjury are very severe. You have been called here today to tell the truth and, if I suspect that you have been lying to this Court I will have no hesitation in ensuring that such charges are brought against you and, if you are found guilty on such charges, you will receive a lengthy custodial sentence. Do I make myself clear?"

Bridget teetered on the brink. She realised this was going horribly wrong. She could hardly speak out now and admit she was lying because the judge had just told her that if she did, she would probably go to prison. Therefore she knew she would have to try to brazen it out. Facing the judge, she said, "Your Honour, I might have made a mistake about the length of time I knew Angela but I am telling the truth about the watch."

Feeling triumphant that she might have cast a little shadow of doubt in the minds of the jurors, Irene Yarwood happily conceded she had no further questions to ask at this time, although she reserved the right to recall the witness to the stand at a later time.

Bridget left the witness box with a distinct cloud hanging over her evidence and she knew it. Inwardly she cursed Detective Sergeant West because it was all his fault and, to make matters worse, she couldn't forget how he'd told her she wouldn't have to testify. One day, she vowed, she would have her revenge on the evil, lying bastard. As she took her seat at the rear of the court, the usher was already calling in the next witness intoning, in the same monotonous voice, "Call Royston Chambers."

The call was repeated down the corridor and all eyes swung to the door as Royston Chambers entered and took his place in the witness box.

Meanwhile, Irene Yarwood was hurriedly scribbling a note to Michael Mulrooney, the defence team's solicitor, asking him to subpoena any bank account details Angela Clarkson might have possessed before she died. As a result of her own cross examination of Bridget Riley it had occurred to her that if Angela Clarkson had purchased the watch then there should surely be some evidence to show that she had that amount of money in her bank account and that she had withdrawn it or, alternatively, she had paid for it by credit card or cheque. She was desperately hoping that if she could find some evidence that the murdered woman had not bought the watch as testified then she could recall this little lying prostitute and crucify her for trying to stitch up her client with false evidence. As an afterthought, she also requested him to contact the agents once again in order to ascertain whether any of the watches had been sold on Merseyside during the crucial time in question. One thing she was quite sure of, whether he was guilty or not, Harry Thompson was going to get as much as she could give in connection with her defence of him.

With Royston Chambers in the witness box, Sir Gordon

did not waste time dwelling on the circumstance in which the witness found himself, besides which, he was beginning to develop a distinct respect for his adversary on the opposite side and he was determined to ensure he didn't give her anything she could sink her teeth into. He hadn't expected an easy ride in this case and he had to grudgingly admit that Irene Yarwood was putting up a spirited performance at the moment even though her opportunities were severely limited. With almost undue haste, he elicited the facts that Royston Chambers was an old lag, currently residing in one of Her Majesty's safe houses of correction and penal servitude whilst he was on remand awaiting his own trial for a serious charge of armed robbery.

Irene Yarwood listened with avid interest as the Crown Prosecutor rushed through this preamble and, before the barrister could fire his first question, she was on her feet shouting and protesting with utmost vigour, "Objection. Your Honour, I must strongly object to the testimony of this man being heard. This man is a convicted felon of many years standing and he is currently on remand on other charges. My client strongly denies ever making any of the statements this man will claim he made whilst both of them were being held on remand. My client explicitly denies that he has ever made any confession, or that he has admitted any guilt relating to the charges he faces. In view of this My Lord, I must ask you to rule that the evidence we are about to hear is inadmissible. Without stopping to draw breath and ignoring the expression on the face of the judge, she continued, "It is also my contention, Your Honour, that this witness has been offered some form of deal or a reduction on his sentence as an inducement to present himself here before you with this confession, *allegedly*, freely given to him by my client. Apart from anything else, how can the jury be expected to rely upon the word of a convicted thief and robber, who now stands before you in order to give this testimony which, I might add, is absolutely and, completely uncorroborated."

Somewhat exasperated, Lord Chief Justice Ewing sat back in his chair. Raising his hands in the air he enquired sarcastically, "Will that be all Miss Yarwood? Have you quite finished?"

She nodded in reply adding, "Yes, Your Honour," whilst hoping she hadn't overstepped the mark. If she had it was too late besides which she had a client to defend. It was of no use to him if the prosecution had got in first with the confession and she reasoned that at least the jurors were well aware of what was coming next. There was no hiding that no matter what Sir Gordon Nuttall-Jones did now.

Judge Ewing motioned both counsel to the bench, and, through clenched teeth, he whispered, "I am going to call a short recess and I want to see both of you in my chambers immediately. Clearly, they both could see he was not amused and he banged down his gavel as hard as he could to announce the delay. As the gavel crashed down the Chief Usher, who had seemed to be all but asleep, leapt to his feet crying, "All rise," and the Judge left the court with a look of thunder upon his face.

The two QCs stood in the Judge's chambers. Lord Chief Justice Ewing rounded upon the defence attorney first, "Miss Yarwood, "Whenever you are in my court, you will kindly refrain from telling me how to conduct proceedings. Regarding your extraordinary outburst in court a few moments ago, am I to understand that you have absolutely no proof that the police have done any kind of a deal with this witness and, if that is so, why on earth did you say it?"

Knowing she was in trouble, Irene relied on a completely honest answer in order to escape the wrath of the judge that she felt certain would descend upon her. "Well, Your Honour, I didn't see that I had much choice. My client maintains the confession is a complete fabrication and there must have been some form of collusion with the police, leading to the witness being offered inducements of some form, otherwise why invent the confession?"

"Well, Miss Yarwood, that is hardly good enough. I can see, and I understand, the dilemma you were in but I have to ask you why the word of your client should be more acceptable than that of the witness? I'm sure, when I ask Sir Gordon whether or not your allegation is true, he will undoubtedly say otherwise and he will also confirm that this man has never volunteered similar evidence on other occasions, neither has he ever been accused of perjury in the past. Isn't that true Sir Gordon?"

Sir Gordon leapt at this heaven-sent opportunity, agreeing vociferously with Judge Ewing and thankful it was his opponent who was bearing the brunt of the Judge's scathing criticism.

"Well, there you are, Miss Yarwood. Now you see my dilemma, I can't refuse to let Chambers give his evidence because, as far as we know, it is factual. Sir Gordon has told us so. In which case I will allow the evidence to be presented and heard."

Sir Gordon was all ready to leave the Judge's chambers but the judge had not finished. Addressing his remarks to him he said, "Now Sir Gordon before we resume, perhaps you can enlighten us by letting us know what steps you have taken to ensure that this confession has not been elicited by any promises from the police or have you and your team simply accepted it as it is, on face value so to speak?"

Sir Gordon was another person who knew the value of the truth in circumstances such as these so he replied truthfully, "Well, er, yes, Your Honour, this was something which just dropped in our laps a short while ago. Obviously it is not something we were involved in and we knew nothing about it until the police advised us that the defendant had confessed to Chambers." Taken by surprise by the Judge's question and, in an effort to recover, he added rather hesitantly, "of course, we will rigorously examine the witness on this point and we expect our learned colleague here to do much the same."

Judge Ewing murmured, "Commendable, most commendable, Sir Gordon but I have to say that I'm going to warn you and, if you have any doubt as to the validity of this confession, you should withdraw the witness. Alternatively, if I have any doubts during his evidence or cross examination, you may rest assured I shall have no hesitation in asking for the evidence to be struck out and for the jury to ignore it. Do I make myself clear?"

"Very clear," said the much subdued prosecuting counsel.

They both left the judge's inner sanctum and made their way in silence to the courtroom. The judge did not keep them waiting and the case was taken up from where it had been left.

Mindful of the judge's comments, Sir Gordon began, "When you were on remand which cell were you in and where was this cell in relation to that occupied by the accused?"

Chambers	"Initially I was held on remand at Warrington but, as it was too difficult for my wife to get there to visit me, I asked if I could be transferred to Walton, Liverpool. I was transferred about four months ago. When I first transferred I was in H wing then, after a couple of days, I was moved to A block where I occupied a cell next to the prisoner."
Sir Gordon	"How did you get to know the prisoner?"
Chambers	"Initially, although he had been pointed out to me, I didn't know him at all. It was only when I moved to A block and I was put

into the next cell to him that I got to know him."

Sir Gordon "Did anybody tell you or ask you to get to know him?"

Chambers "Definitely not."

Sir Gordon "Now, Chambers, let's be quite clear about this. You are saying that you asked for a move from Warrington to Walton but, not from H block at Walton, and, when you were moved to A block, that's the first time you knew you were next door to Thompson. How did you feel about that last move?"

Chambers "Well I wasn't too pleased and I wanted to go back to H block because all the lads reckoned he was off his trolley. When I found out he'd done two of them in, I didn't fancy being that close to him. In the end, after a couple of days we just started talking and it all stemmed from there."

Sir Gordon "Did you mention to Thompson anything about his crimes and, if so, how did he respond?"

Chambers "Well it was a bit funny at first yet, once we started talking, he began to ask me what I was in for so I told him, then he'd ask me about prison life in general and how much time I'd spent inside. Yet when I asked him any questions about himself, he used to go very quiet and he wouldn't say a word. This went on for four or five weeks but, one day after we'd been for a shower, he just came right out with it. He came up to me and, after making sure nobody else was about, he asked me if I had any idea what he was in for. When I said I hadn't got a clue he said, "well you must be the only one in here who doesn't because I'm in for murder. I killed two of them." After that he hardly said a thing and, at first I thought I couldn't report him for saying that because I thought he'd just deny it. Then I had the idea that if he actually confessed I could just let them know. I thought, if he confessed properly, it would help to clear up his case. You see it's like this, thieving is one thing but murder, ugh, that's ugly. Nobody wants to know a murderer because you never feel safe. A few days later, and presumably because I didn't grass him up, he just came up to me and said he had to talk to somebody as he had to get things off his chest, sort of, and, if he didn't he thought he would go mad. With that he launched into this full blown confession about how he killed these two poor women."

Sir Gordon produced some sheets of paper which he handed to Chambers saying "Mr. Chambers, is this the statement that you made in the presence of two police officers whilst you were on remand in Walton Gaol and were there any other persons present when you gave that statement?"

Royston Chambers was in his element. He couldn't wait to tell anybody who would listen especially if he felt it would assist his cause when his own case came up for trial. He knew he had no need to fear any repercussions from Thompson as it was hardly likely he would ever see the light of day on the outside of prison again but that didn't bother him in the slightest as he replied, "Yes this is the statement I gave and signed in the presence of Detective Inspector Taylor, and Detective Sergeant West. There was also one prison officer present and that was Officer Fitzgerald."

"Were you offered any inducements or favours by anyone at all to obtain this confession and, if so, will you please tell this court the precise nature of any favours or special treatment you've been offered to come here today?" Sir Gordon asked.

The witness looked arrogantly towards the judge and then at Sir Gordon, before replying, "None, none at all. When this man Thompson told me he wanted to confess in order to get this off his chest, I considered it my duty to let the authorities know what he had told me. The things he told me almost made me feel ill so much so, I think he must be sick in the mind to do what he said he did."

From the courtroom there came a shout of protest.

Irene Yarwood was on her feet crying, "Your honour, I most strongly object to this. This man has no medical knowledge whatsoever and it is not incumbent upon him to pontificate or express his opinions on the mental state or well-being of my client at any time past, or present. With all due respect, Your Lordship, I must remind the court that the sanity of my client is not under any investigation by anybody in this court. In fact, may I also remind you that my client has entered a not guilty plea to the charges laid and it is fair to say that he has in fact refused to change this plea since his arrest."

The Judge leaned forward. He raised his glasses slightly before ordering the prosecuting counsel to ensure that the witness should keep all such opinions to himself. Then, after telling the clerk to delete the last answer, he ordered the jury to ignore it and motioned to the Crown to proceed.

Thus rebuked, Sir Gordon continued, "What did you do after Thompson confessed?"

A little subdued now, Chambers looked nervously at the Judge before answering, "I requested an urgent meeting with Detective Sergeant West and Detective Inspector Taylor. When they came to the prison I asked to make my statement. At that time they told me they couldn't make any promises about my own case when it came to trial. In fact, they went so far as to warn me that I couldn't expect to receive any special favours as a result. Chambers had recovered his composure a little now and he turned to face the Judge before continuing, "however, they did say that if I came to court to give evidence, the presiding judge might be persuaded to say something on my behalf, to whichever judge heard my case."

Somewhat shocked by these remarks, Judge Ewing began to scribble furious notes on his pad whilst allowing the Crown to continue. At this point, Sir Gordon indicated to Chambers it was time for him to read the confession to the court.

Chambers began, "first of all, Thompson came up to me one Monday after we'd both taken a shower. Without any prompting from me, he said he was inside for killing "two of them." At first I didn't know what to do and I thought I can hardly go and tell somebody because he'll only deny it, and it'll look as though I was trying to cause trouble for him. A few days later, when we were walking back to our cells, he told me he needed to talk to me about the crimes he'd committed. I told him, if he wanted to make a confession, he should get hold of the police officers who arrested him or talk to his barrister, but he said he couldn't do that. He went on to say that he thought he would feel better within himself if he could tell somebody like me about the murders. Somehow, I think he thought this would ease his conscience and that I wouldn't tell anybody so I agreed to go along with it. He told me he killed his girl friend because they had an argument about his sexual performance. During this argument, he struck her on the jaw to try to stop her from screaming then he grabbed her tights and wrapped them around her neck. All of a sudden, he said, he noticed she'd stopped screaming and he thought she was pretending to be asleep. He told me that he shook her in an effort to wake her and, when she didn't move, he realised she was dead. At first he started to cry then he realised he'd have to get rid of the body as he thought nobody would believe his story. He got hold of some black bin liners, together with some rope and he tied her and her clothes in a bundle. Then he drove to a lake somewhere near Preston, where he threw her in. He kept repeating over and over again how he never intended to kill her. Yet later, he told me he was very surprised when they found her body there as he didn't think it would ever be discovered."

Chambers stopped for a moment whilst he took a sip of water. He made the most of this opportunity to weigh up the looks upon the faces of the people he could see. From what he could see, it seemed pretty obvious to him they appeared to be taking it all in."

He began again, "Thompson told me Clarkson was different. She was a prostitute."

Chambers' arrogance was returning and it was definitely showing as he continued, "he told me he was a client of hers. When he saw her in this local bar he said he couldn't believe his luck. He went straight up to her and said he fancied a bloody good screw and he knew she would give him one. They went outside where they got into his car to go to a quiet spot to have it off. When he couldn't manage it, he wanted his money back. This led to an argument and, to stop her screaming the place down, he grabbed her tights, threw them around her neck and throttled her. Once again he said he never intended to kill her and that he only wanted his money back. He made sure she was dead and he pulled her out of the car. After throwing her body and clothes in a ditch, he went back to the car for her handbag, collected the money from it together with her watch, then he threw her bag and the rest of the contents into the ditch with her. After this he went home to bed."

"When he woke up the next day, he realised what he'd done and he might come unstuck if he was ever found with the watch. Because he didn't want to lose it, he thought it would be very clever of him if he handed it in at his local nick then he could claim it back three months later."

Chambers then confirmed that the confession had been freely given in the presence of the two police officers from Merseyside who were in charge of the case, together with a prison officer who had remained in attendance throughout the proceedings.

Sir Gordon didn't see the need to ask the witness any further questions. He considered the confession contained more than enough detail and he didn't wish to risk exposing the witness any more than necessary.

Once again it was the turn of the defence. Irene didn't relish the prospect of trying to discredit the evidence just heard but she decided she had no choice other than to attack the witness in the hope that he might crack or she might be able to show in some way that the evidence was flawed.

"Mr. Chambers, you are aware that my client totally and utterly refutes every word of that confession. In addition my client insists each and every word you have uttered is nothing more than a pack of lies. Earlier today we heard Judge Ewing telling another witness about the penalties for perjury in his court and I have to remind you of the severity of the sentence awaiting you when the truth is known. Make no mistake, Mr. Chambers, the truth will out and you will be punished. Later the jury will have a very simple choice. They can believe your testimony or they can reject it preferring, instead, the testimony of the defendant. In their shoes I know whose evidence I would choose to believe."

"Now, Mr. Chambers, going back to your time at Warrington, who arranged your transfer from there to Walton?"

Chambers "I asked Detective Sergeant West and he said he'd see what he could do."

"That's what I thought," she replied adding, "How long were you in H block and how did you came to be moved to A block?"

Chambers. "As I said earlier, I didn't request that move to A block. I was just told by Officer Fitzgerald I was being moved and I had a new cell in A block so I just collected my stuff and did as I was told."

Miss Yarwood "You didn't think it had been pre-arranged then? In other words it never occurred to you someone from the police might have had a word beforehand and conveniently arranged it? Or, you might consider this, before you occupied the cell next door to Thompson, Thompson would have had ample opportunity to confess to the person who occupied the cell before you, wouldn't he?"

Chambers "Yes, I suppose he would but maybe Thompson wasn't ready to talk then."

"I see," mused the defence lawyer, "now please tell the court whilst you were living next door to Thompson how many visits you received from your friend Sergeant West and explain the nature of these visits to the Court."

Chambers   "Three, I think one was to see if I knew
                  anything about a hold up in St. Helens and
                  the others were to ask me some questions
                  about my own case."
Miss Yarwood   "Well what questions did he ask you in
                  relation to your own case?"

Chambers had already mumbled, "I can't remember,"
before Sir Gordon interrupted with his objection on the
grounds that Chambers was not in the dock and he was there
to answer questions relative to the murder trial and nothing
else.

From his lofty position, the Lord Chief Justice glowered at
Miss Yarwood whilst saying, "sustained."

Irene knew she had been presented with a slight opening
and she was prepared to exploit it by continuing, "I'm sorry,
Your Honour but I'm trying to show that the confession is a
fabrication and, I think, the reply the witness has just given is
an indication of that. I am sure if any one of us was in prison
on a serious charge we would be capable of remembering why
the arresting officer had been to see us and what questions we
had been asked as a consequence."

His Lordship was not the least bit impressed with the
defence, ordering the question, together with the reply, to be
struck from the record. With a rebuke from the Judge she was
allowed to resume her cross-examination.

Miss Yarwood   "Perhaps you can tell the court why you
                  didn't report this alleged confession to the
                  prison authorities? Why on earth didn't you
                  ask any of the warders if you could speak
                  to the prison governor or, failing that, his
                  assistant?"
Chambers   "Well I didn't think I should. I thought it
                  would be better if I spoke to Sergeant West

	and his boss Inspector Taylor."
Miss Yarwood	"Earlier, you told this Court you considered it your public duty to let the authorities know that the person in the next cell had confessed to you that he had committed two murders, didn't you?"
Chambers	"That's correct."
Miss Yarwood	"Then, a few moments later you said, and I quote, 'thieving is one thing but murder, that's ugly, and you never feel safe.' Bearing that in mind and not forgetting your comments casting doubt upon the sanity of the defendant, surely it was in your own interests to ensure that this confession was brought to the attention of the authorities immediately?"
Chambers	"Well that's what I did and why I asked to see the two police officers."
Miss Yarwood	"Well surely that can't be right? Here you are, next door to a crazed killer who has just confessed to you he's committed two murders, yet you can't pass this information to the prison authorities. Are you asking this court to believe you heard this confession and you never considered for a moment that your own life might have been put in jeopardy? That you needed to be moved to a place of safety away from the possible clutches of this maniac?"
Chambers	"I never thought of it like that."
Miss Yarwood	"You never thought of it like that, Chambers, because it never happened as you have testified. Thompson never

confessed to you or anybody else for that matter, and everybody in this court knows it."

Chambers felt the rivulets of sweat running down his back. He knew he was out of his depth here. This was not going according to plan. Despite what he had been told by the police this was anything but easy and, right now, he wanted to be back within the walls of Walton prison enjoying the comforts of his own cell. Fortunately for him his ordeal had now ended and it was a much relieved old lag who stepped down from the dock and into the custody of a warder.

Chambers' testimony was then supported by Detective Inspector Taylor who gave evidence of Thompson's arrest together with confirmation of Thompson's confession. He also confirmed Chambers had given the evidence entirely voluntarily and that he had made no deals with him with regard to his own case when it came to trial."

The Judge signalled this was to be the end of the day's proceedings and the trial was adjourned until the following day.

Michael Mulrooney was waiting for Irene as she came out of the court and she could tell from his expression he had some news for her. Together they made their way to one of the interview rooms set aside for that very purpose. Once inside, Michael told her that the bank details had been faxed to his office. She was not in the least surprised to learn that the murdered girl had very little money in the only account in her name. Indeed it was quite obvious the woman and her associates lived from day-to-day. Banks and saving money played little or no part in their lives. Any money was spent as soon as it was received and it wouldn't go far if you were part of the drug scene. From the bank statements provided, it was all too obvious there was never sufficient cash on hand to allow for the purchase of that damned watch.

The solicitor then confirmed that he had spoken to the watch makers who vouched for the fact that none of their outlets had reported any sales of the same make within the vicinity around the material time. They also confirmed they had been able to account for the purchases of every item, with the exception of one which had been purchased in a London store off Bond Street, some three weeks after the reported death of Angela Clarkson. Armed with that information, Irene Yarwood resolved to recall Bridget Riley to the stand at the earliest available opportunity.

Although the storm was showing some sign of abating as dawn broke over Liverpool the next day, it was still a thoroughly miserable day which greeted citizens and visitors to the city alike. By the time ten o'clock arrived, Judge Ewing had signalled to the court staff, and officials, that he was ready. Proceedings were brought swiftly to order with Detective Sergeant West called to the stand.

Sir Gordon led him through his evidence, which was broadly the same in content to that given by his superior the day before. After eliciting the fact that Chambers had not been offered any deals in return for his evidence, Sir Gordon resumed his seat after stating that he had no further questions.

Yet again there was little relief for the defence as Irene and her team struggled to make any impact on the Sergeant's evidence. Day-by-day as each witness was called by the prosecution, it became apparent that the defence were not making any inroads into the prosecution's case and the strain was beginning to tell upon all concerned. This was no reflection on the team empowered to defend Harry Thompson as it was due entirely to the fact that the evidence presented by the prosecution over the past few days was totally uncorroborated and unsupported. As a result, it proved to be very difficult for the defence team to introduce any challenge.

After another difficult day, Irene and her team, were finally relieved when they heard Sir Gordon Nuttall-Jones advise the court that the prosecution case had been concluded.

<h1 style="text-align:center">Chapter 16</h1>

———

In London, Timothy Harris was feeling pleased with himself as he left the offices of Jerome Woolf and Solomon, solicitors acting for him in his forthcoming divorce action. At this meeting it had been decided that no useful purpose was being served by delaying the institution of divorce proceedings any longer. As he was still very much in the public eye, any action, irrespective of whenever it was brought, was bound to attract more than its share of media attention. It was on this basis his solicitors considered it would be better for the case to go ahead. He had it all worked out in his mind. Tonight, he would take Julie, his parliamentary secretary out for dinner, then, after he'd bedded her he would tell her it was all over. He knew he would have to tell her before news of his impending divorce broke the next day and he would have to be rid of her before he told his wife he wanted a divorce.

In Cheshire, Paula Harris was still deeply troubled. She knew her husband's recent libel case victory was a sham. Although she couldn't prove anything, she knew, without any shadow of a doubt, that he had lied. As a result, two careers had been lost. The life of another person had ended in tragedy and a second person had simply disappeared. She tried to console herself with the thought that, even if she had given evidence against Timothy, the outcome would still have been the same. Now it was time for her to do something about her life and, starting tomorrow, she would take her first tentative steps to trace her first born son. In addition she would speak to Timothy and tell him that, as far as she was concerned, their marriage was over and she wanted a divorce. The gin bottle was handy, and three large gins later, she found her resolve strengthening. She wasn't drunk, she wasn't even merry, she was simply taking charge of her own destiny. She reached for the telephone, talking softly to herself saying, "Sod it and, sod him, the evil little bastard, why should I wait until morning? I'll ring the little shit right now." As she cradled the receiver in her ear, she could hear the telephone ringing. Whilst waiting, she went over the words she wanted to say when the time came. At last the connection was made, and, the receiver was lifted from the hook at the other end.

She got the shock of her life when a she heard the voice of a woman as Julie answered the phone. She recovered from the initial shock with tremendous speed. After all, this was surely the opening she was really hoping for yet another adulterous relationship in their often stormy marriage. At the other end of the line, Julie was also in a state of shock as this dramatic turn of events was something she was totally unprepared for. For the moment, all she could think of was what on earth would Timothy say now? She knew full well he would explode especially since he always insisted she kept well away from the phone. However it was too late for that now and she knew that she had better get rid of this silly, *mithering* bitch before he came out of the bathroom. Recovering slightly and, with the thought rushing through her mind that she and Timothy were now an item, she resolved to get rid of this female tart and any other similar jumped up little farts who caught the eye of Timothy Harris. However, she was brought back to reality as she heard the voice of Paula Harris shrieking down the line, "Get my husband on this telephone immediately and get out of our flat you little prostitute!" Paula stopped midstream as she suddenly realised this was not the way. Yet again this was heaven-sent; it was a golden opportunity too good to miss. In a much more composed and calmer state, she apologised to the person on whom she had been venting her rage and anger. Then, totally in control of her emotions, she requested that, as soon as her errant husband was available, he should return her call in order that they might discuss their impending divorce in a calm and civilised manner. Before she replaced the receiver, she then asked Julie, in a manner which clearly indicated to the recipient that it didn't really matter to her one way or the other, if she would care to reveal her identity. Obviously, it mattered to Julie as she silently replaced the receiver and contemplated her next move.

Timothy came out of the bathroom and Julie could see he was very annoyed. He yelled at her. "How many times have I told you not to answer the telephone in this flat! Just imagine what would happen now if that happened to be my wife! How on earth could I explain your presence here at this time in the early hours of the morning?"

That was as far as he got as Julie angrily retorted, "Well Timothy, I think you'd better sit down because you and I have got something to talk about. That was your wife on the telephone and she wants you to ring her back as soon as possible in order to discuss your divorce in a calm and civilized manner. I suggest you return her call now to see what she has to say for herself. Afterwards perhaps you and I can then discuss our future together. Actually, I think it is all going to turn out fine and, with everything out in the open we can stop all this creeping and pussyfooting around, then get on with our lives together like any other normal happy couple. Let's face it, Timothy, once this is all over and sorted we can get married just as you promised."

"This was news that Timothy did not want nor wish to hear. Paula divorcing him was bad news indeed and he feared it would be even worse if she stated adultery in the grounds of her petition, as it would be a fair bet he would end up liable for all the costs. In a high profile case such as theirs, these costs would be quite considerable without taking into account any financial settlement which might be imposed. Then there was Julie standing here beside him. Bloody stupid Julie who had no idea what this was all about. After one last screw tonight she was supposed to get her marching orders. Yet here she was talking marriage now and all because his divorce was on the cards. One way or another he would have to deal with her first before he made that call to his wife. As he turned to face her, she could see his eyes still blazing with fury as he launched himself into a tirade of anger directed solely at her,

"Julie You just don't understand, do you?" You haven't got the faintest idea what this is all about. For Christ's sake once in a while just think about my position in all this. I can't allow my wife to divorce me because of the effect it will have on my political life and I certainly couldn't allow your name to be dragged through the courts either. I already had it all set up for my wife to receive details of a divorce petition from my solicitors now. Unless I can persuade my wife to back off it doesn't look very likely that will happen. If it did and, if it does, there's a slight chance that it won't generate as much adverse publicity and after a couple of days, it will all die down. In any event don't get carried away into thinking that this clears the way for us to get married because it certainly doesn't. I think the best thing you can do right now is to let me call you a cab and get you off home. After that it would be far better for us not to see each other anymore." Inwardly he was smiling as he spoke. He could see the impact his words were having on Julie as the meaning sunk in and she realised that this was the brush off.

If for one moment, Timothy Harris thought Julie was just going to walk out of the door and out of his life he was very much mistaken. In addition, he had seriously underestimated her character and her strength of resolve, as she hit back at him immediately, "What on earth are you saying? What the bloody hell do you mean? Do you seriously think all you need to say is that it's all over between us and I 'm supposed to get my bleedin' things and walk through the shagging door. Well, let me tell you, Timothy sodding Harris, how frigging wrong you are. First of all, let me tell you once I go through that bleeding door I'll be going straight to the press and I'll soon show you how adverse publicity will affect your political career. By the time I've had my say, you won't have a sodding career worth mentioning, let alone a job in shagging politics. Apart from anything else, your wife will have her adultery petition handed to her on a bleeding plate and I can assure you in no uncertain manner that it won't be my name that will be dragged through the courts, it will be yours. Believe you me, the press will have a bloody field day, especially when they get to know all the sordid details including how you did your best to dump me, knowing only too well that you had got me pregnant. You dirty little piece of useless frigging shite."

Timothy wasn't smiling now. He was trying his best not to panic whilst trying desperately hard to find the right words to say. He had anticipated some kind of reaction but nothing akin to what he had just heard and that last bit, Julie pregnant, Jesus, he knew he would have to handle this situation with extreme care. He knew only too well if she did walk through the door without her thinking the situation had been resolved then, politically, he was as good as dead.

At the moment, she was rushing through the flat like a tornado. Collecting things and shoving items into her bag whilst he followed her from room to room shouting "Julie Julie." Although she heard him it didn't matter for she was determined to get out of the flat as soon and as quickly as possible. In the end he gave up and he positioned himself by the front door in order to stop her from leaving.

A few moments later she came charging through the lounge heading straight for the front door shouting, "Get out of my bloody way, Timothy, I'm leaving. You can have it your way. I realise you are dead right. It is all over now, get out of the way you bastard and let me go."

Timothy stood his ground by the door and, as he opened his mouth to speak, his tone was much softer. There was no trace of anger in his voice. "You are not going anywhere, Julie, not now, not anytime. Obviously, I'd no idea you were pregnant and that changes everything. The first thing you must do is to get yourself to bed and, starting tomorrow and over the next few days, we will sort everything out. I love you Julie and I mean it. I couldn't leave you now and I'm deeply sorry for any pain or hurt I've caused you. I know it's a poor excuse but I've been under a lot of strain these past few months and I'm afraid it's beginning to show. So please let's put this silly quarrel behind us now and sort it out later. Just get yourself to bed and, although it's late, I'll phone home to see what I can sort out there."

Slowly, she allowed her things to slide to the floor then she turned around, and made her way to the bedroom. As she made her way into the bedroom, it was just as well she couldn't see the look on Timothy's face.

He watched her disappear from view and immediately he felt relieved that he'd bought himself some time. How much time he had bought, he could hardly begin to contemplate as, still deep in thought, he began to dial his own home number. As the telephone rang, his mind was plagued with the nagging thought that somehow Julie had to go and, if necessary, the child would have to go with her. The stupid cow, fancy allowing herself to get pregnant!

He heard the sleepy voice of his wife on the other end of the line and he found himself apologising for ringing at whatever unearthly hour was showing on the clock. "I'm just returning your call but, before we go any further, let me put your mind at rest regarding the lady you spoke to earlier. Her name is Julie and, she's my secretary. We've been out for a working meal, and because I have had a number of drinks at various functions throughout the day, she offered to drive me home. That's all there is to it. No hidden romance so please don't go jumping to conclusions. Now about this civilised divorce, I'll go along with that especially since I have already taken steps to start proceedings myself. I know I should have told you earlier so much so, you might even receive some correspondence from a firm of solicitors tomorrow or the day after. Look now listen and please don't get your knickers in a twist. We both know it's all over so, what I'm saying is this. See what the papers say when they arrive and, if you are prepared to go through with it uncontested, then I will pay all the costs. Yes, yes, yours as well, plus any reasonable settlement that we can both agree to. If we do it like this, we can save quite a lot of money on the legal side and, at the end of the day, we both get what we want which is our freedom. Now stop fussing. Let's not start arguing, sleep on it first and think about it. Then we'll talk some more but, remember, if we can't agree on this we're both going to lose out considerably in a financial way." He didn't give her any more time to object or to say anything as he quickly replaced the receiver.

Paula Harris was a little surprised to find the connection broken so abruptly. She felt she had more than adequate grounds for filing for divorce herself which would, if handled properly, result in little or no cost to her but, on reflection provided he kept his word, what the hell did it matter? Right now all that mattered as far as she was concerned was to get the whole thing out of the way. Then she could get on with her own life and take some positive steps to trace her first-born son. The very thought of this, coupled with the excitement it brought within her, ensured a very restless night.

Timothy Harris retired to bed. His mind was no longer preoccupied with the thought of one last screw with Julie, instead, his mind was concentrated on a single thought of how to rid himself of this stupid female and her unborn child.

Chapter 17

Although it had stopped raining, it was still very dull and overcast in Liverpool, and Irene Yarwood shuddered as the thought flashed through her mind it might be an omen. Dismissing such negative thoughts from her mind, she hurried inside the sombre grey building determined that she, and her team, would do everything in their power to defend Harry Thompson and restore his freedom.

Right on time, Judge Ewing settled into his seat and the case for the defence began with Harry Thompson, the accused, taking the stand.

Irene Yarwood had agonized over this moment throughout the trial because, apart from a series of outright denials, the defence had so little to go on. There were no witnesses to either crime. Thompson, her client, had no witnesses to support his alibi and there was nobody who could offer anything in support of his defence. In the end she realised that she had nothing to lose by putting him on the stand. With any luck, she told herself, he might make a more than favourable impression upon the jury.

For both of them it was a triumph. Harry was fully alert giving a first rate performance. His replies to all the questions were clear, concise and, well-directed at the jury. His denials to the crimes were emphatic without being dramatic in any degree. When questioned about his alleged confession, he followed his defence instructions to the letter remaining calm and dignified at all times, so much so Irene reasoned, he came across as a very credible witness. Now it was the turn of the prosecution and the defence could only hold their breath hoping that Harry stood up to his task.

Sir Gordon Nuttall-Jones got to his feet very slowly looking at the accused all the time. Then, he shuffled some of his papers about as if he was becoming nervous but, it wasn't nerves at all on his part. All he wanted to do was to keep Harry waiting as long as possible in an effort to unsettle him. Then it was time to begin and, as he did, his deep, booming voice reverberated around the Court.

"Let me take you back to the time of the disappearance of your fiancée Diane Wilson or, to be more precise, your visit to her parents' home on the first occasion before you went to the police station with your future father-in-law."

In reply to the query, "Do you remember the occasion in question? Harry nodded, and answered, "Yes," wondering where this line was leading as the QC continued, "Will you tell the jury what you said to Mr. Wilson at the time you arrived at the house?"

Thompson   "I honestly can't remember. Presumably, I
                  asked if there was any news about Diane."

The prosecuting counsel paused for a moment before continuing, "No, Thompson that's not true and you damned well know it. As a matter of fact you didn't say anything remotely like that. Would you like me to tell the jury what you said?"

Harry nodded and before he could speak Nuttall-Jones continued, "Is it not a fact, and is it not true that, on this occasion, your words to Mr. Wilson were, "Has she surfaced yet?"

There were gasps from around the court as the impact of the statement registered with those present. Without wishing to lose any momentum from his assault and, ignoring the shouts of objection from the defence, Sir Gordon repeated the question bellowing, "Did you or, did you not, say to Mr.

Wilson, "Has she surfaced yet?"

When Harry confirmed that he had said that or, something very similar, utter pandemonium reigned. It was several moments before the judge could restore order by allowing the defence to object on the grounds that the statement had not been elicited by the prosecution during the examination of the deceased's father at the beginning of the trial.

Before the judge could rule, Sir Gordon was on his feet quickly pointing out that Mr Wilson was still in court and that he could be recalled if necessary, although there did not seem to be much point in it, seeing that the accused had already admitted the statement was true.

With several loud bangs of his gavel, the judge brought order to the proceedings. He solemnly announced that he would allow the testimony to stand and motioned to the prosecution to continue.

Sir Gordon was in his element and he continued to press his advantage for all it was worth saying, "Over the next few months all the country was looking for this poor unfortunate young lady. Only the killer, only the murderer, knew where her body lay. Only one person knew her body had been consigned to the deep waters of the quarry and that person was Harry Thompson, the accused. That is why when he went round on that occasion, he said, "Has she surfaced yet?" He knew very well she had not surfaced. He knew only too well she was hardly likely to be found and he was overconfident and that's when he made his first mistake."

Throughout this tirade Harry Thompson had lost his composure. He brought his fist down repeatedly on the dock rail in front of him whilst he shouted out to no avail that the whole scene and his words had been taken out of context and nothing like that had been intended, let alone implied.

Eventually the scene was over and the defence were

granted a brief recess. During this brief interlude there was no time for recriminations. It was more of an exercise in damage limitation and, although Miss Yarwood was extremely annoyed with recent events in court, she certainly didn't let it show as she explained to Harry that, as soon as the prosecution were through with their cross- examination she would be taking him back through that now crucial part of his evidence in order to impress upon the jury it was, at worst, a completely innocent remark, which unfortunately had potentially disastrous consequences for his case. All too soon it was time for the court to reconvene. Surprisingly enough when they returned to the court the prosecution decided that their cross examination had finished which led the defence to conclude that Sir Gordon did not wish to lose any advantage gained beforehand.

Miss Yarwood rose to continue, "Mr Thompson, during my learned friends cross-examination it was implied, because you used the expression *'has she surfaced yet?'* that you already knew that your girlfriend was dead and you knew where her body had been placed. "Is that true or untrue?"

Thompson.   "Totally untrue, Miss, at that time I had no idea whatsoever what had happened to Diane and I was as anxious as anyone to find her or to discover what had happened to her."

Miss Yarwood. "So in other words you are saying that when you said *'has she surfaced?'* you didn't mean it in that way at all and what you were trying to say was that you were merely enquiring whether or not there was any news or developments in the case?"

Thompson.   "Yes Miss, that's exactly what I meant."

Miss Yarwood   "Now let us be quite clear about this and let us make quite clear that everybody here fully understands that your choice of words was, at worst, most unfortunate as at that time you had no idea she was dead, let alone languishing under water, in a lake, some forty miles away."

Thompson.	"Yes, Miss, that's quite correct."
Miss Yarwood	"Now I will ask you, once again, did you Harry Thompson, kill either of these two women?"
Thompson	"No, I did not and, that's the truth so help me God."

With no further questions Harry Thompson's ordeal was over and it was time to recall Bridget Riley. As the doors opened, all heads turned again to watch Bridget Riley make her entrance. She took her place in the witness box and Miss Yarwood wasted no time in coming straight to the point.

Miss Yarwood.	"Miss Riley, let me remind you that you are still under oath and I have some more questions to put to you. A few days ago, you told this court you had seen Angela Clarkson wearing a very expensive watch which she told you she had bought, and paid for, herself. You also told this court that you didn't know how much she paid for it and you didn't ask her where she bought it."
Bridget	"Yes that's true. I told you all that the other day."
Miss Yarwood	"I must remind you again now, Miss Riley, that you are under oath and there are very serious penalties for those who come before the courts and perjure themselves. I am reminding you of this again because

the defence have discovered that this watch could not have been purchased in Liverpool or Chester, or for that matter, anywhere in the north of England. Therefore, it would have been impossible for your friend to have purchased it herself. Furthermore, I have obtained copies of bank statements of accounts held by Miss Clarkson just prior to her death and she never had sufficient money in her account to withdraw enough funds to pay for such an expensive item of jewellery. According to the manufacturers of this watch, all the items sold have been traced with the exception of one which was purchased for cash in a London store, by an unknown person. This purchase was made a short time after the death of your friend. No doubt, in the fullness of time, the purchaser will be identified, but for the moment it doesn't really matter. What does matter to this court, however, is where your friend obtained her watch, if she ever had one. Miss Riley, I am now putting it to you, once again, that Angela Clarkson never told you that she had bought that watch. I am also putting it to you that you never saw Angela Clarkson wearing that watch or one remotely like it. I am putting it to you that your evidence in this court is nothing but a tissue of lies."

Bridget knew she was in deep trouble over this and she also knew she couldn't afford to admit she had lied. Apart from any perjury charges she would probably have to face, there would be more trouble with Detective Sergeant West once the trial was over. Therefore, she was now faced with a very difficult choice. Either give up and cave in now or stick to her guns and brazen it out.

However, before she could answer, the judge intervened. Taking off his glasses, he leaned across his vast desk then, in a very stern voice he spoke. "I must warn you again, young lady, that the penalties for perjury are quite severe and, in my court, would involve a custodial sentence. Make no mistake I shall not hesitate to bring you back before me if, at some future date, it transpires that you have given false evidence before me in this court. Please think very carefully before you answer the questions put to you by the learned counsel for the defence."

Had the judge not intervened at this point, Bridget would have capitulated and admitted, there and then, that her evidence was false but, once the judge had made his statement, the prospect of prison filled her with alarm and she resolved to give it one last try as she answered, "I am telling you the truth. Angela did tell me that the watch belonged to her. She never told me how much it cost, or how she paid for it. For all I know, when she said she'd bought it, she could well have been lying to me. Well not actually lying but showing off. After all how could I know? All I can tell you is I saw Angela Clarkson wearing the watch a few days before she died and that's the truth."

Noting the shift in the prostitute's evidence, Irene decided there was nothing further to be gained. Suffice to say she had exposed a chink in Bridget's testimony and it would be up to her to exploit it during her summing up. As she prepared to sit down, she advised the judge she had no further questions, and that concluded the case for the defence.

After an early lunch, it was time for the closing statements.

It was the turn of the defence to open and Miss Yarwood made as much as she could of the fact that the DNA sample, although Thompson's, was irrelevant as he had always admitted that he and his girlfriend had sex on their last evening together. Then there was the lack of motive or witnesses to either crime. She made another reference to the DNA sample in the second case which the prosecution had stated and considered to be totally irrelevant, whilst making it all too relevant when applied to the Wilson case. She urged the jury to reject the evidence of Bridget Riley on the grounds that there had been a shift in her evidence when she was recalled and, in her view, she could hardly be called a credible and reliable witness.

Turning to the alleged confession, she pointed out that they, the jury, could hardly take the word of a convicted felon against the word of her client who, up until now, had never even clocked up a ticket for speeding. Throughout her impassioned address, she constantly reminded the jury of the efforts made by Harry Thompson to trace his missing fiancée. Finally, she came to that damning phrase elicited from her client, whilst under cross examination by the crown saying to the jury, "Far from proving his guilt, it only serves to underline the innocence of my client. Think of it this way, if he were guilty of either of these crimes, do you honestly think he would have admitted so readily that he made those remarks?"

"Has she surfaced?" Can you not stop to consider that, if this man was guilty as charged, surely, he would have denied ever making such a statement, knowing full well that it could only be substantiated by the father of the dead girl! In addition, if he were guilty, then such an admission, on his part, could only serve to underline his guilt."

She concluded her submission by asking the jury to find in favour of the accused adding if there was any doubt in their minds, they should return a verdict of 'not guilty.' As she resumed her seat, she nodded to Harry indicating that they had all done their very level best.

Sir Gordon Nuttall-Jones drew himself up to his full height of six foot eight inches. His sheer size, and physical presence, seemed to fill the court as he began. "Ladies and gentlemen of the jury, do not be fooled by the eloquence of the learned counsel for the defence. Throughout this case, we have introduced all the evidence you could possibly wish to hear to show that the person before you is indeed the perpetrator of these terrible crimes. Indeed it is probably a good thing he was caught when he was, because, for all we know, other innocent lives might well have been lost whilst he was still at large. From the time the police discovered the first victim, they only ever considered one man fitted the bill, and that was the person here before you. Remember him, so earnestly pretending to search for his lover. Yet, all the time, he knew she was reposing in that cold, watery grave where he had left her. Why else would he have made that remark to his prospective father-in-law, "Has she surfaced?" Well, I'll tell you. It was because he was the only person on this earth who knew where her body had been left. The defence can say what they like about it simply being an unfortunate phrase, or, choice of words, but you all know better. It was the voice of a guilty man, giving himself away, whilst thinking he had got away with murder. He raised his voice slightly as he added, "and he would have got away with it, had it not been for the intervention of fate."

"Fate played a large part in these trials. After all, was it not fate intervening when Chambers was placed in the cell next door when they were both on remand? Was it coincidence that he confessed to Chambers, or, do you not think he had already tried to confess when he said, "has she surfaced?" The defence has tried to tell you to ignore the evidence of Chambers because he is a convicted felon. Well, why should that make any difference? Why should his word be any less reliable than Thompson's, besides which, for all his criminal activity, he's never been accused of perjury so why on earth should his testimony be ignored?"

"Was it fate that intervened when Thompson found a watch which, to give the man credit, he handed in at his local station, or, was it that he felt that it would be safer to do that, rather than be found in possession of it, if the police came round once the body of Angela Clarkson had been discovered? Was it another turn of fate when one of Angela's friends positively identified the watch as belonging to her, and that she had seen her wearing it before she died. Do not be misled by the defence, making such a play about who had bought it, or, who had paid for it. That is irrelevant. The only fact that matters here is that Bridget Riley has testified that she saw her friend wearing that article shortly before she died. Please do not leave anything else to fate, or chance, return a verdict of guilty on the evidence, and facts, presented before you."

Lord Chief Justice Ewing was waiting with his gavel for the moment when the crown submissions finished. With a swift, sharp knock, he announced a short adjournment to the day's proceedings.

When the court reconvened, Judge Ewing took off his spectacles. He looked earnestly at the jury as he began his summing up. "In this case a number of issues have been raised, and, before you retire to consider your verdict, I think it is incumbent upon me to say a few words about those facts which appear to me to be where you may need a little guidance. First of all, there is the DNA evidence which played a crucial role in the case of the poor Wilson girl. Without that evidence there is no real case against the defendant. With no witnesses the prosecution's case hangs in the balance and you either believe the defendant or you find against him. Counterbalancing this is the evidence of the felon Chambers. As the prosecution pointed out, because he is a convicted thief, that is no reason to assume that his evidence should not be admitted. You have to ask yourself did he stand to gain anything himself by giving this evidence, or, in making it up? The answer to that lies in the testimony of Detective Inspector Taylor who assures this court that there have been no deals made with this witness in order to get him to testify, and I have no reason to doubt that evidence. Now then what of the evidence of the prostitute Riley? Well, there's no doubt that she was well acquainted with the deceased. I subscribe to the view of the prosecution that the purchase of the watch is immaterial. However, it is absolutely crucial that you be satisfied in your own minds that the witness Riley is telling the truth. Be sure of one thing, though, if you are not sure that Riley is telling the truth, then, that link with the defendant is broken, and the case for the prosecution hangs on whether or not you believe the evidence of the witness Chambers, and the alleged confession. In this latter case you also have to be mindful that there is no DNA evidence crucially linking the deceased Clarkson with the defendant. You have to satisfy yourself that the prosecution had no reason to pursue that line of enquiry after eliminating other people from their enquiries."

Finally, and I have left this little bit to the end quite deliberately, you have to ask yourselves, was it just a slip of the tongue, or an unfortunate choice of words that led the defendant to utter those words, *"Has she surfaced yet?"* If you are satisfied that the defendant was simply asking whether or not his girl friend had turned up, and whether or not there had been any developments in the case, then dismiss that piece of evidence from your deliberations. But, on the other hand, if you think the defendant is guilty, then, I myself would consider that choice of words to be very damning indeed, bearing in mind, his choice of grave for her, and, the fact that only the real killer knew she had been dispatched to such a lonely and watery grave."

With the Judge's summing up duly completed, the jurors were dispatched to a place of security and the court adjourned to await the verdict.

The following day, after deliberating for just over three hours, a message was delivered to the court that a verdict had been reached and the jury were returning to the court. Although there was a deathly hush descending on the court there still existed a general feeling of excitement as the jury filed in.

The Clerk to the court rose and asked the jury foreman if a verdict had been reached in the case of the Crown v Thompson and the foreman indicated that they had.

The clerk then asked the same question in connection with the Clarkson case and again the answer was affirmative.

By now the atmosphere was intense as the foreman was asked,

"Do you find the defendant guilty, or not guilty, of the murder of Diane Wilson?" In a low voice he answered, "Guilty."

The clerk continued, without any trace of emotion, "Do you find the defendant guilty, or not guilty, of the murder of Angela Clarkson?" And again the foreman replied, "Guilty."

The Lord Chief Justice banged down his gavel repeatedly in a desperate bid to restore order, and, eventually, the noise subsided as he delivered his sentence. "Harry Marcus Thompson, you have been found guilty of the murders of two young women. Have you anything to say before I pass sentence upon you?"

Harry was standing now. He looked grey faced as he stood before the judge and mumbled, "All I can say is that there has been a terrible mistake, and I did not commit either of these crimes."

The judge was suitably unimpressed as he addressed him once more.

"Quite rightly, in my view, you have been found guilty on two counts of murder by a court of your peers, and I sentence you to two terms of life imprisonment. I also authorise that you serve at least twenty years in prison. Then, with a loud bang of his gavel, he gave the order, "take him down," and the whole procedure was over.

Irene and her team hurried out of court and down below in order to spend as much time as possible with Harry before he was taken away.

Chapter 18

Below the courts it was bedlam. Everybody appeared to be shouting at each other and the officials were trying to hustle Harry Thompson away whilst the defence team were arguing for a few moments' delay. During the ensuing mêlée it was finally decided that his departure would be delayed by fifteen minutes to allow his defence team time to brief him on their plans for launching an appeal at the earliest opportunity.

Harry Thompson was in a deep sense of shock. The trial itself had been an ordeal, but now, with a guilty verdict, and a sentence of twenty years minimum hanging over him, it still hadn't fully sunk in. Irene and Michael kept trying to reassure him they would leave no stone unturned in their efforts to free him, but, nothing seemed to register with him. Although he had made a specific request before the verdict was delivered that he did not wish to see his adoptive mother if he was found guilty, Irene and Michael had ignored his plea, and now she was standing in the small room provided for them. Although he was handcuffed to a warder, and there was another warder present, both Harry and his adoptive mother were crying unashamedly. For a moment, there was nothing either person could say, they were both too upset. Harry felt the heavy hand of the warder on his shoulder, and a voice telling him it was time to go. They had moved away from the interview room provided, leaving Sally behind. Knowing there was little time left he began to issue instructions to his lawyers saying, "Please come and see me as soon as you possibly can. Please ensure that Sally never comes anywhere near the prison. I can't bear the thought of her having to endure that indignity. I've told her I'll write to

door, then she walked straight in.

Facing her was a varnished wooden partition containing a glass window. As she closed the door behind her, she could she a woman walking towards the door directly in front of her. As this door opened, a smartly dressed lady in a matron's uniform quickly introduced herself.

"Hello my name is Edith Farrell and I'm the matron in charge. You must be Mrs Harris. Please, do come in." Showing the way to Paula, Matron Farrell urged her visitor to sit down whilst she arranged refreshments.

Edith Farrell was a typical matron. Like most matrons she had a large round figure, but, she had a most warm, and welcoming, smile. Within minutes she was back with a tray of tea. Once the tea had been poured, Mrs Farrell got straight down to business. "We always ask people, who are tracing offspring, or offspring who are tracing parents, to come down here first. This is not a vetting procedure in any way; it's just that we feel we need to see the people concerned in order to explain to them, face-to-face, what happens next, and how our enquiries are conducted. In addition, we always have to point out not all people wish to be traced. Indeed, we find some people quite resent the fact that they have been adopted, and, in some cases, some children do not get told they have been adopted, so we have to tread very warily at all times. I'm sure you will understand. When you've finished your tea, I'll take down all your details, then you'll have to leave things in our hands. We will then contact the people who adopted your child. Whenever we make these enquiries, we always endeavour to be as discreet as possible, but you must understand that, if your child doesn't wish to make contact, there is nothing we can do in those circumstances, and we certainly cannot divulge any information to anybody."

Although Paula nodded in agreement with this, she was

praying desperately that this would not happen to her.

All too soon, the formalities were completed, and the interview was over. Paula began to descend the depressingly dark staircase, still in a state of excitement, but, with her mind focusing on what developments might lie ahead.

It was six months since the trial, and, it was old news, apart from the fact that Harry Thompson was on hunger strike, and Royston Chambers was just leaving court after being sentenced to five years' imprisonment. Royston Chambers heard his sentence with a sense of alarm, and foreboding, which only increased when he heard that he was being sent to Stafford prison. As he listened to his defence lawyer, Peter Ravenscroft QC telling him he would definitely get his sentence reduced on appeal, his mind was elsewhere. Two years would have been bad enough, especially when he was expecting a minimal custodial sentence, bearing in mind his evidence for the prosecution in the Thompson case, but he had been relying upon Detective Sergeant West to put in a good word for him at his trial, and, for some unknown reason, the detective failed to turn up. Apart from this, Stafford prison was the last place on earth he wanted to serve his time, due to the fact there were at least two people doing time in there who would be very interested in his arrival. As a result, he knew he could anticipate quite a period of time in the sick bay. As he addressed his lawyer he was very agitated saying, "whatever happens, when you get this appeal, you make sure that bent copper is in court. Thanks to that bastard not turning up, I've got to serve five years, in bleeding Stafford of all places, and the chances are I won't survive five frigging weeks. You just make sure that you talk to him and tell him, in no uncertain manner, he owes me and, if he doesn't deliver this time, I'll grass him up. You just be sure to tell him that! I'll withdraw every word of that confession, and I'll tell the press it was all a load of lies, and, bollocks. Ignoring his lawyer's plea for restraint, he continued, "Tell him, and his boss, that I know they were the ones responsible for it, and I don't care who I upset now. Make sure he knows this, and you make certain you speak to the bastard straight away, because if you don't I'll just have to get myself another brief, and the lady I have in mind, will do very nicely indeed, plus she'll be over the bloody moon when she hears what I have to say."

That was as far as he got as the warders appeared on the scene, and he was quickly bundled out of the building, and into the transport which awaited him.

Although quite accustomed to dealing with people from all walks of life, Peter Ravenscroft was still taken aback, not by the outburst, but the information it contained. He knew he was duty bound to lodge an appeal on behalf of his client, but he could hardly go marching into the Merseyside police HQ and threaten anybody, let alone a detective sergeant or his boss, that unless he was prepared to give some support to the appeal cause, the shit was going to hit the fan. Already, a plan was formulating in his brain, which might ensure the presence of the policeman in court, but whether that, alone, would do his client any good was a matter of sheer conjecture and speculation. However, if he gave up the case to another QC, then perhaps, the interests of justice would be better served. Besides which, that would resolve his difficulty concerning the information Royston Chambers had just imparted. This would certainly be in better hands if a certain Irene Yarwood was informed. On his journey back to the office, he resolved to telephone her without delay in order to set up a meeting.

Irene Yarwood sat in the sparsely furnished prison interview room facing Harry Thompson, who had just entered the room accompanied by a warder who then remained by the door. With a curt, "Hello," she opened the interview and, without waiting for a reply, continued, "Harry I have come to see you about your appeal, and, quite frankly, this hunger strike of yours isn't going to help either of us."

She held up her hand to stop him interrupting, saying, "If we can get an appeal hearing what will be the point if you are at death's door? I know I can't order you to stop it, all I can do is ask you to help me to help you." She held her hand up again, because she was in no mood for any interruptions until she finished what she wanted to say. "I also have a message for you from your mother, Sally. She says she is desperate to come and see you, and she wants you to reconsider your decision not to allow her to visit. She noted with interest the change in him at the mention of this, but, before he could reply, she had resumed again, "Let me finish please, then, I'll listen to you. Now, about your appeal. I think we have a very good chance of getting an appeal hearing, but I'm going to try to arrange for your appeals to be heard separately. This way I think we might stand a better chance on the basis of, if the verdict in one case can be overturned, then the other case could be weakened quite considerably, and the second verdict might even be considered unsafe. What do you think about that then?"

Harry sat for a moment before replying, "About the appeal, I'm in your hands there, and I can only be advised by yourself. If you think that's the way forward then, so be it. Regarding myself, I appreciate what you say, but at the end of the day, I'm the person incarcerated here for crimes I didn't commit and, immediately after I was convicted, I resolved to make life difficult for any person in here that I came into contact with. I know I am suffering too as a result, but I'm also suffering as a result of being here, and it may well be that I will achieve as much satisfaction by adopting an approach of non-cooperation, but please leave that to me. Just get me those appeals, and get me out of here. Regarding my mother, Sally, please tell her I really do know what she is going through, and how much she is suffering, but I can't face her coming down here and seeing me in this stinking hole. Please ask her to wait a while longer whilst I see if I can come to terms with the situation myself. If I can, well, who knows? I'll tell you what, ask her to wait until the appeal date has been fixed, then I'll see if I can reconsider. One thing you can tell her though concerns a letter she sent me which she had received from an adoption society in Manchester. Apparently, my real birth mother wishes to make contact with me. I think it's quite ironic, because this was something we had discussed before the case, and it was something I would have liked to pursue, but, under the circumstances, not now. So tell her that I will write myself telling them not to bother."

Straight away, Irene saw this might be just the opening needed to lift the flagging spirits of her client as she countered, "No Harry. I think that could be a mistake. Why don't you write? Say you would desperately like to meet her, but also tell her you can't meet due to your present circumstances. Tell her exactly what those circumstances are, and then she can judge for herself. Don't forget to tell her you are not guilty, and you are going to appeal. This way, it might give you, and your adoptive mother, a little bit of something to cling to."

"Yes," said Harry. "That's a thought, although, I doubt if it will do any good especially with me in here."

Irene stood up to indicate to the waiting observer that the meeting was coming to an end, and, as they parted with a wave, she thought she glimpsed the briefest of smiles cross his face. When she returned to her office in Manchester she found a number of messages waiting for her. One message in particular caught her attention; it was from a fellow QC requesting a meeting for lunch where she would receive important information concerning her client, Harry Thompson. More than intrigued by this message, she dialled the number given, and she soon found herself connected and talking to Peter

Ravenscroft QC. Within minutes she had agreed a time for lunch at the Wig and Gown, a local pub frequented by members of the legal profession. Peter Ravenscroft imparted no useful information during this conversation. As a consequence, she found herself in a quandary regarding the value of any information he might have, and where on earth it could have come from.

She saw him the instant she entered the bar, which was beginning to fill up rapidly, and by the time she reached him he had already secured the drinks. He motioned to a table where they quickly sat down. Without waiting he began, "Just listen to what I have to say, then, after we have had a sandwich or two, I'll let you decide where we go from here. I've just defended a client who figured prominently in your recent murder trial. Yes, you're so right, Royston Chambers, none other. Well, to keep matters short and simple, I couldn't get him off, and he ended up with a five year stretch which caused him a considerable amount of annoyance as he was under the impression that a certain detective sergeant was going to plead on his behalf for a very lenient sentence, taking into account his evidence against your client Thompson. As the detective did not appear, Chambers is firmly convinced that five years is far too long, and the copper has reneged on his promise. As a result, Chambers is now threatening that, if he does not make an effort on his behalf when his appeal comes up, then he's going to announce to the press, not only was his evidence totally false, but it was all set up with the connivance of Detective Sergeant West, and his boss Detective Inspector Peter Taylor.

To Irene, this was earth shattering news, and, if it was true, then at a stroke the evidence against her client in the Clarkson case could be almost wiped out. The fact that there was still the evidence of the prostitute Bridget Riley was of no consequence, because Irene knew that her evidence was a tissue of lies, and armed with this new evidence in court, she was certain she would be able to break her down once she had her in the box again. She could hardly contain herself, and lunch was almost forgotten in the excitement of the moment. "How did all this materialise, Peter, and where does it leave us?"

Peter Ravenscroft thought for a moment before replying, "By allowing you to become his brief, and letting you take the matter from there. I must stress that before he was taken off into custody he was already saying that he had a good QC in mind if I failed to deliver, and I can only assume this was a direct reference to you, so getting yourself appointed shouldn't be too difficult. The main stumbling block here is any part the police may have played in ensuring your client was convicted. Because of this, I'd like to see if I can get some cooperation from Detective Sergeant West when I apply for an appeal for Chambers. The way I see it is, if the detective does give his backing and support to Chambers, it's not going to make the slightest difference. You see, my client is absolutely adamant on this, whether the support is there or not, he is still going to cause trouble. This is because he maintains that he was as good as promised he wouldn't get a custodial sentence for his offence if he supplied the goods against your client, and he certainly did that didn't he?"

Irene thought for a moment before replying, "Yes, he certainly did that. If what you're saying is true, surely if you apply for the appeal and the police appear as requested, he gets out a lot sooner, then presumably, he's still going to come over to our side, because he's continuing to be upset about the police stitching him up. Alternatively, if the appeal fails, he comes over anyway doesn't he?"

"Well that's the chance. Just suppose he wins his appeal, and he does get out how does anybody know he'll do what he says? After all, once he's out, it's a different ball game. Right now, I think I have to proceed with his appeal against sentence and, before the actual hearing, let's just see whether or not things have fallen into place. Once I've done that, we can have a little conference, and who knows we may decide to get the court to order Sergeant West to attend."

With all kinds of possibilities flying through her mind, Irene agreed with the proposal, and vowed to make another visit to Harry in Strangeways Gaol. They shook hands, making a promise to keep in constant touch in order to monitor future developments.

For the next few days, the information she had received dominated the thoughts in her mind. Even at night, she found it difficult to dismiss the case from her mind. As a result sleep was very difficult to come by. All the time, she kept wrestling with the problem of how to proceed with Harry's appeal in the Wilson case. She knew the evidence was circumstantial, and the prosecution had relied on the DNA tests together with the confession. Now, with only the DNA evidence, it left the conviction looking far less safe, but to her it still left that nagging doubt as to whether it would be sufficient to convince the appeal court judges. Over and over again, she told herself there was something else, another way. There just had to be, but what on earth was it? In an effort to resolve the matter, the cases had even been discussed in chambers, but so far she and the other partners had all drawn a blank. During these discussions, her colleagues had been fully supportive of her in connection with the Clarkson case, and they were all of the opinion that, without the confession, that case all but fell apart, provided the defence had Chambers on board.

After another troubled night, she was preparing herself for work. As usual, the radio was playing on the customary Radio 2 station when she heard an announcement concerning the case of Edwin Hurst, due before the European Courts later that day. Although she did not hear the announcement in full, nevertheless, the part she did hear was sufficient to set her pulse racing. Apparently, Edwin Hurst had been arrested by the police in Birmingham, and he'd been convicted and sentenced to a period of imprisonment. However, the most important part, as far as Irene was concerned, related to his appeal being heard in The Hague on the grounds that, under Article Six of The European Convention, his human rights had been abused when he was denied his right to silence when he was charged. The moment she heard that snatch of the bulletin she had an idea that this case might throw up something which could possibly affect the verdict in the Wilson case, and she resolved to arrange to have all the relevant details of the case faxed to her chambers as soon as possible after the verdict.

In turn, this led her thoughts to the Clarkson case and, more importantly, to the procedure to be adopted. She was now aware, with confirmation that the confession was false, that she wasn't really in a position to take over from Peter Ravenscroft QC as this might later be construed that there was a conflict of interests.

As she climbed into her car to make the journey to the prison, she decided that, when she returned to her office, she would contact Peter and ask him to keep the case, and when he next saw Chambers he should tell him in no uncertain manner, that, if he was to persist in his chosen line of defence, he was almost certainly facing a longer term of imprisonment if he was then found guilty of perjury. Before setting off, she made a note to remind herself that the best way forward would be to get Chambers on their side for Thompson's Appeal. Then, after admitting his trial evidence was false, it might be possible to get the courts to view his case with a greater degree of sympathy, should it then be shown he had been coerced into lying by the police. In addition, if it was possible to use the same approach with Bridget Riley, then things would look decidedly better. She made another note to contact Michael Mulrooney in order to ask him to initiate discreet enquiries amongst Bridget Riley's fellow prostitutes to see whether any of them had been approached by the police to provide information to assist the police in their earlier investigations into the Clarkson case.

She started the car and made her way to the office. During the journey, she found it difficult to concentrate due to the constant stream of thoughts and ideas whirling around in her brain. With a minimum of time, she had completed all her tasks and she was soon making her way out of Manchester heading for Strangeways Prison.

Once again, she was in the same dingy prison interview room waiting for Harry to arrive. She didn't have to wait very long before he appeared, and she began as soon as he sat down. "Please sit down," she said quietly. This is simply a quick visit to let you know how things are going right now. First of all, there is a case before the European Courts today concerning human rights violations. Once the verdict has been reached, it's possible that the fall-out from it could affect your verdict in the Wilson case. Secondly, and you must keep this strictly to yourself, we may have a chance to prove that the evidence of Chambers was nothing but a tissue of lies. Now please, don't run away from here thinking all you have to do is appear in court, and this nightmare is over, because, it doesn't work like that at all. Behind the scenes, there's a lot of work to be done, and I wanted you to get this information first hand so that you know we are all still trying to do our bit. Once we get all the pieces in place, we'll arrange for the Clarkson case to be appealed first. Everybody is confident this is really winnable now, especially taking into account the new developments. Afterwards, and if the case before The Hague bears fruit, we'll go through the same procedure after exhausting all possibilities here. In effect Harry, what I'm saying to you is this. If I can find any evidence to show that, during your trial in the Wilson case, your human rights were abused, then the verdict can be overturned and the conviction quashed. This means that you would be free! What do you say to that then?"

Irene sat back, feeling elated. She thought she was beginning to see a glimmer of light at the end of the tunnel. However, she was totally unprepared for Harry's response.

"Well actually I do not like it. You see, first of all the Clarkson case is quite all right because I can see that I might be found not guilty, but this other case that procedure leaves me cold. What you are saying to me is that you might be able to engineer my release on a technicality. Well, I don't want that, and I'll tell you why. If you pursue that line and I get out, I'll always be known, and pointed out, as the man who got away with murder. Quite frankly, I couldn't live with that. I don't want you to think I'm ungrateful for everything you, and the team, are doing for me, but please don't just consider my feelings. At the same time, consider the feelings of Mr. and Mrs. Wilson. How do you think they will feel if they saw me walking out of here on a technicality?"

His statement completely deflated Irene. Whereas she had confidently expected to see some sign of hope from him, there was nothing. She said quietly, "Very well if that's your decision I'll respect it, but you must realise that, at the end of the day, it may prove to be your only way out of here, so, please bear it in mind and give it some thought in the future won't you?"

Harry nodded then added, "I took your advice about the adoption society. I've written to them to say I would like to meet my real birth mother, but I've also told them they must tell her who I am, and exactly what I am doing in here. By doing it this way, she has a choice, either to get in touch or leave me out of her life altogether. Naturally, I have told her

about Sally, my adoptive mother, and I've also told her about
trying to get my case reheard, so now we shall have to wait and
see what happens."

With the meeting over they went their separate ways.

Chapter 19

Paula Harris alighted from the Taxi outside the offices of the Manchester and District Children's Adoption Society. Her hands shook with excitement as she paid the fare, and, as the cab sped off, she took another look at the drab façade and peeling paintwork of the building. Before going inside, she took out the letter she had received from the society, and she checked the date before reading the contents for the fiftieth time to make certain she was in the right place at the right time. As each measured step took her into the building, she could feel the tension mounting within her. Already, the questions were flooding her brain. Has my son said he will meet me? If so, where, and more importantly, when? Where on earth is he living? What does he do? Is he married? Has he any children, and if so how many? What will he say when he knows he has a brother? Then again, the haunting doubts. What will I do if the answer's no? Will they let me write to him if only to explain? As each step took her up toward the offices she had visited a few short weeks ago she stopped, aware that the excitement of the moment was getting to her. Her heart was pounding, and her breathing was coming in short sharp gasps. She stopped again for another brief pause, during which she urged herself to show a little self restraint. Then, she was at the doorway entrance. Another very brief stop for breath, she pressed the bell, and entered.

With a flourish, the yellowing window panel was thrust back to reveal the smiling features of the Matron, Edith Farrell. She recognised Paula at once from their previous encounter, and she immediately opened the door saying, "Please do come in

Mrs. Harris, and take a seat whilst I arrange for a pot of tea. It's so nice to see you again. Now please sit down, and make yourself comfortable. I really won't keep you a moment. Paula sat down as instructed, her thoughts raced through her brain, telling her it was going to be all right. It must be. That's why she's making the tea. It's good news; I know it is, otherwise they wouldn't bother. Within a few minutes, Edith Farrell was back with a tray containing a pot of tea and two cups. Do hurry up, Paula silently pleaded, as it seemed to take an age before the hot steaming liquid was poured, and placed in front of her, together with a plate of biscuits. She lifted the cup to her lips whilst the matron began talking, "as promised we contacted your son by letter. He has replied, and that's why we've asked you to come down here today. You do understand we have to guard against every eventuality, and we ask everybody to come whether the response is favourable or not. Anyway, as I just said, your son has replied, and he has asked us to give you this letter. As she passed the three sheets of prison paper over for Paula to read, Edith Farrell could see she was shaking like a leaf. Nevertheless, she carried on talking by saying, "Your son has insisted we give you this letter to read before we proceed any further, and once you have read it, I'm sure you will understand why."

That was as far as she got. Throughout the Matron's commentary Paula had been furiously scanning the pages, and she began to stand up as the implications of the contents began to sink in. With a cry, which sounded more like a sigh, she fell across the table, sending the contents flying in all directions, as she suffered a massive stroke to her right hand side which rendered her unconscious, blind, and almost, completely paralysed.

The Matron summoned an ambulance, and made Paula as comfortable as possible, pending her transfer to the hospital across the busy Manchester city streets. From today, she would only be able to move the little finger on her right hand and, although she would be able to hear events going on around her, she would not be able to see. Over the ensuing weeks, and months, she would endure many agonising moments, as she desperately tried to come to terms with her illness, and the almost certain knowledge that she would never physically see either of her sons again.

The news of the massive stroke suffered by his wife was relayed to Timothy in the Commons tea bar, and he made arrangements to leave for Manchester as soon as possible. Messages of condolence came flooding in from all parties, and he acknowledged them all with as much grace as he could muster, although deep down he was cursing the fact that, somehow, she had survived. As far as he was concerned, it would have been a lot better, and far easier for him, if she had died. That way, there would be no divorce, he would be even more secure financially, and he could devote more time to Julie, his pregnant mistress, and the problems her presence was causing. As he settled into his seat on the plane, he was still deep in thought about the inconvenience his wife's illness was likely to cause him. He decided that, when he saw the doctor in charge at the hospital, he would ask how long she would be kept alive on the life support system.

Later that evening, Paula was visited by her husband Timothy. Doctor Peter Woods was still on duty when he arrived, and he told Timothy the same bleak prognosis, after which they entered the ward occupied solely by his wife. To the doctor, he was kindness personified, but to Timothy it was all an act, and he found himself wishing it was all over. For his wife, although no one could see it, it was an ordeal, especially since she did not want him near her. Eventually, Doctor Woods led him away to his office where they could talk more privately.

"Tell me doctor, if things are as bad as you say, is there any point in keeping my wife alive? Surely, it would be far kinder to switch everything off now?" Timothy sat back in his chair whilst he waited for the doctor's reply.

Peter Woods was taken aback by the question, and although he knew the decision would have to be made at some time, he was shocked that Timothy had broached the question so soon. Giving the man the benefit of the doubt, and assuming he was tired after his long journey, he answered, "Sometimes miracles do happen, and it's early days yet. Besides, as far as we can ascertain, your wife isn't in too much pain, or discomfort, because she is almost completely paralysed. Consequently, she is devoid of feeling in all her limbs. Rest assured, we'll monitor the situation carefully and review everything on a daily basis. Obviously, we'll keep you informed of any developments.

This reply didn't satisfy Timothy and he put his cards straight on the table saying, "It's all very well for you to say that doctor, but how do you know that she isn't suffering when she can't communicate? Also, I think you should consider my feelings in this matter. How do you think I feel coming in here, seeing my wife in this state? I'm telling you straight, I don't like it, and I won't allow this state of affairs to continue for too long. If there's no improvement soon, I'll be asking you to remove any support systems that are being used to keep her alive. Do you understand?"

Doctor Woods had now taken a firm dislike to Timothy. There and then, he decided and resolved that he would do his utmost for his charge.

Irene had finally arrived home, but the day was far from over. First of all, she telephoned Peter Ravenscroft to see if he had made any progress with Royston Chambers and the police involvement. She was surprised to learn from him, following his own visit to Stafford prison, that Chambers was now prepared to sit it out and take his chance, rather than risk any sentence increase on charges of perjury. What Chambers had not told his lawyer was that he had received a cell visit from one of his fellow inmates, who told him, in no uncertain manner, he would never walk out of prison if he tried to make trouble for a certain detective.

Next she telephoned Michael Mulrooney, her able defence solicitor. When he answered, Irene said she had a job for him, and she proceeded to outline the most recent developments in the case, including the latest admission from Chambers. Irene wanted Michael's help locating friends and associates of Angela Clarkson and Bridget Riley in order to seek additional information about the watch. She also wanted to ascertain whether the police, or Detective Sergeant West in particular, had tried to put pressure upon them in order to obtain evidence. She knew it was a long shot, but she reasoned that, if this had happened, perhaps one of the girls would talk about it. Given the right result, this could provide the ammunition to shoot down Bridget Riley when the time came.

Michael readily agreed to assist and promised to set about it straight away. Before the conversation ended, he enquired if she had heard the news about Paula Harris suffering a massive stroke whilst visiting the offices of the Manchester and District Children's Adoption Society. Irene replied that she hadn't heard the news, and asked Michael why he thought it relevant. She wasn't prepared for the reply. It was perhaps as well she was sitting down as he explained that Paula Harris, the lady in question, was the wife of Timothy Harris, the errant MP who had been the subject of so much rumour and speculation recently.

"Christ, Michael," Irene exclaimed, "This is a whole new ball game now. Something tells me Paula Harris is the real mother of Harry Thompson. Please don't quote me on this yet until I have it confirmed, and even if it does prove true we should still keep this strictly to ourselves, or until such time as we are in court winning our case."

Irene's brain was in overdrive as she thoughtfully added, "One more thing Michael, I think I might even be way ahead of you on this one. As you know, before these cases came to court, all kinds of rumours were circulating that Timothy Harris and the Merseyside police had engineered a cover up in the Clarkson case. In fact, I think it went a little further than that, as I'm almost sure they said a man, not named, had been exonerated from their enquiries. I'll bet you a case of vintage champagne that the person exonerated was none other than Timothy Harris. The picture is beginning to get a lot clearer now, because, if they had named him, it would have probably come out that he was one of her customers, and in all probability he was her client and that he gave her the watch. Now then, Michael, prepare yourself for the big one. I'll bet you another case of champagne that Timothy Harris bought Angela Clarkson that watch. You see, it all fits. It has to be him, and although it doesn't prove that he had anything to do with her death, it certainly puts him right in the frame. She could feel the excitement mounting within her as she continued, "Assume Harris was her last client, also assume that he doesn't kill her. Then the police are looking for a killer and, without the watch, they have no leads. Even when the watch is found, they have nothing on Harry, until that prostitute comes along to say that the watch is Clarkson's. Michael, I'm telling you now, it stinks. Remember, at the time the watchmakers themselves could supply proof of purchase of all the watches sold then with the exception of one, and even in that case they know that it was not purchased anywhere in the north of England.

"I think we'll have to tread very carefully on this now, and concentrate on getting all the information in before we make any moves at all. When we do Michael, boy, will the shit hit the fan, because there's another aspect to this which disturbs me now more than ever. If what we have just discussed is subsequently proved to be true, then Timothy Harris perjured himself in his recent libel action. See what you can dig out from Clarkson's associates, and be very careful, Michael, because something like this could turn out very nasty. As soon as you get something give me a ring, and we'll meet for a chat somewhere. Ok?"

Michael confirmed his agreement, and replaced the telephone having already decided that tonight he would start to look for information.

Later that evening, Michael could be observed walking along Rodney Street in Liverpool. He had taken the precaution of notifying a contact within the Merseyside Police that he was going to be in the area, and the exact nature of his business. He was well aware that the police had tightened up considerably on kerb crawlers, and their like but tonight there didn't seem anything to worry about as there were no girls out. He walked straight on to the "Hookers". He spotted Bridget immediately, then he saw Theresa standing alone at the bar. He edged his way to the bar, and obtained a spot next to her. As the barman placed her order on the bar he swiftly placed a ten pound note on the counter saying, "Let me get those Theresa," and whilst he waited for his change he whispered, "can we talk somewhere quiet? I need some information, and I am quite willing to pay for your time." As the barman returned with his change, he collected it and slipped one of his business cards to her saying, "I'll wait here, and I'll have a drink while you think about it."

He didn't have time to finish his drink before she was back at the bar saying, "Let's take a quick walk and I will see if I can help you, but it'll cost you. Twenty-five," she said smiling at him, "that alright?" He nodded in reply, and they left the bar.

Once outside he told her, "I'm the solicitor who represented Harry Thompson, the man who was convicted of the murder of your colleague Angela Clarkson. We all know that your friend gave evidence, and I'm wondering if your friend was told what to say by the police. We also know the confession produced in court was false, and, without these two pieces of evidence, there is no case against our client. Now I'm sure you want to punish the guilty person, but I'm equally certain you don't wish to see an innocent man punished for a crime he did not commit. I am now asking you to tell me, did you ever see your friend Angela Clarkson wearing that watch? Or did she ever tell you that she had been given a watch, or even bought a watch of that description, before she died?"

Theresa became very nervous before answering, "I don't know anything about that. You will have to ask Bridget about that. After all, she was the one who gave the evidence why don't you ask her? Leave me out of it; I don't want to get involved."

Michael tried a different approach, "Look I am not here to cause trouble for Bridget, but if I can find evidence that she was forced into giving false evidence by the police, she will have nothing to be afraid of. But first, before I can do that, I have to know if the police tried to get anybody else to testify besides Bridget, plus, I need to know whether, or not, you saw Angela with the watch."

Theresa was extremely nervous, she kept looking up and down the deserted street then she said, in a voice barely above a whisper, "I can't tell you anything, do you understand? If you want to know anything ask Bridget, she was the one who testified, not me. Go and ask her, not me, do you hear me?"

She turned and started walking hurriedly away. Although she heard his last question, "Is it because you are afraid?" she chose to ignore it as she strode off into the night cursing him, and that bloody Bridget, for getting her into this mess. Whilst walking away she determined she would sort out Bridget, the stupid cow, for getting everybody involved.

Michael walked slowly back to his car. He didn't consider the evening's excitement a total failure. Theresa's reluctance to answer any questions regarding the matter only confirmed his suspicions she had never seen the watch before, and neither had Bridget. Sooner or later, he knew the truth would come out. It was only a matter of time and patience.

After Timothy returned to London, he was soon under pressure from Julie. She couldn't understand why they didn't make the most of the opportunity to live together. She couldn't see the point in delaying matters especially if his wife stood no chance of getting better. As a result, Timothy was seeing things from a very different perspective, and as much as he reasoned with her, it was increasingly obvious she was becoming a pain in the backside. One way or another, she had to be dealt with, and it had to be soon. The opportunity came when it was least expected. One of her friends was having a party in a local club and Julie asked Timothy to go with her. During this conversation, she declined to mention that she had had an abortion, thinking, if she could get him in the right frame of mind at the party, they might get round to discussing marriage again. With an unwanted child out of the way, she thought he might adopt a more reasonable attitude.

Normally, Timothy would have declined invitations of this nature, but on this occasion he said he would be pleased to attend. In his mind though, he thought it might just present the opportunity he was looking for. Then, with any luck, it might be 'goodbye Julie.' When the evening arrived, he telephoned Julie in order to tell her that some last minute Commons business had turned up. There was no alternative, she would have to go alone and he would join her later. Naturally, she protested, but it was to no avail. He knew he could not take a chance on arriving at the party with her that would leave them both open to idle gossip; besides, his plan would work better if they arrived, and left, alone.

He arrived about ten, and she spotted him coming through the crowd. After a couple of introductions, they detached themselves from the crowd, and he went to the bar where he obtained drinks for them both. His drink, by choice, was a simple bottle of tonic. Tonight was not a night for alcohol as, unseen by anyone, he slipped the ecstasy tablet into Julie's drink and he returned to the table where they were joined by a group of friends. After a suitable period of time spent mixing with various groups of people, he felt it was time to ask Julie for a dance. During the dance, he whispered that he would have to be going shortly, and she would have to go home to her own flat. Naturally, he told her he was very sorry, and he would make it up to her very soon. Shrugging aside all her protestations, and completely ignoring the fact that she had something important to tell him, he said his farewells and retired from the scene, trusting that, if the drug did its job, then his problems would disappear overnight.

Sadly, Julie watched him leave the club. She berated herself for not telling him she had aborted his child. She had only taken this step because, she realised, it would be better for her, and certainly better for Timothy, if they did not have the problems that a child would bring, especially when a high profile figure such as Timothy was involved. By taking this drastic step, the pair of them would avoid most of the unwanted publicity when news of their affair became public, and they either set up home together, or, if it became possible, they eventually married. After watching him leave, she went back to her friends to continue partying.

It was the incessant telephone bell which woke him from

his drunken slumber. He had hit the bottle hard when he got home, and when he came to, he found that he was still almost fully dressed even though he was actually in bed. He groped wildly for the light switch, then the phone rang again, "Hello. Hello who is it. Recognising the voice of one of the party whips, he began to sober up rapidly as the voice informed him that his parliamentary secretary had collapsed at a party, and she had been rushed to hospital in a deep coma as the result of a suspected drug overdose.

He was sobering up very quickly indeed, and making all the right noises, as if to show that he was genuinely concerned for her well-being. He asked the caller if there was anything he could do. Then he elaborated further, telling the caller that he'd attended the same party earlier in the evening but, because of a busy day ahead, had left early. He also let it be known that he had a dance with her and that as far as he was concerned, she seemed to be enjoying herself immensely when he left. He felt a surprising sense of relief when he replaced the receiver. Not a trace of guilt, just relief that she was possibly out of his life forever. Now it was up to the spin doctors, and the party machine to keep his name out of it.

Less than twenty four hours later Julie Catterall was dead! The drug had done its deadly work. Timothy was standing before the Prime Minister, and he was being sympathetically told to take things easy for a month or two as he seemed to be suffering a series of terrible misfortunes recently. With the episode with the press, the libel case, his wife's illness, and now this. His leader thought he might need a break. He was smiling to himself thinking that everything was going to be just fine when the Prime minister remarked in a very casual manner, "By the way Timothy, I suppose you've heard the news about your secretary, Julie?" He didn't have time to answer as the PM continued without drawing breath, "She'd just had an abortion you know. Now all the press are running around like headless chickens trying to find out who the so-called father was. I think I ought to warn you that your name has cropped up more than once already. For your own sake, and for your own good, Timothy, I hope there's no truth in it, because that would be a resigning matter." The Prime minister watched him as he left the office, and although his face bore a slight smile, he had already decided that Timothy Harris was now excess baggage, and his days in government circles were decidedly numbered.

As he left the Commons, and prepared to return to Cheshire, Timothy knew now it had been a stupid mistake to slip that tablet into Julie's drink, but then if she'd told him beforehand she had aborted the child, he wouldn't have needed to do it. He attempted to ease his conscience by telling himself he had only done it in the hope that it might have caused her to have a miscarriage. However, looking at the overall picture now, first and foremost there would be no messy divorce, or scandal. Julie, and her unborn child, were off his back, and everybody was beginning to feel sorry for him again thinking that life was being very harsh and cruel, to him. God, if only they knew?

Sergeant West parked his car in the station yard. He was feeling pretty pleased with himself as he walked across to the entrance and made his way to his office upstairs. Once inside he sat down and waited for the phone to ring to tell him that the girls had been picked up and that they were being held in the cells below. The arrests and their release, invariably without charge, would ensure they would feel indebted towards him. The fact that these arrests were highly illegal didn't bother him in the slightest, after all these girls were just common prostitutes and, as far as he was concerned, they were the dregs. After taking the call advising him that the girls were in the holding cells and asking to see him, he made his way downstairs repeating cheerfully, to himself, "Easy innit?" He reached the ground floor and made his way to the desk where he asked the desk sergeant the names of the persons arrested. In reply he was given the names of Bridget Riley and Theresa O'Rourke, both of whom had been found with a small amount of a controlled substance in their possession. He made his way down the corridor to the first cell where he found Bridget Riley. She rounded on him immediately he entered shouting, "What the bloody hell do you think you are playing at this time Westy? Me, and the girls, are getting a bit pissed off with this routine now and you know full well none of us ever come down on our patch with even a joint to share between us! So what's this all about?"

"Bridget, this isn't a game I can assure you. All I know is that I'm busy working away upstairs when I get a call from the duty sergeant, telling me there are two girls in the cells asking to see me if I'm in the building. The duty sergeant informs me you are claiming the drugs have been planted on you. As you know Bridget, I have helped you and your friends in the past, so I've come down here to see if I can help you once again."

Bridget wasn't a bit impressed, and retorted angrily, "What will you be wanting this time, Westy? Will it be another witness job or is it a quick blow job because, whatever it is, you can go and stuff yourself! I'd rather take my chance in court on whatever charge you bastards try to make stick. Don't forget, I haven't forgotten the last time when you promised me I wouldn't have to give evidence. You sold me down the river then, leaving me almost facing a perjury charge because of you. So, you'd better make up your mind pretty quick this time. Either chuck us both out now, or charge us, but before you charge me, or ask me any questions, I want a solicitor present. Whilst we're at it I can assure you that you won't get much change out of Theresa because, this time, we're sticking together." Still visibly annoyed, and showing no sign of calming down, Bridget continued, "I demand the use of a telephone in order that I can contact Michael Mulrooney. I'm going to ask this gentleman to represent us. You have no right at all to keep us here when we haven't committed any offence."

Sergeant West had not anticipated for a moment he would be put on the spot in this manner. Realising he would have to do something about it very quickly, he walked rapidly out of the cell without saying a word, securing the door behind him. As he walked down the corridor, he could hear Bridget shouting to Theresa that it was going to be all right, and they just had to stick together. When he reached the desk, he went behind to the offices at the rear where he found the arresting officers having a drink. Constables Richardson and Barrett could see from his expression something was amiss. He motioned them to remain seated whilst saying, "Right you two, these girls you brought in on charges of possession, I want to know straight away if you've got the bottle to make this stick? Now, we're not beating about the bush here; I want to hear it from you now that you found small amounts of controlled substances on them, and after each of them was cautioned in the appropriate manner they were duly arrested, and brought here in order to be charged. If you want to make any progress in the force, and especially this division, there comes a time when you have to stand up and be counted. That moment has now arrived. Do you both understand what I am saying?" He looked at them very carefully to see if he could detect any sign of weakness, or lack of resolve. Knowing they were in too deep, and they could hardly back off now, he allowed his gaze to settle on PC Barrett. He'd already determined he was the one who might weaken given time. "How about it then lad?" You're up for it aren't you?" he enquired, trying to sound as nonchalant as he could.

PC Barrett was in a quandary. He knew the drugs had

been planted on the girls as an excuse to get them inside, but it never occurred to him he would be asked to stitch them up. He also knew he was on the horns of a dilemma, because if he didn't go through with it, his career was as good as finished. Desperately, he looked at his colleague whilst searching his soul for the answer, but he found no respite there. In fact, his colleague PC Richardson was trying as hard as he could to avoid eye contact with him in order that he would have to make the decision for them both. If PC Richardson agreed to go along with sergeant West, Barrett knew he would comply as well, but for the moment he was being spared from making that decision.

After what seemed like an eternity to PC Richardson, his colleague finally answered, "Yes sergeant I'm up for it. We planted the stuff on them, and we found it so I suppose we should tie up all the loose ends. That's right, isn't it Rich?" Richardson nodded in agreement. Sergeant West felt quite relieved; the girls could do what they wanted now, but it would make little difference as far as he was concerned. Although it didn't show, he was a little disappointed that his plans had been thwarted, and for the time being, there wasn't an immediate prospect of any sexual favours coming his way in return for organising the release of the girls, but it hardly mattered now. The main thing was for the two arresting officers to complete their work, and let life return to normal. Whoever the girls got to defend them was a simple matter of choice for themselves, and whether they were found guilty no longer interested him. "Before you proceed lads, just let me have a couple of minutes with the girls in turn and then I'll be out of your way for the night. Ok?" As both men nodded in agreement, he made his way to the cells where he told each girl in turn, despite all his efforts, he hadn't been able to get the arresting officers to drop the charges, and if they wished to have a solicitor present he would arrange it before he went home. The two girls stuck together on this, and arrangements were made for somebody from Michael Mulrooney's practice to attend as soon as possible. Feeling satisfied that, despite the setback, he was out of the woods, he said goodnight to the staff, and made his way out of the building.

But Sergeant West was not out of the woods. Far from it! Bridget Riley was absolutely livid, and she had already made up her mind she was going to get even with this evil, lying, and cheating Detective Sergeant West. She was equally sure that, on this occasion, Theresa O'Rourke would be only too happy to assist.

Michael Mulrooney couldn't fathom any reason why two Liverpool prostitutes wanted him to defend them on charges of possessing cannabis, especially when the spokesperson was none other than Bridget Riley. Listening to her story, he concluded that, in all probability she was telling the truth. Even so, that left him with another dilemma. Why somebody in the Merseyside force thought necessary to stitch them up in this manner when it was so much easier to run them in on a prostitution charge which would certainly stick? Because that is what they were, and that was what they had previous convictions for. Hopefully, he sighed it would become a little more clear when he interviewed Theresa O'Rourke the next day.

Theresa O'Rourke was waiting in his office when he arrived the following morning. As she related her story, it was soon apparent that it followed the same pattern as Bridget's story. Both women were denying possession of any drugs, claiming the police had planted the drugs during the search procedure. In addition, the women were claiming this had happened in the past, but then in return for sexual favours; they had been released without charge. Looking at the girls' statements more closely, it was quite apparent this had happened on a number of occasions. He decided to press this point a little further and, as a result, he soon had a number of dates he could check on. He knew if he checked these with dates in the arrest book in the station he would be able to see how many times the girls had been released without charge. He was also aware, even if they had been released without being charged, that information should also be recorded. Obviously if these details were not in place as police procedure dictated, then something was very wrong with procedure at that station. On that basis alone there was a good chance of getting the women off.

Michael explained the procedure and the lines of enquiry he was going to pursue, and he told Bridget he would like to see her and Theresa before any court hearings. Before concluding the interview, he informed Bridget he had already been told, by Theresa, that she had been asked by Detective Sergeant West to testify that she had seen Angela Clarkson wearing the watch which figured so prominently in the recent murder trial. She had refused to give that evidence as she had not seen Angela wearing it. He then asked Bridget to give considerable thought to the evidence she had given in the murder trial. He offered her considerable reassurance. He started by telling her that, if it could be shown that she had been put under pressure by the police to testify, then she wouldn't face any charges of perjury if she subsequently retracted that evidence. Seeing the look of concern on her face, he told her that without her cooperation on this matter, he wouldn't be able to take any action himself, and any decision concerning this matter was entirely up to her.

Bridget could see the way out, and she could also see that this was one way of getting back at this crooked, lying copper, Detective Sergeant West. But, for the time being, it represented a step too far. As she prepared to leave, she told Michael she would give the matter some thought, and get back to him in due course.

Later that afternoon, Michael telephoned Irene Yarwood, and gave her an update on this most interesting day of developments. Irene was more than pleased with this news. Now she knew that she would be able to get at the truth once the Clarkson case came to appeal. All she had to do was find the other pieces of the jigsaw.

As it happened, she didn't have long to wait. Two weeks later, the European Courts of Justice delivered their historic ruling on a prisoner's right to silence. In effect, the courts were saying that, should a person elect to say nothing, then that was their right in law. In addition, by not saying anything it could not be inferred that a person was covering up their own guilt. Just how this would assist Harry Thompson she couldn't say at this stage. All she knew was that she had a deep gut feeling telling her that somehow this was of vital importance to her client. Hearing the news, she determined, irrespective of what Harry Thompson thought about all of it being nothing more than a legal ploy to get him off, she would still bring it to his attention the next time they met.

Chapter 20

It is said by many people that everybody watches, or listens to, the daily news bulletins at some time of the day. Whether they take it all in, or simply assimilate the news within their minds for use at a later time, is another matter. Certainly that was the case on this dull and rainy day, as the television newscaster intoned, "Police have discovered the body of a man believed to be in his late twenties in a disused warehouse in Manchester. We understand the premises in question had been used as a squat, and it was a known meeting place for drug users. The name of the person is being withheld until the body has been formally identified and the next of kin informed. At this stage, foul play is not suspected, and police are appealing for any persons with any information to come forward."

Many people heard the news but paid little attention to it, as it didn't affect them directly, including on this occasion Timothy Harris. To him and countless others, this was just another wastrel who had lost his life needlessly therefore, there was nothing for anybody to lose any sleep over. As he relaxed in his Cheshire home, he poured himself a large brandy, and contemplated his own future which was now being complicated as a result of his wife's illness. Despite his wife's illness, he was still enjoying life, but he realised he had to keep a much lower profile, and it also meant his divorce case was put on hold. This bothered him but, because of his position in the eye of the public, he'd decided this was the best action to take. Besides, if his wife died as a result of her illness, he would save a lot of money because there would be no costly divorce or settlement to pay. All thoughts of Julie had been banished from his mind, and it was almost like being single again as he wallowed in the waves of sympathy which well wishers within the party bestowed upon him.

Despite this, there was something on his mind and although he didn't lose any sleep over the matter, he did find it difficult to accept his wife's illness on a long term basis, and he knew he would have to start the ball rolling at some time if he wanted to get her life support system switched off. Once the courts ruled in his favour on that issue, he would be able to enjoy life to the full. Who knows, he thought, I might even retire from politics altogether, and seek opportunities and pleasure elsewhere. Then his mood changed, there was one thing stopping him. It was that bloody stupid consultant in charge of his wife.

He poured himself another large brandy, and settled himself into his comfortable leather armchair recliner. To relieve the quietness of the house he switched on the television then he picked up that morning's edition of 'The Times.' As he heard the news bulletin again, including details of the body discovered, he found himself saying, "silly pillock's better off dead." The buzzing of the intercom system brought him back to reality.

"Yes he answered in reply who is it?

After a short pause a voice answered, "My name is Chief inspector Mallory and I need to speak to you on a matter of some delicacy, and urgency. If we can come up, we won't detain you a moment longer than necessary."

Almost mechanically, he pressed the button on the automatic security entrance system, and made his way to the front door. Thoughts raced through his mind, was it something to do with his wife? Then he shuddered as another thought occurred, perhaps something has come up about Julie? He dismissed this immediately however because she was dead, and cremated now.

As he opened the door, he saw the frame of Chief Inspector Mallory together with another officer. Mallory produced his identification which showed him to be a member of the Security Services saying, "would you like to sit down I think we have some bad news for you?"

Timothy was convinced this was the bad news he desperately wanted to hear as he enquired, "Is it about my wife? She's dead, isn't she?"

Mallory looked at his colleague a little nonplussed as he replied, "No sir, we haven't come about your wife. We are here about your son Anthony. Our enquiries have revealed that the body of a person, discovered in a disused warehouse, could well be that of your son."

Obviously, this was not the news Timothy was expecting. He was sure there must be some mistake. Surely not Anthony, oh it was true they'd had their ups and downs, and he'd thrown him out of the house some time ago, but no, not this, surely it had to be a mistake. "Was it, was it an accident?" he asked nervously, quite unsure of himself.

"We think it may have been due to an accidental drug overdose, sir, so I suppose you could say that it was an accident, but the body has been taken away for a post mortem examination, and until that's been carried out I'm afraid we cannot say for certain. In the meantime, we would like you to accompany us to the mortuary to identify the body. At the moment there's a complete news blackout on this story, and I'm sure you can understand why. However, these things can only be kept under wraps for a certain amount of time. You can rest assured, sir, if the story does get out we'll appeal to the press to delay publication for a little while. The Chief Inspector was standing now and it was quite plain, however unpleasant the task ahead, it was time to go.

Timothy locked up the house, and climbed into the back of

the unmarked vehicle which drew quickly, and silently, out of the long winding drive.

During the journey Timothy had ample time to reflect. Yes, it was a wasted life, and yes, Anthony was a silly pillock but maybe if he had treated him better things might have been different. He knew he was more than partly to blame. He had always harboured doubts that Anthony might not be his son and this had shown itself on many occasions during their lives. Now he found himself regretting all of this and the subsequent events which had happened.

Their presence was expected and they were taken straight to the mortuary where an attendant slowly opened a cabinet which contained the body. He drew back the sheet to reveal the corpse. Timothy knew instantly and he turned away in an effort to hide his grief. With his voice barely above a whisper, he acknowledged to the silent onlookers that it was the body of his son.

Throughout the journey home, Timothy never spoke a word. He went silently into the deserted house to be alone with his grief. Once inside, he wasn't allowed much solitude, or privacy, as the messages of condolence began flooding in from the Prime Minister, and all members of the political spectrum as well as countless well wishers and friends.

Lying in her hospital bed, Paula Harris was deeply conscious of all the sound and movement going on around her. Her mind was deeply troubled with countless thoughts, and questions for which she never received any answers. She knew she was in a strange environment, but where upon earth was she and how long had she been there? Why couldn't she see anybody, or for that matter anything at all? To make matters worse, why didn't anybody come near her whenever she cried out? Unbeknown to Paula, no sound came from her lips no matter how hard she tried to talk, or scream. Similarly, there was nobody to witness any movement in her body because no matter how much she tried, her body wouldn't respond to any signals that she desperately tried to send from her brain. Despite this each day she strengthened her resolve, and determined one way or another that somebody would realise that she was still alive.

From the different sounds emanating from the ward, she could tell there had been a change of staff and nurses Betty and Brenda were on duty. As they carried out their daily tasks, she heard them talking to each other. She tried to picture their faces whilst trying desperately to make some noticeable movement, but as usual it was to no avail. Today however, they had a new topic of conversation to talk about as she heard the voice of Betty enquiring, "did you hear the news this morning Brenda, about that poor fellow they found in a disused warehouse? Well, it seems that it's her son." She nodded her head in the direction of Paula as she ended the sentence.

"No I didn't hear that. I was too busy trying to get here on time, I didn't even have a chance to put the telly on." replied her companion, "but, if it's true it must be awful. Fancy just lying here unable to see or hear, and yet the whole world and his dog knows your son's dead, and you're completely oblivious to it."

But, Paula Harris was not oblivious to it. She was here and she could hear every word the nurses were saying. Surely, she agonised, there must be some mistake. Please. Please dear God, she prayed, make them say it's all a mistake. Not Anthony – it mustn't be, it can't be true."

As if to punish her further, the voices continued, "well apparently they gave it out that Timothy Harris, yes, that MP, identified the body last night. There'll have to be a post mortem to determine the cause of death, although the papers are saying he was on drugs. All the same it's still a shame isn't it, and it just goes to show, even the best of families have drug problems, not just our kids Brenda. What do you say?"

Brenda readily agreed and gradually, the voices began to recede as the nurses moved out of the ward. Had they stopped to make a final check on their charge, they might have just caught the glimpse of a tear which forced its way out of the corner of their patient's eye as they left Mrs. Harris alone with her new found grief. Neither could they see the movement in the little finger of her right hand which, with great determination, she was trying to cross over her ring finger. With both her arms beneath the tightly wrapped sheets, this tiny movement went unseen by all, then completely exhausted by her exertions, Paula sank into a deep sleep.

Harry Thompson never knew what hit him. One minute he was walking into the shower block on his own. Then crash, all the lights went out, and he remembered nothing more. Now he was in a dream, floating light as a feather, looking down on the world. Only something was wrong: everything was hazy and out of focus. His head throbbed and the pain was getting worse. It seemed as if his brain would explode. Gradually he sensed calm being restored, and he was floating again. This time he was floating on a series of waves, being carried gently to the shore. How long he lay there he didn't know as he drifted in and out of consciousness. In his barely wakeful moments, he was aware he could hear himself talking to different people. Everybody around him seemed to be sifting through masses of papers then, just when it seemed that he was going to get some answers, the lights went out again as he lapsed, once more, into his unconscious state. Events throughout the world passed him quickly by as a result of an attack by another inmate, Lying in his hospital bed he was able to piece together the events of that night and, although he didn't actually see his assailant, he knew who was responsible and, he vowed, when the time came he would exact his revenge.

At that moment the door opened and he could just make out the figure of Bertram Carter, the prison governor, accompanied by a doctor. As the Governor advanced towards his bed, the doctor spoke to him in a soft voice saying, "You certainly seem a bit brighter and it makes a nice change to find you awake. As you can see Mr. Carter, the prison governor, has come to see you and I've told him that he can have a couple of minutes with you."

Bertram Carter stood at the side of his bed. He seemed a little nervous when he spoke, "Er, Hello Thompson. I hope you're feeling a little better now, and, er, by the way, the doctor said you can only improve now although it'll take a little time. I thought you might like to know that there's a full scale enquiry under way in the prison and as soon as we find those responsible, you can rest assured we'll throw the book at them. I don't suppose you would have any idea yourself who was responsible would you?"

Harry shook his head. It wasn't a case that he genuinely didn't know or he was afraid of saying who was responsible. Identifying his assailant would only add to his problems once he was back inside. Once back in the prison, he knew it would only be a matter of time before he came face-to-face with his attacker then it would be up to him to exact his own revenge. For the time being, in an effort to take the heat out of the incident, Harry insisted it was a complete accident, and that he had slipped on a bar of soap. He knew the governor wouldn't fully accept this explanation but he was determined to stick with it, and nothing and nobody would encourage him to change his mind.

Bertram Carter sighed as he realised that Harry was not going to assist him. Before terminating the interview, he asked him if there was anything he wanted or if he wished to see any specific visitors. In reply Harry asked if it would be possible to see Irene Yarwood, and the governor promised to assist, adding he would pass on the message as soon as possible.

Irene reached her own office just as the telephone began to shriek its ugly sound. She quickly lifted the receiver. This time she was pleasantly surprised to find herself talking to Bertram Carter, the prison governor, and she readily agreed to his request to visit Harry that day. During the conversation, the governor told her about the attack on her client and sought her help in trying to get Harry to change his mind about identifying his assailant. En route to the prison, she wondered why she had received this summons, because under normal circumstances, this would have been something for Harry's solicitor to handle but, she knew she would find out soon enough.

When she arrived at the prison, the governor escorted her to the hospital wing where she could see Harry lying in bed. She broke the ice immediately by saying, "don't bother to get up Harry." She was rewarded instantly with a smile, possibly the largest smile she had ever seen upon his face, although that was hardly surprising considering his ordeal over the previous months.

"I must say it's nice to see you again. How are you feeling Harry and what on earth has been going on here?"

Determined to stick to his story, Harry replied, "I had an accident in the shower block. I must have slipped on a piece of soap. The next thing I knew I'm in here. Now, everybody's running round saying I've been attacked by another inmate, but I can assure you it wasn't like that at all. I'm feeling much better now, and if I continue to make good progress then I should be moved back to the prison sick bay within the next week or so. That will be a lot better because at least I will be able to move around a bit. After that, it'll be back to the old cell which brings me to the real point of your visit. Since this unfortunate accident, and whilst I've been lying here, I've given a lot of thought to what you said about getting my conviction quashed on the human rights issue and I've decided to go along with it. Lying here, in this state, has given me ample time for thought and I think you're right. I should go for it because that'll show everybody I have nothing to be afraid of, and I was not the guilty person. Therefore, if you're still prepared to act for me on that basis, I'll be very pleased to do as you say. I have to be perfectly honest and tell you that isn't the only reason. The doctors have told me any type of fall, or another blow to the head, would probably be enough to finish me off. Therefore, I have to take advantage of every opportunity which comes my way. I also have to tell you, even if you are successful, I won't ever stop trying to prove my innocence completely."

Irene was obviously pleased with this news, and she told Harry she was certain that he had made the correct decision. Then she outlined the progress the defence team were making in the Clarkson case. She deliberately stopped short of revealing anything connected to Timothy Harris preferring instead to confine her remarks to the false evidence given at the trial, and although she knew she couldn't guarantee this would overturn the verdict, nevertheless she could see at once the effect this good news had on her client. She urged Harry to have a drastic rethink over his version of events in the shower block, but there was no way he would change his story. After a little light-hearted conversation, the meeting ended and she made her way quietly out of the room. Before leaving she made it known to Bertram Carter, that as far as she was concerned, this attack on Harry was no accident, and he and his staff had to make considerable improvements in the way they looked after, and protected, Harry Thompson whilst he was in their care.

Now that Harry had changed his mind it pleased her no end because it made her job a little bit easier. She could devote all her energy to the task in hand which was to secure his release.

She reached the car and swiftly seated herself and started the motor. The engine started effortlessly, and she drove slowly out of the car park heading back to the office for a meeting with Michael Mulrooney.

The solicitor was already waiting for her when she arrived back and, from the look on his face, she could see something was giving him a little more than cause for concern. As she placed her briefcase beside her desk before sitting down, she asked apprehensively, "Come on Michael is it good news or bad?"

He responded quickly saying, "Well, when I last spoke to you we were both a bit pleased because we thought we might get somewhere if we could appeal the cases individually. Even when we found that this wasn't possible, it looked as though we might be in with a chance especially with Bridget Riley and Royston Chambers about to admit to giving perjured evidence. With Theresa O'Rourke willing to testify and, since she'd also been requested to testify to the same evidence as Bridget, it really did look as though we were going somewhere with this case but now there is this to contend with. With that he pushed a number of documents across the desk whilst continuing, "these came today from the Crown Prosecution team and, on the face of it, it looks as though we don't have one chance in hell. According to this, the scientists at the forensic laboratory have come up with a method of obtaining DNA results from clothing. Until now, this was something which was not possible before. According to these documents, they've carried out tests on the clothing of Angela Clarkson and Diane Wilson, after which they compared the results with the sample from Harry Thompson. The result is, Bingo, it's him. Of course if this is true, he's run us round absolutely ragged and, to make matters worse, he's known all along he was as guilty as sin."

For a moment, the news shattered Irene and she was

completely lost for words. All she could do was read the contents of the correspondence over and over again, unable to believe the message it contained.

Eventually she spoke, "Michael, this is indeed a body blow but it's a good job that we have been given this information now, and that it's not just been dropped on us when we arrived at court. We do have a little time to find our own forensic expert who may be able to contradict this evidence. He might be able to tell us that the tests have not been carried out properly. After all, it's a new procedure and we may be able to cast sufficient doubt upon it. Then, with two of our three musketeers revoking their earlier evidence, we might still be in with a chance. The thing that bothers me about this though is if this is correct, only two things are possible. Either Harry had been with the Clarkson girl earlier or he actually is the killer. Really, I cannot believe it. All this time, all this effort and just when we think we are getting close something like this has to happen. I've just come from the prison Michael, and I've just seen Harry and although he's recovering nicely from the attack that we discussed earlier, nevertheless, he's still adamant he slipped on a piece of soap. That's all I, and the prison authorities, can get out of him. However, as a direct result of the attack, he knows it's in his own interests to get himself out of there as soon as possible, even if it means freedom on a technicality so to speak. On my way back here from prison I was feeling quite pleased thinking we might be going somewhere, and then you come up with this. Jesus Michael, whatever next, eh?"

Michael breathed a heavy sigh as he replied, "Yes Irene I know. This is why I had to get round here straight away because I can't believe it either. "Furthermore, I never thought I could ever be taken in by anybody like this, and I would have bet everything I have that our man was innocent."

Still grimacing, Michael remained unconvinced and

continued, "I know we still have to go through the procedure but, quite frankly Irene, I'm sure it's well nigh hopeless, and I reckon the press will have a field day when this gets out. However, for our sakes as well as Thompson's, I'll get my hands on the best forensic person I can locate. Meanwhile, in the forlorn hope that we might yet be granted a miracle, may I suggest we keep this to ourselves for the time being. That includes not even telling Thompson."

Irene had recovered from her surprise, and her brain was moving into overdrive as she snapped, "No Michael. I don't agree. Please listen. We haven't got much time so first I think you'd better contact the prosecution. Tell them we need samples providing for our own independent analysis. In the meantime, find me the best forensic expert in the country, or even Europe for that matter; somehow, we'll have to dig up something ourselves on this. Meanwhile, I'll go and see our man Thompson to have it out with him, and boy oh boy, he'd better come up with some answers. If I can get him to admit he was one of Clarkson's clients, and she was still alive when he left her, we might be in with half a chance. On the other hand, he might possibly admit to some kind of necrophilia, or similar sexual act if he'd stumbled across her body before the alarm was raised. Either way, he won't come out of it with any credit at all, but at the moment I do not see what else I can do. One thing's certain however, the appeal will still go ahead because I'll also try to get the judges to refuse to admit this new evidence."

She was in full flight now as she continued, "Remember Michael, at the trial, Judge Ewing made mincemeat of me over the fact there was no DNA sample involving the Clarkson case. He stopped me from even mentioning it as the crown were not going to introduce it in evidence. Therefore, if I can reverse the argument now, their lordships might just throw this new evidence out. Even so, I'll go and visit Thompson to see if he'll admit to any involvement, although when I confront him with this he'll have a hard time denying it."

As the solicitor left her office, she looked again at the new evidence lying on the desk before her, thinking it was turning out to be a very bad day indeed. Totally unaware of what she was doing even, she gathered up the papers and made her way to the office of Sebastian Kreiff, the head of chambers. At the moment she felt an urgent need to confide in someone.

Sebastian was kindness personified, and he sat back in his large leather armchair whilst he digested the information which Irene had just given him. He read the forensic report again, then, shaking his head replied, "Well Irene, this looks like bad news. Let's face it, if you can't shake their forensic expert and this evidence counts, it seems to me this is the end of the line for Harry Thompson. Obviously, I'm sure you'll give this your best shot. I wouldn't expect anything else but after this, if the cause is lost, I'd strongly urge you to put the case to bed. I'm sure we can find you plenty of other worthwhile causes in this practice. In the meantime, let me say, irrespective of the outcome of this case, in this practice we are all very proud of you and the way you have conducted this case. Let me tell you Irene, nobody else could have done any better and I really mean that. Remember this, in the case of Regina v Thompson, you took on a hopeless case. One that nobody else wanted to even look at and the odds were stacked hopelessly against you right from the beginning. I can assure you everyone in these chambers is extremely proud of you and your effort in this case."

Thus heartened, Irene Yarwood took her leave, and returned to her own office.

Chapter 21

Theresa and Bridget were walking slowly along Rodney Street. Although it was almost midnight, they were both hopeful they would find another punter or two before they went home. They saw the sleek black car turn into Rodney Street, heading slowly towards them. As the driver switched his lights on and off quickly they knew one of them was in luck. With the car noticeably slowing down, Theresa walked quickly towards the door which the driver had already opened. She entered the vehicle and sat down. "Before closing the door, she said a swift goodnight to Bridget adding, "I'll see you sometime tomorrow Bridey," then the car sped rapidly away into the night. Bridget turned to watch the car disappear then she began to walk towards the traffic lights at the junction, determined to give her shift one last try before going home. At the bottom of the street she didn't notice the car turn into Rodney Street, making its way silently towards her. As the vehicle drew alongside the driver spoke through the open window, "Hello Bridget, have you got time for a quick chat. This won't take a minute and it is important."

Before venturing towards the car, Bridget looked up and down the street but it was still deserted, apart from her and the driver. Cautiously she moved towards the vehicle and spoke to Detective Sergeant West, "If you think you're on for a quick jump or anything, you can think again you bent bastard."

"Bridget," appealed the driver, "just come here. I'm trying to help you and there's no need to get in the car if you don't want to."

Despite recognising the voice, it was still a very nervous

Bridget who moved towards the stationary car and enquired, "Well then, what is it you want, and make it bloody quick?"

Sergeant West held out his hand through the open window and Bridget could see that his outstretched hand held an envelope. She took it quickly and opened it. In order to read the contents of the letter, she leaned through the open window. The letter was from The Chief Constable's Office of the Merseyside Police, informing her she was not to be prosecuted for possession of an illegal substance and she was being let off with a caution.

"How's that for good news then Bridget?" enquired the detective. "I thought things got a little out of hand last time so I put in a good word for you and Theresa, and I persuaded those two rookie cops this was the best way forward under the circumstances. Don't you agree?" Before she could answer, his hand was at her throat, and the electric windows started to push up, trapping her head with the top of the car door. She opened her mouth to scream, but before she could utter a sound, she felt the full force of a blow to the head with the hammer he had concealed beside him. With the windows slowly retracting and the door already open, he had her inert body in the car beside him in seconds. Then unseen by anybody he drove quickly away from the scene. As he drove, he muttered to the still figure beside him, "I'll teach you to try and put the squeeze on me you little bloody tart. After tonight, you won't be telling any bugger anything about me and you won't ever be in a position to cause trouble for me either." He knew he was wasting his breath, because, the girl was already dead but it made him feel better, and it gave him a complete sense of satisfaction. Driving along the deserted streets, heading towards Southport and the sand dunes at Ainsdale Beach, he began to relax as he whispered over and over to himself "Easy innit!"

Chapter 22

It was another grey and miserable Tuesday morning when Michael Mulrooney arrived at his office. He was surprised to find Theresa O'Rourke waiting for him. Just one look at her extremely nervous state confirmed to him that something totally unexpected had occurred, because this certainly wasn't the hard-bitten, streetwise prostitute he had recently got to know. He ushered the woman into his office and asked his secretary to put the kettle on. As they both sat down, he asked Theresa what was the nature of her visit.

Even though she knew they were alone, she kept looking nervously around her before blurting out that Bridget Riley had disappeared.

At once a dozen questions sprang to his mind and from his lips, but her answers were always the same. Yes she'd been there and she'd telephoned here, there, and everywhere but, as far as she was concerned, there was no trace of her friend whatsoever.

"Mr. Mulrooney, what am I going to do now? You see I'm frightened for my own safety. I think it's all something to do with this bloody murder case, and the fact we were going to give evidence against the police." At this point she began to break down, and he realised she really did think her own life might be threatened.

He poured out the tea, and began to talk quietly to her saying, "Come on Theresa, think hard. Tell me when you last saw her, and when did you plan to meet again. Also, do you think it's possible she might have decided to take off for a couple of days without saying anything to anybody?"

Theresa didn't think long, or hard, she looked up at him and replied, "On Sunday night we were both on Rodney Street. It was getting late, but at the last minute I got a client which left Bridget alone. As it was getting late, she said she was going home and that was our signal. Whenever it's getting late and one of us is alone, we make a point of going home leaving the one with the client to telephone afterwards to make sure everything's all right. Later, well in the early hours of the morning, I telephoned Bridget to say all was well but there wasn't any answer. I got up and dressed and I went round to her house but it was all locked up. My first reaction was to telephone you, but I decided to wait until today, just in case she turned up but there's no trace of her. Mr. Mulrooney, what am I going to do now? You see I'm certain she's been killed because it is so unlike her not to keep in touch."

Taken aback by this turn of events, he realised he must do something to placate her. He began by asking if she had voiced her concerns to any of their other friends, or even the police. These enquiries drew a negative response although he noticed that she visibly recoiled at the mention of the police. After a few more minutes, during which time she appeared to become much more composed, he leaned across his desk and spoke softly to her, "Theresa, you must listen to me. First of all, just because you haven't had any recent contact with Bridget it doesn't mean that you can automatically assume she's been murdered, and somehow the police are involved. Think of it this way. Why on earth should a man, with some twenty years service in the force, risk throwing it all away by murdering a person whom he persuaded to commit perjury? Really it doesn't make sense. To me, it seems his most obvious way out would be to brazen out all these allegations in the hope that our appeal will fail, and this will all die a natural death. I think you'll find your friend Bridget is every bit as afraid as you are and she's decided to go away for a few days. Once she's sorted herself out, there's is no doubt in my mind that she'll get in touch with us. Why don't you do the same thing? Take off for a couple of days, keep it to yourself where you decide to stay, and give me a ring at the office each day to let me know you are safe and well."

Theresa dried her eyes once more then, with her voice barely above a whisper she replied, "To you, no doubt that makes a great deal of sense, but I can't see it the same way because I've also received this. She paused for a moment before pulling out a brown crumpled envelope from her pocket. From it she extracted a small typed letter, addressed to herself from the Chief Constable's Office stating, "Following a review of your recent arrest for possession of a small amount of a controlled substance, the authorities have decided not to prosecute in this instance, and they will deal with the matter by the issue of a caution. Should any further offences of this nature be committed, this offence will then be taken into consideration."

"Mr. Mulrooney, I received that letter the Tuesday morning after I last saw Bridget. You can see if she received a similar letter, and she should have done, surely she would have been in touch with me? This is simply that lying bent copper trying to cover his tracks, thinking if we're not charged, then there's nothing to be afraid of and there's no need for her to admit her evidence was false. What you don't seem to appreciate is now she has even more reason to be afraid! Just suppose Westy comes along, after I've left her, and he tells her he wants a quick word. He tells her she's got no need to get into the car if she doesn't want and he gives her a copy of this letter addressed to her. Once she's read it she's no longer suspicious, and she might even have accepted an offer of a lift home."

Brushing aside Michael's attempt to interrupt, she continued, "When I went to her house later that day, there was no sign of a letter to Bridget similar to the one I received. Now, I'll bet you, if you telephone the station you'll find they did send one out. No Mr. Mulrooney, you're quite wrong, Bridget's dead and I am going to take your advice and disappear. You can rest assured that I will keep in touch, and whatever happens now I'll still testify for the defence." With that she picked up her handbag and proceeded to make her way out.

Michael managed to get to the door first in order to let her know he would notify the local police of her disappearance, and he would also ask about the issue of a caution to Bridget. Urging Theresa to take care and, stressing the need to keep in touch, he closed the door quietly behind her.

Once she had left, he telephoned the Bootle police station to alert them regarding the disappearance of Bridget; then he telephoned Merseyside police headquarters, from where he ascertained it was recorded that a caution had been issued and sent by post to Bridget Riley.

A further telephone call was made to Irene Yarwood. She greeted the news of the disappearance with some dismay because, coming on top of the new forensic evidence, it was beginning to look that the appeal would be rejected almost out of hand.

It is often said that the best laid plans of mice and men oft times go astray. So it would prove to be in the case of Detective Sergeant West. He was feeling well pleased with himself since he had received the news of the new forensic tests. Although it opened up new and exciting possibilities concerning the Wilson and Clarkson cases, settling both matters without leaving room for any doubt regarding Thompson's guilt, he kept telling himself it was indeed a pity the news had not come through a few days earlier. Had it done so, he might not have had to kill Bridget Riley. Regarding this matter, he now sought solace from his evil deed by telling himself Bridget had to go because she had told him she wouldn't keep her mouth shut. He went over the events again in his mind. He could see her there telling him in no uncertain manner, that come what may, she'd had enough, and she was still going to go ahead with her action against him and the Merseyside force. With all his years of service behind him, he knew he couldn't afford to allow that to happen, so there was no other option. With one swift and telling blow from a hammer, it was all over in seconds and it was goodnight Bridget. 'Pity,' he sighed, 'but it just had to be.' Now, as a result of receiving the news concerning the new forensic tests, he hadn't gone into the office today. Instead he was enjoying a leisurely drive down to Stafford prison where he had arranged to see an old acquaintance, Royston Chambers. For him the news of the new forensic evidence could not have come at a more opportune time, and he could hardly contain his satisfaction as he drove towards the prison. All that mattered to Detective Sergeant West was matching criminals to their crimes, even if it meant, on occasions, that evidence had to be tailored a bit to ensure the perfect fit.

In this case, that no longer mattered as the end had been justified by the means. He permitted himself another smile as he whispered to himself, "easy innit" and he allowed himself to wallow in his self belief that Harry Thompson had finally been nailed as a scheming, lying, and cold blooded murderer far too incompetent to make a fool of Detective Sergeant West.

As he drove his face wreathed in smiles at the prospect of confronting that old lag Chambers with this latest development, he told himself this would ensure that Chambers toed the line, and now he would forget everything he knew about his own evidence being made up. He was back to his old buoyant self, savouring every moment as he glanced at the report lying on the passenger seat beside him. He told himself this really would be easy. Just let Chambers know there was now irrefutable forensic proof Thompson had killed Clarkson, and the odds were he had also murdered his girlfriend. Therefore, even if Chambers went over to the defence team, there wouldn't be a cat in hells chance of the judges believing his retraction and that the evidence he had given in the murder trial was false. Now, he was going to tell Chambers that he truly was a spent force, and his only hope of any salvation lay in his own hands, and that it was time to do his bird, and try to get some time off for good behaviour.

He parked his car at the gaol, and presented his identification at the visitor's gate. Once his police card had been verified, he was shown quickly inside to the office of the assistant governor.

Whilst waiting to be admitted to see Royston Chambers, he couldn't stop his mind from dwelling on Bridget Riley. It was only temporary and he consoled himself again with the thought that, if she hadn't threatened to cause the trouble over her own evidence, she would still be alive today. Soon back to his own self, he allowed himself another smile as the thought occurred to him that she wasn't going to cause any more trouble for him, or anyone else, in the future. It would only be a matter of time before the body was discovered on the sand dunes at Ainsdale Beach, a local popular beauty spot and, he reasoned, it would also serve as a warning to others not to mess with Westy, even though, he knew that there would be nothing at all to connect him with the killing. He was still smiling to himself, and thinking about how easy it had been to kill her. Once the body was discovered the police would probably be looking for a homicidal maniac, with a pathological hatred of prostitutes. When the assistant governor entered and after a quick drink and a talk about prisoners and prison life in general, it was time to go and see arch criminal Chambers.

When the door of the interview room opened to admit the prisoner, Royston Chambers could see at once that this was not a meeting he was going to enjoy. Detective Sergeant West greeted him in a very curt and abrupt manner. He lost no time telling him that, as a result of new evidence, they now had positive proof Harry Thompson was the killer of Angela Clarkson. He then went on to say, although he couldn't stop Chambers from lodging an appeal, there was absolutely no chance that he would offer any assistance. This was because, with this new evidence against Thompson it didn't seem possible that any judge in the land would believe the story that he, Chambers, had made it all up. "Face facts son," he said, "they will bloody well laugh at you and accuse you of inventing this story just to see if you can get some time off. Well take a tip from me, Roy, just go and forget the whole thing. Before I leave, let me tell you that the only time I want to come down here again is to hear you, telling me, that you've got some hot tips for me. Then, I might be persuaded to try to do something for you. Do I make myself clear?"

Royston Chambers nodded and silently watched as Detective Sergeant West walked triumphantly out of the interview room whispering, "Easy Innit!"

Timothy Harris was seated in the sumptuous office of Jerome Jerome the senior partner of Jerome Woolff and Solomon. He was also feeling pleased with himself, despite the news of the recent death of his son. Today he intended to ask his legal team to drop the divorce proceedings against his wife. It wasn't a change of heart; it was more a case of saving himself the fees involved. A couple of days ago, whilst alone in his flat with a large brandy in hand he realised that, if he went to court and requested permission to switch off his wife's support systems, then there was no need for costly divorce proceedings, and he would be free to enjoy life as a single man again. He, too, permitted himself a wry smile as he savoured the prospect, whilst cursing himself for not thinking of pursuing the matter earlier. The thought never occurred to him that this avenue might have been denied him had Anthony been alive at the time.

Jerome Jerome looked straight at his client; he began on a cautious note, "I can understand what you are saying Timothy, but first of all, you will have to get the divorce proceedings cancelled. After which I would advocate you leave things for a little while, as I don't want us to be in a position where we go before the judge to ask permission to switch off whilst it is still in the eye and the mind of the public that you have been in the process of divorcing your wife. You do understand don't you, adverse publicity and all that. He sat back in his chair in order to allow his comments to sink in, but Timothy was unmoved, and he steadfastly refused to be swayed by such reason as he replied, "Under normal circumstances, I would agree with you, but I hardly think these are normal circumstances. First, consider this, over the past few months I've hardly been out of the public eye, or the press, with one thing or another. You know the allegations, the libel trial, the death of my parliamentary secretary, my divorce action, the illness of my wife, and most recently the tragic death of my son. Therefore, do you not think it feasible that I might still receive more than my share of the sympathy vote from the general public?"

Again Jerome looked straight at his man and said, "that may well be, but what if the judge views this action as a means for you to be rid of your long-suffering wife, rather than go through with your divorce action? Also, remember this, if you were divorced, then this course of action would not be open to you would it?" As Jerome anticipated, the question hit home hard and he noticed the immediate change in his client's facial expression and posture.

At first Timothy merely nodded, as he studied the implications of the last question, then, in a rather abrupt but assertive manner, he issued his instructions as follows, "I don't think I have much choice, because it's quite possible my wife could die at any moment. In which case my position would be unchanged. Secondly, I could have the support systems switched off which leaves me in exactly the same position. Or I can sit back, let my wife suffer in her silent world, secure in the knowledge that, if the positions were reversed, my wife would be doing everything possible to relieve me from misery and any pain and suffering. On the whole, I don't think I have a great deal of choice and I reckon I should take my chances and go for it. If, for any reason it doesn't come off, then I shall have to review the divorce procedure again."

Jerome Jerome finished the notes he'd been scribbling which contained his client's wishes, and the interview concluded.

Chapter 23

The discovery of the body of Bridget Riley amongst the sand hills at Ainsdale beach made the headlines in all the national press. Following the discovery it soon became known that it was the body of Bridget Riley, the prostitute who had given evidence for the crown in the double murder trial involving Harry Thompson at Liverpool not so long ago. Once it became known she had been killed with a blow to the head, probably caused by a hammer or a similar heavy instrument, the speculation that she had been killed by a pathological maniac with a hatred of prostitutes, started in earnest. Naturally, this in turn conjured up visions of the Yorkshire ripper, and whilst the police appealed for the public to remain calm, nevertheless, there was a lot of disquiet amongst those other girls similarly engaged in the profession.

The news was particularly distressing for Theresa O'Rourke although she did stick to her promise to keep in touch with Michael Mulrooney.

For Timothy Harris, time simply flew because of his involvement with so many things. He had attended the inquest on his son's death where the coroner had recorded an open verdict following the medical evidence which concluded that death had occurred as the result of a drug overdose, probably caused by a combination of the drugs he had injected and the use of another drug called Roacutane. This latter drug had been prescribed by his own doctor for the treatment of a chronic acne condition. At the time, the hearing made banner headlines in the press but as Timothy Harris was keeping as low a profile as possible, the press soon had to find something else to target.

In addition, the dropping of his divorce action aroused so little interest it wasn't worth bothering about. Gradually, he set about socialising a little more frequently whilst looking forward each day to some news about the court action to switch off his wife's support system.

Following her meeting with Michael Mulrooney, Irene Yarwood had arranged a hurried meeting with Harry Thompson at Strangeways prison. She was ushered straight into the sparsely furnished ward where he was still being kept under medical observation.

Harry broke the ice saying, "hello I wasn't expecting to see you and noting the expression on her face, added, "I can see something's bothering you so, I think you'd better get it off your chest then, hadn't you?"

Irene nodded and said, "Listen very carefully now to what I have to say, and think very carefully before you answer any questions. Before we go further, let me tell you that I don't want any bullshit, just the plain honest truth, no matter how bad it is, or how much it hurts. In one week's time, we are due in court to try to overturn the Clarkson verdict. This appeal started off quite badly at first as we were not able to get this appeal heard on its own. Then, we managed to find a witness who was prepared to testify she had been asked to give false evidence at your trial, and we were able to follow this up by getting Bridget Riley to admit she gave false evidence concerning the watch you found. In addition, we also had the prospect of Royston Chambers admitting your confession was nothing more than a figment of his own imagination. With all of this, can you possibly imagine how we felt knowing full well that it would be almost impossible to lose? Whilst she was talking she noted, with interest, the look of astonishment on his face. It was as if he couldn't believe that, finally, his luck might be changing. However the smile on his face soon disappeared as she continued, "unfortunately however, it was too good to last, because somebody threw a spanner in the works and Bridget Riley disappeared. Although we thought we could cope with that, we now know that she has been murdered, and that's something we were not in the least prepared for, neither for one moment, did we reckon on anything like this."

She paused for a while in order to take out the latest forensic report, then she proceeded to spit the words out with increasing venom and animosity. "This is a forensic report of a DNA test, carried out on semen stains removed from the clothing of Angela Clarkson and Diane Wilson. According to the expert who carried out those tests, this DNA matches yours. I need hardly tell you, Harry, even if Chambers agrees to testify, no judge in his right mind will believe him now."

She saw the colour drain from his face. She noticed with interest the change in his facial expression, together with his whole body language. To her eyes this was unreal. Here she was, watching him going into a state of shock with disbelief at what she was saying, and again, she found herself thinking if this is an act, then without doubt he should be on the stage. She brought herself back to reality in an instant snapping at him. "you told me that you had never been near this girl let alone with her, but this proves otherwise. Harry, can't you see, once this evidence is presented in court it's all over! The whole case is compromised, you are as good as finished. So now, let's concentrate on the job in hand. We will start with you telling me right from the start all about your involvement with this girl."

Harry Thompson sat there, silent for a moment, whilst he searched for the right words to say. He had thought, after the guilty verdicts in the trial that nothing else could happen to him and that one day, he might escape from this nightmare. He stared straight at her, looking into her cold blue eyes, before speaking, "Miss Yarwood, both during and since my trial I have the utmost admiration for you yourself, and the team you have built around you to assist in my defence. However, I'm as mystified as you are concerning this latest evidence. I've told everybody who will listen that I never met the girl, I had never seen the girl, let alone been with her, so how the hell my DNA came to be mixed up in all of this I haven't got a bloody clue. All I can say is, for some reason, the police must have planted it there."

She was onto him in a flash, "No Harry, that won't do. Why on earth should the police plant this evidence on the clothing of the dead woman when, at the time concerned, they must have known there would be no chance of it being used because, the forensic tests were not available then? If, as you say, and I must confess I can hardly believe you, you never saw the girl, would you admit to seeing her when she was dead, and would you also admit to carrying out some form of necrophilia with her body before the alarm was raised?"

Irene thought she had seen it all with this client, but she was horribly mistaken. Once again she saw the changes taking place within his face and body. There was true hatred and venom in his eyes now as he shouted, "What on earth are you saying? Do you realise that you are now accusing me of having some form of sexual relations with a corpse? Do you really think I am that sick? Do you honestly believe that I could sink that low? Because if you do then I no longer want you to act for me, so we might as well forget all about the appeals now. I'll just quietly pass away the next twenty years and pick up my life when I get out."

Once again, Irene could understand his anger and she could actually feel for him in a sad way, but she still had a job to do and by God she was going to do it. "Harry, she said sympathetically, lowering the tone of her voice, "Believe me, I know it's hard for you but you must look at this from my point of view. With this new evidence, the crown are going to rip you to shreds and there's got to be some logical explanation as to how your sample got there. What I said just now offers one such explanation, however unlikely it may be? Once we get into court, the only chance you have is if the judge refuses to allow the crown to admit this new test as evidence. This is why I'm clutching at straws, because if he doesn't then as far as your defence goes, necrophilia in some form or other may be your last chance."

Once again he glared defiantly at her before saying, "Well I can assure you truthfully and honestly I didn't leave that sample there so you will just have to face up to the fact that the police themselves must have manipulated it, just as they manipulated the confession. If you can't get at the truth exploring those avenues, then I can only suggest you do as you suggested yourself. Get the judge to refuse to admit the test as evidence. Still seething he continued, "why don't you look at it from my point of view and just for once consider the treatment I'm going to receive from the press when it becomes public knowledge that, not only have I obtained my release on a technicality, now you want to rub salt in the wound by getting me to admit I've been shagging a corpse."

With that he turned his back on her to indicate that the interview was over.

Peter Ravenscroft sat facing Royston Chambers. He was here to advise his client on his next move. He took off his glasses as he began, "Well Roy, I think it is very decent of this copper, isn't it? Coming along, after all this time, now he's telling you he's not going to help you get your time inside reduced. Well, I'd be sorely tempted to ask him where the hell he was first time round, because if he'd turned up as promised, you wouldn't be in this predicament would you? He noted the look on his client's face as he carried on, "there's no doubt in my mind, Roy, if he does as he says this time, you'll almost certainly lose your appeal, because if this evidence is produced in this other case, and it does nail Thompson to the floor, then whatever you say afterwards won't carry any weight. However, before we kick the ball into touch, let's consider this. This copper doesn't need you, and what's more there's no logical reason for him to help you now. At least that's what he's saying but he's forgetting one thing. Just suppose this new evidence is flawed, or not admitted, then you come along with your story about being forced into giving false evidence, then you stand every chance of getting away with it. Royston Chambers sat silently for a minute. He even pretended not to hear when his barrister whispered, "of course, that's assuming that the confession wasn't genuine but only you know that don't you, Roy?"

A thin smile pursed the prisoner's lips as he answered, "at the moment the question of the confession doesn't come into things. The only thing I'm interested in is getting out of here in the shortest possible time, and this is a definite possibility. The only other thing that bothers me is if I go along with this and I don't get my bird reduced, then, it's all for sweet FA. I don't care what you believe, I think this fellow West is after something, or he's cooking something up. As you said earlier, why wait all this time before coming forward? To me, something stinks, and at the end of the day I smell even more trouble for myself. So, Mr. legal eagle, advise me on this. Suppose, just suppose, you tell this pillock West, I'm quite prepared to do my time without causing any trouble for anyone, then, when Thompson's appeal is heard, I give evidence at that hearing and take my chances afterwards."

"Yes I can see your point and I quite understand your dilemma," replied the lawyer, "if you get involved with this bent copper again you'll never be free of him, or his ilk. If you do as you suggest, you're still left with a chance after the Thompson appeal. So really, you aren't going to be any worse off. At best now you'll be inside for at least another two or three years, assuming good behaviour. This appeal business might be settled within the next month or so, in which case, your appeal could follow some time afterwards. With these last few words on the subject, Royston Chambers went back to his cell hoping that this time he had backed the right horse.

Chapter 24

Irene and the defence team were seated in the appeal court waiting for the case to begin. Also present were the Crown Prosecution team led, once again, by Sir Gordon Nuttall-Jones. As their lordships took their seats, the noise of the pleasantries between the parties died down and it was time for Irene to open the case for the defence.

"Your Lordships, we are here today to consider the appeal of Harry Thomson against his conviction for the murders of Angela Clarkson, and Diane Wilson. It is the contention of the defence that this man has been convicted on the flimsiest circumstantial evidence ever brought before any court in the land. Throughout the trial, my client always maintained he had never ever seen Angela Clarkson in his life and during the trial the prosecution could not produce one person or one shred of evidence linking the two of them."

"Since the conviction, we have uncovered new evidence that Bridget Riley, one of the main witnesses for the crown, gave false evidence, and you will see before you, her sworn oath that she gave this false evidence under duress and extreme pressure from somebody within the Merseyside Police."

At this moment she was interrupted by the presiding judge, His Honour Lord Chief Justice Stanhope, who asked brusquely and incredulously, "Are you asking this court to believe that somebody in the Merseyside Police Force actually coerced this young lady into going into the witness box in a murder trial, and that she subsequently perjured herself? Young lady, I must warn you that this is an allegation of the most serious kind, and you are going to find yourself in the most serious trouble if you cannot substantiate those remarks." He had now completed his admonishment, and after conferring with his two learned colleagues, he motioned to her to continue.

Although a little more nervous, Irene continued, "The defence had hoped to bring this lady into court today, but I regret to advise you this will not be possible because she has been murdered. However your lordships will find, on page three of the bundle, an affidavit sworn on oath to this effect. Once again, she was interrupted by Justice Stanhope whose annoyance was now evident to the whole court, "Miss Yarwood are you now telling this court that you are not in a position to substantiate this charge directly, and we will only have the sworn statement of a murdered prostitute to rely on?"

Irene didn't give him time to continue. She instantly remembered the rebuke she had received in the original trial concerning the admission of the confession by the convicted felon Chambers, and from the position so far she could see she was going to be in for a very rough ride indeed. Therefore, it was a case of straight in with both feet and all guns blazing.

"Your honour, I would respectfully remind you that, up until the demise of this young lady, she was prepared to come here today and give this evidence before you. Whatever she did to earn a living is no concern of mine, or this court. Just because she was a prostitute, that doesn't mean her evidence would be any less credible, or believable than, say a bus driver, a convicted felon, or even a high court judge." She knew, from the reaction on the faces of the judges, the remark had hit home with a dramatic and telling effect. She also knew she couldn't expect any sympathy from anybody in this court, and from this moment, she would be in for a very torrid time indeed.

As she anticipated and, as expected, the gavel came down with an enormous crash. Everybody could see Lord Stanhope was absolutely beside himself with rage as he ordered her to approach the bench. He leaned forward as far as he could, in order to get as close as he could to this young upstart, who had just insulted him and his learned colleagues, in his own court of appeal.

He didn't just shout at the small figure beneath him, his voice all but erupted, such was the severity of his rage, and his whole body literally shook, "Before I report you to the bar council to be struck off, young lady, I should like to know what on earth you think you are playing at? You cannot come into this court telling me and my learned colleagues, how to conduct ourselves, and I hope you realise I can have you, and your client's appeal, thrown out immediately, as well as having you charged with contempt."

If the judge thought this would weaken the resolve of the defence, then he didn't know Irene Yarwood. Before her now she saw, not a high court judge but a pompous ass so used to bullying and browbeating people, and so accustomed to getting his own way that she was prepared to sacrifice her entire career rather than back down now. She took a deep breath and replied calmly and quietly, "Your honour, I respectfully beg to differ. I can assure you that it wasn't my intention to cause any offence to you, or any of your colleagues. In addition, I am extremely mindful of the fact that I have an appeal to conduct and I am trying to do this in a manner which ensures I represent my client to the best of my ability. If I could draw the attention of this court to page 56 of the bundle, I will quote from the transcript of the records from the original trial. As you will see, I had objected to the submission of a confession by the witness Chambers on the grounds that he was a convicted felon. I would like to point out my objection was overruled by no less a person than his worship Lord Chief Justice Ewing who said, and I quote, 'whether or not Chambers was a convicted felon did not matter one iota. Although he was certainly a dubious character. Nevertheless, as he hadn't been charged with, or convicted of, perjury in the past, it was up to the jury whether or not they believed him.'

"Therefore, all I am trying to say is, whatever the occupation of Bridget Riley, she was still entitled to come here to give evidence before you. If my choice of words offended you when I mentioned high court judges, I apologise most humbly and I can assure you no disrespect was intended. In this case here, I'm sure you will appreciate I was merely trying to illustrate the point made to me by His Worship, Lord Chief Justice Ewing."

The effect of this speech was certainly not lost on Lord Chief Justice Stanhope. He grudgingly conceded that proceedings should continue and, as directed by him, Irene began again.

"As well as the sworn statement, we will also be introducing confirmation of police coercion by way of another witness. This witness was also asked to give false evidence at the murder trial. Fortunately, for herself, she refused to testify."

Again Lord Stanhope leaned across his desk to enquire whether this evidence would be corroborated to which she replied, "no your honour, we will only have her word on oath." Then, as an afterthought, which clearly brought out the devil in her, she added tongue in cheek, "she is here to be questioned about her evidence but, she is a prostitute."

Irene was most relieved to see the briefest of smiles cross the face of Lord Stanhope as he said, "Point taken Miss Yarwood. Please continue."

"I must now draw your attention to the alleged confession which my client strongly denied making throughout the previous proceedings. Without any pressure being brought to bear, and without offering him any inducements, we are going to bring Royston Chambers before you in order that you may hear, for yourselves, his total retraction of that evidence, which was so crucial in obtaining the conviction of my client. Mr. Chambers is well aware that, by coming here today and giving this evidence, he might end up facing charges of perjury and he also could, if found guilty, end up serving an additional term of imprisonment. In this instance, when Chambers is giving that evidence, I will respectfully ask for the court to take into account the fact that at the time he was also being threatened by the Merseyside Police."

Once more, Lord Stanhope halted proceedings whilst he consulted his two colleagues before saying, "Miss Yarwood, these really are the most worrying and disturbing allegations you are making. And, my colleagues and I will insist that you must be able to offer something in the way of backing up these claims. We find it almost inconceivable that the Merseyside Police, in fact any police force, would act in this manner."

Irene responded firmly saying if she could show, and quite clearly she could, that three completely independent people were prepared to come forward to testify, surely that should be sufficient corroboration to make a balanced judgement, not forgetting that one of those persons could face further charges. She had left the most difficult part until the last, and now she couldn't delay any longer her comments concerning the new forensic reports,

She allowed herself a sip of water before continuing, "We will also be presenting our own forensic expert to give his views on the new evidence to be introduced by the crown. No doubt the prosecution will lay this before you very shortly. However, before this evidence is heard, I would like your lordships to rule upon whether, or not, this is admissible because the prosecution are on record as saying in the original trial there was no DNA evidence in the Clarkson case. As an afterthought she added, "on page 37 of the bundle you will find the comments on this subject, made by your very learned and able colleague. Lord

Chief Justice Ewing, when he took me to task on this very issue. Once again, Lord Stanhope permitted himself a faint smile as he whispered, "there's that man again." Irene herself smiled at this rare moment of humour in proceedings before sitting down and at the same time informing the court that was the case for the defence.

Sir Gordon Nuttall-Jones wasted no time at all. Once upon his feet he proclaimed, "Your Lordships, the case for the prosecution is simple. First of all, you have the transcript of the original trial, and upon the evidence contained therein Thompson was quite correctly convicted. Since that conviction, and just prior to this appeal being granted, there was another leap forward in the field of forensic medicine. This meant experts were now able to test samples taken from clothing and match them with samples obtained from suspects. In this case, the killer left traces of semen on the clothing of the dead women but this could not be used in evidence as the technique for lifting DNA profiles from clothing had not been perfected. Well, now it has, and all I can say is this, if we had been able to use this evidence during the original trial, then I doubt very much that we would be here today. We will be able to show your Lordships that this evidence is conclusive, and all the tests were carried out properly. We have again asked the forensic scientist, Professor Guy Whittingham, to be present for examination of this new evidence, and he will be able to explain everything to your complete satisfaction. Earlier you heard my learned opponent asking you to reject this evidence. I would respectfully suggest you ignore that plea because the results of the tests are so compelling, it is just as though Thompson had confessed to the crime himself. I am equally sure, once you have listened to the evidence, you will remain as convinced as before that the correct person has been convicted, and society in general feels a lot safer with him behind bars. I am also convinced, when you come to reach your conclusions, you will put behind you all this ridiculous talk you have heard concerning the conduct of certain members of the Merseyside Police force. They did a magnificent job in hunting down this most vicious killer. In my book, it goes without saying the two principal officers deserve commendations for their efforts in bringing Thompson to justice. My lords, I leave matters in your hands, and await your decision regarding the admission of the forensic evidence."

The three robed figures withdrew to make their deliberations and also to recess for lunch.

Across London, in another court, Timothy Harris sat with his legal team. They were attending a high court hearing to determine whether, or not, the life support systems keeping Paula Harris alive could be switched off. During the morning's proceedings, Timothy had kept in the background leaving his legal team to do all the work, and so far everything appeared to be going to plan. His barrister Jerome Jerome had spent the best part of the morning explaining to the judge that Mrs. Harris was totally blind, completely deaf, unable to move a muscle, and quite incapable of any bodily movement. As a result he argued it was fair to say the poor woman was only alive thanks to the working of the life support system. In addition, as her husband Timothy Harris was her only known, and closest relative, the decision to terminate her life could only be taken by him. Jerome assured the judge they had considered this case from every angle possible, but with no prospect of a return to anything like a normal life, it was now considered to be in the best interests of the patient to take this step."

The defence team, aided by Peter Woods the consultant in charge, had stoutly resisted all the arguments. They had insisted that more time was all the patient needed, although they did reluctantly conclude they couldn't hazard a guess as to how much time might be needed, and how long Mrs. Harris might remain in this state.

All eyes were now centred on the judge as the court reconvened after lunch and he began, "This is indeed a sad case. A very sad case indeed and may I also point out, it is also one which cannot be taken lightly. For the taking of another person's life is a very, very serious business indeed. I must be very honest with you all, I find the prospect quite daunting but, even so, I am going to find for the plaintiff Mr. Harris. Although I do not know the gentleman, nevertheless, I understand he has had rather a hard time of it recently, that is if one believes some of the things which are published in the press, and taking into consideration the fact that his name has been within the public's eye on a number of occasions recently."

"Although deserving of sympathy, that is not the reason for my judgement in his favour. I have reached this difficult decision by taking into account the fact that the defendants have been very honest and open about the true state of the health of this unfortunate woman, and they are unable to give any estimate of if or when she might be expected to improve.

Court observers now noticed a distinct change in his tone of voice as he continued, "However, I am bound to say that in the belief that sometimes miracles do happen I'm quite prepared to delay the implementation of my decision for twenty-eight days. If, during that period of time, there has been no recognisable improvement in the condition of the patient, then the support systems may be switched off."

Turning to the defence, Judge Martin Russell addressed his remarks specifically to the doctor, Peter Woods, saying, "Let there be no doubt in your mind whatsoever, if you can show this court, together with medical evidence, that there has been some improvement in the condition of your charge, then I shall be more than happy to review or even rescind my decision."

Jerome Jerome looked at his client and smiled briefly saying, "Well there you are Mr. Harris. This means, I come down here one week from today, and eventually if there's not been any improvement, the judge signs the order, and the hospital have to comply with the wishes of the court and yourself. I trust for your sake you've made the right decision, because if the roles were reversed, I don't think I would have had the bottle for it. Please don't misunderstand me, I'm not criticizing you, or your motives, I am merely reiterating what the judge said earlier."

Timothy Harris merely nodded, and they left the court together engaged in earnest conversation.

In the Appeal Court things were not going too well for the defence. After the lunch recess, and much spirited argument, their lordships ruled the new evidence was admissible. Sir Gordon Nuttall-Jones had just finished his questions to the forensic expert, Professor Guy Whittingham, and now it was the turn for the defence.

Irene began her cross examination without any hesitation.

"Tell me, Mr Whittingham, how sure can we be that the forensic evidence is correct, and is it not at all possible for this evidence to be flawed in any way because this clothing, or those extracts from the clothing, have been stored for a considerable length of time? In addition, surely some contamination was bound to have occurred when the Wilson girl, together with her clothing, was immersed in water at the quarry. With regard to Angela Clarkson, her body and clothing, were left in a ditch exposed to all the elements, and we know there was at least one torrential downpour before her body was discovered."

"Yes, I agree," countered the professor, "I can assure this court that the samples have been stored under clinical laboratory conditions, and, although I did find some sign of deterioration in the samples available to me, I didn't find the deterioration to be a significant factor due to any exposure with water. With regard to the Clarkson woman, although the clothing had been exposed to the elements, after analysis and comparison, the only conclusion I could come to was that these samples matched the sample I had tested originally in the Clarkson case. And that matching sample could only have come from Thompson."

"That may all be very well, Professor, but this sample, as you said, was obtained from clothing, which doesn't prove Thompson killed the girls now, does it?"

Before he could answer, there came the all too familiar voice of Sir Gordon crying out, "objection, your lordships, what my learned colleague is forgetting is this definitely proves he was present at the scene."

Lord Stanhope agreed with this, and motioned to Irene to continue. Irene knew that the appeal was as good as lost, but she was determined not to give in without a fight. Although there was still the defence expert to call, she felt there was very little else which could be achieved by doing so. He had already informed the defence team he would not be able to disprove the claims of the prosecution that the samples were from Thompson. All he could hope to do was throw some doubt in the minds of the judges, concerning the contamination of the samples. It was then her eyes caught her own notes which she had scribbled during the address made by the prosecution. For a moment she couldn't continue as she read, then reread, the words she had written. "It was just as though he had confessed," these words went over and over in her mind, together with the ruling in the Hurst case under Article Six of The Human Rights Act. She became acutely aware that the judges were anxiously waiting for her to continue as these thoughts rapidly crossed her mind then a plan of attack presented itself to her.

She allowed herself one last quick glance at her notes before continuing, "One final thing professor before you go, did I and their lordships, hear you correctly just then, when you said the sample you tested came from the sample provided by my client in the original murder enquiry into the Clarkson case?"

Full of his own sense of importance, and quite convinced his evidence was irrefutable he answered, "Yes, that is most definitely correct. I used the same readings from that sample against the samples obtained from the clothing of the deceased women."

"And tell me, professor, were these new readings identical to the readings you obtained before?" She enquired.

Still full of his own belief and importance, the professor replied, "Well they were certainly close enough for me to say they came from the same person, and that person has been identified as Harry Thompson."

"So professor, we are again talking about 300 million to one are we?"

"Yes," agreed the witness, "it has to be read in that context, although, to allow for the slight contamination of the samples taken from the clothing, I would reduce those odds somewhat, to…" for a brief moment he hesitated in order to reassess the odds, then he added, "say, 200 million to one."

Now the knife was honed to perfection, and Irene was ready to plunge it straight in the jugular, "Surely Professor, that wasn't the correct thing to do was it?

He frowned at her, and the question, before replying, "I'm afraid I don't understand you. I can assure you, and this court, all the correct procedures and tests were properly conducted, and scientifically carried out."

"No. They were not, professor!" she thundered, "These tests could not have been carried out properly, because in the first instance you should not have been in a position to compare those new tests with anything. My client's sample, after comparison with Clarkson, was ordered to be destroyed along with the two hundred other samples which were given voluntarily at the start of this murder enquiry. If that had been done, you wouldn't have a sample to compare it with. Perhaps you can tell this court why this sample was not destroyed?"

Although a little subdued, he was still quite composed as he replied, "At the time none of the samples were destroyed on the orders of the officers leading the murder enquiry so quite naturally I thought it quite in order to continue testing, especially when the new techniques came out. Throughout it all I kept the crown prosecution service well informed of all developments."

Sir Gordon was on full alert and addressed the judges, "My lords, where on earth are we going here? It is painfully obvious that my learned friend is clutching at straws, does it make one jot of difference where the sample first came from, or, from where it was obtained? Surely, all that matters is a sample from Thompson, provided by Thompson, matched samples found at the scenes by the forensic team. The clothing exhibits have been shown to yourselves and you've been able to satisfy yourselves they had been properly tagged and recorded in evidence. What on earth will be proved or achieved if these samples are rejected and Thomson is asked to provide another one? The end result will be identical and it will show without a shadow of doubt that Thompson is the man."

Irene was determined not to be outdone. Still visibly annoyed she countered this outburst by proclaiming, vehemently, "Your lordships, my learned colleague is overlooking a simple, but very fundamental point which is this. My client had a right to silence in a court of law, and that right has been denied to him because of the incorrect action of the prosecution in not destroying his voluntary sample. I would respectfully ask you to go back to the transcripts at the beginning of this hearing, where you will find my learned colleague saying to you, and I quote." She paused for a moment to look at her notes, then she continued, "The results are so compelling it is as though Thompson is confessing his guilt. My client has never confessed his guilt, and I have witnesses here today to prove it, and this proves what I am saying. Under European law, my client has a right to silence which has now been denied to him. If you wish to study this for a while might I suggest you look at the recent verdict in the Hurst case which was before the European courts very recently on this very issue. Once again I must ask your lordships to reconsider your own decision to allow this evidence in court today."

Announcing a short recess, their lordships withdrew to reconsider their decision. In the courtroom, the antagonism continued. Sir Gordon could hardly contain himself as he raged at Irene, "What on earth do you think you are playing at. Surely, your own common sense should tell you that you haven't got a leg to stand on? Your man is as guilty as sin, and this evidence proves it. What difference does it make when, or where, the sample came from? All that really matters is that the sample is his, and it had been correctly obtained in the first place.

Although short in stature, Irene drew herself up to her full height of five feet two inches, and even though she could barely reach a couple of inches above his navel she was not deterred in the least as she launched into another onslaught. "Have you ever considered that, if suspects are denied their right to silence, it won't be long before we're back in the dark ages torturing people in order to obtain confessions.

"Don't be ridiculous," he angrily retorted, "the way you are going you are trying to pervert the course of justice. Anyway you won't be allowed to get away with it as I am sure their lordships will reject your submission out of hand as well they should."

The usher brought the arguments under control when he signalled to the court that their Lordships were about to return. Once Lord Stanhope was satisfied that his colleagues were comfortably seated he began, "We have discussed the point of law raised by Miss Yarwood for the defence, and, whilst we have to agree that it does indeed touch upon a new point of law, we are satisfied that it has no relevance here today. Therefore, we will allow this evidence to stand. He then nodded approvingly for Irene to continue.

Because she had now moved the impetus of her examination away from the new forensic techniques, she decided that it would not be in the best interests of the defence to call Sir Martin Littlejohn at this stage and, after a brief discussion with this witness together with her legal team, she urged him to continue his own tests and experiments in an effort to find something which might be of some use at a later date.

She resumed her defence by calling Michael Mulrooney in order to question him about his interview with Bridget Riley. He was able to confirm the affidavit shown to the court had been sworn in his office, and that Bridget Riley also attested to the truth of the contents. After a brief examination by the prosecution, Lord Stanhope intervened again to say that he wanted a transcript of that evidence, and all subsequent evidence on the subject forwarding to the Home Secretary. He made it quite plain it would be up to that gentleman to institute further enquiries into the allegations.

Theresa O'Rourke followed the solicitor into the box and she gave her evidence in the same manner. Yet again, the proceedings were interrupted by Lord Chief Justice Stanhope reminding her in no uncertain manner that the repercussions for perjury were extremely severe. He went on to say that it was most likely she would be questioned further by the authorities on the questions of coercion and police irregularities, once this appeal had been heard.

Sir Gordon took an instant dislike to Theresa O'Rourke as a witness. It showed immediately in his demeanour and the sarcastic manner he put his questions to her. He asked her why she hadn't volunteered to come to the aid of the defence with a similar statement when the trial took place.

In reply, Theresa told him that she was too afraid of that "bent copper," Mr. West.

"Well now," sneered the arrogant QC. "Your friend Bridget wasn't afraid was she? Why did you think she came forward?" Without allowing her time to answer, he continued, "I'll tell you why. She came forward to help Angela, your friend, who was so brutally murdered."

"Bridget didn't give evidence to help Angela or her memory or the police. I'm telling you Bridget gave that evidence because she was so afraid of that rotten copper stitching her up on a charge of possession, and her being sent back inside. That's what we were both afraid of, and look what has happened to her now." After this little outburst, Theresa glared at Sir Gordon. She was challenging him to speak ill of the dead and her departed friend if he dared.

"Come on now, Miss O'Rourke, are you seriously asking this court to believe that this detective has had something to do with the death of your friend? I have to tell you that that is a very serious allegation to make."

Theresa looked long and hard at this sneering individual. She wished she could meet him on a cold dark night, thinking, 'a good hard kick in the balls is what you need,' before replying,"I am not saying that. All I am saying is that we were all afraid of this man, and we'd recently been to see a solicitor to make a complaint for wrongful arrest. My friend Bridget, and myself, were adamant this time he wasn't going to get away with it.

Now she's gone and whilst I can't say that he had anything to do with her death, you can't stop me having my own suspicions."

Lord Chief Justice Stanhope who had been making furious notes during this exchange, again intervened saying angrily, "Young woman, whatever suspicions you have concerning your late friend, or anybody else, please keep them to yourself or report them to the police. Kindly note, I will not have such baseless and completely groundless accusations, made in my court, especially when one is trying to involve the police. Do I make myself clear?"

"Perfectly your Honour," she answered.

"You may step down now," commanded Sir Gordon adding, "I have no further questions."

Theresa left the court room deep in thought and wondering if she had done the right thing in coming here in the first place.

Royston Chambers stood in the witness box. Before Irene could begin, the senior judge delivered a severe admonishment to him, "My colleagues and I have studied your evidence in the trial very carefully and, before you give any evidence here today, we wish to impress upon you that you could well be facing serious trouble retracting your evidence from the original trial. By coming here today, you are telling this court that the evidence you gave before was nothing more than a figment of your own imagination, and you perjured yourself in giving that evidence. As a result, you could end up with an additional sentence to serve on top of the one you are currently serving. I trust these remarks are not lost on you, Chambers."

Following this outburst from the bench, it was obvious before Irene asked her first question, Royston Chambers was wishing he was back at Stafford and he had made the gravest mistake of his life coming here today. But it was too late now as Irene began, "Mr. Chambers will you please confirm that you are at present serving a term of five years imprisonment at one of Her Majesty's penal institutions, and whilst you were on remand you became acquainted with Harry Thomson, who had been arrested and charged with the murders of two people?"

Chambers "Yes that is correct Miss."

Miss Yarwood "During your time on remand, did you ever come into contact or conversation with Harry Thompson?"

Chambers "Yes Miss I came into contact with him but I hardly ever spoke to him at all."

Miss Yarwood "How close did you get to him?

Chambers "Well I was moved into the cell next door and we were neighbours so to speak for up to six months, but, during this time other than to say hello, I hardly ever spoke to him."

Miss Yarwood "Did he ever speak to you, and did he ever confess to you that he was guilty of these two crimes?"

Chambers "No never, not ever, and that's the absolute truth."

Miss Yarwood "Will you please tell this court how you came by this so called confession."

Chambers "Well Miss I had received a couple of visits from Detective Sergeant West. During these visits, he kept telling me I was facing at least seven years in gaol this time, but, if I could help him by getting Thompson to confess, he would come to my trial and try to get my sentence reduced."

Miss Yarwood "And did you help him?"

Chambers "No, not at first, because, Thompson wouldn't talk to anybody, let alone me."

Miss Yarwood "So what did the Sergeant do. Did he

	threaten you at all?"
Chambers	"Well actually, thinking about it, he was very clever, because, he just kept suggesting that, if I didn't get him this confession, he wouldn't help me. He also kept telling me that, if I didn't do it then I would also be in trouble with his boss, Detective Inspector Taylor. That's when I knew it was getting really serious, and, if I didn't give them what they wanted, they could well end up framing me for another job as well."
Miss Yarwood	"So what did you do next?"
Chambers	"Well I gave in didn't I?" I gave them a confession which was just what they wanted but I made it all up, every single word."
Miss Yarwood	"As a result of this, are you aware that, without your confession and without the false evidence from Bridget Riley, Harry Thompson could well be a free man, able to walk the streets at will?"
Chambers	"Yes I am, Miss, and that's why I have volunteered to come here today because, whilst I have been in prison, I have had a visit from Mr. West telling me not to come here today. He reckons nobody will believe me, and with this new evidence against Thompson, it will be a waste of time. He also said, because of this new evidence, the right man was in gaol, and he no longer felt obliged to help me in my appeal."
Miss Yarwood	"Thank you Mr. Chambers. I have no further questions but if you will wait there

I am sure Mr. Nuttall-Jones will think of something to ask you.

Sir Gordon was already on his feet and he moved quickly into the attack, "Come on now, Chambers, you know full well that this isn't true. Admit it man, there isn't one grain of truth in any of your allegations whatsoever. First of all, let me remind you, you are under oath here, and I would like to take you back to the trial where you swore, on oath, that the evidence you gave was the truth the whole truth and nothing but the truth. At that time, you never mentioned anything about being pushed into this by anyone in the police force, and that can only be a malicious falsehood on your part."

Chambers	"No, The only truth is what is being said here right now."
Sir Gordon	"Well I think it's something different, and I'm putting it to you that you have come here today to try to cause trouble for a man who has devoted a lifetime serving the public and to solving crime within the Merseyside area. I am also putting it to you that you've come here today with this cock and bull story in the hope that, if somehow you are to be believed, you might get a reduction in your sentence. Well I can assure you Mr. Chambers, that it is not going to wash and you'll end up in very serious trouble. Think about that."
Chambers	"I already have and, with the evidence presented here today, there's probably quite a lot of truth in what you say. In which case, I say to you, why should I come here today to take such a risk? Well, I'll tell you. As far as I am concerned, I've got nothing

to lose, and, eventually, when the truth
does come out, I might have something to
gain."

Sir Gordon addressed the bench before indicating he had no further questions, "Your lordships, I would like this court to consider that, if you do not believe the evidence of this witness here today, then, he has without doubt, committed perjury. On the other hand, if you think that he has told you the truth today then he undoubtedly committed perjury at the murder trial. Either way, he cannot have it both ways, and it is my contention, his sole purpose in coming here today was to try to make such an impression that he might have been able to secure a reduction in his sentence. Then, as he resumed his seat, he continued to glare at the hapless figure of Chambers leaving the court.

With the proceedings over, the three robed figures left the court to consider their verdict which would be announced two days later.

Chapter 25

After the high court hearing, with the day coming towards its conclusion, Timothy Harris found himself the centre of attraction. The baying hounds from the press refused to leave him alone as his own case before the court was prominently featured on the television.

Lying in her bed in the private hospital, Paula Harris could hear all the activity around her. In fact, she had been aware of it almost from the start of her ordeal. The trouble was she couldn't see where she was, and nobody took a blind bit of notice whenever she spoke. It never occurred to her that nobody could hear her because no sound came from her lips. She knew she was in hospital and she knew her bed had been made for she had heard the nurses saying to each other, "Roll her on her side, now lift her this way etc. Under normal circumstances all this effort would make a patient feel a little more comfortable, but, as in Paula's case, when your body is completely devoid of feeling, nothing at all felt different.

This daily ritual was interrupted by the sound of the telephone ringing. Paula heard the voice of Sister Brenda speaking in reply, "Hello, hello, oh it's you Mr. Woods, yes I can hear you. No, Matron has just left the ward, and we're making Mrs. Harris as comfortable as possible. At this point her voice faltered momentarily, as she said, "No doctor, there hasn't been any change in her condition, and there's still absolutely no response from her. In fact, everything remains the same as before you left, and we look forward to seeing you when you get back. By the way, is it possible to say how you got on at the high court today? She gave a sharp intake of breath as she received the news that, barring a miracle, her charge had twenty-eight days to live. Shocked by the news she had just heard, she clumsily replaced the receiver whilst calling anxiously to her colleague, "Betty, Betty quick that was Mr. Woods on the telephone speaking from London. According to him, it's practically all over for Mrs. Harris. Apparently, the judge has ruled if there is no medical evidence of any improvement in her condition within the next twenty-eight days, her support systems will be switched off."

Betty heard the news with alarm. "My God, she exclaimed. "That's terrible news, and her lying here like this not knowing anything about it, and to make matters worse, not even knowing her son was buried last week. Tell you what, Brenda, it makes you realise just how lucky and well off people like us really are."

Brenda readily agreed, and commiserated with her colleague as they both set about the completion of their allotted tasks.

Trapped in her inert state, it was impossible to describe the pain now felt by Paula Harris as she digested the news that she was on a life support system, and at best she had only four weeks to live. This coupled with the confirmation that her son Anthony had died set her mind racing with a hundred and one questions which could not be answered. Once again, she agonised to God that it could not be true. Please. Please dear God, she prayed, don't let it be true about Anthony or the life support system. With all the strength she could muster she was trying to scream the place down. Surely, she thought, somebody will hear me. God Almighty, why can't somebody hear me, but it was no use, no sound issued from her lips. Despite all her efforts, her limbs refused to respond to her commands to move. As she lay there, utterly exhausted from her efforts, the two dedicated nurses left the ward. As they left, they were unable to see, the single, salt laden tear, which had formed within her eye before beginning it's painstakingly slow journey down her cheek. Beneath the bedclothes, she moved the little finger on her right hand with agonising slowness trying to mount it across her index finger. After another supreme effort, she finally succeeded then, as the medication administered by her dedicated nurses began to take effect, she lapsed into a deep sleep, still praying to God, still hoping against hope this was nothing more than a bad dream, from which she would escape when she finally awoke.

Relaxing, in her little flat, in the parish of All Saints, Manchester, Edith Farrell had just poured herself a refreshing cup of tea when she heard the announcement on the television about Timothy Harris and his case in the high court concerning the switching off of the support systems keeping Paula Harris alive. She knew at once this case referred to the Mrs. Harris who had suffered a terrible stroke whilst visiting herself at the premises of the Manchester Children's Adoption Society. Hearing this sad news upset her badly, because somehow she knew instinctively, Mrs. Harris desperately wanted to contact her son. If it were true her support systems were going to be switched off, she was acutely aware this would not be possible. Edith Farrell could not live with herself if she allowed that to happen and, her own conscience demanded that she take action. Normally, under adoption society rules, unless both parties specifically agree to contact, then contact cannot take place. This rule ensures that any person wishing to forget about that period in their lives is free to do so. She knew she was taking a chance, and if she was found out it could also mean she would lose her job as well as her pension rights, but she felt she could not stand idly by and let somebody turn off her support system. In addition, Edith Farrell was also aware that Mrs. Harris's first born son also wished to make contact, and if that opportunity was denied him now, he would never get the opportunity to meet his real birth mother. At first she was in a quandary about how she should proceed then, after giving the matter some considerable thought, she decided she would write a letter to the lawyers who had handled the defence of Harry Thompson. She reasoned, quite correctly, that she should be able to obtain that information from The Law Society the following morning, then she would be able to post her letter straight away.

She wrote as follows:

I wish to advise you that I received correspondence some time ago from one of your clients who was trying to trace his birth mother. It so happened that his birth mother had expressed similar thoughts, and arrangements were being made for these two people to be put in contact with each other. At this stage, I must point out that this contact related only to contact between mother and son, as there was no mention of the name of the father on the birth certificate. Therefore, my society would not be in a position to offer any further assistance should your client wish to pursue the matter further.

As you are aware your client is at present serving a prison sentence, and he insisted, before any personal contact was made, his mother had to be made aware of all the relevant facts as he felt his incarceration might make his mother change her mind about the whole thing.

With hindsight, that is something we will never really know for the poor lady suffered a terrible stroke, whilst making a visit to our offices, and the effect of this illness has left her in a terrible state, completely unable to fend for herself.

Today, I have learned that there was a high court hearing to determine whether, or not, the support systems keeping Mrs. Harris alive could be switched off. I realise that I cannot allow this to happen whilst I know that she has a blood relative who, in all probability, would dearly like to be put in touch with her.

Perhaps, this is something that you could discuss initially with her doctors at St. Margaret's BUPA Hospital Manchester.

This issue is further complicated by the adoption society rules which state contact can only be established if it is the wish of both parties, and in this instance this condition has not been fulfilled, due to the stroke suffered by Mrs. Harris.

In addition, I should also point out that, in writing to you, disclosing this information I am putting my job on the line together with my pension rights. Despite this, I can't sit idly back, allowing this lady to die without her knowing everything possible had been done to reunite her with her child. My own conscience simply will not allow it. All I am asking is that you treat this matter in the strictest confidence because, so much and so many people, depend upon it.

Yours sincerely,
Edith Farrell,
Matron,
Manchester and District Children's Adoption Society

Chapter 26

As usual Betty Oldroyd was in a happy mood as she reported for duty on ward 7. In order not to waste time, Brenda and she had a set routine which involved the first person to arrive collecting the tea tray from the ward station and taking it straight to the ward which housed Paula Harris. Brenda had seen her making the tea, and as a result she had gone straight to the ward. After opening the door she proceeded to open the windows in order to allow the clean fresh air to permeate the room, then it was time to roll the bedclothes, part way down, before they both sat down for their early morning tea.

She had just attended to the covers, when the door opened and Betty entered, with the tray. She turned around and wished her colleague "Good morning. Then she turned to say the same to her patient. It was at that moment the words froze on her lips, and she let out a scream. The tea tray went up in the air, returning to earth with a resounding crash, scattering the scalding contents all over the room. For a moment her colleague was transfixed by the scene, then she shouted, "Betty, good heavens, what is it? What on earth is the matter?" Betty was rooted to the spot. All she could do was point her finger at their inert charge. Unable to see at once what had given her colleague the shock of her life, she repeated the question, "Betty what is it?"

Released from the spell, Betty took three quick strides to the bed and pointed to Paula Harris's hand, crying as she did, "look Brenda, her little finger it's moved!" See, look at it, it's resting on her ring finger. She must have done that last night or sometime after we left. Betty was almost in tears as she continued excitedly, "Brenda, it's a miracle, it's a miracle I tell you. Ring for Mr. Woods immediately. As her colleague picked up the telephone in order to convey the good news, and to request the urgent attendance of that person, Betty reached out, and put her arms around the still body crying, "Mrs. Harris, Paula, please don't worry. It's going to be alright. Oh God, you poor thing, I do wish you could hear me. As doctor Woods arrived on the scene, he was confronted with the sight of two of his senior nurses, crying unashamedly as they tried to explain to him the discovery that their patient had some movement, irrespective of how minute it might be.

After a quick examination of Mrs. Harris, he brought the two of them quickly back to earth, explaining this did not mean that she was going to fully recover, neither did it mean she could understand, or hear, what was going on around her. For the next few minutes, he busied himself requesting the attendance of other colleagues in order that a full and proper clinical reassessment of the patient's condition could be carried out. At this stage, although he dare not show it to those present in the ward, he was also hoping this might prove to be sufficient improvement to allow Judge Russell to change his mind.

Michael Mulrooney was seated in his office. He was reading through the morning mail which had arrived on his desk. One letter in particular had caught his eye. It was a letter sent by Edith Farrell, Matron, at The Manchester and District Children's Adoption Society, and it clearly Identified Harry Thompson as the child of Paula Harris. As he reread the letter, he began to realise the implications, and the effect, the contents could have on the lives of quite a few other people. Potentially, it opened up a whole new can of worms. Out of interest, he found himself posing a number of questions which he thought might be of some relevance. What if, Timothy Harris wasn't the boy's father and if that were the case, how would he react when the news broke, as it surely would, at some given moment in time. Worse still, how would Timothy Harris react if it transpired he was the father of Harry Thompson, and he wasn't aware of this? Almost immediately, he dismissed this scenario from his mind, as he couldn't envisage a situation such as this arising with Timothy Harris being totally unaware of this fact for all these years. Still he, mused, it would be ironic if that were the case, especially with his involvement with Angela Clarkson, the subsequent libel case, and finally, his own son being convicted of the Clarkson murder. He shook his head at the thought, and whispered aloud, "No that's too far-fetched to contemplate. His thoughts now turned to Mrs. Harris, and her position especially since she was under virtual sentence of death. Finally, his thoughts turned to his own client, Harry Thompson. How would he react to the news? In addition, there was also the question of secrecy. Already, he could sympathise with Mrs. Farrell, and the dilemma she faced, and he realised that above all else she had to be protected and her name kept out of the public domain.

A man of quick decisive action, he picked up the telephone and rang the number of Irene Yarwood's mobile phone. One way or another, she had to be informed immediately. Together they would consider the implications, and plan the next moves to be taken.

Irene listened intently as he read the contents of the letter over the phone. She grasped the nettle straight away, telling him, "Michael, the first thing you must do is set up a meeting with the legal team representing the hospital. The knowledge that Mrs. Harris has a son might be sufficient reason to allow the judge to reverse his decision. I know this is taking a chance on Mrs. Farrell being exposed, but I don't think anybody has much choice in this matter especially if the judge rules that the improvement described still doesn't warrant her support systems being left on. Looking at it from another point of view, just suppose Harry Thompson knew that Paula Harris is his birth mother. Don't you think he would be saying to the judge, "kill my mother if you dare!" I know one thing, Timothy Harris won't be pleased to hear this news, and the press will have a field day when they learn, Harry Thompson is his stepson. Go ahead, make contact and set up a meeting as a matter of extreme urgency. If I were you, I think I would go via the consultant who is responsible for her at the hospital, because he will know who best to contact regarding the legal aspect. You might have to put him under a little bit of pressure, as I agree with you we must do all that we can to protect the anonymity of Mrs. Farrell. But I'm sure we'll be able to come up with some way of keeping it secret. Anyway, telephone me later at the office or, if you are free, come down to the Wig and Gown for lunch. Ok? Goodbye and I'll see you later. Thanks."

As requested, Michael telephoned the hospital and arranged to see Doctor Woods without delay. Later that morning, he was shown into the consultant's office where the doctor asked him how he could help.

Michael hesitated, then he decided to put his cards on the table, "I've come to see you about one of your patients, a Mrs. Harris. I think we may have a joint interest in her wellbeing and welfare. I have received information today that this lady has a living relative. In fact it is her son who was adopted many years ago. Strictly speaking, I can't, under any circumstances, reveal the source of my information, but I can assure you that the source is absolutely impeccable, and the information will withstand any test in any court of law. Besides, it's better that you don't know, then you cannot be questioned about it later. I'm sure if you pass this information to your legal representatives and we can arrange a meeting, perhaps something can be done to prolong the life of Mrs. Harris."

Throughout this opening speech, Dr. Woods had studied his visitor intently now he spoke, "Well first of all Mr. Mulrooney, let me thank you for coming here with the news about my patient. I have to say that I find it all very mysterious to say the least. Here we are, with positive information which might prolong the life of my patient, and you can't disclose the source. I must confess I am intrigued to say the least. However, let me put you in the picture. This morning, when my staff and I reported for duty, we were astonished to find there had been some improvement in the condition of Mrs. Harris. Two of the dedicated nurses discovered she has some very slight movement in one of her little fingers. Following on from this and after carrying out further tests, we have been able to ascertain that the lady can hear. Throughout the day we shall be carrying out all manner of tests in an effort to establish if there is any other part of her body which is able to function. Naturally, I have already been in touch with our legal advisers, and we are hopeful that this improvement alone will enable the judge to reverse his decision. Therefore, I'll give them a ring now to see if we can meet as soon as possible in order that we can compare notes. Following a brief telephone conversation Michael found himself driving to the city centre and a meeting with the hospital's legal team. The meeting was short and the discussion brief. It was decided that the appeal would be lodged on the basis of the new medical evidence and, if that tactic did not succeed, then an approach from Harry Thompson would be made, on the basis that he had an interest in the case being the son by birth. It was also agreed the name of Matron Farrell should well be kept out of all matters if it was at all humanely possible. Feeling well satisfied with the morning's work, Michael made his way to his luncheon appointment at the Wig and Gown with Irene Yarwood.

After a pleasant lunch, during which he brought Irene up-to-date with the morning's proceedings, they made their plans for another trip to London to the Court of Appeal for the much awaited the judgement of their lordships. For safekeeping, he deposited the letter from Matron Edith Farrell with Irene, and they both agreed, once it had been established that it had served its useful purpose, it would be returned in person to that upright and stalwart individual. She could then destroy it herself with the knowledge that it could never come back to haunt her in any way.

After lunch, Irene returned to her chambers where she was pleasantly surprised to find Sebastian Kreiff the senior partner waiting for her. He came straight to the point of his visit, "I take it that you'll be going down to the Appeal Court tomorrow, and I wondered if you could do me a great favour.

"Certainly," she responded, "What is it you want me to do?"

"Well, he replied, the Crown Prosecution Service has asked me to defend the appeal of the Latimer Brothers' conviction, and I wondered if you would be able to pick up the court transcripts of the trial from the Central Records Office and bring them back with you. This will ensure I have as much time as possible to study the case. You won't have to wait or anything as I'll get my secretary to telephone the Records Office in advance, and they should have all the relevant files to hand when you get there."

"No problem, she replied, "I'll be in London anyway so I should be able to do that for you and I wasn't planning on stopping over after the verdict, so consider it done. Will that be all Seb?"

"Yes, he answered, "that's all for now, but whilst I'm here, just let me ask you something. Where on earth did you get that idea about Thompson's right to silence, and what on earth made you tie it in with his human rights being abused?"

"To tell you the truth, she answered, I was literally clutching at straws. You can imagine the picture. The crown had just presented this new evidence about lifting DNA from clothing and I knew I didn't really have a leg to stand on. As a result, I was most reluctant to call our forensic expert there and then as I didn't consider I could introduce sufficient doubt in the minds of their lordships, and I thought I had nothing to lose passing him over at this point of the proceedings. Whilst this was going through my mind, I couldn't help thinking about something the prosecution had said earlier, something about this evidence being so compelling my client might just as well have confessed to the crime initially. Had I not have read about the Hurst case in the first place, I probably wouldn't have thought about it, but those words kept going round in my mind, and the next thing I knew I was asking the questions."

"Now I know it hasn't got us anywhere yet, but if the appeal verdict goes against me, then I shall ask for permission to appeal to the House of Lords. In that case, I'll be praying that permission is denied so that I can lodge an appeal with The European Courts. This will be on the basis that when a sample from Harry Thompson was tested without his permission, he was effectively denied his human right to silence, and this was a denial of his basic human rights."

Sebastian looked at her incredulously whilst she continued, "No doubt a lot of people will argue this is trying to get Thompson off on a technicality, but Seb, isn't this what the law is all about? Also we mustn't forget that, if the crown had done its own job properly in the first place, this opportunity would have been denied us.

Finally, allowed an opportunity to speak he asked, "Are you serious about this Irene?"

"Of course I am, and it won't do you the slightest bit of

good trying to persuade me otherwise. Don't forget, my duty is to my client, and nobody else."

"Irene," replied Sebastian, "I wouldn't dream of it. In fact, please let me tell you I think it's absolutely brilliant and I'm praying that it succeeds for you because you certainly deserve it."

"Thanks Seb, I really appreciate that. I really do because, at one stage, I thought I might have blown it but if this comes off then I know it will all have been worthwhile. Incidentally, one last thing before you go, I'll bet you didn't know that Harry Thompson's mother is Paula Harris!" She saw another expression of surprise on his face as the news sank in, and his legal mind went into overdrive, as he too realised the implications and repercussions this could well have on the case.

Whilst he was still thinking about these matters she continued, "Of course that doesn't mean Timothy Harris is the father, but even so I am sure you can imagine the complications which could arise before we've finished with this case."

About to take his leave, Sebastian wished his junior partner good luck, and a pleasant journey before adding, "It just goes to show, Irene, it's a very small world indeed. He was still shaking his head in disbelief as he walked down the corridor to his own office, repeating to himself, "Harry Thompson and Mrs. Harris, mother, and son, who would have believed it?"

Chapter 27

Irene left the office early and returned home in order to collect her overnight bag and her personal things for her trip to London. After checking she had everything she needed she walked to her car and started the motor. She drove slowly out of the drive and headed towards the motorway, and London. Knowing she had at least a four hour drive, she determined to make as much time as possible by keeping to the outside lane with her foot pressed firmly on the accelerator. There was quite a lot of traffic on the road together with the usual borders of colourful plastic cones, and contra-flow systems to admire. Despite this, she continued to make good progress towards her destination, which was the Park Hotel in Finsbury Park. As she entered the building and headed to the reception desk, a quick glance at her watch confirmed she had been travelling for just over four hours. Check in procedures completed she made her way to her room on the first floor.

After a quick shower to freshen up, she proceeded to the restaurant for a light evening meal, before retiring to her room in order to be ready for the events of the following day at The Court of Appeal. Before retiring, she made a brief telephone call to Michael Mulrooney to let him know she had arrived, and, she would see him at the court building in the morning.

Michael was already there when she arrived, and they entered the building together. In due course, the other protagonists arrived, which heralded the usual exchange of greetings, then, as the usher solemnly intoned, "all rise" in his familiar dull and monotonous voice, following which the three robed figures took their places, it was time for the proceedings to get under way.

Lord Stanhope made himself comfortable, turned to both of his colleagues to ensure that all was well, then, with a quick cough to clear his throat he opened the proceedings. "In the Appeal Courts of justice in the case of Regina versus Thompson, this court has unanimously decided that this appeal must fail. My colleagues, and I have reached this verdict irrespective of the new evidence provided by the defence. We are united in our opinion that the correct verdict was reached in the original trial, and there was nothing new in the evidence presented by the defence to enable us to come to any other decision."

"We were not at all swayed by the evidence of the witness, Chambers, who attempted to retract the evidence he gave at the original trial, neither were we suitably impressed with the witness O'Rourke. Regarding the evidence of these two persons, we have ordered that full transcripts of this appeal be sent to the proper authorities in order to ascertain whether any other proceedings should be taken. We have taken a very poor view of the efforts of the defence to smear, and slander, the Merseyside police force with allegations of misconduct and because these allegations have been made, we have issued instructions that an investigation ought to be carried out, if only to clear the good names of the officers involved.

With regard to the new evidence introduced by the prosecution, the defence made a spirited effort to have this evidence rejected. This was bound to fail. Once produced, this evidence only sought to underline the fact that justice was not only seen to be done, but the correct person responsible had been tried, and punished for it. It goes without saying, if this evidence had been available at the very start of this case, then, there would have been no grounds at all for allowing an appeal of this nature.

As Lord Stanhope began to close his papers to indicate the proceedings were over, Irene sprang to her feet, "Your worship", she cried, in an effort to catch his attention, "Is it possible to have the permission of this court to take this appeal to the House of Lords?"

Looking down at her from his lofty position on the bench, Lord Stanhope thundered, "Certainly not permission denied."

Then, to the doleful voice of the usher proclaiming, "All rise" the three judges strode purposefully from the court.

The court cleared very quickly, Irene, and Michael, were left alone. "Well Irene he said "that was short and sweet wasn't it, although, in a way, I'm glad it's all over.

"Yes", she replied, "and, as I told you before today's hearing began, the verdict wasn't unexpected. Now, we just go straight on with the appeal to the Court of Human Rights. Come on let's face it it's not the end of the world, let me buy you a quick drink, then, I'll have to leave you because I have to collect some papers for the boss from the criminal records centre." One hour later they both went their separate ways.

Irene paid the taxi driver, and walked across the car park to collect her car. She drove out of the hotel car park, and despite the heavy traffic, she reached her destination just over an hour later. Alighting from the car, she glanced at the building which housed the Central Criminal Records Office, then she entered the building, and proceeded, as directed, to the first floor.

Sergeant Gerald Crowther was feeling quite smug, and very pleased with himself. Today was his first day of work at the Records Office. Even though he'd only been there a couple of hours, and despite the fact that it was a very mundane job to say the least, nevertheless, he was enjoying every minute of it. Not for him the unrelenting shifts, and station life with all its rules regulations, and, bullshit, no, this job suited him down to the ground. A regular day job, no real loss of pay to speak of, just turn up on time each day, do your eight hours, enjoy your breaks, lots of opportunities to skive off for a smoke and no inspectors or superintendents to worry about. Throughout this first day, he'd reflected many times on his good fortune at landing a cushy number such as this and, considering he'd been on sick leave for almost twelve months with early retirement looming, he had to keep pinching himself in order to convince himself he wasn't dreaming. Another bonus for him was the never ending stream of women calling at his counter, in order to deposit or take away bundles of legal documents. Because he always fancied himself as a ladies' man, this gave him ample chat up opportunities which he positively relished. At this very moment, all he could see were the ample curves of Irene Yarwood approaching his counter. Flashing his broadest smile he enquired "Yes Miss can I help you?"

"Yes," Irene quickly responded, "I'm here to collect some crown prosecution papers for Sebastian Krieff QC. He's been asked to take the Crown Prosecution case against the Latimer Brothers appeal and, I understand the papers are here awaiting collection by myself. Whilst she was talking, it occurred to her the sergeant did not appear to have his mind fully on the job, and an idea flashed through her brain. She resolved to exploit the situation adding, "I don't think I've seen you here before have I? She waited with baited breath for his reply praying she hadn't blown it but, she needn't have worried as he responded, "No miss, actually it's my first day here; I'm sort of feeling my way about so to speak."

The idea in her brain grew enormously as she realised this was indeed a heaven- sent opportunity. What on earth prompted her, or, where the idea sprang from she didn't have a clue. All she knew was she had to go along with it, and she said, as casually as she could, "and Mr. Kreiff would also like the papers on Regina versus Thompson Liverpool 1988. He might not have gone through the channels for those papers as he only rang me whilst I was making my way here." Irene flashed him a warm inviting smile whilst awaiting his response.

She didn't have to wait long. His reply was almost instantaneous. He was well and truly hooked, and he returned her smile with one of his own together with a wink, saying "Don't worry about it Miss, I'll go and get those first then we'll sort things out from there. He turned away, swaggering along the corridor thinking to himself, "this job's a bloody doddle. Who knows, I might even be in here."

He returned a few minutes later with the bundles of documents which he placed on the counter, saying as he did, "I'll be back in a few minutes. I've just been told my boss wants a quick word, and, as it's my first day, I don't want to risk upsetting him."

"Take all the time you want," she replied, unable to believe her good fortune. Irene watched him disappearing down the corridor and, with her brain pounding and her hands trembling, she began to look at the files he had left. As soon as she saw the third folder, she knew she had hit the jackpot. It was boldly emblazoned with a white sticker containing the words Not To Be Disclosed To The Defence. When she saw this, she was almost in a state of shock, and she realised the only thing she could do was borrow it, and hope the stupid oaf hadn't counted the files before leaving them. She reasoned thatonce outside the building she would have ample time to look at it, and if there was nothing of any great significance, she could return it immediately without harm. She looked around quickly, to ensure there was nobody about, then she placed the file beside her brief case on the floor. She busied herself searching the other files, wishing all the time the sergeant would soon return. A quick glance through the other folders gave no insight to any additional information concerning the case, although there was a note from the crown prosecution legal team rejecting Theresa O'Rourke as a witness on the basis that she might prove unreliable and this could possibly have a damaging effect upon the testimony of Bridget Riley, and Royston Chambers.

When Sergeant Crowther returned, he was pleased to see Irene busily scribbling her shorthand notes. He placed the transcripts of the Latimer Brothers case on the counter, and enquired if she would be taking away the files on the Thompson case.

She gave him another dazzling smile as she answered, "Well actually, it would be better if I could. I really wanted to get back to Manchester tonight in order that Mr. Krieff might look at them but, if that'll give you a problem, I might just as well stay here and make some more notes.

Thoroughly captivated, desperately anxious to please and make a good impression, Sergeant Crowther volunteered his services to book the additional files out for her, even though he knew the request and subsequent arrangements, should have been made beforehand.

Irene couldn't believe her luck as she quickly gathered up all the files on the counter. She placed them all on top of the file she had secreted, and picked up her brief case before smiling once more at her hapless victim saying, "Thank you very much sergeant you've been most helpful. Obviously I'll get these back to you as soon as possible. If I can't get back myself I'll send them by express courier." Another smile, then she was rushing through the door.

Despite the fact that she didn't want to draw undue attention to herself, she still found herself almost running to her car and she had to force herself to slow down. Once safely within the confines of the vehicle, she knew she had to resist the deadly urge within her to look at this mysterious file there and then, as it was imperative to get away from this place. With her heart still thumping and pounding away, she started the car and drove slowly out of the car park. As she drove, she kept telling herself not to panic, and all she needed to do was concentrate on her driving until she found a safe place to stop where she could look at the file in much greater detail.

Gradually she regained control of herself, and began the long drive back to Manchester along the motorway. When she saw the sign for the first service station she didn't hesitate. She moved smoothly off the busy road, and into the parking area. She didn't get out of the car. Instead she reached for the file. Her hands continued to tremble as she opened it to reveal the information the police and the prosecution had strived so very hard to conceal from the defence.

She certainly wasn't disappointed. The file contained all the details of the police interview with Timothy Harris. It clearly showed he'd been with Angela Clarkson, and confirmed he had paid her for sex. His statement also confirmed that he'd given her the watch, or a watch identical to the watch shown on the Crime Watch programme on television. Then there was the DNA evidence, confirming he'd been her last client. After reading the statements of Timothy Harris and the manager of the Roundhead Hotel, it soon became clear why he had been excluded from the murder enquiry. It was equally obvious, and apparent to Irene that, had this evidence been available to the defence at the time of the trial, Harry Thompson would have stood an excellent chance of being found not guilty. She also knew, with this evidence before the appeal judges, his appeal might even have been successful. However, that was water under the bridge now as that issue was clouded by the admission of the new forensic evidence. Damn that bloody DNA sample, and damn that bloody judge Lord Stanhope. She cursed silently to herself. If it wasn't for that, this case would be as good as finished. Still, never mind she thought, I can still get there through the European Courts so it isn't the end of the world yet.

She had reached the end of the file and thoroughly digested the contents. Now, it was abundantly clear Timothy Harris had lied to parliament, and he had perjured himself in his libel trial against the press. With some reluctance she closed the file, and made her way to the cafeteria where she bought herself a much needed drink. Apart from the drink, she needed time to think and clear her brain before she could face the long journey home. Taking out her mobile phone she called Sebastian Krieff as she thought it was of the utmost importance to advise him of these dramatic developments in the case. Once the connection was made, Sebastian couldn't believe what he was hearing, "Just take your time getting back. I'll wait here until you do Irene," he urged, "In the meantime I'll let Michael Mulrooney know, although, on second thoughts, maybe you should do that; after all it's you that has earned it. Before leaving, she telephoned Michael with the good news, then she resumed her journey back to Manchester.

Four hours later she arrived back at the office where she found Sebastian waiting as promised. She was also surprised to find the other two senior partners present together with Michael Mulrooney. Sebastian explained to Irene that the news of her discovery had travelled quickly through the practice, and although congratulations were not yet in order, nevertheless, they all felt the occasion was worthy of some celebration. In addition, everybody wished to see if there was any contribution they could make. To Irene, the fact that her colleagues were prepared to put themselves out in this manner, without being asked, pleased her immensely, and she was delighted at the thought that, she had joined a practice where her partners really cared. Naturally, all concerned wanted to see first-hand the mysterious file, especially since something as sinister as this was almost unknown in legal circles. In fact, they could only recall one other instance relating to a case in the Midlands many years ago, where the defence had been denied access to vital documents.

Whilst the persons assembled in the chambers waited for copies of the file to be distributed, Sebastian produced a bottle of champagne, and he proposed a toast to the successful conclusion to the case. Then, returning to the serious side of the business, he addressed everybody, "This case is not over yet, and whatever is discussed here tonight must remain within these four walls. I want you all to be quite clear about this, Irene has done a magnificent job, but it's far from over. Also, please remember, she's taken a tremendous risk in bringing out these papers that is why I want this to be kept strictly under wraps. This is Irene's case, and how she proceeds from here will be entirely up to her, but if anybody in this office can come up with any specific form of procedure which may assist our colleague, I'm sure it will be greatly appreciated. The only thing which bothers Irene and me is we will all sleep much happier once these files have been returned to the Central Criminal Records Office, so, it goes without saying that the original file must be returned by motor cycle courier first thing in the morning. With that he handed the meeting over to Irene.

Irene thanked those present and then began "As you know I've just been to the appeal court where my client's appeal was denied as was permission to appeal to the House of Lords. I was expecting that, and now it leaves the way clear for me to appeal this case direct to the European Court of Human Rights. Just in case you're not familiar with this, I must add that this stems from the verdict in the recent "Hurst" case, whereby Mr. Hurst was denied his right to silence when a DNA sample of his was taken from him, and used without his permission. During my appeal, the thought occurred to me that because

Thompson had not given his permission for a DNA specimen of his to be used then his right to silence had also been taken from him. Using the same argument, it will be my contention that this was an abuse of his human rights. A successful appeal on this basis will be sufficient to get the verdict against him overturned, and then, I'll go back to the appeal courts to have his other conviction overturned. In this latter case, there was so little evidence against him I'm more than hopeful their lordships will rule that conviction unsafe."

"Whilst waiting for all of this to take place I now have to consider what to do concerning this file. Quite clearly, we all know now that although Timothy Harris was eliminated from the murder enquiry there was a cover up by the Merseyside Police to keep his name out of the press, and we also know it was Timothy Harris who gave that watch to Angela Clarkson. If that's true then it's abundantly clear Bridget Riley couldn't possibly have seen her colleague wearing that watch at any time. Therefore, this proves without any shadow of doubt somebody from the Merseyside Police leaned on this woman in order to get her to commit perjury. Knowing this, I can now turn to the evidence of Royston Chambers, because, his confession also includes the watch, and if Thompson had made any kind of confession at all then there would not have been any reference to any kind of watch in it. Therefore reference to the watch in the confession could only have come from one source, and that source was the Merseyside Police.

"Following the loss of the appeal, Lord Chief Justice Lord Stanhope insisted the transcripts of the appeal be sent to the Home Secretary to see if further charges are to be brought, and to order an enquiry into the allegations of the activities of the Merseyside Police. At first, I was going to consider taking no action on this matter until the results of these actions were known, but on reflection I don't think that's the best way forward. With an investigation under way, I can't see a better chance of bringing this out into the open. So I think it would be a good idea to turn this information over to the Home Secretary's department and let matters take their course from there.

"With particular reference to Timothy Harris, it's abundantly clear from the file, he committed perjury during his libel trial against the London Independent Newspaper Group where he was awarded a record sum in damages. I need hardly remind you that, in addition, he lied to parliament. It is because of this, I think I should contact the lawyers acting for the London Independent Newspaper Group because I'm sure they will be more than pleased with this information, and they should have no difficulty whatsoever in reversing that verdict. However, that will be entirely up to them."

"All of these charges are of a very serious nature indeed, and at the conclusion of all the cases there are going to be quite a few lives in ruins. Quite rightly one of these will be Timothy Harris.

"Finally, I'd like to thank you all for being here tonight and as Sebastian said earlier, if anyone has any thoughts on procedure please feel free to let me know as soon as possible." Feeling quite tired, Irene made her excuses and withdrew from the scene, leaving her colleagues in earnest discussion about all aspects of the case. As she descended the stairs she couldn't help reflecting that she'd certainly given them food for thought, as well as, plenty to talk about.

Chapter 28

Suitably refreshed after a good night's rest Irene awoke early to the sound of the morning paper falling on the mat. As she had expected the paper contained the story of the failed appeal but the main focus had shifted to the allegations against the Merseyside police force. The editorial comment column was particularly vitriolic, singling out the defence team for the worst of the criticism with banner headlines proclaiming justice had been done, and it was a pity hanging had been abolished. This in turn was followed by an attack on the legal system which, through the legal aid system, not only allowed, but actually encouraged appeal cases such as Thompson's which were almost certainly doomed to failure. It highlighted the cost to the taxpayer of yesterday's case, pointing out it was a total waste of money, and the whole system was in need of reform. Irene smiled to herself as she read, and re-read, all the nonsense written in the name of journalism thinking to herself. 'Boy if you only knew what is coming tomorrow,' and how these moaning editors will be forced to eat their words. In a very good mood and high spirits, she set off for the office determined she was going to have a good day, and that she was going to enjoy every minute of it.

Timothy Harris was in consultation with Jerome Jerome at the High Court. They were awaiting the pronouncement from the judge that it would be in order to switch off the support systems keeping his wife alive. As they were unaware of the most recent developments in the case, they were under the impression this was just going to be a mere formality.

In due course the proceedings began, and Doctor Peter

Woods was called to give evidence before the presiding judge, His Lordship Martin Russell.

"Now Mr. Woods," began his lawyer, "Can you tell this court what improvement, if any, you have found in your patient since the last hearing?"

His voice was loud and clear as he answered, "Yes I can. Since I attended the last hearing I have to advise you there has been a significant change in the condition of Mrs. Harris. First of all we have established, beyond any shadow of doubt, this lady can hear everything which is going on around her, and she has some movement which allows limited communication. When I say some movement, please allow me to clarify that by saying that Mrs. Harris is able to use one finger; the little finger on her right hand, and through this she is able to communicate with those around her. It's very limited, and very time consuming. However, we are hoping this is just the start of a much bigger, and general improvement in her well- being."

The impact and effect of this testimony was very dramatic, and the atmosphere in the court became electric. Amidst the noise, the judge banged his gavel repeatedly shouting, 'order, order.' Eventually, order was restored.

The judge looked at the plaintiffs and enquired, "Have you got any questions Mr. Jerome about this most wonderful news?"

"Yes, Your Honour, I have. "On behalf of my client I would like to protest about this so-called improvement in the condition of the patient, on the basis that she is still totally dependent upon those same support systems for life. It is not her hearing, or the movement in her little finger which is keeping her alive now is it? Furthermore, the good doctor here cannot possibly guarantee there will be any continued improvement now, or in the near future, can he? Because of this, I respectfully submit you conclude this hearing in favour of Mr. Harris."

"Hold on now, Mr. Jerome, the judge replied, "When we were here the last time, I ruled if there was no improvement in the condition of Mrs. Harris within twenty-eight days, I would grant the order in favour of your client. At the time I made that pronouncement, I said that I did so with the utmost regret as I might be seen to be taking life away from somebody, and I found that a very difficult matter for my conscience to live with. I must point out, Mr. Jerome, when I gave that judgement, you made no effort to ask me for any clarification on the point, or question of improvement, or even the degree of it. You did not stand up before me in this court and ask how would any improvement be made, or measured. In fact, you were more than prepared to leave it up to me. Now you see the consequences of leaving the matter in my hands. Thanks to some kind of minor miracle, I am completely satisfied there has been some improvement in the medical condition of Mrs. Harris, and your client's petition is denied."

"Bbut Your Honour," stuttered Jerome.

That was as far as he got, "No buts about it Mr. Jerome. I came here today with a very heavy heart. I am leaving now in the best of spirits, knowing full well a most difficult decision has been taken from me by some form of divine intervention. Consider an appeal if you must, but I must warn you, the mere fact that Mrs. Harris can hear will weigh very heavily against you."

The jubilant defendants rushed from the court eager to telephone the good news to all concerned.

Once again, the hounds of the press pack were sharpening their pencils in readiness of another field day. Timothy Harris was in the news again, but this time for the wrong reasons. As he left the court building accompanied by his legal team, it was obvious to all observers that Timothy Harris was a far from happy man. Ignoring his lawyer's advice about hostility from the press, he was busy issuing instructions to reinstate divorce proceedings without delay.

Irene had completed a hectic morning. She had been in contact with the London Independent Newspaper's legal team, and as a result of the information she had sent by fax, one of their senior lawyers had boarded the first available plane for Manchester and he was due to arrive any minute, via the fast car which had been sent to meet his arrival at the airport. Arrangements had been put in hand for an appeal to the Court of Human Rights, and although this would take quite some time before it would be heard, the process had to begin somewhere.

Elsewhere, things were hotting up. There had been an announcement via the news bulletins that the government had ordered an enquiry into the actions of the Merseyside Police following the allegations of coercion, and corruption, made by the defence. This enquiry was going to be led by officers from the West Yorkshire Police force, and this news was being welcomed by those concerned on Merseyside. In addition, the announcement of the enquiry attracted a great deal of comment in the lunchtime editions of the press which were just beginning to hit the streets.

The car turned into St. Mary's Parsonage, Manchester, the home of the chambers and offices of Messrs. Kreiff Kreiff and Isaacs and the sole occupant alighted.

As the car sped away, Irene stepped forward offering her hand in greeting saying, "Mr. Atherton, my name's Irene Yarwood, I'm very pleased to meet you."

Malcolm Atherton returned the greeting and introduced himself allowing Irene to lead the way to the offices which were normally occupied by Sebastian Krieff. All in good time, the formalities were dispensed with and the meeting got under way. Irene produced the copy of the file which her visitor began to devour with amazing speed, making many remarks and comments as he did so. At times, he could hardly contain himself as he digested the information contained therein and considered the effect on those persons mentioned. When he had finished, he placed the file on the table beside him whilst he found the right words to say, "Well Irene, this is absolute dynamite. How on earth did you get hold of that?"

"Christ Almighty, to think with his lies, that evil little rat Harris almost closed our paper, won record damages, and one way or another, was responsible for the death of the editor of the paper. A fine man who was a close and very personal friend of mine, so I have more than a personal interest in nailing this little lying bastard. My God I just can't wait to get him in court now."

Irene could understand how he felt because, to some extent, she shared the same feelings about Timothy Harris and it was certainly time for him to be brought to justice. She smiled briefly as she spoke, "Well Malcolm, that's what you've come all this way for, and that is your certified true copy." All that remains is, for you and your colleagues to set the wheels in motion with the launch of your appeal against him. We'll turn the file over to the West Yorkshire Police who think that they have been sent over here on a rubber stamping mission. You can imagine their reaction when they get their grubby little hands on this lot."

"Indeed I can, he replied, "believe me, I just can't wait to get started. He stopped briefly to look at his watch, then he said, "I suppose this really calls for a celebration. Why don't you let me take you out for a spot of lunch? Then I'll catch the five o'clock shuttle back to London."

Irene readily accepted this invitation, and offered to allow him to sample the lunch- time delights of the Wig and Gown.

Once the lunch was over, Irene said goodbye to her companion for the day, wishing him every success for a speedy conclusion to his newspaper's appeal. In return, he did the same and they went their separate ways, both filled with eager anticipation of events to come.

Chapter 29

The following day, the London Independent formally lodged their appeal in the libel case against Timothy Harris. The lodging of the appeal caused a sensation, but that was nothing compared to the interest generated by the London Independent. As the information filtered into the public domain, the resultant storm slowly gathered strength, it reached hurricane level when it became clear that Timothy Harris had lied to, and misled, parliament. There was no need for any baying hounds from the opposition benches this time. The Prime Minister was the first to react to the news. The errant MP was swiftly summonsed to the Prime Minister's private office in the commons, there he was told in no uncertain manner he was being sacked, and removed from office with immediate effect. This time, no amount of pleading by Timothy would allow the Prime Minister to relent. Neither was he content to leave his decision in abeyance until such time as the London Independent News appeal was heard.

In all the press, editorial comment on his dismissal followed the same pattern, 'Good Riddance to a bad apple, rotten to the core.' For a change, MPs, on all sides of the political spectrum were united in their condemnation of a man who had let the House down in such dramatic fashion. This was mirrored by party supporting newspapers, praising the Prime Minister to the hilt for acting so decisively and with such speed in getting rid of him. Although Timothy Harris was rank bad news, the baying hounds could smell blood; now they wanted blood.

In no time at all it was the day of the libel case appeal. People had come to the courts from all over the country and many had slept out overnight in order to ensure they got a seat. So great was demand, limits were placed on the press allocation and when the court opened it was soon packed to capacity. There was a loud and continuous buzz of excited conversation as everybody waited eagerly for the case to begin.

The appeal was being heard before His Lordship Sir Campbell McKenzie the judge who presided in the original libel trial. Once again the London Independent's lawyers were Robert Jackson QC and Elizabeth Collins QC. With Jerome Jerome and co. acting for Timothy Harris the stage was set for the finale.

"All rise," intoned the dull monotonous voice of the usher allowing Sir Campbell McKenzie to stride purposefully into court. Today, it was quite apparent he wasn't very pleased, and that was an indication to all concerned not to get the wrong side of him.

Without wasting any time, and, equally anxious not to suffer the wrath of this judge, Robert Jackson QC opened the case for the appeal, "My lord, this appeal has been brought before you on the basis that, in the previous libel case, the witness Harris lied on oath and perjured himself, in order to secure the verdict against my clients. During that trial, the defendant Harris denied he had been in the company of Angela Clarkson on or about the night she died. We now have evidence which we shall lay before you, that this was the first lie, perpetrated by Harris. Harris also stated, in his evidence, he had not given Angela Clarkson the gift of a watch, and he allowed a watch to be produced as evidence here before you, knowing that was also untrue. Before I go any further, I should like to point out this new evidence, which is now before you, has been provided by the defendant himself, when he sought to extricate himself from the murder enquiry into the death of Angela Clarkson. So, there can be no doubt whatsoever about the authenticity, or, the validity, of my client's case."

Sir Campbell's face had a look like thunder, and it was clear the source of his displeasure lay in the defendant Timothy Harris. Before anybody could speak, and, in order to silence anybody who dared, his gavel came down with an almighty crash. "Silence!" he ordered, "Silence in this court." He fastened his gaze upon Timothy Harris, then his gravel filled voice filled the room as he spoke, "Mr Harris, these are very grave and serious charges you are facing, and before this case continues any further, I feel it only fair to warn you that I don't have much time, or sympathy, with those who come before me and perjure themselves. Let there be no doubt in your mind, if that is the case here, you will be facing a long custodial sentence. After your victory in my court, I can recall the jury awarding you a record sum in damages, and should you suffer any reversal here I will be mindful of that, when I make any award against you. As a result of this and, for the duration of this case, I am going to make an order, before this court, freezing all of your assets. Do you understand?"

Whilst Timothy nodded, Jerome was on his feet. He asked the judge for permission to approach the bench. The judge gave his approval to this request, and both counsel made their approach.

"Well man, what is it? The judge snapped impatiently.

"Your honour I was wondering if we might be able to have a word in chambers about this. My client is fully aware of the wrong he has committed, and he is most anxious to put matters to rights. Even to the extent of admitting his guilt here, and now. He is acutely aware, with his police statements in the possession of the defence, he cannot possibly defend these allegations against him. He would also like to state this is something he will always have to live with and, to his everlasting shame, it is something that he will always regret.

In mitigation, he simply wishes to say all this stemmed from his wish to keep his name out of the papers during the police enquiry into the death of the poor Clarkson girl, because of his position in public life. He is most genuinely sorry he did not come into the open at the time, and he now realises, had he done so, none of this would have happened and, whilst he might have had to resign his position in government, he would at least have earned some respect for doing so, even if it meant he sacrificed his career."

Sir Campbell listened to this impassioned plea, without a trace of emotion, or any change in his facial expression. Announcing a recess whilst he conferred with both parties in his chambers a hush descended on the courtroom as they hurriedly left the court.

Once in the privacy of the Judge's chambers, Jerome continued from where he had left off, "Your honour, it goes without saying, my client will repay the sum he was awarded in damages, together with accrued interest, and he will also pay the full legal costs of both hearings. Furthermore, if we can reach some agreement here, then there will be quite a considerable saving in costs, but if we have to go through a lengthy, and protracted hearing, there will be a dramatic escalation in costs, which might mean my client would not be able to meet all his obligations."

Sir Campbell McKenzie looked inquisitively at Robert Jackson QC. and posed the question, "What do you think about this. It's your clients who have brought the action, and if they will be satisfied with the offer, it's up to them. However, personally, I don't think that is the end of it. Is it Mr. Jerome? If you, and your client are thinking this will square matters then, you'd better think again. In the first place, this man had the temerity to come into my court and commit perjury. I don't mind the two parties striking a fair deal, but there will be no negotiations on any other matters. Do I make myself clear, Mr. Jerome.? Once this hearing is concluded, the papers will be passed to the Director of Public Prosecutions in order to ascertain whether a charge of perjury should be brought against your client."

A nod from the judge indicated to Robert Jackson QC. that it was his turn to make a contribution to the hearing. He quickly responded, "On behalf of London Independent Newspapers may I say that, if the offers mentioned were put on the table, together with a public apology, then, I don't think my clients will object. If this case went the full distance, my clients would not benefit by another penny piece, and as we have just been advised, there may not be a big enough pot if the case is prolonged. In that case, if you will let me confer with my clients on that basis I will see what I can do to secure their agreement."

Sir Campbell was, at last, beginning to mellow, "Well Mr. Jerome," he said quietly, "I think you'd better go and have a word with your client as well. Tell him what his options are and ensure he fully understands the future which awaits him. Then, we'll reconvene after lunch." With a dismissive wave of the hand, Sir Campbell allowed both men to leave for their own consultations.

When the court reconvened after lunch, it was a very different man who appeared in the dock before his Lordship. Timothy Harris looked a completely broken man. He knew before the hearing started that the future for him looked bleak to say the least, but he hadn't expected it to be as bad as Jerome senior had painted it. By the time this hearing was over, he would be lucky to have any money left at all, added to which there would still be the divorce costs, together with whatever settlement was made.

During the recess, both parties had come to an agreement

covering all financial matters. All that remained was for the judge to confirm his agreement to the details. He coughed slightly before he began his address, "Ladies, and gentlemen, in the case of London Independent Newspapers versus Timothy Harris, agreement has been reached with the plaintiffs for the repayment of the sum of two million pounds damages, plus accrued interest. In addition, the defendant Timothy Harris, has agreed to pay all of the costs of the plaintiffs covering both hearings and amounting to one million two hundred and fifty pounds. Mr. Harris has also agreed to issue a public apology to all concerned. All monies were to be lodged, and deposited, with these courts offices within the next seven days. Any non compliance of such agreement will be met with the issue of a warrant for immediate arrest."

Before bringing this case to a conclusion, I have to point out that the papers are being sent to the Department of Public Prosecutions in order to consider whether, or not, to bring charges of perjury against the defendant Harris. Coming to the end of his speech, he motioned to the usher that proceedings were drawing to a close, and the usher's familiar cry of, "All rise," echoed around the courtroom.

This prompted a mad scramble from the assembled press and television reporters to convey their stories to the waiting public. Timothy Harris was now very big news indeed, but for all the very wrong reasons.

The conclusion of the hearing dominated the news and the whole of the national press for quite some time, and it certainly gave the Prime Minister more than a few anxious moments in parliament.

However, this was only the tip of the iceberg. The West Yorkshire police force had descended on Merseyside but this was not to be they easy whitewash they had at first anticipated. Now the file was out in the public domain, some very serious and embarrassing questions were now being posed. Almost immediately, it was announced that the Chief Constable was being suspended on full pay until such time as the investigation was concluded. The same treatment was given to Detective Inspector Taylor as well as Detective Sergeant West. In turn, this led to even more embarrassing questions being put to the government, and the Home Secretary.

Over the next few weeks the press had a feeding frenzy, during which time they devoured every morsel which came their way. Never before had so many had so much to write about because these topics covered greed, corruption, sex, lies and genuine sorrow. Even so, each revelation seemed to add a dimension of its own. Interest in the three suspended police officers had waned a little after it was announced that they had all been certified sick, and too ill to attend the enquiry when summonsed. The feeling amongst the general public at large was with the passage of sufficient time, this would peter out, and the principals concerned would retire to oblivion.

Just as everybody had resigned themselves to a normal life, suddenly, the glare of publicity erupted again. Once again, the spotlight was on Timothy Harris. He was to be tried for perjury, and this was to take place in three months time before his Honour Sir Campbell McKenzie. Following the announcement of this news, Timothy Harris held a series of urgent consultations with Jerome Jerome. He was told, in no uncertain manner, his position from a legal standpoint was almost hopeless, and he should spend his time up to the trial putting all his personal affairs in order, and to prepare himself for the worst.

As a result of the furore caused by the news surrounding the Merseyside police enquiry, no less a person than Lord Chief Justice Stanhope had been in contact with Irene Yarwood. As he had insisted upon sending the transcripts of the appeal hearing to the authorities for investigation, he felt morally obliged to keep himself fully informed of all developments surrounding the case. As a result, he had studied a copy of the secret prosecution file, and he had been appalled at what he saw. As soon as he had read the contents he could see the allegations made in his court concerning perjury, and the false confession, possessed more than a ring of truth about them. If that were the case, then leave to appeal to the House of Lords should have been given to the defence at that hearing. First of all, he communicated with the two judges who had also heard the appeal, and once they confirmed their own agreement that they concurred with this decision, he wasted no time communicating this to the defence.

This news came as a tremendous surprise to Irene, and the defence team. She began by submitting the defence application to that body, citing, under Article Six of The Human Rights Act, the rights of Harry Thompson had been abused when his DNA sample was wrongly used for comparison without his permission being obtained. In support of the application, she also included the evidence of malpractice by the Merseyside Police.

Chapter 30

Today, Irene was keeping an appointment with Matron Edith Farrell. She felt she owed this lady a personal visit, and she also knew this visit was long overdue. She was going to return the letter which the matron had written concerning Mrs. Harris, and she was determined to do this in person in order that Mrs. Farrell would then be completely reassured that her secret was entirely safe, and she had no need to worry herself any further about the contents being divulged to anybody.

She reached the building and began to climb the wooden stairs. From the light of the single bulb, she could see the peeling paintwork on the ceiling, and she felt she could almost taste the nicotine which coated the once pastel painted walls. As she reached the second flight, she tried to avoid holding the varnished handrail, which was sticky to her touch, and she felt herself shuddering at the thought of so many young women who had ascended those stairs in days gone by, and the harrowing stories, and heartache, which lay behind the visits of them all. Eventually, she reached the first floor, and found herself outside the door marked 'Manchester and District Children's Adoption Society.' She obeyed the instruction on the sign which read, "Please Enter" to find herself at a bare counter, which housed a sliding glass panel. As she tried to acquaint herself with her surroundings, this panel was suddenly thrust open and a thoroughly bored voice, enquired "Yes?"

She turned round to face the person and answered, "I have an appointment with Mrs. Farrell."

"Take a seat," the voice urged, "and I'll see if she's free."

The panel closed almost immediately and Irene did as

requested. On the small table in front of her there were a number of magazines and to pass a few moments she idly gazed at them. One such magazine caught her eye; it was an old edition of The Cheshire Times. It contained all the gossip among the county farming and country set. There were announcements of Hunt Balls, Point to Point race meetings and society weddings. Her eyes were inextricably drawn to the personal and advertisement columns where she spotted a notice announcing the funeral of Anthony Harris. Intrigued rather than curious she began to read it. It said quite simply, 'Anthony Harris aged 27 years born January 1961 died September 1988, dearly loved son of Paula Harris and Timothy Harris MP. The funeral will take place at St. Martyns Church, St. Martyns under Peover, on Friday 2nd February at 3 pm. No flowers and no members of the press admitted. Admittance Strictly Limited to Family. Close friends by personal invitation only. Members of the public are asked to respect the wishes of the Family.'

In her mind's eye she found herself picturing the sad scene. The grieving family including the despicable Timothy Harris, but alas no place for Mrs. Harris the poor mother of the deceased. She pictured the quaint country parish church where, no doubt, all the locals knew one another, the green fields surrounding the church, the vicarage, and the *olde worlde* village. Her thoughts were swiftly interrupted with the yellow glass panel being thrust open once again and the voice proclaiming, "Mrs. Farrell is free now would you like to come straight in?"

She entered the room where she was warmly welcomed by Mrs. Farrell who escorted her to the privacy of her own office. "Good Morning," she said, "My name is Irene Yarwood. I spoke to you earlier on the telephone and you said it would be convenient for me to call to see you today." Whilst continuing to talk she had already extracted the letter which she was returning from her brief case and now she carefully handed it over saying as she did, "I thought, in view of the contents of this letter that it would be far safer in your hands. As you have probably heard Mrs. Harris has made some slight improvement and, as a result the threat of switching off the life support system has been lifted so there was no need to involve anybody else."

Matron Farrell took the letter and Irene could see instantly the relief which flooded her face friendly face which became transformed with a warm smile. "I would like to say thank you very much indeed I really do appreciate this and if there is anything I can do to help in the future please don't hesitate to let me know. You know I was really at my wits end when I wrote that letter. All I could think about was that poor dear woman just lying there unable to move and I felt that I had to do something."

"Well, Mrs. Farrell, because of the situation my colleagues and I who are handling the defence of Mrs. Harris's son have not told him anything about this up until now so you have no need to worry about there being any breach of the confidentiality code operated by the society. Although now that her doctors have achieved this breakthrough it is more than likely that she will wish to have some communication with her son but we appreciate that confirmation of this will have to come from Mrs. Harris herself."

Edith Farrell took a deep breath and sighed, "It's a very strange world isn't it? I mean, as if she hasn't got enough on her plate as it is and now this – her son in prison for murder. In a way it might have been a blessing if she had died when she had that terrible stroke."

"Yes, Irene sympathised, but you mustn't forget Harry Thompson has always maintained he's innocent of all charges and I, and his defence team are still working on that. Once again Irene's brain had spotted an opening, the faintest glimmer of a chance which she fully intended to exploit. "By the way, Matron, would it cause any problems if I were to ask Mr. Thompson whether or not he would like to reconsider his decision not to be put in touch with his mother whilst he is still in prison and, if he has changed his mind then I could let you know. This way it would leave it up to you and the society to establish contact with Mrs. Harris through the Hospital and there would not be any breach of society rules would there?"

The Matron thought for a moment and then she said, "No I can't see anything wrong with that. I'll wait until I hear from you." Then she enquired "Will that be all?"

The past few moments had given Irene a chance to think about the idea swiftly germinating in her mind as she responded, "Can you tell me something, Mrs. Farrell. It's nothing really. It's just to satisfy my curiosity but do you keep any records here about the mothers and their children? In other words what records would you have of Mrs. Harris and her child both before and after adoption? She noticed the change of expression on the face of the matron as she answered,

"Well strictly speaking everything we keep here is strictly confidential. Why do you ask?"

"It's nothing really," Irene replied, I just wondered if perhaps you kept copies of birth certificates, or any information on Harry Thompson such as where he was born, but if you can't tell me anything I can quite easily obtain it elsewhere. You see, I thought I might be able to save myself another journey."

"Well, Miss Yarwood, I can tell you that Mr. Thompson was born at St. Mary's Hospital which is just along the road from here. If you can tell me how old Mr. Thompson is I can look up the entry for him in the record book for that year. This entry will also confirm the actual place of birth, and I think in those days we also recorded the name of the doctor who Mrs. Harris would have attending her at the time. You know it must have been pretty awful in those days for young girls like that."

Irene nodded in agreement and added, "I think it would be sometime in December 1960. I know he is 28 years of age. In an instant which belied her age, the matron was on her feet searching for the book in question. "Ah, here it is she exclaimed rather excitedly and, er let me see now. Yes there it is Bibby Harry Marcus 9th December 1960. Mother's name Paula, Father unknown, well not unknown you know that used to happen a lot in those days. They wouldn't always declare the name of the father. Yes, see there it is, the name of the doctor. Doctor Macmillan. Very young in those days, all the nurses fancied him. In fact, I'll bet some of them still do because he's still there you know. Is there anything else I can help you with?"

"No, replied Irene you have been very helpful indeed so I will get along now because I am sure you're very busy and I've already taken up far too much of your time. Unfortunately, even though I am in the vicinity I don't think I will be able to visit the hospital to see your handsome doctor for myself as I have got to get back. So I will say cheerio for now."

She was deep in thought as she left the building and proceeded along the busy road towards the car park. During her walk she kept thinking how life really was strange. Of all the days, and of all the places to visit, she had to choose to come here today and the first thing to catch her attention was the funeral notice for Anthony Harris. Anthony Harris she mused. What a tragic waste of a young life; 27 years of age and he would never know he had a brother thirteen months older than himself. The same thoughts echoed through her mind as she collected her car and drove towards her chambers. As well as the names in her head, she now found the numbers running around in her brain so much so she was finding it difficult to concentrate on her driving but, try as hard as she could, these thoughts refused to leave her troubled mind."

It was the silly clown on the left trying to push in who brought her back to reality and as she slammed hard on her brakes to avoid a nasty collision she knew something was wrong. She realised it was pointless to remonstrate with the idiotic university student who had almost rammed her and, instead, she tried to collect her scattered thoughts. For a moment her mind went back to her own law student days and old examination papers where students were deliberately given false information. It might only be the incorrect addition of a column of figures but, if you did not spot it, you were losing marks and, surprisingly enough, there were those who didn't despite being warned beforehand. It was then that the penny dropped. That was it, no wonder the figures were haunting her almost to the point of distraction. The figures were wrong. One person born early December and the other person born in early January that would put one person only weeks older than the other and not thirteen months as she had originally surmised. Clearly something was wrong and, whilst she could not see how this would assist her in the defence of Harry Thompson, nevertheless it represented something which had to be checked out just in case it proved to be anything of real significance.

The moment she reached her office she rang the number of Michael Mulrooney. As soon as the call was answered she said excitedly, "Michael I want you to do something for me. I know you might think it rather odd but I need a copy of the birth certificate of Anthony Harris. Yes that Anthony Harris – the very same one. All I can tell you that I spotted something today which, if it were true, would mean that Harry Thompson would only be about four to eight weeks older than his late brother. Now we know that can't be true, so I need a copy of his birth certificate. No, I'm sorry I don't know myself where this is leading to I just wish I did. All I know is that Anthony was born in Chester so if you could do that for me I will be ever so pleased and, whilst you're doing that I will be making some enquiries of my own."

She put the phone down and sat back in her chair in order to think as clearly as she could. Today she had seen the entry in the Adoption Society records for Harry Thompson so those details had to be true; there was absolutely no doubt about that. In that case, she reasoned to herself, it must have been a misprint in the Cheshire magazine. It had to be and so she dismissed the thoughts from her mind.

She found it very difficult to concentrate on the documents left on her desk by the practice manager requesting counsel's opinion on a range of issues simply because she could not dismiss Harry Thompson or his late brother from her mind. There was something niggling her about this and she had to get it sorted once and for all. After a few moments' thought she put out a call to St. Mary's Hospital and asked if she could speak to Doctor Macmillan.

When asked who was calling and the nature of the call, she replied, "My name is Irene Yarwood QC and I have reason to believe that doctor Macmillan may be able to give me some information regarding a birth he attended almost thirty years ago. If this is true, the information could benefit my client and aid his defence."

The voice at the other end of the line interrupted her, "I'm sorry madam but I don't think that would be possible due to the fact that all personal information regarding doctor, and patient, is strictly confidential. I don't wish to appear rude or unhelpful, but I am sure you wouldn't be pleased if we gave out any of your details over the telephone."

Irene did not expect this rebuff, and, she continued, "I can understand what you are saying and the reasons for it, but all I want to do is to ask Doctor Macmillan one simple question. If he chooses not to answer on the grounds which you have just stated then I will have to go back to the mother in question, and arrange for her to order the good doctor to tell me what I need to know. If that were possible now, I would ask the mother direct, but as she has suffered a stroke and she is unable to speak, I have resorted to this approach. Failing this, I will have to apply to the courts to subpoena the doctor to attend a hearing in order to drag it out of him. Now I'm certain neither of us wishes to do that do we?"

This latter statement had the desired effect as a much more subdued voice responded, "Please hold the line one moment whilst I see if I can connect you. A few moments later she was rewarded with the sound of a male voice saying "Macmillan speaking, how can I help?"

"Good afternoon, Doctor Macmillan, please let me introduce myself. I promise I won't take up too much of your valuable time. My name is Irene Yarwood QC. And I represent a person called Harry Thompson. Almost thirty years ago you attended his mother at a birth in St. Mary's Hospital, I think her name at the time was Paula Bibby. Immediately after the birth the child was given up for adoption. However, something about this doesn't ring true because I've discovered recently this child had a younger brother, but if the information I have is true, then this younger brother would only be three to four weeks his junior. She heard the soft intake of his breath and his soft Scottish brogue whispering, "After all this time, my moment of fame denied me returns to haunt me. Well all I can say is Christ Almighty that Mrs. Bibby!"

"Can you recall the birth after all these years?" She asked.

"Well, Miss Yarwood I could hardly forget it. You see I'd only been at the hospital a short time when this young lady came in to give birth. The birth of the baby was fine but it was after the birth that things went wrong for her, because, that's when I had to tell her that she was going to have another child!"

"What shouted Irene in utter disbelief, "Twins?"

"Well not exactly. They are still twins but, instances of this are what we call staggered births, and they are very rare indeed. However, they can, and do, happen. It means that at the time Miss Bibby conceived her first child she continued to ovulate, and she became pregnant again. I was most concerned for her wellbeing at the time, but Miss Bibby insisted upon discharging herself and having the first child adopted. She was so upset at the thought of having two children, and her fiancée totally rejecting her, all she could think of was to give the first child up for adoption, and see if the boyfriend would do the decent thing, and marry her. Later, she wrote to me to tell me that she was getting married, and from that I assumed everything was all right. Naturally, at the time, she begged me not to say a word about this to a living soul, and because of the state she was in at the time, I agreed to it. Had word got out at the time, the pair of us would have been celebrities, and it might have given my career a boost, but what does it matter, my conscience is clear knowing I did the right thing at the time. The only condition I placed upon her was that I insisted, when she went in to the hospital for the second child she let me know where she was, and which doctor she was under. In the end, I persuaded her to come back here again for the birth of her second child and that's what she did. You can tell how rare this condition is because, if my memory serves me correctly, I think there had only been some twenty recorded cases. In the case of Miss Bibby, the contractions had stopped naturally, so it was safe from a medical point of view, to leave the second baby in the womb for as long as it was considered safe to do so. In her case, I advised her that as long as she was under medical supervision she would be safe. Then, when I decided it was time for the child to be born it was delivered by Caesarean section. So, tell me now, how does this tie in with your defence of her son?"

"Harry Thompson as he is now known, was arrested and convicted on two counts of murder.

There was a loud intake of breath as he muttered, "Jesus."

She wasn't distracted and continued, "My client has always maintained he was completely innocent of both charges and we now know, the police conspired to have false, and perjured evidence, produced against him at the murder trial. At present his appeal is going to the House of Lords, and we're hopeful this time it will be upheld. With this information, together with some expert forensic help, I think we may be able to secure his freedom. There's one other thing I think you should know, that is Mrs. Harris as she is now known has suffered a massive stroke which has left her almost completely paralysed, and she is kept alive only by a life support system. In view of what you told me earlier about your pact with this lady, I can assure you I shall only use this information with her permission. All I can say now is thank you for your help. No doubt if you read the press you'll see how it all unfolds in the future."

Irene put down the phone to find she was almost shaking with disbelief and, utter relief. Tears of joy began to fill up her eyes as she realised for the first time, in a very long time, that, Harry Thompson her first client in a murder trial, just might have been telling the truth, and he wasn't guilty after all. Before going home utterly exhausted, she contacted Michael Mulrooney.

"Michael Oh Michael," she said, "you're not going to believe this when I tell you. It really is the most wonderful, yet bizarre, piece of news. The odds are that Harry Thompson is innocent and I think we may be able to prove it. Harry and Anthony, are more than brothers, they're twins! Although they're twins, they're not twins as you, and I know it. In fact, they are known as staggered twins since they weren't born at the same time. They were born within four weeks of each other, and I've just spoken to the doctor who delivered both of them. He's just told me, although it's very rare, it does happen occasionally. So what I need now are DNA samples from Timothy and Paula Harris to confirm they are the parents of the two boys, plus a sample from Anthony Harris deceased for comparison with the Clarkson girl. Hopefully then, we can clear this thing up once and for all. I know we're still going to try to get the new evidence ruled inadmissible, but if we can show later, from these samples, it's possible that the real perpetrator of the crimes was Anthony Harris, then, I think the case against Thompson vis-a-vis the Wilson case will simply fall apart. Michael, can you imagine the reaction from Timothy Harris when this news becomes public, and the field day with the press if it transpires that Harry is his son."

"Irene, he said, "that really is the most sensational news I have ever heard. Please tell me how on earth did you come by this information? I mean it's absolutely mind blowing and in all the years I have been practising law, I have never heard of such a thing. How you got hold of this is beyond my comprehension. I tell you Irene I still can't take this in."

Irene paused for breath before replying, "I went to see the Matron at the adoption society and I just happened to be reading a magazine about Cheshire life, when I came across the funeral announcement for Anthony Harris. At the time, I didn't think anything about it as I was assuming quite incorrectly that these two were brothers born thirteen months apart. But, on my way back, it suddenly occurred to me there were only four weeks separating the pair. So, I got hold of the doctor who is still at the hospital, and he gave me all the information. It really is the most wonderful news, isn't it Michael?"

"That goes without saying he replied, but right now I can think of a few people who won't be at all pleased. Anyway that's life, and I'll get on with your requests. As soon as I have got everything I'll let you know. One last thing before I go, I think we'd better start to collect as much information as we can on Anthony Harris."

"That's my boy, she responded, "you get on with it, and I'll be in touch. Take care of yourself, enjoy what's left of the day. Bye for now." She replaced the receiver still deep in thought about the wonderful news.

Chapter 31

Sir Campbell McKenzie viewed the crowds outside the court buildings with dismay, and a good deal of disdain. 'Bloody sharks,' he muttered to himself as he wove his way through the throngs of people milling in front of the building. Nothing but bloody sharks come to feed on the humiliation of one of their own kind. 'They won't get too much joy here today,' he grumbled to himself, 'leastways, not in my court.' He knew what it was all about. In fact, the probability was the whole country knew, that today Timothy Harris was due to appear before him to face a charge of perjury. What the public at large did not know was, this wasn't going to be an ongoing circus for the next two or three weeks, with Timothy Harris battling to save his career, or even himself. This was something which would be over within the hour at most for Timothy Harris intended to plead guilty to the charge. With the discovery of the prosecution file marked *Not To Be Shown To The Defence*, there wasn't any point in him pleading any other way as his statements contained within that file proved, without any shadow of doubt, he had lied about everything in his libel action against the London Independent Newspaper Group. He finished his pot of tea then nodded to the usher that he was ready, whereupon, he followed that person to the door then as the usher issued his familiar cry, he strode with a great sense of purpose into the overcrowded court.

Straight away, all of those present could see he meant business today. Picking up his gavel, he brought it crashing down with a tremendous thud, to indicate to one and all his court was now in session. The chief clerk to the court rose from his seat and commenced proceedings by addressing Timothy Harris with the preamble, "In the case of Regina versus Timothy Harris, you are charged that at an earlier Libel case hearing in this court, before his worship Sir Campbell McKenzie, you gave false evidence at that hearing in order to secure a favourable verdict for yourself, and as a consequence you committed the crime of Perjury. How do you plead in answer to that charge – guilty, or, not guilty?"

Although there was complete silence in the court, his reply was almost inaudible as he answered with one word "Guilty."

From his lofty position on the bench, Sir Campbell glared down at the hapless figure before him. When he began to speak to Timothy, he spoke with a voice of great authority yet he betrayed no sign of emotion.

"Have you anything to say before I pass judgement upon you?"

At this point, the counsel Jerome got to his feet, and indicated he would be speaking on behalf of his client. "Your Honour," he said, "My client has said all that he can say in his defence, and in mitigation at the last hearing before yourself. He can only reiterate that he is both deeply sorry, and ashamed, to find himself in this position which is I must say one of his own doing entirely. At the start of the murder enquiry, my client insists he did only what any other person would have done if they found themselves at risk of being linked to the case, even though he was totally innocent. It was only because he was a member of the present government that he wished to save himself, and his party, from any embarrassment should it become known he had conducted an extra marital affair whilst attending to constituency matters. Now, with hindsight, he totally regrets taking the action he did at the time, because he is fully aware of the lives he has blighted, and if it were possible to turn back the clock, he would do so without any hesitation whatsoever. Therefore, all my client can do now is throw himself on the mercy of this court and ask your worship to be mindful of any effect a lengthy custodial sentence might have upon him."

The glare on the face of the judge was still there for all to see, and to those who knew him, it was quite obvious he was far from pleased. "Mr. Jerome," he said, "Let me thank you for that eloquent speech on behalf of your client. Now, let me put matters in perspective. First of all, I think the only remorse felt by the defendant is due to the fact he has finally been found out. If he felt truly ashamed about his conduct, and his association with a common prostitute, he should have come clean and said so at the time, but he didn't. Instead, he chose to lie to parliament. Then, as if that wasn't enough, he chose to come here, and to commit perjury in order to prevent the truth from coming out. I think it is fair for me to say that, had he not lied to the house, it follows that he would not be here today facing such a serious charge. In fact, had he chosen that course of action, he would have found that, although his political career might have suffered along with his reputation, he would still have his freedom."

"I cannot find any extenuating circumstances in his plea for mercy, put forward with such eloquence by his learned counsel, and I am going to pronounce sentence accordingly."

Timothy Harris had remained standing throughout the short proceedings. Now, the judge addressed him directly.

"Timothy Harris, I take exception to any person who commits the act of perjury. I find it even more disagreeable when a person commits such an act in my court. Although I am mindful of the fact that you have chosen to come here today and plead guilty, I cannot allow that to sway my judgement in this case. In view of this, I feel I have been left with no alternative, but to sentence you to serve six years in prison.

During your period of incarceration, I trust you will find ample time to meditate upon the actions which have brought you here before me, and prior to your release, you will have spent as much time as possible preparing to rehabilitate yourself to fulfil a useful role within society."

With a nod to the bailiffs who were present in the court, he cried, "Take him down."

Barely able to stand, Timothy Harris was led away from the court supported by the bailiffs on duty.

Once again there was another mad scramble by the assembled members of the press to get their stories into print in the shortest time possible. It was going to be another story which would figure prominently in the papers for quite some time. Timothy Harris was in the news again but, for all the wrong reasons.

With the perjury trial completed, attention swung towards the Merseyside Police enquiry being carried out by the West Yorkshire Force. Despite numerous attempts, the three protagonists, aided and abetted, by their own police federation, successfully avoided all efforts to give any worthwhile statements to the body carrying out the enquiry. All three had been certified as being under too much stress and illness to attend the proceedings and, one by one, they were allowed to leave the force on the grounds of sickness which ensured a more than generous payoff together with their police pensions intact.

In their report, the investigators singled out the Chief Constable for some stinging criticism, not for being a party to the contaminated evidence presented at the trial, but for not coming forward to reveal that Timothy Harris, his brother-in-law, had lied during the libel trial. The report concluded that, by not exposing Timothy Harris at the earliest opportunity when he was in a position to do so, some of the more serious matters could well have been avoided.

Detective Sergeant West bore the brunt of the blame. The authors of the report found, in their opinion, he was the person who ensured Royston Chambers produced the false confession when it was needed most, just before the beginning of the trial. In addition, they found he had coerced Bridget Riley into giving evidence, which he knew to be completely false. Close examination of the station arrest book, followed by internal enquiries, revealed many occasions where suspects had been arrested, and subsequently released without charge yet no details of the alleged offences were found in the arrest book. Almost all the complaints investigated related to Detective Sergeant West being instrumental in having known prostitutes arrested on charges with false evidence planted upon them. These victims were almost always released without charge, usually at the behest of Detective Sergeant West, although it was noted that all of the prostitutes interviewed claimed there was usually some form of payment in kind at a later date.

As a result, Detective Sergeant West was arrested, and charged with attempting to pervert the course of justice. Although the charges were laid against him, they remained on the book due to the serious deterioration of his health.

Detective Inspector Peter Taylor was exonerated on all charges as there was nothing to indicate that he had played any part in the affairs concerning Timothy Harris, neither could he be traced to having any links with the arrest, and release of the prostitutes, or the confession supplied by Chambers. Within a week, the report had been consigned to the waste paper baskets, and life returned to normal within the force without the services of the corrupt officers.

Michael Mulrooney had been kept very busy indeed. Apart from his normal caseload, he had been to see the consultant at the hospital. The purpose of his visit had been to see if the consultant could communicate sufficiently with Mrs Harris for information about the birth of her sons to be disclosed in order that investigations might continue. She was also asked to approve an exhumation order to remove the body of Anthony Harris to allow DNA samples to be obtained in order to assist with the enquiry. Although able to hear, and understand the questions posed, this was no easy process. Everybody was well aware of the tremendous strain this imposed on Paula, and each session was conducted with as much sympathy and compassion, as was humanly possible. Despite this, all concerned found it a very trying experience and they were mightily relieved when it was finally over.

Michael had also been to see Harry Thompson in prison. At this visit, he had arranged for him to supply DNA samples for analysis. He had also been to see the lawyers acting on behalf of Timothy Harris, where he acquainted them of the fact that, if Timothy Harris was the paternal father of Anthony Harris deceased, then it was almost certain he was also the father of Harry Thompson. In support of this claim, he presented them with the evidence of the birth of the son Timothy Harris had never met. Initially Timothy Harris refused all requests to cooperate until it was pointed out to him, permission had been given by his wife for Anthony's body to be exhumed and this could be carried out without his involvement. The news concerning his other son hit him the hardest of all. Without the evidence provided, he wouldn't have believed it, and this caused him a great deal of pain and anguish. Alone in his cell at night, he found himself reduced to tears as he finally came to terms with his losses in terms of real life. At times almost suicidal, he blamed himself for the incarceration of his new found son. How he wished now, he'd never met Angela Clarkson, and become so besotted with her, and dozens more like her. With so much time on his hands, he had ample time to reflect upon the mess he had made, not only of his own life but of so many others. For Timothy Harris life was hardly worth living now.

With all the good luck messages still ringing in her ears, Irene Yarwood had arrived in London for the appeal to the House of Lords. As a result of the recent turn of events, the only issue in doubt concerned Article Six of The Human Rights Act, and whether, under that Act, the human rights of Harry Thompson had been abused. If their Lordships found that they had, then the Clarkson verdict should be overturned, following which, there was a strong possibility the Wilson verdict would then be deemed to be unsafe. She knew that a verdict in favour of her client was bound to provoke outrage in all the press, none more so than those papers which were bitterly opposed to Britain being in Europe, and the Common Market. She was quite prepared for all the criticism which would be directed at her, and her client. She permitted herself a wry smile at such happenings, especially in view of the fact none of them knew that once the new DNA results were to hand, they would alter the hard held views of them all once these findings were made public. This would happen soon enough once the application to exhume the body of Anthony Harris was heard. For a moment, she shuddered nervously at the thought, and the immense attention it was bound to attract from the media, and the press.

At the appointed hour, their Lordships took their places, then, with all eyes upon her, Irene began, "Your Lordships, the issues here before you are relatively simple. In these cases, I represent the defendant, Harry Marcus Thompson, who was found guilty of the murder of Miss Angela Clarkson, and Miss Diane Wilson. My client has always maintained he was innocent of these charges, and to a large extent, this conviction has been thrown into doubt with the publication of the West Yorkshire

Force enquiry into malpractice at and within the Merseyside Police force. This enquiry has revealed the witness, Bridget Riley, committed perjury against my client when she gave her testimony at that trial. The enquiry has also revealed she only gave that perjured evidence under duress following the threat of arrest by a serving officer on the Merseyside Force."

At the trial of my client, the Merseyside Force colluded with a Mr. Royston Chambers, a felon with many previous convictions, to produce before the court a confession, allegedly given to that person by my client. My client has always maintained he never made any confession, of any kind, and it was nothing more than a figment of the imagination of Royston Chambers. This gentleman has since appeared before an appeal court, and retracted every word of that confession. Enquiries by the West Yorkshire Force have now revealed this was indeed the case, and the prisoner was coerced into making the whole thing up by the same serving member of the Merseyside Police Force. Take away these two vital pieces of evidence from the prosecution case, and there is almost no case left for my client to answer."

"Once the murder enquiry was announced, the Merseyside Police launched an appeal for local male persons to come forward voluntarily to provide DNA samples for analysis. This was in order to eliminate as many people from the murder enquiry, with the promise that all non-matching samples with those obtained from the deceased would be destroyed. We now know, from evidence before your lordships, this did not happen in the case of the sample provided by my client. Out of all the samples provided by the public at large, my client's sample was the only one retained in the end. As you will see from the new evidence before you, samples were taken from the dead woman Clarkson, and these showed a positive match with the sample supplied to the police by her last client,

Timothy Harris. This man admitted to having sex with this woman, but subsequently, the police were able to remove him from their list of suspects. Despite the fact that the sample taken from the dead woman did not match that supplied by my client, the police did not authorise the destruction of it, and had they done so, they would not have been in a position to compare it with a sample recently taken from the clothing of both women. At this stage, I need hardly remind you that all of the other samples, voluntary provided by the members of the public, had already been destroyed as promised by the police."

"When this, the Clarkson case, came to trial, the prosecution stressed they were not offering any DNA evidence against my client, relying instead on the perjured evidence before you."

"Later, during the appeal hearing, the prosecution were allowed to introduce DNA evidence taken from the underwear of the dead women, and according to their expert this new evidence proved to match the sample from my client which had not been destroyed. I respectfully submit that this piece of gross deception was a breach of the rights of my client under article six of The Human Rights Act."

"During this appeal, and as you will see from the transcripts before you, the counsel for the prosecution stated, and I quote, 'With this new evidence which was not available at the murder trial, it was just as if Harry Thompson had gone to the police and confessed to the crime. I respectfully submit that this serves to underline that breach of my client's human rights because, under Article Six of the said Act all people, not just my client but all people have a right to silence, and this right, was taken from my client."

"In making this appeal, I must now refer your Lordships to the recent ruling in the European Courts, which ruled that all people had a fundamental right to silence, and the exercise of this basic right should not be held against them in any court of law."

"In conclusion, may I say if you find in favour of my client on this basic issue, I trust you will bear in mind my earlier remarks regarding the perjured evidence, produced at the trial, which weighed so heavily against him."

As Irene sat down, Sir Gordon Nuttall-Jones rose from his seat. He cast a long look around the court which took in their lordships who were waiting for him to begin. He cleared his throat quite loudly, as if he needed to summon all eyes upon him, then rather tentatively, he began, "Your Lordships, You have just heard from my learned friend that much of the evidence presented at the trial of her client was perjured, and false. With the benefit of hindsight, which none of us had at the time of the trial, and after reading the evidence produced in support of this, I have to say without any hesitation, I agree with her. I need hardly say more than, if this had been known at the time of the trial, then it is highly unlikely her client would have been found guilty of anything, let alone murder. In these circumstances, however, that would have constituted an even bigger travesty of justice because a murderer would have been found not guilty.

"It is only now, with the superior knowledge available to the forensic scientists, that human samples can be taken from clothing and analysed. In this case, samples of semen, collected from the undergarments of the deceased women, were found to match a sample from Harry Thompson which proves conclusively that he was at the murder scenes and it is impossible for him to deny it. Quite simply, those facts cannot lie."

"Whilst I can support the Human Rights Act as being an important piece of legislation, albeit long overdue, I must plead with your Lordships that the interpretation which you are being asked to place upon it today borders upon the ridiculous. Here we have open and shut cases, proving that a person who may well have escaped punishment in the first instance due to the circumstances already stated, may well be acquitted simply because somebody did not ask him, or his defence team, whether or not his sample could be used in another test. Obviously, I need hardly point out, had this same test been available from the start, then this issue could not have arisen and my learned friend's client would be stuck behind bars where he clearly belongs."

"All I can say is, if you find for the defence on this issue, it will be a very sad day indeed for British justice." As he sat down, he looked across at Irene and the look on his face said it all.

Irene sat there listening impassively. She made no move to object to anything which had been said by Sir Gordon, she knew she could have stepped in when Sir Gordon remarked about her client being at the scene, but this wasn't the time, or the moment. First, and foremost, there was still work to be done regarding other people, and other suspects so, for the time being it was simply one step at a time.

With the legal arguments, and submissions, out of the way, it was up to their Lordships to consider their verdict. The chairman was the first to leave, closely followed by his fellow members, then the protagonists slowly drifted away from the chamber and the building. Without being over-confident, Irene was in an ebullient mood. She thought things had, more or less, gone her way and, because of the ruling in the European courts on the Hurst case there was an established legal precedent already on the books. Therefore, she was reasonably certain that their Lordships would rule in favour of her client. She also knew she could show that there was no material or credible evidence, which could be shown against Harry in relation to the first charge of murdering Diane Wilson and his conviction on this charge was decidedly unsafe. In this case, all anybody had to go on was the fact they had sex at some time during that day, and later that day she was subsequently and mysteriously killed."

When their Lordships returned to deliver their verdict, although all persons present studied their faces intently, none of them gave any clue regarding their deliberations. The presiding judge sat down, and after ensuring his colleagues were also seated, he began, "These appeals have proved to be extremely trying in that my learned colleagues and myself believe that, even though the defence have shown, quite rightly I might add, that a right to silence exists we feel it is not beyond criticism when applied to appeals of this nature. However, we have to add that, in these cases, had the prosecution done their homework properly and had they followed their own promise to destroy all of the samples provided, then, we do not think we would be here today. Now, it is not incumbent upon us to criticise the defence for bringing this action, albeit due to a loophole, provided in chief by the prosecution, but in delivering our verdict, we do so in the hope we are not merely opening the floodgates for cases of a similar nature."

"As there are two issues before us, it stands to reason that we shall deliver two judgments, and these are as follows.

"In the case of Angela Clarkson, we subscribe to the view that at the original trial, the evidence of the prosecution was so tainted by perjury, and falsehood, no jury in the land would have found Thompson guilty without that tainted evidence. In this case, we have to bear in mind, at the time of the trial there was no DNA evidence linking the defendant to the victim, so we must conclude Thompson should have been found not guilty of the murder of Angela Clarkson. This verdict is unanimous, and in addition, we have reached the conclusion that, at the appeal of this case, the accused's right to silence, under article six of the Act, had been violated, and the new evidence should not have been admitted. However, we are sure, if the appeal judges had possessed the evidence of perjury and falsehood, there is no doubt in our minds that their Lordships would have reached the same conclusions as ourselves."

"With hindsight, we now know the crown have turned up new evidence, which would tend to indicate the possible guilt of the accused but as we all know, a person cannot be tried twice for the same crime."

The excitement within the defence team was reaching unbearable levels as the implications of the judge's verdict began to sink in, and they waited with baited breath for the next judgement as the judge continued,

"In the case of the murder of Diane Wilson we are drawn to a different conclusion. By a majority decision we were unable to agree that there are sufficient grounds to declare that verdict unsafe. I need hardly remind anybody here, in this case, after discounting the false confession, all anybody has to go on is the fact that Harry Thompson was probably the last person to see this young girl alive apart from her killer. It is fair to say here, the police were totally unable to link her disappearance and subsequent death with any other living person. In this case, the accused admitted quite freely that, after sex, they quarrelled, and it is on this basis alone, we think the police were quite correct to establish a prima facie case against Thompson. In this trial the DNA evidence was not called into question, presumably on the basis that, if Thompson admitted to having sex with the girl, and his sample matched that taken from her, then, it was indeed his. Now, we are faced with the vexed question of the discovery of samples taken from her clothing. Evidence which was not available at the trial, and we have to ask ourselves how did it get there? Was it during intercourse, immediately afterwards or some other time? Does this discovery violate Thompson's right to silence? The answer to that is, by a majority decision we think that it does, and we also rule his right to silence had already been breached at his original trial. In fairness, we have to say this is where we feel this Act falls down and it is a cause of great concern to us here. With the benefit of hindsight, we can all sit in judgment, but who would have thought that, at the outset of the original trial, the use of Thompson's DNA in the Wilson case would be ruled invalid at a later date simply because his sample had been specifically donated for testing in the Clarkson case. We hasten to add, had another sample been obtained, and tested this defence, and our ruling here today, would not have been possible."

In court, the atmosphere was pure electric. Nobody in their wildest dreams could have predicted any such outcome. Despite repeated calls for order, it took quite some time before order was restored, and the judge was able to continue,

"If there are any more outbursts of this nature, I shall clear the court without a moment's hesitation. These are very serious issues which are being decided here, and, they go right to the heart of British Justice."

"Before I conclude this verdict, both my learned colleagues and I are of the opinion that the papers on this case should be sent to the presiding judge hearing the case against the prisoner Chambers, as he may feel, as a result of that person's contribution in coming forward voluntarily before the appeal court to admit he had been forced to perjure himself, then some reduction in his sentence might be called for."

The presiding judge then turned to Harry and, addressed him as follows, "Young man, it goes without saying that you will be released from custody with immediate effect, but I hasten to add, you will have to live with your conscience for a long time to come. I am sure you will realise your release, from years of incarceration, is due solely to the diligence and expertise of your defence counsel. You are indeed a very fortunate young man to have found such a very able person to defend you."

Once the judges had left the chamber it was sheer pandemonium. All the reporters, and photographers, jostled each other for pictures, and statements, and it was with great difficulty they reached the sanctuary of one of the inner interview rooms. Everybody was in a tremendous state of euphoria, for a few moments nobody could speak. Then, as the mood gradually subsided, it seemed as though everybody wanted to speak at once. Eventually, they all gave way to Irene, who was, without doubt the heroine of the hour.

Irene's address was short and sweet, "To everybody here who has worked so hard on behalf of Harry and myself, all I can say is we are all totally indebted to you. When we finally leave here, let me warn you we saw nothing here compared to the reception which awaits us once we venture outside. All I ask is, we try to keep the press away from Harry as much as possible, and we get into the cars with utmost speed to try to put some distance between us, and them. I know it's difficult for the press, but they will have ample time later to get their stories, besides which, they will all be very busy right now sending off the results of the appeal."

"I know this is a time for celebration, and everybody wants to have a word or two from Harry, but first of all can you leave Harry in the capable hands of myself, and Michael Mulrooney. We both have something to say to him which can't wait, which we hope will have a significant bearing on the events which have just taken place."

Harry wondered what on earth was going on as everybody vacated the room leaving him in the company of his principal defence team. As the door closed behind them, Michael leaned against it as Irene spoke to Harry.

"Harry, as of now you are a free man but Michael and I have to tell you this is not quite the end. Although you've gained your freedom on what will, without doubt, be called a technicality, legally there is nothing anybody can do about it, but we have to tell you it's a rod you might not have to bear for the rest of your life. We can't guarantee anything at this stage although we are more than hopeful that we will clear your name. First of all, we have to tell you that until a few months ago you had a twin brother."

Harry looked at Irene, and Michael. It was quite apparent this news was coming as a complete shock, and it was very visible in his facial expression, and body language. He put his hand on the table in order to steady himself and prepare for whatever came next, as Irene continued, "I know this is coming as a complete shock, but, we've got to get all this out of the way before we leave here. Your mother, when she became pregnant, continued to ovulate, and she also became pregnant with your twin brother Anthony. In medical terms, this is a very rare occurrence. It's known as a staggered birth. For a moment now, I want you to think about the state your mother must have been in at the time. Being pregnant outside of marriage was one thing, and to give birth to twins was even worse, but to conceive twice like this, with all the attendant and unwanted publicity, it was too much for your poor mother to bear. This is why you were given up for adoption then, following a pact with the doctor who attended your birth, she went home to tell her husband to be that she was expecting his child. Four weeks after giving birth to you, she came back to hospital to give birth to your brother, Anthony, after which, she and her fiancée, got married."

I have to tell you it wasn't the happiest of marriages, due mainly in part to your father resenting the fact, to some extent, he had been forced into the marriage, so there were frequent flare ups involving your mother and your brother. She could see Harry was becoming decidedly nervous, and it was quite apparent, he was more than anxious to find out who his actual parents were. She deliberately paused for a moment, urging him to sit down, saying as she did so, "I'm afraid it doesn't get much better, Harry, so please be patient with me."

"Your mother wrote to you whilst you were in prison, and you replied insisting that you couldn't agree to any contact, let alone a meeting as long as you were in prison. Whilst reading that letter, your mother suffered a tremendous stroke which left her blind, deaf, and completely paralysed. As a result, she exists now only with the aid of a life support system." She paused again because she knew she was coming to the hardest part, and she was willing herself to stifle the emotion mounting deep inside her. Your mother's maiden name was Paula Bibby, and her married name was Harris – Paula Harris. I don't suppose that means a lot to you, but when I tell you who in all probability your father is, things might look a little more clear. This is because we think your father is Timothy Harris, the disgraced MP, who was recently sent to prison for committing perjury. We can only say we think he is your father because the tests haven't yet been conducted, but we are hopeful this will take place sometime next week. As you will have read in the press, Timothy Harris was also involved with Angela Clarkson, and it was he who gave her the watch which you subsequently found. It has to be said that, as a result of the cover up which followed, you were drawn into the murder inquiry. Had there not been any cover up, or had Timothy Harris come forward, then you would not have become implicated in the Clarkson case. Having said that it doesn't mean that the police wouldn't have arrested and charged you with the murder of Diane, but it would have meant that the case against you was a lot weaker and for now there's no point in us wasting valuable time speculating upon what might have been."

"Well, what about my brother? he asked?"

She knew she had to answer, and she knew she had to face him, no matter how hard, or painful, she found the ordeal,

"Well, I was just coming to that because your brother Anthony died a few months ago. Apparently, he dabbled with drugs, and he was also on medication. The combination of the two caused a reaction, as a result of which he died in a coma but we'll deal with that later. Now look at me Harry," she said, with her voice quivering with emotion, "we have an application going before the courts to exhume the body of your brother in order to carry out DNA tests as it's our belief that your brother Anthony is the murderer of your girlfriend Diane Wilson, and also Angela Clarkson."

Almost at breaking point, she continued, "before we can do that we need to establish first and foremost, that your real father is Timothy Harris, because if it turns out that he isn't, then the forensic tests already carried out cannot lie. You understand what we are saying now, don't you Harry? For your sake, I hope and pray to God that he is because, if he isn't there's no point in continuing with the exhumation in an effort to prove your innocence. This is because, in these circumstances, Anthony's DNA will not match those taken from the clothing of the two women."

Harry was no longer in the mood for celebrating; the shine had been well and truly rubbed off the victory. He sat there, motionless, with his head in his hands almost oblivious to the things going on around him, still wondering if there was ever going to be an end to this nightmare. Then he became aware of Michael standing in front of him saying,

"We think you had better look at these pictures of your brother. We have to say the resemblance is absolutely uncanny, so much so even though you were born weeks apart, you're both truly twins, but not 'Identical' twins in the accepted sense as you were both conceived with separate eggs. So we're hoping, and praying, for the best possible outcome. Before we go any further, we have to tell you that we couldn't introduce any of this fresh evidence in court, as we felt that we might be overstepping the mark insofar as we had objected to the prosecution bringing in fresh DNA evidence. Not only that, but we have our own forensic expert waiting to testify that the new evidence could, and I emphasise the word "could," be flawed, or contaminated."

"You see you mustn't run away thinking, just because you have an identical twin brother, that his DNA will match yours exactly. According to our expert, if the pair of you are identical, then, a match of 90/95%, would be considered to be more than sufficient, taking into account any deterioration which could have occurred due to exposure to the elements. After this, you then have to face up to the fact that your brother killed both of these women and it was his DNA which was left behind. Although Anthony's death was drug-related, we have to tell you that according to the autopsy report, it was due, in part, to another drug he was taking for medicinal purposes. Apparently, the combination of the two drugs caused him to go into a coma, and he literally drowned in his own vomit. His badly decomposed body was not discovered for a long time afterwards."

"Going back to your mother, we also have to tell you that she and Timothy Harris, had agreed to divorce but following your mother's illness, Mr. Harris applied to the courts to have her life support system switched off due to the fact that she appeared to be totally incapacitated. The judge hearing the application ruled, if there was no improvement in her medical condition within seven days, then she would be allowed to die. Fortunately for both of you, the medical team discovered that she could hear, and she had limited use of the little finger on her right hand. By this means, she is able to communicate with those around her but it's strictly on a limited basis, and it's very time-consuming. When you get back home you can make arrangements to see her, bearing in mind as far as we're aware, she hasn't been told of the outcome of today's proceedings. We thought this should be something very private between the two of you."

"Irrespective of whether or not, Timothy Harris is your real father, you will have to consider the fact that you will have a say in the decisions to keep your mother alive. As her son by birth, legally, this decision can't just be left in the hands of your father. All we can say regarding this is, according to the medical team, she's not in any pain as far as they are aware. How long her condition will remain in this state is a matter of pure speculation."

Michael indicated to Irene he'd finished, and she asked Harry if he had any questions to ask about the news they'd just imparted. He didn't look up to face them, and merely shook his head whilst continuing to stare at the floor. She moved a little closer to him, saying, "Harry we know it's been a long hard day. You must feel as though you have been put through the wringer, but you have to appreciate that there was no other way for us to tell you. We had to tell you at this very moment because, there's so much going on, and so much more which still has to happen."

"Before we go, I must warn you what to expect from today onwards, and in the near future. As a result of the verdict today the press will have a field day at your expense. In all probability, you'll see banner headlines in the papers proclaiming, "double killer freed on a technicality. Killer freed to strike again, and countless other variations on the same thing. Unfortunately, there's nothing we can do to stop this type of thing happening, so, for your own sake, you're going to have to keep a very low profile indeed. To this end, we've arranged a safe house for you, and we can't stress too much how important it is for you to stay there keeping out of sight."

"Dealing with the press of tomorrow is one thing, but you will also have to contend with the press of the future, and, by this, I mean the eruption which is bound to follow once the exhumation order becomes public knowledge, coupled with an explosion which will be created if and when it's confirmed that Timothy Harris is your real father. Believe me, there's no way you can escape any of this, and it certainly won't be an easy ride. Then, you will also have to come to terms with reality after all the tests have been concluded. Hopefully by then, we will be able to prove to everybody that you weren't guilty, and this will set off another mad scramble with press, TV interviews, and all manner of things. Strictly speaking, you aren't going to have anything like a normal, or a private life, for quite a considerable period of time. Whilst all this is taking place, you will also have to consider the impact all of this will be having on your adoptive mother. Don't forget, since the trial she hasn't seen or heard from you, and I know she's taken events so far very hard indeed and it's only going to get harder still for her."

Still staring at the floor, Harry finally spoke but his voice betrayed no sign of emotion whatsoever as he said, "Before we leave here let me say to both of you, I really do appreciate everything you have done for me during this terribly dark period of my life. As you said, it has been a very trying day and I realise my ordeal is far from over. I also realise I am deeply indebted to a lot of people, and I'll do my best to ensure that their trust, and belief in me, has not been misplaced. Right now, the news you have given me has only just begun to sink in and I'm finding it very difficult to come to terms with. All I want now is to be allowed to go somewhere quiet, and peaceful, whilst I contemplate and reflect upon my life before deciding where I go from here. At some stage, I know I have to face the press, and the public, so I think it would be better if we prepared a short statement for those persons from the press waiting outside on the basis that no questions will be asked or answered. Following that release, we should be allowed to leave in peace without being hounded. After Michael had prepared a statement for the press they made their way to the exit.

Once the great steel studded doors were opened, the press surged forward as one. The agreement was totally forgotten as question upon question was hurled upon them, and, flash followed flash, as each person present endeavoured to secure the best pictures. Surrounded on all sides, but still making slow, but painful progress to the waiting car, Michael read out the press release.

"My client is truly grateful that his period of incarceration is now behind him and he is pleading with everybody here to allow him some privacy so that he can pick up the remaining threads of his life. Throughout his ordeal, my client has always maintained his innocence, and he continues to do so. At the present moment, he regrets that he is unable to answer any questions, or arrange any interviews, but in the fullness of time, he will be more than willing to face all his detractors, and answer any questions raised."

"Please understand, this has been a momentous day, and, allow us all to leave peacefully." They had reached the safety and sanctuary of the car and once inside, they were driven quickly away with the press trying to follow in hot pursuit.

Chapter 32

Although the madding crowd had been left behind, none of the occupants felt they could relax. They cast anxious looks behind themselves on countless occasions to ensure they were not being followed. As they became more secure they did relax however and, one by one, they fell asleep exhausted by the day's events.

They awoke to the sound of the car being driven on the gravel of a long winding drive. The car drew up outside the impressive front entrance of a very large house, and they were quickly ushered inside where Harry and his companions, found the welcoming figure of Sebastian Kreiff. With a minimum of fuss, drinks were produced and served, together with refreshments. When he deemed it appropriate, Sebastian rose from the table to announce a toast, "Ladies and gentlemen, will you please allow me to propose a toast in honour of our partner, Irene Yarwood, who has done such a magnificent job in securing the freedom of her client, Harry Thompson. Glasses were raised in her honour to cries of *speech*, and Irene duly responded,

"Sebastian, Ladies and Gentlemen, first of all let me thank our host for having so much trust in me at the start of my career. I think I was very fortunate in having such a high profile case thrust upon me. I must thank everybody who has helped and assisted me during this long saga which is still not quite over. I really am indebted to you all. Finally, to those of you who have not yet met him, let me formally introduce you to Harry Thompson who has been through such an ordeal, and who has mercifully been freed by the judges today. Let me assure all of you here now that this fight, Mr Thompson's war, still goes on and he won't rest until he has been granted a Queen's pardon. This is the only thing which will lift the stigma with which he will be associated for some considerable time to come."

The strain of the day's proceedings had really begun to tell on all of the persons assembled, and it was a welcome relief when Irene and Michael, could take their farewell, leaving Harry, in the capable hands of Sebastian and his wife.

One thing was sure, the next day the hounds were certainly in full cry and baying for blood, in fact anybody's blood. All the press carried thick, black banner headlines proclaiming a person's right to silence as the 'criminals' charter.' Most of the broadsheets led with lurid headlines laying claim to, "Crazy Killers being allowed to roam the streets," "Guilty Man Walks Free," "Serial Killer Granted Licence, May Kill Again," and many more, all destined to strike fear into young and old alike.

The leader and political columns did no better and, to the public at large, it must have seemed justice had been turned on its head as the press united on a solid front against the government, and the legal profession, for allowing, what they could only perceive to be such a gross miscarriage of justice. In some of the tabloids, Irene, came in for more than her fair share of criticism, being named in an attempt to shame her as being the instigator of a gross manipulation of the law; calls were made for her to be banned from practising law altogether.

The team had received the results of the DNA testing which proved, beyond any shadow of doubt that Timothy Harris was indeed the father of Harry Thompson, and, as the days passed allowing some form of normality to return to the scene, the hunt took on a different direction, with the tabloids leading with stories such as, "Where is Double Killer Thompson, £5000 reward for sighting of Thompson."

"Double Killer Thompson too afraid to come out of hiding. Later, as the press interest began to wane, the inevitable happened when news broke about the hearing for the exhumation order, to enable the tests to be carried out, on the samples taken from Anthony Harris deceased.

Like rats out of a sewer, journalists appeared from the length and breadth of the country, sensing with an extraordinary acute perception, that this was to be no ordinary occasion. Any exhumation order carries with it the prospect of a story, but this was going to be something so much bigger. Something told them it had to be, due to the fact that Anthony Harris was the son of Timothy Harris. The MP who had been involved in the Clarkson case cover up, and this latter item had spilled over into the Thompson murder trial. One by one, they started to accumulate snippets of information and, like a jigsaw, they began to build up their own pictures.

Once again the banner headlines appeared, screaming, What is Double Killer's Link with ex MP's son? They led with highly controversial comment, "What is the mystery surrounding the exhumation of the body of Anthony Harris, the late son of the ex-MP Timothy Harris? Surely with his father behind bars, and his body being interred over six months ago, why all the secrecy surrounding the application?"

"And, what on earth do the police hope to gain by allowing such action?"

'Despite this particular reporter spending most of the morning at the court, not one person would offer any explanation to this dramatic turn of events, and yet it must indicate a lead, or a different line of enquiry into an ongoing case, or even cases, which have remained unsolved on the files for some considerable time? When our reporter put this to the officer in charge, the only response received was a polite request to move away, and to direct all questions to the Chief

Constable's office. For the police to behave in such a heavy handed way, only fuels speculation there are going to be some dramatic events taking place very shortly."

Throughout it all, Harry Thompson had followed his instructions to the letter; keeping a very low profile, he had remained out of sight at the safe haven provided by the senior partner in the chambers. Owing to the pressure applied by the media, he had only minimum contact with his adoptive mother, Sally. Arrangements for them to meet had been planned like a military operation, because, the media had all but taken up residence outside his former home, in the hope that Sally would lead them to his hideaway. However, with a couple of swift car changes on dual carriageways, the bloodhounds of the press had been thwarted. Such were the attentions of the press however, it was decided it was far too risky at this stage to repeat the operation.

A tight security blanket had been thrown around the hospital where his mother remained, still cocooned in her inert state, and although his mother had been told of his release from prison, she had also been told he would not visit her until his name had been fully cleared. With no further improvement in her condition, Paula Harris lay there in a highly charged emotional state despite the constant attention of the dedicated staff devoted to her care and well-being. Her consultant, Peter Woods, was in constant touch, and arrangements were in hand for him to visit immediately, should anything untoward occur. With a twenty-four hour news blackout, it was hoped that Paula, and the events and happenings of the outside world, could be strictly controlled, and monitored. This was in order to spare her as much anguish as possible.

Chapter 33

Tuesday, the second of April, had proved to be a particularly exhausting day for all concerned. During the early part of the morning, Irene and Michael had kept in constant touch with Harry because this was the day the results were expected, and each time the telephone rang they were all so highly charged that they were jumping out of their skins. With agonising slowness, the clock face showed that the appointed hour for lunch had passed them by, but food was the last thing on their minds at the moment. At half past two, Irene was to be found seated in the office of Michael Mulrooney. Neither person spoke; instead they sat there, willing the phone to ring. Praying that the caller would convey the results they were so absolutely desperate to hear. All the staff had been specifically told they were not to be disturbed, and if any persons other than Sir Martin Lttlejohn rang they were to be informed that Michael was away from the office, visiting clients

With a sound which would have awakened the dead Michael's private telephone shrieked into life. His hand shot out instantly to remove the receiver from its place of rest. With what appeared to be a single movement, the phone was in his hand, and cradled against his neck as he whispered nervously, "Mulrooney here." From his facial expression, together with the look in his eyes, Irene knew instinctively this was the call they had waited so long for. Even so, she was still praying that it would contain, and convey, the news they desperately longed to hear. She listened with eager anticipation to Michael saying, "Wonderful, that's great that's absolutely wonderful news, and there's absolutely no doubt about it. Please send me a fax as soon as you can, then we'd better see about a press release. Just let me have five minutes with Irene, she's with me in the office; then I'll phone you back Ok?"

Flushed with excitement, he replaced the receiver shouting, "Irene, it's official the tests confirm it. Sir Martin said that, from the tests he conducted, he can prove that the samples taken from the clothing of the dead women, match the samples obtained from the body of Anthony Harris. His opinion, along with that of the police forensic scientists is, even allowing for some contamination due to exposure, and they all stress there was some contamination, it is almost impossible to distinguish between the samples of Harry Thompson and Anthony Harris. This means that Harry's conviction would be ruled unsafe, and the verdict would be overturned in any court in the land. Irene, I'm telling you, it's finally all over."

Michael was out of his chair, dancing round the office, then he opened the door, and told all the staff present, "Spread the word Harry Thompson is innocent."

Irene brought him down to earth temporarily, reminding him he still had to phone Sir Martin back in order to discuss the press release through Merseyside police. "Meanwhile," she said excitedly, "I'd better telephone Sebastian with the good news, then I suppose we had better fix up some interviews with the media and Harry, because, this truly is a historic day, and it belongs as much to Harry as it does to us and everyone else." Irene waited with some anxiety whilst Michael spoke to Sir Martin, then she spoke to Sebastian.

Immediately the news was received at the offices, Sebastian despatched a car to collect Harry from his safe house in order that a press conference could be arranged after the news had been divulged to the press. For this purpose, Irene was hastily recalled to the office along with Michael Mulrooney. Fortunately, they all arrived before the press, and a statement was speedily prepared. It was a simple press release as follows, read by Irene Yarwood.

'As a result of DNA tests carried out on samples voluntarily donated by the Harris family, including Timothy Harris, we have to tell you that the results prove conclusively, Timothy Harris is the father of Harry Thomson. After comparing these samples, with samples taken from the body of the late Anthony Harris, we can also confirm that Harry Thomson, and the deceased, are twin brothers. Further tests have been carried out on the clothing samples taken from the two women involved in the Thompson murder trial, and the police forensic scientists have today confirmed to us that, as a result of those tests, they can no longer say that Harry Thompson is the only person who could have committed those crimes. We anticipate a much more detailed statement will be made later through the offices of the Merseyside Police Authority following their discussions with the forensic scientists, and pending receipt of that report and discussions between ourselves. We have nothing further to add, apart from the fact that this good news proves, beyond any shadow of doubt, that Harry Thompson is innocent of all charges. Obviously we shall be applying to the Home Secretary to grant a full Queen's Pardon to Mr. Thompson who has undergone a most terrible ordeal. And as soon as all the formalities are completed Mr. Thomson will be seeking adequate compensation to take into account his arrest, and subsequent incarceration. Meanwhile, Mr. Thompson wishes me to make it known to everyone he is extremely thankful that his ordeal is now over and he asks each, and every one of you, to respect his privacy.'

Ignoring the clamour for answers to the many questions hurled at them from the waiting press, the party made their way back inside the offices. Once inside however, Irene sensed at once that the mood had changed. Everybody was happy, and congratulating them all over again. Somehow, Irene sensed rather than felt that the air was tinged with anticipation. She told herself this was something she was imagining but the feeling persisted, refusing to go away.

Then, all of a sudden, she was aware that the noise was quickly subsiding; she found herself looking at Sebastian Kreiff, and, the other senior partners in the practice.

Without any hesitation, Sebastian stepped forward to speak to Irene and the assembled, who now included Harry and Michael. He was saying, "Irene, on behalf of myself and everybody here, I would like you to accept this little gift as a token of our esteem. Also, our regard for you following your successful defence of Harry Thompson. It goes without saying that not one person in the entire legal profession thought you had a ghost of a chance, but you proved them all wrong. It gives me great pleasure to ask you to accept this small token of our regard. Here's to the future, and to many more successful briefs. With that he handed her a small oblong velvet case. As the onlookers began to clap, Irene opened the case with a great deal of nervous anticipation. Inside the box lay a brass plate inscribed,

'KRIEFF, KRIEFF, ISAACS, and YARWOOD'

It was at that precise moment that it finally dawned on Irene that she had truly proved to everyone in the profession that she had fully earned her position and the right to the letters 'QC' beside her name. This was together with a full partnership within the chambers.

It was also at this moment in time that she suddenly caught a glimpse of Harry and, observing the way he was standing with his arms wrapped tight around his body, the words of Professor Love flooded back into her brain. Instantly reignited were all her doubts concerning him in the murder trial as it was instantly replaced by a much stronger feeling that she had just turned a multiple killer loose upon society. There and then she vowed to herself that, if their respective paths ever crossed again, she would make certain that he ended up where he belonged…

BEHIND BARS.

www.ingramcontent.com/pod-product-compliance
Lightning Source LLC
Chambersburg PA
CBHW051009180726
48291CB00006B/2040